Bookworm IV

Full Circle

ALSO BY CHRISTOPHER G. NUTTALL

The Mind's Eye

Bookworm series
Bookworm
Bookworm II: The Very Ugly Duckling
Bookworm III: The Best Laid Plans

DIZZY SPELLS SERIES
A LIFE LESS ORDINARY

Royal Sorceress series
The Royal Sorceress
The Great Game
Necropolis

Inverse Shadows Universe
Sufficiently Advanced Technology

Bookworm IV

Full Circle

Christopher G. Nuttall

Elsewhen Press

Bookworm IV: Full Circle
First published in Great Britain by Elsewhen Press, 2015
An imprint of Alnpete Limited

Elsewhen Press, PO Box 757, Dartford, Kent DA2 7TQ
www.elsewhen.press

British Library Cataloguing in Publication Data.
A catalogue record for this book is available from the British Library.
ISBN 978-1-908168-84-9 Print edition
ISBN 978-1-908168-94-8 eBook edition

Designed and formatted by Elsewhen Press

To My Beta Readers, With Many Thanks.

You Know Who You Are.

Prologue

The Witch-King had thought that time was meaningless.

He was a lich, after all, a dead body held permanently in suspension by magic. He had waited for a thousand years for his plans to come to fruition and he could have waited another thousand, if necessary. What did the passage of time mean to him when there were minds to bend and living people to manipulate like pieces on a game board? Indeed, part of him would even *miss* the sensation of covertly steering events from his lofty vantage point, ensuring that matters went the way that best pleased him.

But now ... time was moving again.

Deferens – the Emperor, his tool – had taken power and was readying himself to deliver the magic that would end the Witch-King's long rest and bring him back into the world of men. Other pieces, carefully groomed for their roles, were already playing their parts, spreading chaos across the world. There would be no organised resistance as the Empire slipped into civil war, nothing to stop the Witch-King returning to the Golden City to take power and finish the work he had begun, thousands of years ago. The hour of victory was at hand ...

And yet, randomness was the enemy.

He'd always known that randomness might disrupt his plans. His ability to influence even the greatest magicians was limited, while his ability to steer the paths of mundanes was non-existent. Sheer random chance had impeded his plans before ... but then, he'd always been able to pull back, secure in the knowledge that his existence, let alone his influence, remained unsuspected. Now, a handful of people *did* know of him; knew of him, feared him and intended to destroy him. Their prospects of success were laughable, at best, and yet the thought nagged at his mind. He'd seen too many carefully-constructed plans fall apart as randomness took hold, to dismiss them entirely ...

… And now, he couldn't pull back and wait for centuries before trying again.

They could destroy me, he thought.

It wasn't something he wanted to contemplate. He'd gone further than anyone else in his studies of magic, exploring vast vistas that most magicians refused to consider even existed – and he'd succeeded. The simple fact that he'd survived over a thousand years without going mad was proof of his success. But now there was another magician, who understood the deeper layers of magic, bonded to a young man who had no idea of the true nature of his powers. The tools to destroy the Witch-King were at hand, if they knew how to use them, and they'd been spared the contamination that would have opened their minds to his influence.

He was vulnerable. He could be destroyed.

Part of him regretted what had to be done. He had never talked to a true equal since he'd hidden himself away, fearing what would happen if a newcomer learnt his true nature. It would be nice, perhaps, to bandy words with them before killing them, to talk as equals across a table …

… But not at the cost of his own survival. And he'd lived too long to place his life at risk now.

He reached out with his mind, feeling the threads of magic that linked him to hundreds of magicians. Deferens, his mind permanently on the brink between sanity and madness, was his puppet, even though he would never know it. The ambition that burnt through him was easy to steer to a new target, feeding an obsession that had no logical cause. His forces would swoop forward and claim the Principality Ida, then hold it while the Witch-King rose from the shadows and took power. Nothing would be allowed to get in the way.

And yet, matters were so close …

Standing at the cusp of godhood – or nemesis – the Witch-King waited.

He could do nothing else.

Chapter One

The dragon didn't like her.

Charity, former Head of House Conidian, quivered as the dragon's massive eyes turned to follow her. It was an immense beast, easily the size of a small house, with giant bat-like wings and eyes that glowed like embers of coal. Its teeth were sharp, covered in stains that *had* to be blood; its claws flexed, tearing great holes in the ground. It was hard, so hard, to stand close to the creature and not turn and flee. She was *convinced* that the only thing saving her from becoming a tasty snack was the iron will of her master, Emperor Vlad.

"Get up," the Emperor ordered, curtly.

Charity swallowed as the oath she'd sworn to him forced her forward. It grew hotter as she approached the dragon, the warmth a reminder of the fire in its belly, but the scales on its back were surprisingly cool. Somehow, she managed to scramble up onto the dragon's back and sit there, clinging to the scales for dear life. The Emperor snickered, then turned to his men and glowered at them.

"If a mere woman can do it," he growled, "so can you."

Bastard, Charity thought coldly, as snowflakes drifted down around her. Cursing him in her mind was the only thing she could do to keep herself sane, after everything he'd done to her. Making her wear a harem outfit that was utterly unsuited to the cold weather was the least of it. *You don't have them under obedience charms and oaths.*

She looked down at the Emperor, feeling bitter hatred and helplessness curdling in her gut. He was a tall muscular man, wearing a red shirt and kilt; a wand, a sword and a handful of daggers glinted at his belt. His long black hair hung down around his shoulders, wild and unkempt; the neatly-trimmed beard provided an odd contrast, a message Charity didn't really understand at all. But she knew him too well to feel any attraction; he'd killed the Grand Sorceress, claimed the throne and then offered her a flat choice between serving him or immediate death. In hindsight, death would have been preferable.

The Emperor smirked as his men – the red-robed magicians, the oath-bound Inquisitors and a number of his private guards – climbed onto their dragons, then he scrambled up beside Charity and sat in front of her. Charity was almost relieved, even though she would sooner have cuddled up to a man-eating yeti than the Emperor. At least she wouldn't be riding the dragon alone.

"Up," the Emperor commanded.

Charity braced herself, just in time. The dragon unfurled its wings, flapped them once and hurled itself into the air. Charity looked down as they rose higher, feeling an unaccustomed sense of vertigo as the Golden City shrank beneath them. The skies echoed with howls from the dragons, a sound unheard for nearly a thousand years. It had been a long time since the very last dragon was exterminated. Now, even though the Emperor was bringing them back into the world, there was no one alive who knew how to stop a dragon. They'd torn through the wards of a dozen Great Houses as though they were made of paper.

The air grew colder, rapidly, as they rose above the Seven Peaks and stared down at the remains of the Watchtower. Once, the Inquisitors had watched over the Golden City, their firm but fair judgements respected by all. Now, the Watchtower was gone – and no one knew *how* it had been destroyed – while the Inquisitors, oath-bound to serve the Emperor, followed Vlad and did his bidding. They couldn't break their sworn oaths and live.

Magic crackled around them – the Emperor let out a whoop of pure glee – as the dragons flew over the mountains, heading straight for the nearest city. Knawel Haldane stood only a bare couple of hours from the Golden City – less, if one rode the Iron Dragons – and it had always been loyal to the Empire. But now, with rumours flying everywhere and hundreds of Court Wizards either dead or trapped in the Golden City, the Empire was coming apart. Kings were declaring independence, rogue magicians were carving out states of their own …

… And everyone else was caught in the middle.

Charity shuddered at the thought, helplessly. She'd never really cared about the mundanes, about those unlucky enough to be born without magic. Indeed, she hadn't cared *that* much about her Powerless brother … and hadn't *that* turned into a joke, now Johan had become a dangerously powerful and unstable magician? Who *cared* about the opinions of people who were helpless against even the mildest compulsion hex? But now, her enslavement – and she was a slave, no matter her official title – showed her just how the mundanes must have felt, when they looked at her powerful family. Helpless, unable to do anything to protect themselves …

Jamal enjoyed wielding his power, she thought, bitterly. It was true; her eldest brother had been a bullying sadist, picking on everyone weaker than him. *But was I really that much better?*

It was an uncomfortable question. She'd expected to find herself married off to an older magician, not to find herself Head of House Conidian. Jamal would inherit the title, after all; everyone else would be expected to deport themselves to support him. And so she'd spent her days going to parties, shopping and generally having fun. There had been no thought of preparing herself for any other life. But now House Conidian was in ruins, her two younger siblings hostages and she was a slave.

"Knawel Haldane," the Emperor said. "Burn!"

Charity felt her stomach rebel as the dragon swooped down, opening its mouth to spew out a raging torrent of flame. The guardhouse below exploded into fire, the handful of guards and makeshift defences incinerated before they had a chance to do anything … as if there was anything they could do. She shuddered as the dragon pulled up, then blasted a stream of fire into a line of houses, exploding them one by one. An arrow glanced off the dragon's scales as someone tried to fight back, only to be vaporised by a blast of fire a second later.

"A real man," the Emperor said. His deep voice was tinged with heavy satisfaction. "But also a fool."

Magic flickered around them, again, as a handful of wizards tried to mount a defence, shooting off hexes and curses from their tower. The Emperor snickered as five of the dragons detached themselves from the rest and threw themselves on the tower, ripping it apart with casual ease. A lone figure, standing on top of the tower and waving her arms as she tried to cast a protective ward that might stand against the dragons, fell to her death in the flames. Charity felt a stab of pity, but she knew there was no point in saying anything. The Emperor regarded female magicians as abominations, wastes of potential when a powerful woman should have been having powerful sons. It made her wonder if he intended her to have children sooner or later, choosing her husband to suit himself. It was a terrifying thought.

The dragon rose, soaring up into the air. Charity looked down; half the dragons had taken up positions outside the gates, their human riders raising wards intended to trap the population inside the city, while the remainder flocked over the city, breathing down fire on anyone foolish enough to challenge them. Several large fires were raging through the houses, although many of the wealthier parts of the city looked untouched. Their homes would be warded against flames, Charity knew. They'd be untouched unless the dragons targeted them specifically.

But the poor will be forced out of their homes, she thought. *And then they will die.*

"We land," the Emperor said.

The dragon dropped down and landed before the remains of the first gatehouse. Charity gagged as she smelt the burning human flesh, then followed the Emperor as he jumped off the dragon and landed neatly on the remains of the road. His followers bowed to him; he nodded back, then turned his attention to the city. Behind them, Charity could hear the sound of his marching army advancing from the Golden City. It wouldn't be long before Knawel Haldane was completely surrounded. Resistance would be utterly futile.

She looked up as she saw a handful of people picking their way through the gatehouse and walking towards them. The leader was a middle-aged man wearing a merchant's outfit;

here, away from the Golden City, a man didn't have to be a magician to rule. Indeed, unless she missed her guess, the man *behind* the leader was a magician. He was definitely carrying a wand on his belt, although he was careful to show that he wasn't holding it at the ready. The last three men looked like bureaucrats, probably tax collectors. They never visited House Conidian, of course, but anyone without the power to stand up to them would find himself plucked like a chicken.

"Well," the Emperor said. He took a step forward, his red cloak spilling out behind him as he struck a dramatic pose. "Kneel."

The representatives hesitated, then dropped to their knees. Charity felt another pang of pity, mixed with helpless outrage; they weren't under any spells and yet they were kneeling in front of the Emperor! But the dragons were a convincing argument in the Emperor's favour and the representatives had already watched them tear through the city's puny defences as if there was truly nothing standing in their way. They had to know there was no point in further resistance, not when the city was surrounded. The Emperor could burn their city to ash whenever he chose.

"So," the Emperor said, coldly. "Who comes to speak with me?"

"I am Goodman Chaney," the leader said. Merchant or not, he couldn't keep the unease out of his voice. "I speak for the City Fathers."

"Good," the Emperor said. "I want your complete and total surrender."

Chaney blinked. "But sire ..."

"You are at my mercy," the Emperor said. She couldn't see his face, but Charity was sure he was leering. The Emperor enjoyed watching people squirm. "I have orders for you. If they are not carried out, your city will be burnt to the ground and any survivors sold into the most unpleasant slavery."

He allowed a moment for his words to sink in, then leant forward. "Every young man between fifteen and twenty is to report to my camp, where they will be conscripted into my army," he said. "Every magician in the city, from the lowliest hedge witch to the highest sorcerer, is to report to my magicians for induction. Any magical artefacts within the city are to be handed over, regardless of who owns them. Knawel Haldane itself is to provide everything my army might require, including food, military supplies and billets. Your families, in particular, will be handed over to us so we have hostages for your good behaviour."

Charity winced, inwardly. The Emperor wasn't doing *anything* to soften the demands, not even offering Chaney a chance to rise in the new order in exchange for doing what he was told. But then, the Emperor probably held a mere merchant in contempt. He was no magician, no warrior ... nothing the Emperor might find admirable, even if he could be useful. And Chaney had no cards to play unless he was willing to countenance the destruction of the entire city.

"It will be done, Your Supremacy," Chaney said, bowing his head.

"Good," the Emperor said. "Send a messenger to your families. I expect your wives and children – and those of the other City Fathers – to be here within half an hour. Should they not be here ..."

He patted the dragon, affectionately. The dragon's mouth lolled open, revealing his cruel teeth and long tongue. Chaney paled still further, then turned and hurried off, followed by the rest of the representatives.

"You could have given them more time," Charity said, before she could stop herself.

"They would have had time to plan an escape," the Emperor said. He looked past her to General Vetch. "General. Organise the troops to occupy the city, once the hostages arrive; billet them in prosperous houses. The dragons will provide support, if necessary."

Charity followed the Emperor like a stray dog as he moved from group to group, issuing orders, patting the dragons and generally keeping himself on top of what was going on. No one looked at her, not overtly, but she could feel their gazes following her, their eyes mocking her silently. They knew who she'd been, before she'd bent the knee to the Emperor; now, she was little more than a whore and they rejoiced in her fall. No doubt they came up with all sorts of stories about what the Emperor made her do, although he'd never touched her. But how could she blame them? She'd been so far above them that they could only watch her with envy, before the fall.

"The hostages have arrived, Your Supremacy," General Vetch reported.

"Excellent," the Emperor said. He strode over to where the hostages were waiting eyeing the dragons nervously. Charity followed him, feeling her heart sink. She had a nasty feeling the Emperor had something horrible in mind for the hostages. The little cluster of wives and children standing next to their husbands and fathers almost broke her heart. "Order them to be outfitted with slave collars. We might as well make some use of them."

Chaney stared in horror. "Your Supremacy ..."

The Emperor smiled at him. "Are you defying me?"

He waved a hand dismissively. One of the dragons moved forward with astonishing speed and opened its mouth. Chaney had no time to scream before the dragon swallowed him in a single gulp. A woman fainted – his wife, Charity assumed – while her children started to scream in horror. The Emperor showed nothing but cold amusement as he surveyed the remaining City Fathers. They looked as if they were torn between mounting a suicidal resistance and complete submission.

"Have them fitted with collars," the Emperor ordered. He nodded at the woman lying on the ground. "And have her thrown to the men. She's useless."

The City Fathers offered no further resistance, even when the slave collars were fitted and the hostages were marched off to an unknown fate. Charity hoped they'd be treated reasonably well – there was something to be gained from treating them as guests – but she knew the experience would be horrific. A compulsion charm could be fought, even broken, by a person of strong will and determination; a slave collar was almost impossible to resist. And if their husbands and fathers chose to resist later, they could simply be ordered to cut their own throats.

"Have the magical artefacts brought to my tent," the Emperor ordered, curtly. "My aide" – he nodded at Charity –

"will inspect them."

Charity was almost relieved. Poking magical artefacts ran the risk of being hexed or killed, if the owner had placed security charms on them, but at least she'd be away from the Emperor for a few hours. She didn't trust his temper – or his sense of humour – and she knew, all too well, just how cruel he could be. He was worse than Jamal ... who, at least, had never had her helplessly at his beck and call ...

But he had the maids at his command, she thought, as she made her way towards the royal tent. The soldiers were putting together a large camp outside the city, although a number of the men would be billeted inside the town. She hoped the civilians would keep their heads down and stay out of trouble. *What did he do to them?*

She sat down, inside the tent, and waited for the first box of artefacts to arrive. They all looked common, something that didn't really surprise her. Anything really old or powerful would be hidden, rather than tamely surrendered. She picked her way through a case of old wands, then checked a handful of basic spellbooks. None of them were more complex than anything she'd seen during her first year of schooling, although one of them had a number of scrawled annotations that made her smile. Clearly, whoever had owned the book had been something of a genius. But, if he or she had joined in the battle, they were probably already dead.

And the dead magicians might be the lucky ones, she thought. She knew what the Emperor had in mind for the magicians of Knawel Haldane, those who weren't strong enough to be helpful. They'd be sacrificed, their power fed into storage crystals and used to summon more monsters from the other realms. *They won't have to see what the Emperor does to the rest of the world.*

She pushed the thought aside bitterly – she was helpless and enslaved – and turned her attention to the next box. An old Hand of Glory, burnt and useless; a Ring of Power, the gem cracked and broken; a Soul Drainer ... she shuddered, remembering how her father had insisted on using one on Johan, hoping to spark his magic; a knife that felt oddly familiar ...

It *was* familiar! The Conidian Crest was emblazed on the

hilt, while magic – *family* magic – crackled around the blade. She remembered watching, years ago, as her father had presented it to Jamal, on the day he'd turned sixteen. The blade was charmed; it would be lethal, instantly lethal, to anyone it cut, unless they were a close relation. *Charity* could hold it safely, she knew, and even cut herself … but anyone else?

And if it's here, she asked herself slowly, *how in all the hells did it* get *here?*

Jamal had carried the blade everywhere, she knew. She was sure it would still work for him, even after he'd lost his magic. The blade was linked to the family's bloodline, not his magical signature, yet the blade *still* thought Jamal was its master. And that meant … her older brother was somewhere in the city, alive and well. She hesitated, unsure if she wanted to ask the Emperor for permission to look for him, then rose to her feet. Perhaps he'd give her permission to find him …

… And if he did, at least she wouldn't be alone any longer.

Chapter Two

"That's Falcone's Nest," Dread said. "Dead ahead."

Elaine nodded, cursing her weakness under her breath. Two days of hard riding had left her tired, sore and bruised in places she hadn't known she had. Horses didn't like her, as far as she could tell, and they didn't like the spells she used to make the ride a little easier. She'd been lucky to have avoided falling off more than twice.

"It's different," Johan said. She could sense his admiration through the apprenticeship bond they shared. *"Very different."*

Elaine smiled as she looked down the road towards Falcone's Nest. It was a mid-sized town – absently, she estimated that the population couldn't be larger than ten thousand souls – built on the far side of a river. The district of the town facing her was dotted with shipyards and harbours, packed with ocean-going galleons and large barges for the inland canal network, the latter loaded with goods for trade. It looked reassuringly normal, although she could see a handful of armed City Guardsmen watching warily as the riders cantered up to the bridge, backed up by a pair of magicians. They had to know that *something* was badly wrong.

They could have had word passed to them from the Golden City, she thought, grimly. The Emperor had taken down the network of linked crystal balls that bound the Empire together, but there wasn't any shortage of powerful magicians in the Golden City. One of them could easily have sent a message to a friend via magic. *Or someone could have ridden ahead of us while we were trying to escape Dread.*

She winced at the memory, looking up at the former Inquisitor. Magicians who lost their magic tended to go mad – or die – very quickly, but so far Dread seemed to be almost unchanged by the experience. His hard face – rugged, scarred after years on active service – showed no hint of emotion, no doubt or fear about the future. She envied him his confidence, even as she mistrusted the soundness of his judgement. Two days ago, he'd been one of the most powerful and capable magicians in the world. Now, he was just another powerless mundane.

But that doesn't make him helpless, she reminded herself, sharply. *The Levellers proved that when they brought down the Watchtower.*

Johan pulled his horse alongside hers. "You're being depressed again."

Elaine felt herself flush. Johan could sense her emotions as easily as she could sense his; indeed, the mere fact that they were closer in age than most masters and apprentices made them *more* open with one another. It was embarrassing to feel so naked in front of him, even though she was wearing a shirt, a pair of long trousers and a travelling cloak. But then, he felt the same way too.

"I just worry," she said. They hadn't seen any signs of pursuit since they'd stolen Dread's magic – as far as he knew, he was the only person sent after them – but she knew that would change. The Witch-King wouldn't be content to let them vanish into the countryside, not if he suspected what she knew. Deferens would send his entire army after them rather than risk utter disaster. "Don't you?"

"I don't have time to worry," Johan said, shortly.

Elaine gave him a sharp look. Johan had wanted to drink himself senseless at the first inn they'd reached, which she'd forbidden. They'd argued backwards and forwards until Daria had threatened to bang their heads together, but they'd apologised to each other in the morning. Now, Johan seemed almost as driven as Elaine herself. Discovering that he had a relative who'd died almost as soon as he'd met her – and that his family was enslaved – had changed him.

"Watch what you say," Dread warned, as they approached the bridge. "You never know who might be listening."

He spurred his horse forward, pulling up just in front of the guardhouse. Elaine watched the magicians eying him sharply, then turning away. She knew they would never have shown such blatant disrespect for an Inquisitor but, as far as they knew, Dread … was just another mundane. In some ways, it was a relief, yet she knew it had to hurt the older man. He'd spent his life building up his magic, only to lose it in a split-second.

But he would have remained a slave if he'd kept it, she thought, numbly. *And if we tried to restore it, who knows what would happen?*

Johan leant his head over to hers. "You think they're buying the cover story?"

Elaine shrugged. There were five guardsmen and two magicians; Johan's odd magic *might* be enough to take them both out, along with the guards, but it would attract attention. Deferens would hear of it and know precisely where to look for them. And then … she shook her head, tiredly. As humiliating as it was to tell people that she was being married off to a magical family on the other side of the continent, it was a reasonably plausible story that explained her small escort. No bandits in their right mind would attack a magician and her guards.

And if I try to assert my authority, she reminded herself, *they might refuse to accept it.*

She shook her head. Had it really only been seven months since she'd become Head Librarian, as well as a Privy Councillor? She'd had power and position that would have been considered unimaginable to the poor orphan girl she'd been, because she wasn't a very powerful magician. But the knowledge in her head more than made up for her lack of power, if she had time to cast her spells. She rubbed her forehead, feeling the weight of centuries of accumulated knowledge pressing against her mind. If she fell into Deferens' hands …

He has the Great Library now, if he can get through the wards, she thought. She'd locked the wards in place when she'd left, but she knew all too well that *any* ward could be broken, given enough power and determination. *Does he really need me any longer?*

"Come," Dread called.

Elaine cursed mentally and spurred the horse onwards, Johan cantering beside her while Daria – in wolf form – brought up the rear. She was no less pleased than Elaine at pretending to be an oversized wolfhound – Elaine was mildly surprised that *anyone* was fooled – but it did give them an additional wand, if necessary. Besides, horses disliked werewolves far more than they disliked Elaine. Daria wouldn't have been able to ride a horse without using magic to force it to obey.

"I used to dream about sailing the seven seas," Johan said, as they crossed the bridge. "It wouldn't have been *that* hard to get a berth on a merchantman, then work my way up the ranks. But father ..."

He shook his head. Elaine sensed his sudden pang of guilt, mixed with a bitterness that had never faded, and winced in sympathy. Johan's father hadn't killed Johan outright, as he'd had every right to do when one of his children was born without magic, but he'd kept Johan inside House Conidian and firmly under control. And when Johan's magic had exploded into life he'd done everything he could to bring Johan *back* under his thumb. Johan resented his father – and hated him too – yet he still felt guilt for stealing his father's magic. It had crippled House Conidian when it needed strong leadership.

She reached out and squeezed his arm. "Don't worry about it," she said. It wasn't enough, but she'd never been good at knowing what to say when someone needed comfort or reassurance. "We can go sailing later, if you like."

A dull rumble echoed through the air as an iron dragon crossed the closest bridge, heading west towards the Golden City. Elaine wondered if the passengers knew that most of the lines were broken, or if they intended to stop well before they reached Knawel Haldane. Or even if they wanted to go to Knawel Haldane itself. Had the city been attacked and taken? She knew little about military strategy, but Knawel Haldane was the major gateway to the Golden City. It was unlikely that Deferens would leave it alone.

"I'd like that," Johan said, giving her a shy smile. "Or we could just go riding instead ..."

"Not on your life," Elaine said. She looked down at the horse's mane, then shook her head firmly. "The sooner I can stop riding, the better."

"You just have to get used to it," Johan said. "It's easy

once you have the confidence to look the horse in the eye and make it obey.”

“I’ll take your word for it,” Elaine said, as they reached the far end of the bridge. The smell of salt water was pushed aside by the aroma of rotting fish. She swallowed hard, then cast a spell to protect their noses from the stench. The thankful look Daria tossed her made the small effort worthwhile. “Maybe you just have to be tougher to make the horse obey you.”

She sensed Johan’s amusement, although he managed to keep it off his face. “My baby sisters rode horses,” he said. “I ...”

He broke off, a sudden sense of guilt, regret and melancholy echoing through the link. His little sisters had bullied him mercilessly, as soon as they’d come into their powers; he still carried the scars from hundreds of pranks and japes that were only funny if the victim had the magic to undo the spells. He’d hated them and he’d enjoyed scaring them with his new reputation, but Cass’ letter had made him think about just what sort of person he wanted to be. Now, she knew he’d want to see his sisters again, if only to ensure they were safe.

“We’ll see them again, I’m sure,” she said, gently. “You can take care of them ...”

“If they’re still alive,” Johan said, quietly. “What if Deferens has killed them?”

Dread cleared his throat. “The guards said we could stay in the city for five days, but we’d have to leave after that unless we register and pay a tax,” he said. “Where do you want to go from here?”

Johan frowned. “The Jumping Jody,” he said, after a moment’s thought. “That’s the name we were given back in Knawel Haldane.”

Elaine smiled. “They do seem to like using inns as bases, don’t they?”

“Practical,” Dread grunted. As an Inquisitor, it had been his job to hunt the Levellers down; now, the Levellers were about the only people who could help. “Inns are good places to hear the latest news, while no one is surprised when guests pack their bags and leave in the middle of the night. And we can probably change our horses there too."

"Good," Elaine said. The horse under her shivered, as if it knew she was looking forward to getting off. "Did they buy the story?"

"Didn't question it very much," Dread said, as he swung the horse around. "You're clearly a magician, while there aren't enough of us to cause real trouble. They're not likely to question us as long as we don't attract too much attention."

He cantered down a cobbled road that was badly stained. Elaine followed, allowing Johan and Daria to bring up the rear. Falcone's Nest was crowded, but there was an undertone of fear in the air that worried her, even though she knew the cause. A herald was caterwauling in the square as they passed, telling everyone within earshot that five men and two women were in the stocks for spreading false rumours. Elaine caught sight of the prisoners and winced in sympathy – the crowd was already gathering to throw rotten fruits and vegetables at the unlucky prisoners – but she knew there was nothing she could do. Besides, it was quite possible they deserved their punishment.

Let's hope they don't start throwing stones, she thought, shivering. The orphanage staff had taken the children to watch prisoners in the stocks once or twice, just to make sure they knew what fate awaited anyone who ran afoul of the law. Some of the crowd had pelted a false witness with stones, breaking his nose and leaving blood spilling into the streets. *It would kill the poor bastards.*

Johan slipped up beside her. "We could break them free at night ..."

"And then get caught ourselves," Elaine said. She shook her head. "Bad idea, I think."

She sucked in her breath as the Jumping Jody came into view. It was a large wooden building, carefully structured to pack as many people as possible inside; behind it, she could see a cookhouse with signs advertising food from all over the world. A handful of dogs sat outside, their tongues lolling out of their mouths. She guessed, as Dread dismounted and helped her down to the ground, that their owners were inside the inn.

"Wait here," Dread ordered curtly. "I'll go speak to the

innkeeper."

He turned and strode inside. Anyone who looked at him, Elaine was sure, would know him for a dangerous man, although they'd never see him as an Inquisitor. Dread could simply have commandeered everything they needed, if his skull-ring had still worked for him. But it didn't, forcing them to buy what they needed. She had a nasty feeling that they would run out of money, sooner or later.

Johan dropped down beside her, holding the horse's reins in one hand. "You think the beds will be comfortable?"

Elaine shrugged. She hadn't stayed in many inns and only one of them, as far as she could recall, had been reasonably comfortable. The others had had itchy bedding, cold water and insects scuttling across the floor when she'd doused the lamp. There was no reason to expect anything better from the Jumping Jody. The dogs started to bark in unison and she looked up, sharply. A man with faintly canine features was walking past them, his eyes fixed firmly on Daria.

"We're further up the river," he said, so quietly that Elaine had to strain her ears to hear his words. Daria's ears, sharper than any normal human, would have no trouble. "Come see us, sister."

He walked on, leaving Elaine staring after him. Daria showed no visible reaction, but sniffed once or twice, as if she was testing the man's scent. Dread reappeared and led them into the inn, tapping his lips gently when Elaine made to speak. Walls had ears, even when the innkeepers weren't magical. She gritted her teeth as she smelt beer in the air, then averted her eyes as she saw dozens of men quaffing down ale as though it was on the verge of running out. Two fights were taking place, the fighters surrounded by several other men who were placing bets on the outcome; a handful of women, wearing beer-stained aprons, were quietly collecting used glasses and placing them back on the bar for reuse. It didn't *look* as though they were being washed first.

"I ordered a single large room, in keeping with our cover story," Dread said, shortly. He stopped outside a door, opening it with an iron key. "There should be enough room for all of us."

Elaine sensed a flicker of mixed emotions from Johan as

they stepped into the room and glanced around. It wasn't particularly clean, although Elaine had been expecting worse; a pair of beds, a handful of lamps and a window allowing them to look out onto the streets below. She glanced through a paper-thin wooden door and saw a tiny bathroom, complete with bucket, iron bath and pump. Clearly, the fad for indoor plumbing hadn't reached Falcone's Nest yet. Even the orphanage in the Golden City had had hot and cold running water, as well as real toilets. She hastily cast another spell to hide the worst of the stench, then slipped back into the bedroom.

"Elaine and Daria will get the beds," Dread said, as he locked the door. "I ..."

He stopped, grimly. "Elaine, can you ward the rooms?"

Elaine nodded, drawing her wand and casting a handful of spells of her own design. Most of them were breakable – most magicians outshone her as the sun outshone the moon – but their true strength lay in the fact they were almost impossible to perceive, except at very close range. A magician who tried to spy on them from a distance would find it very difficult ... and if the wards started to fail, Elaine would know about it at once.

And Dread would have done it for himself, once, she thought, bitterly. *Now ... now, he can't.*

"I'll share a bed with Daria," she said, as her friend snapped back into her human form. The men hastily averted their eyes as Elaine passed Daria her robe. "You two can have the other bed."

"I'll be taking the first watch," Dread said, gruffly. He didn't *sound* as though the loss of his magic was working on him, but she knew it had to be affecting him badly. "You three get some sleep, if you need it."

"I need a bath," Elaine said. She could heat the water using magic, if she tried. "Do you have a plan for contacting the Levellers?"

"We have code phrases," Johan reminded her. He turned to look out of the window. "They don't know, do they?"

"They know *something*," Dread grunted. "That's another reason to go for a wander, once we've had a rest. We need to know what they know."

Elaine looked at him. "Could they do anything if they did know?"

"I don't know," Dread admitted. He didn't sound as though he believed his own words. Vlad Deferens had dragons, hundreds of magicians and an entire army. Falcone's Nest had nothing more than a handful of magicians and the City Guard. "But at least they can try."

Chapter Three

The guards outside the Emperor's tent bowed to Charity as she approached, then allowed her to step through without searching her. It wasn't a sign of respect, Charity knew; it was a sign of contempt, a reminder that she literally *couldn't* pose any threat to her master even though she was carrying a wand and a charmed knife. She pushed the tent flap aside, then stepped into the chamber and hastily prostrated herself while waiting for the Emperor to notice her. She'd learnt the hard way that Emperor Vlad didn't like interruptions.

"There are riots in the Western Hills," General Vetch was saying. He glanced briefly at her, then looked back at the Emperor, dismissing Charity as unimportant. "And the citizens in Rising Shadow have overthrown their king and declared independence."

"It isn't an important matter," the Emperor said, curtly. He was looking down at a map on the table, as if he wasn't quite listening to his General. "We can reclaim control of Rising Shadow later, once we hold Ida."

"Ida isn't a major state, Your Supremacy," General Vetch said. He sounded as though he was pleading, expecting the Emperor to listen to him. Charity knew it was futile. The Emperor seemed dangerously obsessed with Ida, almost as obsessed with the tiny state as he was with the Head Librarian. "Rising Shadow controls trade and transport links to a fifth of the continent. If we lose control of the state, we run the risk of losing the other states ..."

"I have *dragons*," the Emperor snarled. "Are they going to stand against *my* dragons?"

"Dragons are not invincible, Your Supremacy," General Vetch reminded him. "They *can* be beaten ..."

"One or two dragons can be beaten," the Emperor snarled. "I have *dozens*."

He rose to his feet. "See that the men are well-rested," he

added, nastily. "I intend to march onwards within two days. We'll leave a garrison in the city to ensure it behaves itself."

General Vetch turned and stalked out of the tent. Charity thought, for a chilling moment, that he was about to kick her before he walked onwards. The Emperor glowered after him, one hand flexing in a manner that suggested he was about to cast a spell, then peered down at Charity instead. She hastily pressed her face into the tent floor in absolute submission, hoping he wasn't feeling sadistic. He'd once left her in that position for hours.

"Rise," the Emperor growled. He stamped back to his seat and sat down. "Pour me a drink."

Charity obeyed, feeling a glimmer of sympathy for the maids and servants who'd worked for House Conidian before the fall. The Emperor took the glass she passed him, drank it hastily and slammed it down on the table so hard it cracked. Charity looked at the map, trying not to make it obvious, and frowned inwardly. If the map was correct, Rising Shadow wasn't the only state intent on breaking free of the Empire. Five more were also about to collapse into chaos.

"The General does not understand the true importance of our work," the Emperor said, his voice icy cold. Charity had the odd feeling he wasn't talking to himself, even though the words weren't aimed at her. "His concerns are purely mundane."

"Yes, Your Supremacy," Charity said.

"I should send a swarm of dragons to Rising Shadow and burn their capital to the ground," the Emperor mused. "It would convince them to behave themselves, would it not?"

"Of course, Your Supremacy," Charity said.

The Emperor's eyes sharpened, suddenly. "What are you doing here?"

Charity swallowed, then held up the knife. "This belonged to my brother," she said. "And the link between it and its owner is still alive."

"Johan?" The Emperor asked. His face twisted with an emotion she didn't recognise. "He's *here*?"

"No, Your Supremacy," Charity said. "Jamal."

"How nice," the Emperor said, after a moment. He took the knife, turned it over and over in his hand, then passed it back to her. "And so?"

"The records say the knife came from a slave warehouse," Charity said. There was no way to be sure that Jamal was still there – and she had no idea what he was doing in a slave warehouse anyway – but it was a good place to start. "I could go find him. If he's still alive ..."

"You could torment him as he tormented you," the Emperor sneered. "He's powerless now, is he not? Why *not* attempt to make him suffer?"

His face twisted into a leer. "Is that what you want?"

Charity hesitated. She couldn't lie to him ... and yet, she wasn't sure *what* she wanted from Jamal. Revenge? She could humiliate him, if the Emperor let her, but at least he would be safe from everyone else. And yet, she knew Jamal didn't deserve to be safe. If he hadn't been such an unpleasant bully, would Johan have gone off the deep end too?

"I want him to be safe," she said, finally. "Having him know his safety is dependent on me will be revenge enough."

"How like a woman," the Emperor said. "Very well. You may go find him, if you wish, and bring him here. I will have a use for him."

"Thank you, Your Supremacy," Charity said. She looked down at the gauze covering her breasts. "May I change first?"

"I think not," the Emperor said. He smiled at her, nastily. "But you may use magic to defend yourself against all threats, save for me. Now go."

Charity turned automatically and walked out of the tent, her legs moving of their own accord. Outside, it was growing darker, but not dark enough to hide the harem outfit. She hesitated, cursing the Emperor in the privacy of her own thoughts, then drew her wand and cast an illusion spell over herself. Most magicians, seeing the glamour, would assume she was hiding a mole or making her clothes appear finer than they were, rather than hiding her body beneath an illusion. She just hoped that no one tried to cancel the spell for a joke. One of the students at the Peerless School had ended up naked after using magic to dress herself in finery, rather than buying them with her own money. Her enemy had cancelled the spell in the middle of class.

She turned and walked through the camp, ignoring the long lines of inductees, slaves and magicians being hauled over to the sacrificial altar. The Emperor hadn't hesitated to start killing magicians, particularly the weak ones who were of no other use to him. She shuddered as she passed a line of children, their magic not yet awake; they'd be dead long before their magic came to life. The red-robed were watching them carefully, ready to use spells or brute force to keep the children in line. There was no hope of escape.

The remains of the gates, manned by a handful of soldiers, loomed up in front of her. She held up the token the Emperor had given her – it felt like years ago – and they stepped back, allowing her to pass unmolested. Knawel Haldane seemed almost deserted, the handful of people on the streets hidden under hoods as they slipped through the darkness, trying to remain unnoticed by the soldiers. Charity had heard enough to know precisely how the soldiers were treating the civilians, particularly anyone unfortunate enough to be young, female and vulnerable. She clutched her wand tightly as she strode past a tavern, then cursed inwardly as a handful of drunken soldiers staggered towards her. Gritting her teeth, she raised her wand and turned them into snails.

The Emperor may punish me for this, she thought. The spell wouldn't last long, but there would be ample time for something to happen to the soldiers before it wore off. *But he did give me permission to defend myself.*

No one else tried to block her way until she reached the slave warehouse. She'd never been to one before, not when her father preferred to enslave servants using his own magic. The faint stench of human waste touched her nose as she tapped on the solid door, wondering if the dealer was still at work. No doubt there was something to be said for the chance to sell slaves to the army ...

She shuddered, feeling the cold wafting across her unprotected body. How was *she* any different from the poor bastards in the underground cages, just waiting for a buyer to take them home?

The door opened, revealing a fat man carrying a wand. He relaxed slightly as he saw her, although his piggy eyes never left her face. It wasn't a lustful look, more of a wary one; he could sense her magic, she was sure, even though he probably didn't know who or what she was. A gust of warm air blew out of the building as she stepped inside.

"I carry a message from the Emperor," she said, as she pulled the knife from her belt. "He wants to find the person who gave you this blade."

The slaver gave her a surprised look. "You mean Lot #453? He was telling the truth?"

Charity frowned. "What did he tell you?"

"That he was a magician and that he was from a powerful family," the slaver said. His pudgy face started to look nervous as he waved her into an office, then motioned for her to take a seat. "*Was* he telling the truth?"

"Partly," Charity said. "Where is he now?"

"In the cells," the slaver said. "We assumed he'd stolen the knife."

Charity took a breath. "What happened?"

The slaver stumbled over a long and complex explanation that reminded Charity of studying at the Peerless School, where something that could be said in a dozen words was often stretched into a dozen sentences. She had to resist the temptation to order him to get to the point, fearing it would only make matters worse. Eventually, she figured out that Jamal had fled the Golden City – without ever trying to recover his possessions from House Conidian – and made his way to Knawel Haldane, where he'd started a fight in a bar. Without his magic, he'd been beaten to a pulp and – as he didn't have the money to pay for the repairs – he'd been sold into slavery. His knife had been taken and kept by the slaver, then handed over to the occupation force when it had arrived.

"And it was a right waste of money," the slaver concluded. "*No one* wants him! No one! Not even as a drudge slave! I'll have to sell him to the mines!"

Charity snickered, despite herself. She had no trouble believing that no one would want Jamal, even as a spellbound slave. The mines would probably have taken him, eventually, and worked him to death. He'd really been quite lucky that his knife had fallen into her hands.

"Bring him here," she ordered, shortly. "I'll take him with

me when I go."

The slaver hesitated. "There is the matter of the money I paid for him …"

"The Emperor wants him," Charity said, cutting him off. "And seeing you're here, without being conscripted … I'd bet you don't really want to change that, do you?"

She smiled as the slaver turned and hurried away. He *was* a magician, although a very minor one; she was mildly surprised he hadn't been added to the magicians awaiting their turn on the sacrificial altar. But then, his speciality – enslavement spells – might come in handy for the Emperor. He'd probably find himself leaving with the army, when the time came, and practicing his art on prisoners of war. Given what he'd done to his victims, she found it hard to feel sorry for him.

It was nearly thirty minutes before the door opened again, revealing the slaver – and Jamal, wearing a slave's loincloth and a collar around his neck. Charity almost didn't recognise him; he'd once been tall and reasonably handsome, but now he looked dirty, hungry and thoroughly unshaven. He'd never learnt how to shave himself, not when he could use magic to do it; hell, he'd been *dependent* on magic for almost everything. His eyes went wide when he saw her.

"Kneel," the slaver said. Jamal, compelled by the collar, fell to his knees. "Is this the person you expected?"

Charity hesitated, caught in a complex whirlwind of emotions. How often had Jamal humiliated her in front of her friends and family? How easy would it be to use the collar to force him to humiliate himself? Or simply whip out her wand and show him exactly what it felt like to be at the mercy of someone with more power than himself? Her hand itched; she knew a dozen spells she could use and she'd laugh while she cast them. But … he was her brother, even though he was a horrible bully. Part of her was horrified to see what he had become.

"Yes," she said, when she trusted herself to speak clearly. "He's … he's the person I expected."

The slaver nodded, slowly. "I can remove the collar, if you wish," he said. "Or do you want it left in place?"

Jamal's eyes flashed with sudden hope, but Charity shook

her head. "Leave it," she ordered, shortly. "Transfer master authority to me."

The slaver pressed his hands together and bowed, then touched the collar while murmuring a spell under his breath. "Hear this," he said. "Your servitude is transferred to this young lady, who will be your mistress. Hear her orders and obey them."

He waved a hand. Jamal's body froze.

"Touch the collar to establish the link," he said. "And then you may do what you like with him."

Charity touched the collar, feeling a flicker of magic as it accepted her command over its victim. Jamal looked up at her, seemingly torn between hope and fear; Charity kept her face as impassive as she could, even though part of her just wanted to rub his situation in as much as possible. The slaver thanked her, then released the spell on Jamal and indicated the door.

"Thank you," Charity said. She looked at Jamal. "Follow me. Do not speak without my permission."

Jamal followed her as she strode back through the streets, always keeping two paces behind her. Charity couldn't help feeling a cold sense of pleasure at his predicament, even though he was helpless. No doubt he'd tried to force a woman when he'd entered Knawel Haldane and discovered, the hard way, that he no longer had the power to protect himself. She smiled at the thought as they entered the camp and walked to the Emperor's tent. Jamal said nothing – he couldn't escape the commands she'd given him – but she sensed his burning curiosity as she told him to wait outside, then stepped into the tent.

"I found my brother, Your Supremacy," she said. "He's a slave."

"Good," the Emperor said. He waved a hand in the air. A guard stepped into the tent seconds later. "Fetch Moeder from her tent."

"Yes, Your Supremacy," the guard said.

The Emperor looked at Charity. "And what condition is he in?"

"He seems reasonably healthy," Charity said, "but he has a slave collar …"

"Then we can bargain," the Emperor said. "Bring him into the tent."

Charity obeyed, wondering just how Jamal would react to discovering that she was practically a slave too. But then, what *could* he do? His eyes widened as he saw the Emperor, then he knelt in front of Charity. The Emperor seemed amused at his expression.

"So passes a once-great House," he said, softly.

The flap opened again, revealing a middle-aged woman with long brown hair and a thin expression that Charity found oddly familiar, even though she was *sure* she'd never seen the woman before. She prostrated herself in front of the Emperor, but there was something in the way she moved that suggested she was not under any form of compulsion. She'd offered her loyalty freely …

… And that was odd. A man, sure; Charity knew that thousands of men had pledged their loyalty to the Emperor. But a woman? And clearly one of some resource … it didn't make sense. *She'd* been forced to give *her* oath to the Emperor.

"Jamal Conidian," the Emperor said. "You are a slave. There is no hope for freedom, unless you pledge yourself to me."

Charity blinked. He *already* had Jamal as a slave. It wouldn't be hard for the Emperor to make *her* pass command authority to him. He didn't need Jamal to do anything.

"I have a task that needs doing, one you can perform," the Emperor continued. "If you complete the task to my satisfaction, you will be freed."

He looked at Charity. "Tell him he may speak freely."

"You may speak freely," Charity said to Jamal.

Jamal stared at her. "What happened to you?"

"She is mine," the Emperor said. "And so are you. Do you accept my offer?"

"Yes, sir," Jamal said.

"That's *Your Supremacy*," the Emperor said. He didn't sound annoyed, merely amused. But then, Jamal had left the city before he'd claimed the Golden Throne. "The Head Librarian is ahead of us, heading towards Ida, in company with your brother. You, Moeder and a squad of my guards will intercept them. Moeder will deal with the Head Librarian while you kill your brother. If this task is completed properly, you will be freed."

Jamal nodded, immediately. "I will do it."

"I imagine you don't like being a slave," the Emperor said. He reached out and touched the collar gently, very gently. "You will swear oaths once the collar is removed, oaths binding even on a powerless mundane. And if you betray me, you will suffer in ways deemed unimaginable."

He smiled, coldly. "Charity, take your brother to your tent, clean him up and make sure he gets some sleep," he ordered. "We'll swear the oaths tomorrow, then he can depart."

"Yes, Your Supremacy," Charity said.

Chapter Four

Johan didn't sleep well.

It wasn't Elaine's fault, he knew; indeed, the sense of her presence at the back of his mind was comforting. But there were some problems he wanted to deal with himself, without help, which made the bond between them awkward at best and embarrassing at worst. He waited until Elaine had slipped into sleep, then sat up and climbed out of bed. Dread gave him a sharp look, then tapped his lips sharply. Johan nodded, glanced at where Elaine and Daria were sleeping, then walked over to the window. Outside, night was falling over Falcone's Nest.

There are still hundreds of people on the streets, he thought, slowly. *What are they doing now?*

Dread came up behind him, walking so quietly that Johan didn't hear him coming. He wouldn't have known the former Inquisitor was there if he hadn't seen the reflection in the mirror. The older man moved with surprising stealth for his age. But then, he would have spent most of his career chasing Dark Wizards and Rogue Mages. He wouldn't have survived if he hadn't been very good at sneaking around.

"You should get some sleep," Dread said, very quietly. "We might need to leave in a hurry."

Johan turned to look at him. "You think we'll be attacked?"

"A team of soldiers could cover the distance between Knawel Haldane and Falcone's Nest in less than a day, if they exchange horses at each coachhouse along the way," Dread said, flatly. "We stayed off the main roads too, while they can take the direct route. They could be searching for us now."

"But they won't find us," Johan said. "Will they?"

Dread shrugged. "You'd be astonished just how much gets noticed," he said, dryly. "A person asking the right questions in the right place may locate us very quickly."

Johan swallowed. "We told the guards that Elaine was going to be married," he said, ignoring the odd feeling in his chest at the words. "They're not going to connect a high-born magical brat with the Head Librarian, are they?"

"Depends on what they think they're looking for," Dread warned. "The cover story won't hold together if someone starts asking the right questions."

"Like just who she's going to marry," Johan said. He'd known his father had planned to organise marriages for his siblings, marriages that could easily have taken his sisters away from the Golden City; surely, he wouldn't have sent them off without telling them who they were going to marry. "And the dowry and other matters."

"The first question would be bad enough," Dread said, wryly. He shook his head. "We'll go downstairs once the girls wake up and try and make contact. If we fail, we head onwards tomorrow without waiting any longer."

Johan nodded, slowly.

"But enough of that," Dread said. "How are you feeling?"

"I should be asking you that," Johan said. His father and Jamal had been broken when he'd taken their magic, but Dread ... seemed almost unchanged. "How are *you* feeling?"

"You didn't have a choice," Dread said, curtly. "I told you that, remember? I can't blame you for taking my magic."

"My brother would consider it a fate worse than death," Johan muttered.

"Which suggests a lack of imagination," Dread commented. "There are *far* worse fates than losing one's magic."

He met Johan's eyes. "How are you feeling?"

"Odd," Johan confessed. "I keep thinking about my sisters. Cass ... Cass told me I was being nasty to them, that I was being like *Jamal*."

"You probably were, if she called you out on it," Dread said. He didn't try to offer any false reassurance. "Cass was always very perceptive."

"I wish I thought she was wrong," Johan said. "Will I end up like Jamal?"

"Make a choice," Dread advised. "And then stick to it."

Johan gave him a sharp look. "That makes no sense."

"It makes plenty of sense," Dread said. "You have power. What you do with that power is up to you. Using it to torment your sisters is a choice. So is using it to heal the sick and save countless lives. You're not" – he glanced around the darkening room – "a cockroach, scuttling helplessly across the floor. Make a choice about what you want to do with your life and stick to it."

He shrugged. "But I think you *know* what it's like to be helpless," he added, after a long moment. "Do you really want to make anyone *else* feel that way?"

Johan shook his head, quickly.

"You're talking too loudly," Daria said, sitting up. "I can hear you even in my sleep."

"I'm sorry," Johan said, quickly. He felt a tingle in his mind as Elaine awoke too. "I didn't mean to wake you."

"Stay here," Dread said. "Johan and I will try to make contact with the Levellers. Keep the door closed and don't open to anyone, except us."

"Understood," Elaine said. She rubbed her tired eyes as she sat up next to Daria. "Good luck."

Johan had to force himself to look away. Elaine was cute, rather than pretty … and yet he felt a surge of attraction that surprised him. It struck him, a moment later, that she would sense his feelings … flushing bright red, he opened the door and stepped outside, glancing up and down the darkened corridor for any signs of life. Dread followed him, closing the door firmly. Elaine's wards would keep out anyone without magic who wasn't already keyed into them.

"Follow me," Dread ordered. "And keep one hand on your pouch at all times."

"Yes, sir," Johan said. There was something about Dread that just compelled respect from him, even though he was no longer an Inquisitor. "Shouldn't I be carrying a sword?"

Dread gave him a sharp look. "Do you know how to *use* a sword?"

"No," Johan said. "You point the sharp end towards the enemy, right?"

"It's a little more complex than that," Dread said, sarcastically. "Unless you spend hours training with a mundane blade, you're not going to be anything more than dead meat if you get into a swordfight. I'll try and teach you a few tricks, if you like, but you won't find it easy."

He led the way down the stairs and into the bar. A handful of men were still boozing, but most of the patrons seemed to have left the bar and headed home. Dread looked around, then headed straight towards the bartender. The blonde-haired girl standing behind the bartender eyed them both sourly, her eyes promising mayhem if they even *dared* try any games with her. Johan stepped up next to Dread, then cleared his throat.

"Knowledge is power," he said.

The bartender scowled. "Oh, piss off."

"But power is knowledge," the girl said. Her eyes glinted with sudden suspicion. "I don't recall seeing either of you before."

"We're from the Golden City," Dread said. "And we need to talk."

"Hawke sent us," Johan added.

"I'll take them into the backroom, father," the girl said. Her voice was brisk, rather than harsh or subservient. Indeed, she sounded like someone who was used to taking control. "Can you close up here?"

Johan looked from one to the other, puzzled. He'd assumed the bartender would be the Leveller, but it was the girl? On the other hand, he had to admit that no one would *believe* she was a Leveller. Bar wenches weren't expected to do anything more than hand out the beer, take the money and put up with being groped by drunken patrons. It was the perfect cover, assuming someone was prepared to tolerate the job. And the girl *looked* tough; her long blonde hair and dirty dress didn't disguise the muscles on her arms. Johan wouldn't have cared to get into a fight with her, not without magic.

The girl led them into a backroom, then closed the door and waved her hand. Johan's ability to sense magic was very limited, but it was clear she'd cast a privacy ward of some kind. The door locked of its own accord a second later, keeping everyone else out. It didn't escape Johan's notice that they were also locked *in* with a magician of unknown power. If the meeting went wrong, they could end up in deep trouble.

He closed his eyes, gently touching Elaine through the bond. She'd be looking through his eyes, for all the good it would do. Maybe, if the meeting went badly wrong, Elaine and Daria could escape before it was too late. He felt a flicker of concern on the other end of the link, then nothing more than calm patience. Elaine had always been more patient than him.

"My name is Sarah," the girl said, shortly. "The reports from Knawel Haldane are not good."

Dread leant forward, urgently. "What do they say?"

"The city has been attacked by dragons, werewolves, basilisks and hundreds of other creatures out of legend," Sarah said. She didn't sound particularly concerned. "We don't know how seriously to take them."

"The Emperor is using dragons, summoned using the magic of sacrificial victims," Dread said, flatly. "I imagine he won't have any difficulty summoning other creatures, if he wishes."

He cleared his throat. "And does that convince you," he added, "or do you want to keep the truth spell up?"

Johan blinked in surprise. He hadn't *sensed* the truth spell! How had Dread known it was there? Did he have some residual sensitivity to magic? Or had he recognised her casting the spell? Or had he tried to lie and found it impossible?

"I'd prefer to keep it for the moment," Sarah said. She gave them a crooked smile. "You'll be surprised just how many infiltrators have tried to sneak into our ranks."

"I wouldn't be," Johan said. He cleared his throat. "I saved Hawke's" – he tried to say *son*, but failed – "daughter. He was willing to pass on code words to us in exchange."

"So I hear," Sarah said. She studied him for a long moment, as if she was attempting to peer under his skin. "Did the Watchtower really fall?"

"It did," Dread said. He cleared his throat. "The Emperor is advancing towards Ida, for various reasons. There is ... *something* ... hidden there, we believe, that will utterly change the world. We have to get there first, before his army. However, we also need to slow the army down as much as possible.”

“And recruit other magicians,” Johan added. It was an insulting question, but it had to be asked. “How powerful are you?”

Sarah gave him a nasty look. “Would you like boils on your bum?”

“I’ve had worse,” Johan said. It was true. Jamal had once tested a torture curse on him, back when he’d been home from school. “I’ve met nastier sadists than you.”

“I was taught by a friend here,” Sarah said, after a moment. “I never went to the Peerless School … or any school, really. My wand is a hand-me-down that doesn’t always work.”

“And you cast the truth spell on the whole room, rather than just the two of us,” Dread said, flatly. “You don’t have the power to isolate a couple of subjects …”

“I have enough to keep the patrons from doing anything too bad,” Sarah said.

“You’re a magician,” Johan said. “Why are you also a Leveller?”

Sarah’s face darkened. “Do you think it’s easy being a very low-power magician when there are hundreds far more powerful and capable?”

“No,” Johan said. He thought, suddenly, of Elaine. She could have been like Sarah if things had been a little different. Enough magic to make her different, but not enough to become truly great. And yet, given enough knowledge, Elaine had managed to start rewriting her spells to do more with less. “I know it isn’t easy.”

“I am a Leveller, first and foremost,” Sarah said. She waved a finger at Johan, threateningly. “Do you want to question me further?”

“No,” Dread said. “We do, however, need to discuss planning with you.”

Sarah shrugged, then sat down on a hard wooden chair and scowled at them. “What do you want us to do? Bear in mind that we aren’t going to risk our lives too far.”

Dread met her eyes. “First, tell me what the political situation here is like.”

“The City Fathers are in a mess,” Sarah said, after a

moment's thought. "They've been hammering everyone who dares to repeat rumours from Knawel Haldane, even though the entire city knows. The City Guard is on alert, but they don't know who or what they're going to fight. Us? We've been keeping our heads down and trying to decide what to do about it."

"I see," Dread said. "Do you have any allies on the City Council?"

Sarah snorted, rudely. "Do you really think that any of *them* would ally themselves with *us*? We do have a handful of allies in the City Guard, but no one with enough power to force the City Fathers to see reason."

"I'll give it some thought," Dread said. "How many of you are there and how many are magicians?"

"I would prefer not to answer that question," Sarah said. She waved a hand in the air, dispelling the truth spell. "I *will* tell you that I'm not the only magician."

Johan leant forward. "Is there anyone significantly more powerful than you?"

"Some," Sarah said, flatly.

"There are spells we could teach them, new spells," Dread said. "You might find them useful."

"I'm sure," Sarah said. "Enough to stand up to a dragon?"

Dread looked uncomfortable. "I would prefer not to allow those spells to become common knowledge," he said. He cleared his throat. "Do you have any way of taking over the city?"

"Probably not," Sarah said. "We'd wind up with a civil war."

"Then we need your magicians to come with us," Dread said. "In the meantime, we also need to bring down the bridges and make it harder for the enemy to ship his men across the river."

"Correct me if I'm wrong," Sarah said in a tone that reminded Johan of Charity in a snit, "but dragons *fly*, don't they? There's nothing stopping one flying over the river and bathing the city in fire. Or do you think a dragon will refuse to fly over the water for fear of its wings suddenly failing and plunging into the icy waves?"

Johan felt himself flush, angrily. His power, his strange

power, rose to the forefront of his mind. He could humble her, he could break her, he could strip her magic …

Calm, Elaine said, through the link. *Take a deep breath and be calm.*

I'm trying, Johan sent back, *but* …

He forced himself to take a long breath, calming down. It wasn't easy. No one had talked to him like Sarah had since he'd gained his powers. It brought back all the bitter memories of endless humiliations at the hands of his family, the people who should have loved him no matter what happened. And it would be so easy to revenge himself on them.

"The Emperor wishes to push an army at Ida," Dread said, calmly. "The nearest natural ford on the Lug River is ninety miles to the north. Taking down the bridges will force him, at the very least, to divert men and material to build pontoon bridges. Unless" – he quirked an eyebrow – "it's possible to swim the Lug?"

"Not here," Sarah said. She smiled, rather coldly. Johan couldn't help thinking of a predatory animal moving towards its prey. "The river looks deceptively tranquil, but only a complete idiot would attempt to swim it. There are all sorts of nasty currents towards the middle. I know sailors who turn pale at the thought of trying to navigate through the river."

She frowned. "But what's to stop him from bringing his men over on dragons?"

"Very little," Dread said. "But it will take a *very* long time for him to merely move them from one side of the river to the other, if he's completely dependent on dragons. Anything that slows the main body of his army is worth doing, I think."

"Maybe you're right," Sarah said. "He'll still take it out on the city, won't he?"

Johan took a long breath. "Yes, he will," he said. "But I don't think you can expect to be treated well in any case."

"The rumours from Knawel Haldane make that clear," Sarah agreed. She stood, brushing her hands down her filthy dress. "I will, of course, have to discuss it with my fellows. Those of us who are magicians will be interested …"

"I would hope so," Dread said. He frowned. "There really

isn't much time. I imagine they could be here within hours if they wanted to merely rely on the dragons."

"I'll tell them," Sarah assured him. "You'll be safe in your room, for the moment."

"Thank you," Johan said. He hesitated, then asked the question that had been nagging at his mind ever since he'd realised that Sarah was a magician. "Why do you work *here*?"

Sarah shrugged. "My father owns the inn," she said. "It's a good place to hear what's going on – and besides, without me, one of the fights would burn the whole building to the ground soon enough."

"But can't you get a better job?" Johan asked. "Somewhere where you can use your magic?"

"Not when I barely have enough to light a candle," Sarah snapped. "I don't even have enough to be interesting on the marriage market."

She opened the door and nodded to the stairs. "We'll be in touch within the next couple of hours," she added. "Don't leave the building; if you need food, ask one of the other wenches to get it for you. I wouldn't advise eating anything from here unless you want to spend the next few hours on the pot."

Johan shuddered in disgust. Sarah smirked at him.

"You're a long way from the Golden City," she said. "Welcome to how the rest of the world lives."

Chapter Five

"I can still talk," Jamal said, once he and Charity were alone in her tent. "What happened to you?"

Charity glowered at him. "You left me in charge of the family, you *bastard*," she said. The nasty part of her mind wondered if Jamal *was* literally a bastard. But no, her father would have tested him as soon as he was born. And besides, he *looked* more like his father – and Johan – than any of them would have preferred. "I didn't have a choice."

Jamal looked at her, sharply. "To do what?"

"To pledge myself to the Emperor," Charity snapped. "To become his pawn – his puppet – in exchange for the safety of my remaining siblings."

"*Our* remaining siblings," Jamal said.

"You're a slave," Charity said. "You *have* no siblings."

Jamal smiled, rather thinly. "So are you."

"Shut up," Charity ordered. Jamal's mouth snapped closed. "Don't say another word until I say otherwise."

She glared at her older brother. His eyes seemed to be glimmering with amusement, although a single word from her could have had him cutting his own throat. And yet, the Emperor had a use for him. She could no more defy the Emperor than Jamal could defy her – and he knew it, the bastard. A slave had no kin, a slave was nothing but property … and she was a slave too. Jamal had been quite right.

"The Emperor wants you to kill Johan," she said. "Do you think you can?"

"I don't seem to have a choice," Jamal said, taking her question as permission to speak. "I want to be free."

"Yes, it *is* awkward having to do what you're told," Charity sniped. She might have felt sorry for him if he hadn't cast compulsion charms on her while she was growing up. "Do you really think the Emperor will free you?"

"He said he'd remove the collar," Jamal reminded her. "Are you *allowed* to suggest he might break his word?"

"I haven't been told otherwise," Charity said. She picked up a bell from the table and rang it, once. Moments later, a maid – the slave collar around her neck clearly visible – stepped through the flap and into the tent. "Fetch a large basin of warm water, a cloth, a towel and some commoner clothes for my brother."

"Yes, Your Ladyship," the maid said. She looked Jamal up and down, silently gauging his measurements, then turned towards the flap. "I will be back as soon as possible."

"Now there's someone obedient," Jamal remarked. "She hardly needs the collar."

Charity shook her head in disbelief. "Have you forgotten the collar around your neck already?"

She allowed her voice to harden. "Tell me what happened after you lost your powers – and don't try to hide anything."

Jamal's face twisted as he tried to fight the collar for a long moment. Charity watched him absently, wondering if Jamal was strong enough to defeat the enchantment – and what she would do if he was. But he had no magic and force of will alone wasn't enough to defeat such an intrusive spell. In the end, he couldn't hold out any longer.

"I fled through the tunnels and out into the countryside," Jamal said. His voice became a whine. "There were too many people who would want revenge. I reached Knawel Haldane and rented a room at an inn while I tried to decide what to do. But I ran out of money very quickly and they refused to extend any credit! They didn't know who I was!"

"Of course not," Charity said, nastily. "Everyone knows that House Conidian only produces powerful magicians, not Powerless."

Jamal glowered at her. "They took me, shoved me into a cell and snapped a collar on me," he added, bitterly. "And then no one would even *buy* me!"

Charity laughed, even though it wasn't particularly funny. If the Emperor hadn't attacked Knawel Haldane, Jamal would eventually have been sold to the mines – or worse – and worked to death. The thought of her snooty bully of an older brother slaving away deep underground, digging up coal or gold, was surprisingly amusing. No one would ever have known what had happened to him, nor would anyone have really cared. House Conidian was better off without him.

"It must have suited you," she said, finally. "And it was precisely what you deserved."

"I am the Prime Heir to House Conidian," Jamal said. "I …"

"You were the Prime Heir right up until the moment you lost your magic," Charity said. Their father might have stripped Jamal of his position anyway – the gods knew the old man had been running out of patience, once Jamal had been arrested by the Inquisitors – but it no longer mattered. "A Powerless can't be Family Head."

Jamal flushed at her words. How often had he thrown them at Johan, before casting a spell that had left the younger boy humiliated? Losing his magic had to be the worst fate Jamal could imagine, if only because of all the people who'd want revenge. Charity wouldn't have bet a single bronze coin on his surviving longer than a week. But he had, barely.

He would have been worked to death in the mines, she reminded herself, as the tent flap opened and a pair of male attendants carried in a large washing tub. She'd heard stories about the mines and none of them were good. *He wouldn't have survived more than a few weeks.*

"Undress, then wash yourself," she ordered. The servants bowed to her, then turned and left the tent. "I want you completely clean, so don't forget to wash the collar. And keep your mouth shut, unless you have an urgent question."

Jamal's face burnt with humiliation. "I need to … ah … take a shit."

Charity flushed in embarrassment. "There's a bucket in the washroom," she said. Trust Jamal to get under her skin, even when she held all the power. "Do your business there, then wash yourself. Once you are clean and dressed, call for me."

She touched her wand at her belt, then headed through the flap into the next room. The maid would give Jamal the clothes, once they were ready, and the collar would keep him from doing anything she'd find objectionable. Until then … she sat down at her desk and stared at the handful of remaining artefacts, wondering what surprises *they* might hold. But as she started to work her way through them, it became clear that they simply weren't particularly interesting.

At least the knife might be useful, she thought, touching it gingerly. She might not have been its mistress, but the charms on the blade would work for her too. *I can use it, if necessary.*

It was nearly an hour before Jamal called her name. Charity sighed, then rose to her feet and stepped back through the flap. Jamal was standing in front of the maid, wearing a long brown outfit that reminded her of the farmers she'd seen before the family had headed to the Golden City … and fallen apart. It was cleaner, though, than anything a farmer would wear and would probably attract attention. She had to force herself to resist the urge to order Jamal to roll in the mud a few times before taking him back to the Emperor. Instead, she settled for beckoning him to follow her as she strode out of the tent.

Night had fallen completely, but the camp was lit up by hundreds of glowing lanterns, throwing shadows everywhere. She hesitated, then led Jamal towards the sacrificial pits, where a dozen red-robed sorcerers were systematically butchering the magicians unfortunate enough to live in Knawel Haldane. Their hands chained with magic-resistant cuffs, the poor sorcerers didn't have a chance. One by one, they were marched to the block and beheaded, their magic extracted from their body and channelled into the Emperor's crystals. Their dead bodies were carried off by slaves to a nearby tent, where the bodies were stripped of anything useful for dark rituals. The sorcerers didn't stop being valuable after their deaths.

She smiled, inwardly, as she heard Jamal gag. He'd been an asshole, all right; he'd bullied his younger siblings and anyone who didn't have the magic to stand up to him. But he'd never killed, as far as she knew, and he'd certainly never set out to slaughter hundreds of lesser magicians for their magic and blood. He knew, as well as she did, just what one could do with the remains of a dead magician. To see what the Emperor was capable of …

It might make him think, she thought, although she suspected it wouldn't. Jamal was a slave, helpless and trapped. He'd do anything to escape that fate, no matter how vile. By now, Johan's death would seem a minor price for freedom. If *she'd* been offered the same choice, Charity asked herself, what would she have done? Killed Johan ... if, of course, it was *possible*. Johan's magic was so strange that no one really understood how it worked. *Jamal might end up dead instead.*

"Let me go," a voice screamed. Charity looked towards the line of magicians and saw a girl who couldn't be much older than herself, struggling helplessly against her restraints. "Let me go!"

A red-robed sorcerer pointed a wand at her and she screamed in pain, falling to the ground and thrashing helplessly. Her fellows made no move to help her, but then ... there was nothing they could do. The red-robed sorcerers, their robes the colour of blood, picked the girl up, threw her over the altar and nodded to the headsman. A second later, her head hit the ground and a surge of magic flared into one of the crystals. Jamal swallowed, loudly enough for Charity to hear, as the remains of her body were taken away.

"I never asked," Charity muttered, as they slipped away from the bloodstained altar. "Why did you keep picking on us?"

Jamal's face contorted as he struggled to keep his treacherous mouth shut. "Because it was fun," he said, finally. "I *liked* watching you all under my power."

Charity wished she was surprised. She'd been told at the Peerless School that a certain amount of bullying was acceptable, if only to encourage young magicians to learn how to defend themselves. Jamal had once even had the nerve to tell her that the itching hex he'd hidden on her robes was for her own good. But Jamal had taken it far too far ... and the only reason he'd done it was because he *enjoyed* it. Their father had never tormented Jamal merely to force him to become better.

"You're sick," she said, finally.

"Fuck you, little sis," Jamal snapped back. "Which of us

pledged herself to the Emperor?"

"Shut up," Charity snarled. He was right, of course; his collar could be removed, but her oaths were binding until the day she died. "And pinch yourself as hard as you can."

Jamal grunted in pain. Charity felt a brief moment of satisfaction before it was washed away by despair. Jamal would be freed; *she'd* remain a slave for the rest of her life. It wasn't fair … she pushed the thought aside as she stepped into the tent, then prostrated herself in front of the Emperor. He was staring into the distance, his face oddly slack. For an odd moment, she was half-convinced she was prostrating herself in front of the wrong person.

"Charity," the Emperor said, shaking himself out of his funk. "Is Jamal ready to depart?"

"Yes, Your Supremacy," Charity said. "All he needs is the collar removed."

"So he does," the Emperor said. He waved a hand at Jamal and the younger man froze, unable to move. "We will start with a blood oath."

He produced a dagger from his belt and carefully placed the blade against Jamal's neck, breaking the skin just enough to produce a tiny line of blood. Charity watched, torn between fascination and horror, as the Emperor muttered the words of a spell, magic flickering around the cut and shimmering into Jamal's body. She'd never seen anything quite like it, but somehow she wasn't surprised the Emperor would use such a ritual. Blood was the single most potent magical substance that could be extracted from the human body.

"Your task is the death of your brother Johan," the Emperor said. "This oath will push you onwards until your brother is dead, whereupon it will break and you will be free."

At least he mentioned Johan by name, Charity thought. Their younger brothers were at the Peerless School, reasonably safe … or as safe as they could be, with a mad Emperor on the Golden Throne. An oath that didn't specify *which* brother had to die could be subverted quite easily. *Jay and Jolie will be safe.*

She shuddered in horror. The Emperor had made *her* take

children from the Peerless School, children who had been used in a ritual for summoning entities from beyond. Yes, they'd been newborn magicians, with no families to complain ... but the Emperor was now so powerful that the remaining Great Houses didn't have a hope in hell of stopping him. He could take Jay and Jolie from the Peerless School if he wished, unless the Administrator stood up to him ...

And that isn't going to happen, she thought. *He doesn't have a backbone, let alone the support of the staff.*

The Emperor muttered another set of words in an unknown language, then smiled. "You may remove the collar."

Charity groaned inwardly, then reached for the collar and pulled it off effortlessly. She *was* its mistress after all. Jamal didn't move, of course; the Emperor's spell was still holding him in place. And then the spell broke and he lunged at her, only to be thrown back by her protective wards. His body hit the side of the tent and fell to the ground.

"I hope you will be more careful when attacking your brother," the Emperor observed, as Jamal slowly picked himself up from the ground. "Trying to attack your sister when she has her magic ... my, *what* an idiot you are."

He looked at Charity. "Hurt him."

Charity lifted her wand and cast a simple spell. Their mother had taught her the spell when she'd started her menses, telling her that it was an effective deterrent to any man who thought he could force himself on her. Jamal's eyes widened, then he grabbed for his crotch, screaming in pain. Charity pushed more power into the spell as he hit the ground again, curling up into a ball. It didn't matter what he did, she knew. He had no magic to counter the spell.

"Enough," the Emperor said, quietly. He smiled at her, showing impeccable teeth, as Jamal slowly pulled himself back to his feet. "Did you enjoy that?"

Charity didn't want to answer, but she had no choice. "Yes."

"Good," the Emperor said. He clapped his hands together, once. "Moeder!"

The rear flap opened, revealing the older woman. Charity stepped aside as she nodded to the Emperor, wondering –

again – at the odd sense she *knew* the woman from somewhere. The woman ignored her completely, her dark eyes travelling over Jamal and clearly dismissing him. Jamal looked back at her, then glanced at Charity. His eyes were wide with fear.

It hurts, Charity thought, vindictively. *Doesn't it? To be helpless as someone hurts you because they can.*

"Jamal has a blood link to Johan," the Emperor said, curtly. "You will take a dragon and move ahead of us, towards Ida. Once you have a clear line to Johan, you will close in on him and kill him, then capture the Head Librarian. You know what to do then."

"Yes," Moeder said.

She didn't offer any honorific, Charity thought, shocked. *Who is this woman?*

"We won't fail you," Jamal stammered. "I won't let you down."

"See that you don't," the Emperor said. "The consequences will be very unpleasant if you do."

He closed his eyes for a long moment, summoning a dragon, then led the way through the flap and out into the field. A large dragon settled to the ground moments later, beady eyes inspecting the passengers as though they were nothing more than a snack. Charity had to smile at Jamal's reaction – he wouldn't have seen the dragons as they tore through the city's defences – and then stepped backwards as the dragon looked at her. Like the one that had carried her earlier, it didn't seem to like her.

"You should be able to get there before daybreak," the Emperor said, as the guards mounted the dragon. "I don't want the dragon seen, if possible."

"We will do our best," Moeder said. "But by now rumours will be spreading everywhere."

"Of course they will," the Emperor said. "Will they be believed?"

Probably not, Charity thought. The last dragons, as far as anyone knew, had died out hundreds of years ago. Dragonhide cloaks, capable of repelling almost any curse, were worth literally *millions* of gold coins ... if, of course, one could find a seller. *No one will believe there are more dragons now, not when they don't know where they come from ...*

The Emperor turned to her. "Do you want to say anything to your brother?"

Rot in hell, Charity thought.

She cleared her throat. "I hope I never see you again," she said. "And you are no longer part of House Conidian."

Jamal opened his mouth to say something cutting, but Moeder pushed him onto the dragon and then scrambled up after him. The dragon flapped its wings, then leapt into the air, leaving nothing but warm air behind. Moments later, it had vanished completely in the darkness.

No one will see it, Charity thought. She wondered, briefly, what Johan was doing, then shook her head. *No one will see the dragon until it's far too late.*

Chapter Six

"Welcome to one of our lairs," Sarah said, as Elaine followed her through the door. "I trust I can rely on you to keep your mouth shut?"

Elaine nodded, looking around with interest. The Leveller base was really nothing more than a private school, one of the places where middle-class children received an education that might – might – allow them to aspire to rise in the world. A handful of orphans had won scholarships to similar schools in the Golden City, she recalled; she'd hoped to win one herself before she'd discovered she already had a place at the Peerless School. And if she'd been a little different, she might have ended up like Sarah.

The schoolhouse had four classrooms, she discovered as they walked through them, and a single large hall for games. She puzzled over it for a moment – there was plenty of space outside for the children to burn off energy – and then realised it provided an excuse to have a large space that could double up as a training room. A handful of wards brushed against her awareness as she passed through the door, spying seven other magicians sitting on the floor waiting for her. Five of them had their faces hidden behind glamours; the other two, both young women, were staring at her defiantly. She wondered if she would recognise them, but when she took a closer look neither of the women were familiar.

"This is Elaine," Sarah said. "I believe she has something to teach us."

"I do," Elaine said.

One of the glamoured magicians snorted. "What can a librarian teach us?"

"You would have been taught spells designed for magicians with far more power," Elaine said, bluntly. There was no time to be polite. "Like me, you will have had real problems making them work because you don't have the magic to smooth over the cracks. This put you all at a major disadvantage when facing more powerful magicians."

She took a breath. She disliked talking to strangers, let alone trying to teach them something important. Vane had handled all such matters in the Great Library. But Vane was dead or enslaved, Daria didn't know the material and Dread couldn't teach magic any longer. Hell, he couldn't have mastered *her* spells even if he'd still had his powers. She was the only hope they had.

"I've spent the last six months devising spells that use less power, but have the same effects," she continued, carefully. "There's no reason why you shouldn't be able to use those spells too."

The first magician snorted, again. "I was told that was impossible."

Elaine raised her wand and cast the first spell, generating a ball of light hanging in the air. If she'd used the standard spell, it would have begun to flicker very quickly as it took a toll on her magic; now, it just glowed permanently. The speaker made a spluttering sound, then drew his own wand and cast a diagnostic charm. There was hardly any link between her and the ball of light, now it was drifting away from her.

"That's impossible," he said.

"No, it isn't," Elaine said. She hesitated, then took the plunge. "Your tutors didn't really comprehend *how* their magic worked. They never really realised that there were ways to cut down the power requirements."

Sarah stared at the light, her face transfixed. "But *how*?"

Elaine took a moment to think of an example. "Pretend you want to build a bridge over a river," she said. "You can cut down a tree and use it as a bridge – one solid piece of wood – or you can build the bridge up from many smaller components. My spells" – she nodded to the glowing ball – "are composed of a number of small spells, working together to produce a perfect result. The overall power requirements are much weaker than casting the whole spell in a single effort."

"You'd need a great deal of concentration," the first speaker said.

"She has it," Sarah said. "And so do you, Brian."

"No names," Brian hissed.

"We all pledged ourselves to secrecy," Sarah reminded him. "And if we get caught, we're doomed anyway."

Elaine nodded. The Empire hadn't cared much about the Levellers – although it was growing increasingly clear that that had been a mistake – but the Grand Sorcerers would be horrified at the thought of *magicians* turning against the Empire. Sarah and her allies might be weak magicians, yet they were *still* magicians. They couldn't expect anything other than an unpleasant death from the Grand Sorcerers, let alone the Emperor. But then, with the Empire falling apart and the Witch-King preparing to return to the world, it was quite possible that no one would be around to care.

"I have a number of other adapted spells," Elaine said. She'd planned to teach them at the Peerless School, before Johan had come into her life. Light Spinner had seen the value, even if many other traditional magicians had not. "I can teach them, if you are willing to learn, but there's something we need in exchange."

Sarah gave her a sharp look. "And that would be …?"

"We need you to come with us," Elaine said. "Some of the spells I devised will be too revealing if used before we're ready."

"That would mean abandoning my wife and family," Brian said, coldly. "Or do you expect them to come with us?"

"If they will," Elaine said. Given Brian's level of power, it was unlikely he'd married into a magical family. His wife was probably a mundane and his children … either weak magicians or mundanes themselves. Would they count as Powerless? Probably. "I have spells that should take down a dragon, but if they're used too early the Emperor will be able to take countermeasures."

"Dragons," Brian sneered.

"They're real," Elaine said, quietly. She'd had nightmares about the creatures wheeling over the Golden City. Inquisitor Cass and Lady Light Spinner had been killed by the dragons, according to Dread, and they'd both been powerful magicians. "The Emperor intends to use them to crush all resistance."

"He's likely to succeed," one of the girls said. "What do we have here that can stop a dragon?"

There was a long pause. Elaine worked her way through the knowledge in her head, but the only solution the ancients had found involved either sacrificial magic or dragons of their own. A dozen magicians working together might *just* kill a dragon, if they managed to hold together long enough, yet while they were killing *one* dragon the others might tear them apart. And dragons were *tough*. Swords, spears and arrows just glanced off their armoured hides. A lone man on a horseback had about as much chance of surviving as would a mundane at the Peerless School.

"We could always try to drown them," Sarah offered, after a moment. "A simple spell would make them *much* heavier, plunging them downwards. If we cast the spells at the right time, they'd go straight into the Lug."

"And then the spell would be countered by the Emperor and his servants," Brian pointed out, rudely. "We *could* use water bubbles."

"They'd breath fire and the water would turn to steam," the girl snapped. "Unless it was a *lot* of water."

"Flame-repelling charms might work," Sarah said.

"They breathe magical fire," Elaine said. Part of her was enjoying the session – it was the kind of brainstorming she'd never really had at the Peerless School – but there just wasn't time. "They'd go through charms and burn their way through wards."

"We could ward parts of the city," Sarah said.

"It wouldn't last very long, even if every magician got involved," Brian said. "We just don't have the power to seal off the entire city."

He cleared his throat. "I will send my family out on a boat," he said. "We have relatives on Casaubon. My wife and children can stay there, for the moment, while I leave the city with you."

Sarah lifted her eyebrows. "You've changed your mind."

"Shut your mouth, wench," Brian said, without heat. "If we can't stop the dragons, we need to get out of here before it's too late. My wife will be safe enough without me, for the moment, as long as she's well away from here."

Sarah looked from face to face. "I can send a messenger to our families," she said. "Is there anyone here who doesn't want to accompany our friends to their final destination?"

"I can't leave the city," one of the other glamoured magicians said. He – no, Elaine realised, *she* – rose to her feet. "I'll take the messages, if you wish."

Elaine sat back, silently gathering her thoughts, as the magicians hastily wrote out messages for their families. She hoped the families readied themselves to leave at once – surely, the Levellers would have plans to escape the city the moment word got out – and left by the end of the day. There was no way to know what the Emperor was doing, but it wouldn't take long for a handful of dragons to fly to Falcone's Nest and attack. Dread wanted to leave tomorrow, whatever happened, and he'd made it clear that he thought they were cutting it fine.

"Very well," she said, once the six remaining magicians had settled down in front of her, ready to learn. "This is the first defensive spell ..."

It took nearly an hour for them to master the first spell, not entirely to her surprise. They'd been taught to put too much power into their spells, which was inconvenient when they simply didn't have the power to make it work. She had to go through the spell, component by component, demonstrating how it went together to form a seamless whole before pushing them into trying to cast it for themselves. It was a well-chosen spell, she thought. Anyone trying to cheat would find themselves rapidly running out of magic.

"It's a weird effect," Brian said. He'd been the first to master it. "Like a thousand *little* spells rather than one."

"That's the point," Elaine said. "Think of it as sharing the weight amongst those spells ..."

"Like having three other people help to pick up a box, rather than carrying it yourself," Sarah said. She sounded frustrated. *Her* spell wasn't working out so well. "You might have to coordinate properly, but at least you won't be doing all the work yourself."

"You're still trying to force your way through," Elaine said, gently. "Don't push so much power into the spells."

Sarah gave her a nasty look. Elaine understood; Sarah had

been told, years ago, that she had to force the spells to work, even though she didn't have the reserves to make them stick. It was a lesson that had plagued Elaine too, right up until she'd learnt how to rewrite the spells herself. But then, if she'd been as determined to prove herself as Sarah, she might have pushed herself to breaking point trying to coax more magic out of her body.

"You're either overbalancing or destroying the spells," she added. "Let the magic flow naturally, once the spells are ready."

"There," Sarah said. "It works."

"And you're not even being drained," Elaine pointed out. "Just think about using these spells in combat."

Sarah frowned. "What's to stop them doing the same? The Emperor's forces, I mean. These spells aren't *that* difficult."

Elaine bit down on the temptation to point out that Sarah had been the last magician to master the spell. She doubted Sarah would thank her for pointing it out. Instead, she tapped the scorch marks on the floor where Sarah's spells had disintegrated into light and heat.

"They had the same training as you," she said, "but they weren't so frustrated. Right now, making magic work through force of will is second nature to them. They wouldn't see any downsides because they have power to spare."

She had to fight down a stab of envy. Dread had had power to spare; Light Spinner and the Privy Council had been among the most powerful magicians in the world. Millicent – her oldest enemy – had been powerful enough to get courted by dozens of magicians, including a number who were considerably older than her. But Elaine had never had those power reserves and, no matter what she did, there was no way to gain them without courting madness. The powerful magicians would always have an unfair advantage.

Bitterly, she forced the feeling aside. "They won't be able to alter the way they cast their spells easily," she added, as reassuringly as she could. Sarah and she had had *far* too much in common. "Even if they start learning my rewritten spells, casting them would force them to unlearn everything they'd mastered at the Peerless School."

"They could do it," Sarah said.

"Not easily," Elaine repeated. She took a breath. "They'd really have to go all the way down to bedrock, while they'd see their greater power reserves as a way to jump forward. It would take them years to master *my* spells to the point where they can use them to save energy while casting the more powerful spells."

"I hope you're right," Sarah muttered.

Elaine smiled. "Do you remember how the more powerful students always used to have trouble with their potions?"

"I didn't go to the Peerless School," Sarah snapped. "And I never had any talent for potions."

"They had real problems mastering the art of using their magic to blend the ingredients together," Elaine said. She'd known, intellectually, that Sarah wasn't formally trained, but she hadn't really believed it. But then, she hadn't grown up outside the Golden City, where magical students were identified before their magic came to life. "It was the middle-ranked students who tended to be best at brewing potions."

"I'll take your word for it," Sarah said. She cast the spell again, shaking her head in disbelief as a glowing orb of light appeared in front of her. "What else can you teach us?"

Elaine smiled.

It was, she decided afterwards, one of the most interesting experiences of her life. She'd never been nominated to tutor anyone at the Peerless School – she simply didn't have the power reserves to cow a first-year student, let alone anyone else – and she honestly didn't like the idea of tutoring *anyone*. And yet, there was something about watching them cast her spells and make them work that thrilled her. She rubbed her eyes, feeling the glamour in place that hid her eyes from casual inspection. If it wasn't so tiring, she might even have suggested they stay at work right up until dusk.

"There's dinner in the upper room," Sarah said, straightening up. "Make sure you eat as much as you can."

"Yes, mother," Brian said.

Sarah jabbed her finger at him; he raised a defence, just in time, as the spell splattered into his protections and flashed out of existence. Elaine sighed, inwardly; she'd wondered if

Brian had been the one to teach Sarah, but it was clear she didn't *treat* him like a tutor. Brian, at least, had had some formal schooling. The thought made her smile as she followed Sarah up the stairs and into the dining room.

"I meant to ask," she said. "Do you teach magic here?"

"Not officially," Sarah said. She gave Elaine a wintery smile. "But we do watch for students with potential and try to steer them towards us. If we'd known about your spells …"

She paused, suddenly. "Do the Inquisitors know about them?"

"I'm not sure," Elaine said, honestly. *Dread* knew, of course, but had he discussed the matter with anyone other than Light Spinner? Come to think of it, had *Light Spinner* talked about it with her advisers? Elaine doubted it – powerful magicians wouldn't have wanted to consider spells that might make lesser magicians their equals – but it was possible. "I was talking about them with a few people, but I don't know how many others they might have told."

"You should have kept them for yourself," Sarah said, curtly. "Or shared them with us."

"I didn't know about you at the time," Elaine said. She'd only heard vague rumours of the Levellers before Johan had met Hawke … and she'd never taken them seriously. "And we were short of trained magicians. Too many died in the Golden City."

"Good," Sarah said. "The Empire is rotten to the core. It needs to die."

"There will be war," Elaine said. "Kingdoms will declare independence, then wage war on their neighbours. Dark Wizards will tear through entire countries …"

Sarah smiled as she passed Elaine a plate of food, wrapped in a stasis spell. "Tell me," she said, sweetly. "What exactly do you have sitting on the Golden Throne?"

"A monster," Elaine said. She had no doubt of that, not after Deferens had cast a spell on her that would eventually have worn her down, if she hadn't managed to free herself just in time. And he'd sacrificed *children* to summon the dragons back into the world. "Deferens is a monster in human form."

And he has the Witch-King pulling his strings, she added, silently. *Everything Deferens has done must benefit him in some way.*

"Exactly," Sarah said. "Or, in other words, a Dark Wizard."

Elaine sat down and began to eat, barely tasting the food. The Empire had ruled the entire world for over a thousand years. Indeed, most people believed the Empire to have been around for far longer; Elaine suspected that only the Witch-King and she knew better. But now, with a tyrant on the Golden Throne and the Inquisitors at his beck and call ... the Empire had become a nightmare. Perhaps it was time for it to go.

But if we can't hold it together, she thought, remembering when she'd been on the Privy Council, *what will take its place?*

Chapter Seven

"So that's how you did it," Dread said, looking down at the barrel of Firepowder. "And there's no magic here at all?"

"None," the chemist confirmed. He hadn't shared his name; indeed, he'd refused to meet their eyes as he showed them the Firepowder. "And I can't make any more either."

Johan cursed under his breath. "There's three bridges," he said. "Do we have enough to bring them all down?"

"The first bridge can be burnt," Bill said. Sarah had introduced him to them, then headed off with Elaine to learn magic. "It's the other two that are the real problem. I don't think we have enough Firepowder to wreck them both."

Johan turned to look at him. He was fat and bald, although there were muscles rippling under his arms that suggested he would be a nasty customer in a fight. Johan suspected, from the way he had looked at Sarah, that he had a crush on her, although there was no way to be sure if it was anything more. They certainly hadn't *acted* like lovers, but that might not mean anything.

"Getting onto the bridge will be a problem," the chemist said, bluntly. "There aren't any Iron Dragons at night, but the bridges are guarded at both ends."

Dread leant back, thinking hard. "We couldn't just blow a hole in the middle," he said, slowly. "That could be repaired quickly, perhaps even before the enemy arrives. We'd need to wreck the spans."

"There are other ways to produce fire," Johan said. *His* power could produce *something*, he was sure. "Couldn't we go out there and see?"

"We might have to," Dread said. He looked at Bill. "Can you take us near the bridges so we can inspect them?"

"Of course," Bill said. "What do you want to do with the Firepowder?"

"Leave it here, for the moment," Dread said. He threw a

glance at Daria, still in wolf-form, then nodded. "We'll come back for it if we see a way to put it to use."

Johan followed Dread and Bill out of the hidden workplace and down through the streets towards the river. The smell of rotting fish grew stronger; he had to force himself not to gag as they passed a market, the tables strewn with fish, shellfish and even a single giant whale being slowly cut down into its component pieces. Bill explained, as they headed onwards, that Falcone's Nest sent out a handful of whaling ships, although the whales tended to be very good at fighting back. It wasn't uncommon for whalers to vanish somewhere in the cold ocean.

He looked down the river towards the sea as it came into view, then tilted his head to look at the bridges. They were spectacular, strange mixtures of wood, stone and iron – the final one quite resistant to magic – that dominated the river. It must have been an immense task to build even one of them, he reasoned; the cost in lives must have been terrifyingly high before the river had finally been tamed. And yet … he peered towards the waters and shuddered as he saw the currents, out in the midst of the river. Sarah was right. The Lug was still a treacherous piece of water.

"Guardhouses at both sides," Dread said, quietly. "And reinforcements on call, ready to intervene if we did anything. Those structures may even be tougher than the Watchtower."

"And the blast needs to strike the spans," Bill added, equally quietly. "Firepowder doesn't work like blasting hexes, sir. If you put a barrel beside the span the blast will follow the path of least resistance."

"Then we'd need to get the Firepowder inside," Dread reasoned. "But how?"

He shook his head. "I need to consider the possibilities," he added. "Can you give us some time here?"

"Sure," Bill said. "Just meet up with us at the inn."

He turned and strode away, whistling cheerfully to himself. Dread sat down on a wooden bench, stroking Daria's fur absently. Johan had to fight to keep the amusement off his face; Daria was, after all, a werewolf. Surely, *someone* had noticed by now. It wasn't as if she was the same size as a regular dog.

But few werewolves would pretend to be normal, he reminded himself. *They might refuse to believe that a werewolf could act like a dog.*

"I don't see any way to do it, unless your magic can work," Dread said, softly. "Do you think you can damage the bridges?"

"I'm not sure," Johan admitted. On one hand, his power cut through normal wards and protections as if they weren't there; on the other, he'd never tried anything so large. A normal magician could summon fire and use it as a weapon, but would it be enough? "Do you think I should try?"

"I think there isn't any other choice," Dread said. They'd talked a little about his power in the days since Dread had lost his, although it hadn't been a pleasant conversation for either of them. "We'll try at night, unless you want to try now."

Johan nodded. "We'd have time to warn the others," he said. "Will they try to close the gates?"

"That's a problem," Dread agreed. "But we can probably slip out, if necessary. There's usually a tunnel or two running under the walls."

They rose, then returned to the inn. Daria snapped back into human form as soon as they were safely in their room and headed for the bathroom, while Johan lay down on the bed and watched darkness slowly descending over the city. Dread spoke briefly to Sarah – and an exhausted Elaine – and then ordered food for the rest of them. Elaine, it seemed, had already eaten. Johan watched her sleeping for a long moment, then turned his attention to Dread and Sarah.

"The families are already out of the city," Sarah said, shortly. "Those of us who are magicians are going to be coming with you, as you wanted. The others ... are going to be making themselves useful when the Emperor arrives."

"You can't stop him," Dread said.

"We can at least *try* to make his life miserable," Sarah said. "The City Fathers will bend the knee to him at once, should they live so long. We, on the other hand ..."

"Very good," Dread said. He leant forward. "We'll slip out of the inn once it gets completely dark."

"Just make sure you stick to the shadows," Sarah advised.

"Can either of you cast a glamour?"

" ... No," Dread said.

"Then make sure you take some coins to bribe the Watch, should they catch sight of you," Sarah said. "You don't want to spend the rest of the night in the pokey."

"Of course not," Dread agreed. "Can you get me some equipment? I need a rope and a set of janitor's tools."

Sarah smiled. "Planning a spot of burglary? They hang thieves here, you know."

Johan shuddered. It wasn't a pleasant thought.

They set out again an hour later, picking their way through the darkened streets. Johan couldn't help feeling that the streets were darker than before, as if the city was slowly becoming aware of the danger confronting it. There were only a handful of lanterns, while many of the citizens seemed to be heading indoors as fast as they could. The marketplace, so full of life when he'd seen it earlier, was now deserted; he slipped on a piece of fish and swore quietly as he almost landed on his rear.

"Careful," Dread hissed. "You don't know if there's anyone on guard."

Johan nodded as they slipped down to the river and peered into the darkness. It was eerie; he could see a handful of lights, where a number of boats floated in midstream drifting up and down with the tide. The bridges themselves were illuminated by lanterns hanging down from the railings, indicating their positions to anyone foolish enough to try to sail up or downriver in the pitch darkness. And, on the other side of the water, he saw nothing. There wasn't even a single light shining out in the shadows.

"There could be anything out there," he breathed.

"You're getting the idea," Dread said. There was a grim note to his voice. "The Emperor could have moved advance scouts to the Lug under cover of darkness."

Johan looked up. The stars were twinkling overhead. Were there dragons up there too, unseen and unheard, just waiting for the command to attack the city? It would be hard to hide something so big from detection, but if the magicians weren't *looking* for dragons who knew if they'd sense *anything*? Did dragons *have* a magical signature? There was no way to know until one of them crossed a ward intended to sense magic-users ...

Dread touched Johan's shoulder. He jumped.

"There isn't much time," Dread warned. "Try to take out the bridges now."

Johan nodded, taking a deep breath. No matter what Elaine said, his power just didn't work normally. Using it was difficult, nothing like Elaine's careful building up of spells for maximum effect. Indeed, it only worked well when he really – *really* – wanted something, be it freedom from Jamal or revenge on his cursed family. And he didn't really *want* to destroy the bridges. They were *brilliant*.

He clenched his fists, summoning hatred. They were *dangerous*. The Emperor could use them to ship troops across the Lug and take Falcone's Nest, then advance onwards to Ida. It could not be allowed. He forced himself to think of the innocent civilians who were in deadly danger, concentrating his anger on the bridges. Again, there was a strange shimmer of power ...

... And he *hated*. He *hated* the bridges.

The first bridge went up like a fireball, the heat so intense that steam boiled up from the water as the bridge melted like a snowflake caught in bright sunlight. Johan heard someone screaming as night turned to day, but he had no time to care as he switched his hatred to the second bridge. It was easier, now, to generate the rage that boiled through him, tearing through the bridge and sending great gouts of flame spewing in all directions. The third and final bridge seemed made of stronger stuff, for a long second, and then it too melted as the flames grew hotter and hotter. The heat slapped his face, setting a dozen wooden ships on fire, their sleeping crews trapped beneath the decks as flames roared through their boats ...

... And he was *killing* them.

He sagged to his knees, anger gone. How many people had he just killed? The Levellers had been sure there were no people on the bridges at night – apparently, it was a guaranteed whipping to be caught trying to sneak across under cover of darkness – but they hadn't bargained on him incinerating the boats. Guilt stabbed him, a bitter guilt that tore through his rationalisations. The bridges had had to die – of that he was sure – but did the innocent civilians deserve to die too?

"Impressive." Dread said, neutrally.

Johan looked up. The first bridge was gone; little remained, save for a handful of foundations poking out of the water. Flames crackled along the water's edge, incinerating the remains of the guardhouse. Beyond it, the second bridge was a twisted ruin – the iron, it seemed, had survived the fires – while the third bridge was still burning brightly. Somehow, Johan doubted that *anything* could cross now. All the City Fathers would have to do to keep themselves safe – or safer – was round up the boats and move them to their side of the Lug.

He saw a burning boat and shuddered. How many had he killed?

"We can't stay here," Dread said. Someone had started to ring the bells – and, in the dark hours before dawn, it could only be to warn of danger. The fires were dying down, throwing the riverside back into darkness, but it wouldn't be long before guardsmen were scouring the shoreline for signs of who – or what – had destroyed the bridges. "They'll catch us."

Johan barely heard him. He reached out for Elaine's presence in his mind, but she was sleeping. There would be no comfort from her … if, of course, there *was* anything she could say to make him feel better. He'd just killed at least a hundred innocent people to save thousands more. He didn't deserve comfort, he deserved punishment. How was he any different from Jamal?

"Come on," Dread snapped. "They're coming!"

He pulled Johan to his feet, then up towards the darkened streets as the sound of running footsteps echoed through the air. They were just in time; a long line of armed men ran past, heading down to the shore. The bells were growing louder as more and more temples added their bells to the chimes, alerting the population to … what? Johan wondered, as Dread pulled him further into the darkness, if the City Fathers would finally believe in the dragons. A dragon could easily rip a bridge to shreds if it wanted.

Or if the Emperor ordered them to cut the links between Falcone's Nest and the other riverside, he thought. *Maybe he'd want to keep rumours from spreading further.*

"Keep quiet," Dread ordered. "And stay in the shadows. We don't want to be caught anywhere near the riverbank."

Johan nodded and followed Dread as they returned to the market place. A handful of men carrying improvised weapons stood in the centre, looking for potential threats. They didn't look very professional, but he knew that didn't stop them from being dangerous. Gritting his teeth, he stayed low and followed Dread as he crawled under the tables and into the alleyway at the far side of the marketplace. The smell of fish faded, to be replaced by the smell of humans trying to find a place to stay for the night. A handful of men were huddling together against the wall, wrapped in blankets. He felt a stab of pity as they crawled past them and onwards, back towards the inn.

"Hey," a voice bellowed. Johan jumped. "Stop!"

Dread muttered a curse as Johan turned to see a City Guardsman running towards them, club in hand. There was a nasty expression on his face as he approached, a strange combination of glee and fear. Johan puzzled over it for a moment, then realised the guardsman must be torn between the rewards and dangers of catching the people responsible for destroying the bridges. But would they have the slightest idea what had happened?

"Show me your papers, now," the guardsman demanded. "Why are you out this late?"

"It's like this, officer," Dread said. "I ..."

He slammed a fist into the guardsman's throat, crushing it instantly. The guardsman, already dead, fell to the ground like a sack of potatoes. Dread checked the unfortunate man's pouch, removed a handful of coins and a small wallet of papers, then dragged the body into the shadows and dumped it there.

"The body will be stripped by the homeless when they find it," he said, when he noticed Johan staring at him. "They'll mess up any signatures a magician can use to track us, if they even try. Guardsmen die all the time."

Johan shuddered, fighting hard not to lose his dinner.

Dread had killed the man so ... so *casually*. Johan had killed far too many people when he'd taken down the bridges, but that had been different. Dread had done it with his bare hands. It ...

"I don't think we're going to be able to get back to the inn," Dread said, as he pulled Johan further down the maze of alleyways. The noise of an alerted population was growing louder and louder. It wouldn't be long until they stumbled over the body. "I wonder ..."

He looked up at the windows, then nodded to himself and scrambled up the side of the wall like a monkey. Johan had no time to do more than stare as Dread opened the window, slipped inside and vanished. Moments later, he stuck his head back out of the window and dangled a long line of rope down to Johan. Bracing himself, Johan gripped hold and climbed up the wall and through the window. Inside, it was a musty room with a tiny bed. A young man lay there, staring at them in horror. Dread had tied his hands and feet, then shoved a cloth in his mouth.

"We're not going to harm you," Dread whispered, "as long as you answer a few questions truthfully. This is a doss-house, right?"

The man nodded, frantically. "Good," Dread said. He reached into his pouch and produced a pair of gold coins. "You stay quiet and don't do anything and you can have this when we leave."

Johan blinked. "I ..."

"Tiny room, communal bathroom and little else," Dread said, curtly. "Just the sort of place for an apprentice craftsman until he graduates. And no one pays any attention to any of them, as long as there isn't a riot underway."

"Good," Johan said. Outside, he could hear running footsteps. "What happens tomorrow?"

"We'll see," Dread said.

Johan nodded, then froze as he sensed a sudden flash of alarm from Elaine. Something was wrong. She was in danger!

"What happened?" Dread asked. "Johan?"

"She's in danger," Johan said. "I have to go to her."

"It's suicide right now," Dread said, grimly. He looked

down at the dirty floor. "They must have started rounding up outsiders, people from outside the city. Shit!"

Johan swallowed. The cover story, already flimsy, wouldn't last very long when Elaine's captors realised her two guards were missing. They had to get back to her …

… But with so many people on the streets, it would be impossible.

He closed his eyes, reaching for her presence in his mind. *I'm sorry*, he sent. *But we'll be there as soon as we can.*

Chapter Eight

Elaine started awake when she heard the bells.

For a moment, she thought she was back in the Golden City. The bells had woken her when she'd been an ordinary librarian, with little to look forward to beyond endlessly shelving books. Not that it had been a bad life, she had to admit; boring, perhaps, but it was all she'd ever wanted. And then she recalled just where she was and sat upright, feeling her head spinning in pain. She'd drained herself too far teaching magic to the Levellers.

Daria snapped back into human form and walked over to the window. "There's a riot outside," she said, peering through the murky glass. "And flames in the distance."

Elaine sat upright. Her ears were nowhere near as sharp as Daria's, but she could hear hundreds of people shouting, barely audible under the deafening sound of the bells. She grabbed for her wand from where it was hidden, under her pillow, yet she barely had the energy to produce a spark of magic. She gritted her teeth, then reached for Johan's mind through the mental link, but all she sensed was a flurry of odd feelings. Her tiredness had weakened the link.

"Shit," she muttered. "What are they rioting about?"

"I'm not sure," Daria said. "But the flames seem to be coming from the bridge."

Elaine massaged her temples. Dread and Johan had set out to wreck the bridge and, judging by the flames, it looked as if they'd succeeded. And the people below were rioting …? Did they think the enemy was at the gates?

"We might need to get out of here," Daria said, sharply. The sound of the crowd was turning nasty. "Someone's shouting about dirty foreigners."

There was a crashing sound from downstairs. Elaine swung her legs out of bed and stood, despite the tiredness in her muscles. The shouting was growing louder, the sound of the crowd as it surged out of control echoing in her ears. It made no sense – Falcone's Nest was a trading town; there were hundreds of foreigners within the walls – but it was happening. She remembered the rioting in the Golden City and shuddered, just as the entire building shook violently. Here, there were no Inquisitors to stop the riot.

"They're crashing upstairs," Daria said. "We need to get out of here."

She snapped back into wolf form and sniffed the air, growling faintly. The sound sent shivers down Elaine's spine. She'd never really been scared of Daria, not after learning her long-time friend was a born werewolf, but now she understood why so many people were terrified of werewolves. She gritted her teeth, then raised her wand as the sound of running footsteps grew closer. There didn't seem to be any easy escape.

The door burst open, revealing four wild-eyed men. They looked at Elaine and stared, their mouths dropping open in horror. It took Elaine a moment to realise that she'd forgotten to renew the glamour on her eyes and it had faded when she'd fallen asleep. To them, she had to look like a monster – or worse. Daria growled and lunged forward, teeth and claws ready to fight; one of the men raised a wand and slammed a spell into her, tossing her right across the room. She landed on her feet and came back, teeth bared, but the second spell threw her right through the window. Elaine desperately reached for a spell, even a tiny one, yet her magic was too drained to respond. She scrambled backwards in terror and fell, tripping over her own feet. There was a dull thud as her head hit the wooden floor and everything blurred out for a long moment …

"Kill the bitch," someone growled.

"No," another voice said. "You heard the boss. Take the foreigners to the pit."

"She's a monster," a third voice said. "Red eyes are *never* good."

Elaine fought to reorder her thoughts. Her head was spinning madly, a dull ache reminding her that she'd banged her skull against the ground. There was a heavy weight on her shoulders, leaving her wondering if her entire head was dead or numb. It took her several minutes, in her confused state, to reason out that she would be dead, if her neck had been snapped. No magic could keep someone alive like that for longer than a few minutes …

And they'd seen her eyes. It was too late to try to hide them, even if she could. The third voice had been right; red eyes were *never* good. They almost always marked a brush with wild magic. And … did Deferens know she had red eyes? Dread knew, but had he told Deferens during his unwilling servitude? Or had Light Spinner told him when he'd asked – as Elaine knew he had – why Elaine was serving on the Privy Council? Did he *know* he was looking for a woman with red eyes?

Her hands weren't working; her eyes were puffy. Slowly, despite the pain, she forced her eyelids open, fighting down the urge to squeeze them shut. She was kneeling on the floor, a wooden block resting on her shoulders; it took her a moment, through the haze, to realise that her hands were trapped in the block, holding them firmly in place. The runes carved on the wood, combined with keeping her hands largely immobile, would make it very difficult to use magic … if, of course, she'd had a spark left. It would be hours, at best, before she regained the ability to cast even the simplest spell.

She felt sick and had to swallow hard to keep from throwing up. Healing wasn't one of her skills, but she was fairly sure she had a concussion. She swallowed again, then looked around as best she could. Five others, three men and two women, were kneeling against the wall, their hands blocked up too. A pair of children, a boy and a girl, sat next to them, their eyes wide with fright. Judging by their clothes, they too were outsiders.

Johan, she thought, trying to speak through the bond. *I* …

A wave of nausea overcame her, forcing her to stop trying to reopen the bond. She wasn't sure if it was the blow to the head, or the charms on the block, that were keeping her from touching Johan's mind, but it didn't matter. All that mattered was that she was a prisoner … she looked past the other prisoners, trying to see their captors. A handful of grim-faced young men were leaning against the wall, one of them holding Elaine's wand in his hand as he looked around. The magician? She had no way to sense his presence without magic of her own.

"Get them on their feet," the magician snapped. "Hurry!"

One of the male prisoners sneered at him. "Do you think there's going to be a trade deal after this?"

"Dirty foreigner," the magician said. He nodded to one of his men, who punched the prisoner in the stomach, then dragged him to his feet and shoved him against the wall. "We don't *need* your trade!"

The statement was so absurd that Elaine stared at him in disbelief. Falcone's Nest *depended* on trade. Ships would dock, bringing trade goods from all around the world, and depart carrying trade goods from the Golden City or any of the inland states. There was no way Falcone's Nest could survive for long without trade. Attacking foreign traders – and long-term residents – was nothing more than a fancy way of committing suicide. What were they *thinking*?

She scowled inwardly as she was helped to her feet. The plank made it damn near impossible to do anything more complex than standing straight; if she fell, she'd be unable to break her fall. Her captors sneered at her as she was pushed against the wall, then searched her quickly and efficiently. The magician poked at her pouch carefully before pocketing it. Elaine knew there was no point in trying to protest, even though there were a dozen gold coins concealed within the pouch. There was no hope of escape until her magic recovered and she could make contact – again – with Johan.

I should be used to this by now, she thought, feeling an odd flicker of amusement. *At least they haven't hit me with any spells.*

The thought jarred a memory loose from her mind. Daria had been blown out of a window ... and then, what? A werewolf could survive anything short of powerful magic or a silver blade – her brain offered a dozen ways to use magic to overwhelm a werewolf – but it had been a long fall, right into the midst of an angry crowd. Was she all right? Had she had the sense to run and hide? She could find Johan and Dread and lead them to Elaine with her nose ... or was she sneaking around somewhere, waiting for an opportunity?

There was no way to know.

She pushed the thought out of her mind as her captors started hustling the prisoners forward, through the door and out into the bar. The innkeeper – Sarah's father – met her eyes for a brief moment, but said nothing as she walked past him. His clients weren't so restrained; they hooted and jeered, while one of them threw a mug of beer at one of the captive women. She lowered her head as much as possible as the beer soaked into her thin nightdress, leaving it clinging to her skin. Elaine silently promised herself the chance to hex the man, when her magic returned, then braced herself as the doorway was pushed open. Outside, the sun was just starting to rise.

I must have been out for hours, she thought, numbly. It had felt like seconds, but she had a feeling her judgement was unreliable. *It was dark when the riot started, wasn't it?*

The streets were jammed with people, staring at the foreigners as they were marched out of the inn and into the middle of the road. Elaine cringed inwardly as more insults – along with a handful of rotten vegetables – were thrown at her and the other captives. She gritted her teeth as she saw an egg strike one of the children, the thrower snickering loudly, as if he'd done something worthy of applause. The crowd laughed as the little boy started to cry …

This isn't normal, Elaine thought, numbly. *Something's forcing them to act this way.*

But was that true? She'd seen hangings – and other public punishments – and the crowds watching hadn't behaved any differently. They'd jeered at men walking towards the gallows, they'd laughed at women placed in the stocks for the night; they'd even hurled stones at criminals who were particularly unpopular. Maybe it was human nature always to mock the weak, just as she'd been mocked in the Peerless School. Or maybe the Witch-King was behind it, urging the crowd on. He had to know where they were going, after all, and a purge of foreigners might well catch one or more of them.

It did catch one of us, Elaine thought, as they were herded into a public park. *It caught me.*

"Stand still," the magician growled. He held her wand in

front of her, then snapped it effortlessly. "Would you like these pieces inserted where the sun doesn't shine?"

Elaine did her best to ignore him, pretending to be in shock. They didn't know she could do wandless magic; hell, if they had bothered to calculate her potential, they'd be damn sure she *couldn't* do wandless magic. It wasn't easy to cast a spell without using a focus – a wand was really nothing more than a stick – but she could do it. If, of course, she managed to get her hands out of the block.

She closed her eyes for a long moment, steadying herself, then looked at the wood. The runes were designed to direct magic away from the wood, breaking the spell down into nothingness. It wasn't a bad piece of work, she had to admit, but it was outdated. The Inquisitors had devised far more capable handcuffs for magical prisoners. Given time, she was sure she could overpower the runes and escape …

If they give me the time, she thought, glancing around. The park was slowly filling with prisoners, all clearly foreigners. Men, women and children, many looking terrified as the crowd stared at them, anger and hatred written over their faces. Were they going to be publicly lynched? Sold into slavery? Or merely left here to rot as the crowd jeered and threw things? *What are they doing*?

"Kneel," the magician ordered. "Get down on your knees."

Elaine scowled, but resistance was clearly futile. The grass was muddy and stained her trousers, leaving her feeling cold and powerless. She was trapped … which, she knew, was how they wanted her to feel. Gritting her teeth again, she kept studying the runes. Breaking free would be simple enough, if she could muster the power …

She frowned as she saw a man, wearing dark blue robes, levitating himself into the air and clearing his throat. He must have used an amplification spell; she had no difficulty in hearing his words, even over the roar of the crowd. And he must have been important, because as he started to speak the crowd quietened down. Even the hail of rotten vegetables and pieces of mouldy fish came to a halt.

"For too long, we have been dependent upon foreigners," he said. His voice was so compelling that Elaine *knew* he had to be using magic. It was almost hypnotic; anyone who thought, even slightly, that he might be right wouldn't be able to avoid falling under his spell. "They have taken our wealth and what have they given us in return? Nothing!"

"NOTHING," the crowd echoed.

"They have even destroyed our bridges, our pride and joy, our triumph over the Lug," the speaker continued. "The entire world hated and feared the power we showed when we tamed the river and opened the far side of the continent to trade. Now, they have ruined our bridges and ruined our lives.

"I, Alfred of House Godwin, say NO MORE!"

"NO MORE," the crowd echoed.

"Today, we purge the dirty foreigners from our city," Alfred screamed. His dark moustache wobbled as he spoke. "Today, we obliterate all foreign interference and return to the days of our forefathers! Today, we show them the power that tamed the Lug!"

Elaine stared at the crowd, feeling sick. They couldn't believe it, could they? But they *wanted* to believe it. Falcone's Nest really wasn't *that* important, save as a trading post; they had to resent their position even as they valued the money it brought. As far as she knew, the city didn't really produce anything, apart from dried fish. But the crowd *wanted* to believe him and, as long as they wanted it, they were easy prey for his spell.

They don't have a hope, she thought, bitterly. *Even if Deferens wasn't a few days away, they'd never be able to survive. There are five other states dependent on trade links through Falcone's Nest. It wouldn't be long before an invasion force brought the trading post to heel.*

She cursed, inwardly, as she saw the plan. Falcone's Nest would have a civil war, sooner rather than later, making it easier for Deferens to enter the city. Yes, the bridges were gone – at least, she *hoped* they were gone – but he'd still be able to fly troops over the river and land outside Falcone's Nest. The city wouldn't have a hope of mounting a defence.

The Witch-King is clearing the way for his tool, she thought, as she peered at Alfred. Even from a distance, it was clear the sorcerer wasn't entirely in his right mind. Like Hawthorne, he'd been touched by the Witch-King; like

Deferens, he was sacrificing his own advantage for the Witch-King, probably without having the slightest idea that he was being manipulated. *This city would be a great place to slow him down, if the City Fathers could be convinced to mount a defence.*

She wondered, again, just how the trick was done. Most compulsion spells tended to be blindingly obvious, at least to an outsider, but the Witch-King's spells were undetectable. Or so she assumed. Any reasonably capable Great House would regularly check its own people for traces of outside influence – and, she assumed, Deferens' family would have done the same for him. And yet they'd found nothing. She wondered, briefly, if she'd have the chance to examine Alfred, then dismissed it as unlikely. There was no way he'd sit down and let her poke and prod at his mind for a few hours.

"The dirty foreigners will be paraded around the city, then butchered in the pit," Alfred said, loudly. "They will see – the entire world will see – just how we defend our rights!"

Elaine shuddered as the crowd roared its approval. It was madness, absolute madness. Once word got out – and it would – there wouldn't be a single ship docking at Falcone's Nest. And the friends and relatives of the dead would be furious. Alfred was likely to wake up in a few days and see an army approaching his city …

Another army, she thought, ruefully.

"On your feet," the guards snapped. "The city wants to see you."

"Please, no," a woman shouted, as Elaine rose. "Please …"

The guards ripped her shirt away, revealing her bare breasts. Elaine looked away as the crowd cat-called, mocking the poor woman. The guards prodded Elaine with their staffs, forcing her to stumble forward. She reminded herself that she'd survived worse – Millicent had been *very* inventive, back at school – and shuffled forwards. Once she had her magic back …

And the others are still out there, she reminded herself. *They're free.*

Chapter Nine

"It's Alfred," Sarah said, curtly. "The bastard launched a coup."

Johan scowled. They'd left the apartment at daybreak, after stealing a set of clothes from their unwilling host, and made it back to the inn, only to discover that Elaine and a number of other foreign guests had been marched off by the crowd. Johan had spent several minutes trying to reach Elaine through the mental bond, yet there had been no response beyond a vague feeling she was still alive. He'd wanted to go rushing off after her at once, but Dread had told him to wait, eat and see what the Leveller spies found out. They'd need a plan before they risked a rescue mission.

"I'm not familiar with the name," Dread said, after a moment. "Who *is* he?"

"A magician," Sarah said. Her voice dripped disdain. "Claims to be a first-rank sorcerer; I don't know if it's true or if he's just posturing. He was born here, but lived in the Golden City for at least ten years before returning and setting himself up as an adviser to some of the City Fathers, eventually getting himself nominated to the Council despite being" – her lips twisted – "a dirty foreigner. In some minds, at least."

"He was born here," Johan said, crossly.

"Anyone who doesn't spend his entire life here can be called a dirty foreigner," Sarah said, darkly. "It's stupid, but it's the way it is."

She glared down at the table as if it had personally offended her. "He must have had some kind of contingency plan, because he had his people out on the streets within moments of the bridges going up in flames and most of the rest of the Council in his grasp," she added, after a moment. "Right now, he controls the City Guard and a small army of baboons who hate foreigners and want to kill them all."

Johan sucked in his breath. "I thought this city *depended* on foreign trade."

"It does," Dread confirmed. "And how long will it be before others start an uprising against Alfred?"

It took Johan a moment to work out the implications. "Civil war," he said. "The city will be torn apart."

"Leaving nothing to stop Deferens from walking into the remains and taking over," Dread said, curtly. He looked at Sarah. "Have you found Elaine?"

"Not yet," Sarah said. "A number of the prisoners are being paraded around the streets, just to make it clear that they're being purged. Alfred ... isn't particularly subtle about how he wields power."

Johan looked up as Daria stepped into the room, looking tired. "Daria!"

"It's good to see you," Daria said. She wore a robe that was several sizes too small for her, but looked too tired to care. "Elaine's been taken."

"We know," Johan said.

"She was in the park, held captive," Daria said. "I don't think she's in a good state."

"So we rescue her," Johan said.

"It won't be easy," Daria said. "There were over a hundred guards and at least three magicians, counting Alfred himself. They snapped her wand."

Dread took a moment to gather his thoughts. "Alfred is trying to trigger a civil war," he said, shortly. "If he was determined merely to take and hold power for himself, he would have rounded up all his possible opponents. Instead, he's left a number of them free while gathering all the foreigners in the city. He hasn't even taken *hostages!*"

"That's our conclusion," Sarah said. "It won't be long before the merchants start building armies and fighting back. The city will die without trade."

"But that's what he wants," Dread said. "The only way to win this is to cut off the head of the snake – in this case, Alfred himself."

"Good luck," Sarah said, sarcastically. "He's a powerful magician and he's always surrounded by guards."

Dread's lips twitched. "A powerful magician *wouldn't* be

surrounded by guards," he said, dryly. "He'd know far more useful protections than swordsmen."

"My father never had guards," Johan agreed. He looked at Dread. "I could go after him …"

"And get yourself killed," Dread said. He looked at Sarah. "Where is Alfred now?"

"He spent some time addressing the crowd, then returned to the City House," Sarah said. "I assume the rest of the City Fathers are inside, but we don't know for sure. The handful of staff has been told to stay home and wait for further orders."

"But we know where he is," Dread said, slowly. "Could you get something into the building?"

Johan looked at him, sharply. "That barrel of Firepowder?"

"Yes," Dread said, shortly. "It worked on the Watchtower, where there were so many protections woven into the walls that I would have bet my magic that nothing dangerous could break through easily. Here … I imagine the explosion would be an even greater surprise."

Sarah looked doubtful. "You'd be practically advertising what happened to the Watchtower to *everyone*."

"I don't think we have a choice," Dread said.

"We could try to free Elaine instead," Daria offered. "You two could pose as guardsmen, then slip up to her and break her out of the pillory. There's no reason to stay here any longer …"

"They'd know you didn't have permission to free her," Sarah countered. "Alfred was very insistent that all dirty foreigners remain imprisoned until they could be killed."

"Instead of simply killing them all immediately," Dread said. He shook his head, slowly. "Alfred definitely wants a civil war."

Johan closed his eyes, reaching out to Elaine again. This time, there was a faint hint of a response before it faded away into nothingness. She was alive, at least, but not in a good state. What had happened to her?

If they've hurt her, I'll kill them personally, he vowed. Elaine had been the first person to show any concern for him, unlike his family. *I'll make them suffer …*

"We need to see the City House," Dread said. "Can we pass unnoticed?"

"As long as you don't open your mouths," Sarah said. She rose to her feet, smoothing down her dirty dress. "You both sound as though you're from the Golden City."

"I don't," Johan protested. He'd only spent a few months in the city before they'd fled and the only people he'd spoken to, really, were his family. Not that he'd *want* to sound like Jamal in any case. He'd need to stick something smelly under his nose if he wanted to try, then walk around with his head in the air. "I sound like …"

"It doesn't matter," Dread said. He deepened his accent, sounding alarmingly like Sarah's father. "Keep your mouth closed unless it's urgent."

Johan nodded, reluctantly. "Yes, sir," he said.

The streets seemed darker, somehow, as they walked out of the inn, Daria following them in wolf form. Small groups of people were gathering together, muttering so quietly that he couldn't hear anything beyond a faint sound, but Daria looked alarmed. It took him a moment to realise that very few women were on the streets. He couldn't help remembering the nightmarish days when they'd hidden from Deferens' forces in the Golden City. Were they doomed to keep their heads down for the rest of their lives, knowing that a single mistake might betray them? Or would they find the Witch-King and destroy him?

Maybe not, if we can't get out of the city, he thought. *We might end up trapped here until Deferens arrives to kill us.*

He gritted his teeth as he saw a handful of prisoners, their hands trapped in wooden planks resting on their shoulders, being marched down the streets. Elaine wasn't among them, thankfully, but his heart went out to the helpless men and women. He'd been helpless far too often in his life, thanks to Jamal, and he knew he'd hated it. And the prisoners had done nothing wrong, beyond being in the wrong place at the wrong time. They didn't *deserve* to be treated like this.

"Hold your peace," Dread whispered. "You don't want to be caught."

City House came into view slowly, a brooding mass that reminded him of some of the guildhouses in the Golden City.

A dozen guards stood outside, weapons in hand, watching as a team of craftsmen slowly put together a giant gallows. It was larger than any Johan had seen – it wasn't common to hang more than one prisoner at a time – but there could be no doubting its purpose. The foreigners were going to be ruthlessly purged from the city …

And he's moving supplies into the building, Johan thought, as he saw a cart being unloaded at the side entrance. There was enough food there to feed a small army, while a dozen other carts were waiting to be unloaded. *Is he planning to hold a party or stocking up in expectation of a siege?*

Dread watched the guards for a few minutes, then led Johan on a circuit around the building and back towards the inn. Daria followed, the werewolf sniffing the air constantly, as if she were searching for Elaine. Johan reached for Elaine again, mentally, and felt a stronger pulse. She was alive, but trapped. Something was interfering with the bond.

"We're going to have to get the barrel into the building," Dread said, once they were back at the inn. Bill and Sarah met them there. "There's nothing magical in the Firepowder, is there?"

"No," Bill said. "But they'd certainly think something was odd if they saw it."

Dread looked at Sarah. "Where's he getting the food?"

"His men have raided a couple of foreigner-owned warehouses," Sarah said, shortly. "A herald announced that everyone is invited to a party, after the foreigners are butchered."

"So he isn't even preparing for a siege," Dread said. He smiled, rather darkly. "How many barrels of beer do you have here?"

"Twenty-five," Sarah said. She smiled at his shocked expression. "My father believes in maintaining a stockpile."

"We need to donate some to Alfred," Dread said. "Put the barrel of Firepowder in the middle of the load, then surround it with barrels of beer. There won't be any magic on the barrel to alert him when it passes through his wards, so the guards will only take a cursory look."

"Particularly if it looks as though we're trying to curry favour with him," Sarah said. "But my father will be furious."

She sighed. "And once we get them into City House," she added, "how do we set up the explosion?"

Dread hesitated. "I can ... *Daria* can brew a very basic heating potion," he said. "We can buy the ingredients at the apothecary. Done properly, it won't register as dangerous magic, but it will catch fire at the right time. And that will trigger the explosion."

"Too chancy," Sarah objected. "The explosion might not go off at the right time – or go off at once, if you blunder with the potion."

"I won't blunder," Daria said, angrily.

Dread gave Sarah a long look. "Do you have a better idea?"

"Use a timed candle," Sarah said. "I have several here for guests. It shouldn't be hard to rig an oil dish to catch fire when the flame reaches the bottom, triggering the explosion."

"Test it," Dread ordered. He didn't sound convinced. Johan wasn't surprised. Magic was reliable, but Firepowder was something else. "The rest of us will start loading up the cart."

It was nearly thirty minutes before the barrel of Firepowder was placed in the centre of the cart and surrounded by eight barrels of beer. Sarah's father, as she'd warned, had been furious when he'd heard the plan, although he was clearly determined to stop Alfred before he could kill off the tourist trade. Johan privately doubted that *anyone* would want to visit Falcone's Nest after foreigners had been rounded up, publicly humiliated and then prepared for execution, but he kept that thought to himself. Given that Deferens was only a few days from the city, it was very likely a moot point anyway.

"It seems to work," Dread said, doubtfully. Sarah had rigged up an oil dish for the candle, then worked out a way to hide it within the barrel. "And if it fails ...?"

"We can sneak back into the building and try something else," Sarah said. "At worst, one of us can drop a lighted taper into the barrel."

"Blowing yourself up too," Dread pointed out.

Sarah rounded on him. "I understand the risks," she

snapped. "And I understand what will happen to us if Alfred keeps his hand on the city's throat. So shut up and let me work unless you have a better idea."

Johan sighed. "Calm down, everyone," he said. Dread had been used to spending days without sleep, when he'd had his magic. Did he realise he couldn't do that any longer? Johan had once tried to stay awake for three days, but by the time the third day began he'd been zoning in and out constantly and eventually collapsed. "This isn't the time to fight."

"Very well," Sarah said, tartly. She glanced out of the window. "It's midday. We'd better get this cart out before it's too late."

Dread nodded. "Let's go," he said. "Johan?"

Johan closed his eyes, trying – again – to reach Elaine. It felt strange; there were brief bursts of emotion, ranging from boredom to humiliation, which faded out as he tried to contact her directly. For a moment, his head swam and he felt sick. Something was badly wrong with her, even if she wasn't in immediate danger.

"I can feel her, but I can't touch her," he said.

Sarah gave him an odd look. "What?"

"They have a bond," Dread explained, curtly.

"Better not tell anyone else," Sarah muttered. "It would be hard for you to convince them that Elaine's marrying someone on the other side of the world."

Johan flushed, brightly.

Sarah laughed, then led the way out to the cart. Johan scrambled up beside the barrels – the Firepowder barrel looked normal, just like the others – and squashed into the railing as Dread climbed up and sat next to him. The former Inquisitor looked surprisingly comfortable wearing the clothes Sarah had provided, even if they were unfortunately rank. Johan disliked them – even as a Powerless, he'd worn finer clothes – but he had to admit they looked the part of a pair of workmen. Maybe he'd be taken as Dread's son …

He could hardly be a worse father than mine, he thought, suddenly.

The cart rolled to life, picking its way through the crowded streets. Several people seemed to have started small parties, handing out beer and snacks while they waited for news from the City House. A number were even talking about how wonderful it was to be able to live without dirty foreigners; Johan wondered, absently, if they were hired shills, people paid to endorse Alfred and his extermination plans at every opportunity. His father hadn't taught him *much* about politics – no one had ever expected him to become a politician – but Johan had learnt a few things. Alfred had probably learnt more at the Peerless School.

He nudged Dread as a thought occurred to him. "Did Alfred go to the Peerless School?"

"I don't know," Dread said. "I did wonder, but it would be hard to fake the graduation paperwork."

"He isn't in the Golden City," Johan objected.

"He isn't on the other side of the world either," Dread pointed out. "One of his political enemies could easily send to the Golden City to check his records, if he wished."

The cart rolled to a halt as it turned into City Square. Johan watched the guards strolling towards them and braced himself. If they were caught …

"I've brought beer for the party," Sarah said, cheerfully. She'd adjusted her dress so it showed off more of her cleavage. The guards didn't even *try* to pretend they weren't looking at the sight. "Where would you like me to put it?"

"Everything's going into the hall," the guard grunted. "Is it good beer?"

"The best," Sarah assured him. There was a flirtatious tone to her voice Johan wouldn't have believed possible, if he hadn't heard it. "My father wants his name on the official record."

"Then report to the office when you're done," the guard said. He gave the cart a cursory once-over, then waved them through. "Call us if you happen to need any help, sweetheart."

"Sweetheart," Sarah muttered, as soon as they were out of earshot. "I'd sooner kiss a pig."

They parked the cart behind another, then waited until it was their turn to unload. Johan and Dread carried the barrels, one by one, into the hall, then lit the candle as soon as the last barrel was in place. Johan wanted to run at once – he was uncomfortably aware that the candle wasn't anything like as accurate as magic – but Dread kept a hand on his arm as they walked back out of the building. The guards looked at them and snickered unpleasantly.

"Make sure you get a lot of work out of him," one called.

"My son wants to see the dirty foreigners," Dread said. "But he's going to help me bring the rest of the beer first."

"Don't worry, young man," the guard said, as his companion laughed. "The prisoners will be marched past the gallows in all their glory before they're finally killed. You can see them die."

Johan – somehow – managed to keep his mouth tightly shut as Dread shoved him back onto the cart. Elaine was in danger and he could do nothing, but wait. And if something went wrong …

We could die here, he thought. He tried to reach Elaine again, but couldn't do more than feel a faint echo of her emotions. *And if we do, the Witch-King wins.*

Chapter Ten

"Stay on your knees," the guard shouted. "Don't move a muscle!"

Elaine kept her face impassive as she tested the runes, one by one. Millicent had taught her *something* about keeping her mind on task, even when she was being repeatedly humiliated; it galled her to be grateful, but in some ways it had been good training for being taken prisoner. Being covered in rotting eggs and smelly fish was a minor annoyance. The magician had watched her for several hours, then clearly decided she was trapped and stalked off to inflict himself on someone else. He would have been less confident, Elaine was sure, if he had known she was practically the mistress of small magics.

She smiled to herself as she carefully unlocked the magic binding hers in place. It wasn't particularly subtle, after all; the designers, she suspected, had thought in terms of holding someone behind a locked door. But she preferred to think of her magic as water, pouring through a sieve and searching for weaknesses. Inch by inch, she wore down the magic bindings and prepared herself to strike.

"Let me go," a woman screamed. "Please!"

"Silence," a guard shouted back, as he hauled her to her feet. "You're the first to face the noose."

Elaine gritted her teeth. The magicians were gone, but they'd be back the minute she revealed she could break out. If she moved now …

She sensed a sudden flicker of anticipation from Johan, followed by a deafening explosion that shook the ground. A colossal fireball rose up from the direction of City House, sending waves of magic through the air. Elaine didn't hesitate; she unlocked the remaining bindings, sent the wooden plank crashing to the ground and rose to her feet. A dozen guards drew their weapons, but they seemed stunned, almost uncoordinated. Elaine threw a stunning spell at them, realising dully that Alfred had to be dead. The complex layers of compulsion he'd woven with his voice and magic were gone.

"Help us," someone called. "Let us go!"

Elaine braced herself, then cast a second spell. The mundanes in the crowd weren't bound in any runic planks; their stocks fell off, instantly, as the spell did its work. A handful of rushing guardsmen came face to face with angry prisoners, who were scooping up weapons from the men Elaine had stunned. She turned and hurried, limping slightly, towards the remains of City House as the guards clashed with the former prisoners, who weren't in any mood to show mercy. Half of the guards seemed so utterly perplexed that they were dropping their weapons and running for their lives.

Good, she thought, as she shaped a third spell. A magician, running towards her with wand raised, fell to the ground as her spell struck him, tearing into his protections and turning them against him. His wand hit the ground; she picked it up, tested it lightly and then cast a greater spell. *Let's see how they fight without their master.*

A large shape leapt across the field and came to rest beside her. Elaine smiled as she recognised Daria's wolf-form, then hurried after her as the sound of fighting grew louder. A set of confused-looking guardsmen were staring at the weapons in their hands, as if they weren't sure what to do with them. Elaine stunned them quickly, before they had a chance to make up their mind, and followed Daria towards a large cart parked by the side of the road, with Dread and Johan standing next to it. She smiled in honest delight – and relief – as she saw them.

"You stink," Johan said, as he wrapped his arms around her. "Are you all right?"

"I've had worse," Elaine said. She smiled at the thought. Compared to Deferens, Alfred hadn't been a particularly unpleasant captor. But then, he hadn't known who she was. "What did you do?"

"Smuggled a barrel of Firepowder into the building," Dread said. "Alfred is dead, I believe."

"I sensed his compulsion web collapsing," Elaine said, as

Johan let go of her gingerly. "Most of his victims are going to be a little bit confused."

"And his prisoners are breaking free," Dread observed. "Now what?"

"Some of us are poised to try to take control, given that most of the City Fathers are dead," Sarah said. "You four, however, are going to a safe house."

Johan held up a hand. "Shouldn't we stay to help?"

"Better not," Dread said. "The locals will need to sort this mess out for themselves."

Elaine nodded, too tired to argue. Her shoulders were aching badly, even though the plank had been dumped back in the park. And her shirt and trousers were covered in muck … she swallowed, silently grateful she couldn't smell herself. It was easy to see that Daria had carefully placed herself as far from Elaine as she could, while remaining on the cart. Her sense of smell was probably a liability now.

Johan reached over and held her hand, gently, as the cart rocked to life, heading towards the Merchant Quarter. Elaine closed her eyes and tried to relax, then opened them again as the cart came to a halt. They'd stopped outside a middle-class house, a small building that would be utterly unaffordable in the Golden City; she smiled, tiredly, at the thought as Sarah opened the door and shooed them into the building.

"There's a small ward around the doors and windows," she said, once they were all inside and the door was shut. "I'll send someone around with new clothes, but otherwise I just want you to wait. Hopefully, you can leave tomorrow with the rest of us, as planned."

Elaine nodded. "Thank you," she said. "Good luck."

"There's a bathroom upstairs with cold running water," Sarah added. She turned to look at Dread. "If I don't come back within a couple of days, assume the worst and head out of the city on your own."

"Understood," Dread said.

Elaine yawned, then turned and stumbled up the stairs. The house was nicely decorated, but there was no sign of any occupants. She puzzled over it for a long moment, then decided that the Leveller creed would probably appeal to a great many merchants. Hawke had been a merchant too, she recalled; a wealthy man with no hope of laying claim to any political power. And his daughter had been brutalised by a magician while he'd been forced to watch, helpless to save her. Blowing up the Watchtower, for him, must have been a dream come true.

The bathroom was larger than she'd expected, the bathtub itself easily large enough for two people. She turned on the tap, then tore the remains of her shirt and trousers away from her body. The stains wouldn't come out, even with magic. It went against the grain to throw away anything – the orphanage had repaired everything, passing it down from child to child, until it was nothing more than rags – but she didn't think there was any choice. She dumped the tattered remains in the basket and looked at herself in the mirror. Her face was pale, her hair looked a mess and there were nasty red marks all over her shoulders. It looked very much as though someone had been beating her.

And my eyes are far too noticeable, she thought. Maybe they'd spared her the worst of the abuse, while she'd been a prisoner; the mundane guards had kept a sharp eye on her, but they hadn't done worse than parade her around the city. *They'll be telling everyone about them now.*

She placed her fingers in the water, using a tiny spell to warm it, then carefully stepped into the bath and sat down. It felt heavenly to just relax and let the warmth work its way through her skin, but there wasn't time to enjoy it for more than a few minutes. She splashed warm water through her hair, using magic to work out the remains of the rotten fruit, and then removed it from the water with another spell before washing her body down with soap. The other prisoners wouldn't have any way to do it, without washing themselves thoroughly. She felt a stab of pity as she realised they'd be smelling for days.

They would have killed every foreigner in the city, she thought, numbly. She'd known the Empire wasn't perfect, but it still shocked her to see so many people turning on their fellow citizens. And Falcone's Nest *needed* the people it wanted to kill. *They would have doomed themselves by exterminating the foreigners.*

She shook her head slowly, then climbed out of the bath. Her body looked bruised, so she cast a handful of spells to speed up the healing. She'd pay for it later – everything came with a price – but she needed to be back up to normal as soon as possible. Taking one final look in the mirror – and casting a glamour to hide her eyes – she donned a dressing gown and walked out of the door. Daria was waiting outside, looking relieved.

"You smell better now," she said. "But you should take another bath tomorrow."

Elaine yawned. "Tomorrow," she said, firmly. "What happened to you?"

Daria shrugged. "Landed amongst the crowd, ducked down and made my way out between their legs," she said. "A couple of them took stabs at me with knives, but I survived."

She paused. "Elaine, there's a Traveller meeting post nearby," she added, rising to her feet and following Elaine. "I think I should go there. They may be willing to help."

"Or at least spread the word," Elaine mused. A werewolf could move far faster than a human, even on horseback. "Will they get involved?"

"I don't know," Daria said. She sighed. "You know how they're treated, sometimes."

Elaine nodded as she walked into the bedroom. Born werewolves had near-perfect control, even when the full moon was in the sky, but made werewolves turned violent when the moon rose. Normally, they were controlled by their families, assuming they *had* a family. A feral werewolf could be incredibly dangerous. No one in their right mind wanted to live close to a werewolf camp, for fear of getting bitten. It would, at the very least, ruin the victim's life.

"Tell them that Deferens won't hesitate to kill them," she said, as she dropped the gown and climbed into bed. It was large enough for them to share, without being uncomfortably intimate. "He won't, you know."

"I know," Daria said, irked. "But they may prefer not to believe it."

She leant forward. "I'll leave once we get out of the city," she said. "How are you feeling?"

"Sore," Elaine said, curtly. "But I've had worse."

Daria gave her a sharp look. "If you want to talk about it," she said, "you can always talk to me."

Elaine sighed. She *didn't* want to talk about it, not when she *had* had worse. Deferens had tried to break her, body and soul. He would have succeeded, too, if she'd been anyone else; she'd have been nothing more than a mindless slave. The prospect of mere death, even after public humiliation, seemed rather less worrying. And yet …

"I can't believe how quickly everything came apart," she said, slowly. "Alfred must have had the whole scheme planned in advance, then … then he just took advantage of us destroying the bridges."

"Unless there's a spy in the Levellers," Daria said. "Alfred must have decided to let us go ahead, rather than try to stop us. If he believes the crap he was spewing out, he might have figured that losing the bridges wasn't a complete disaster."

Elaine shook her head. "He'd still have had only a few hours to lay the groundwork for his coup," she said. "Getting the City Fathers into the City House alone would have been difficult."

"But not impossible," Daria said. "He did it."

"I know," Elaine said. She looked up at her friend. "Is the Empire really that fragile?"

Daria considered the question for a long moment. "You were born in the Golden City, weren't you?"

Elaine nodded, shortly.

"And you haven't seen many places outside it," Daria added. "Falcone's Nest isn't the only city with delusions of grandeur about the past, or the only one that resents the Empire's absolute dominance. You know who wields the *real* power in the kingdoms."

"The Court Wizards," Elaine said.

"They're appointed by the Grand Sorcerer and sent out to rule, in all but name," Daria said, softly. "Don't you think that's resented? There are places that have been reduced to poverty because of decisions taken in the Golden City – or because of decisions that were then blamed on the Golden City. Someone convinces the Grand Sorcerer to support *them* and hundreds of other people get the short end of the stick. Their taxes go to the Golden City and what do they get in return?"

" ... Government," Elaine said.

Daria smiled. "Do they need it?"

She met Elaine's eyes. "That hatred was always under the surface, but held in check by fear," she said. "The Golden City always controlled the vast majority of sorcerers ... as well as the road network, the shipping and the crystal balls. Holding the Empire in its grasp wasn't *that* hard. But now, the Court Wizards are largely dead, the Inquisitors are weaker than they've ever been and the last Grand Sorcerer is dead. The smaller kingdoms have never had a better chance to break free."

"Except for the minor detail that Deferens has a swarm of dragons under his command," Elaine pointed out, curtly. "They'd need more than *luck* to overcome them."

"They think the dragons are rumour," Daria said. "And all this chaos only benefits the Witch-King."

Elaine nodded. The only hope of a coordinated response to the Witch-King lay with the Empire ... and the Empire had already been subverted, placed under Vlad Deferens. He had to realise he was weakening his own position, but did he care? The Witch-King had presumably made sure he *didn't* realise just how dangerous his position had become.

But it may not be that dangerous, Elaine thought, slowly. *A swarm of dragons would be enough to cow most of the kingdoms, certainly the ones without magicians of their own.*

"Then we have to leave tomorrow, whatever else happens," she said, firmly. "Thank you for coming for me."

"You broke free on your own," Daria said. "You'd have been fine without me."

Elaine shrugged. She had her doubts.

"I hope so," she said. "Goodnight."

"I want you to try to contact Johan first," Daria said. "He was near-panicking over losing touch with you."

Elaine closed her eyes. *Johan?*

Elaine, Johan sent back. There was a wash of relief – and something else – that made her smile. He *cared* about her. *Are you all right?*

I think the blow on the head scrambled my thoughts, then

the runes scrambled them a little more, Elaine sent. *Are you all right?*

There was a long pause. She could sense his doubts – and hesitation – before he finally answered.

I'd like to talk about that tomorrow, he sent, finally. *You need your sleep.*

"He wants me to sleep," Elaine said, out loud. "I'm not a child, you know."

"But you've been through hell," Daria said, firmly. "Sleep."

I will, Elaine sent. *Goodnight.*

She reduced the link until Johan was nothing more than a reassuring presence at the back of her mind, then looked at Daria. "Goodnight."

"Goodnight," Daria said. She rose and headed for the door. "I need to check with Dread, then go for a bath. I'll sleep on the floor, so don't worry about me."

"You can share the bed," Elaine protested. A thought struck her. "Or do I smell *that* bad?"

"Goodnight," Daria said, firmly.

Elaine closed her eyes, but sleep didn't come easy, despite her tiredness. Alfred's face kept flashing in front of her mind, mocking her pretensions that the Witch-King could be defeated by mere mortals. She could have died in the crowd, crushed by the throng or stoned to death, and no one would ever have known what had happened to her ... and, without her, could the Witch-King be stopped? Even with her, she wasn't sure what to do. There was so much she didn't understand ...

He's a lich, she thought. There couldn't be any other answer, not when any form of stasis would have held his thoughts in suspension along with his body. The Witch-King had to be awake and aware. *Magic must be keeping him alive – or undead. And that means magic can stop him.*

It was an odd thought, but she thought there were clues. She'd been turned into objects often enough and there were safeties woven into the spells to make sure she didn't go insane, no matter how long she stayed utterly immobile. Millicent had been fond of turning her into a statue and just leaving her there, knowing *Elaine* would be blamed for not freeing herself. It was odd, but could the Witch-King have used similar spells to keep himself relatively sane, if inanimate? She was sure he had to be sane or he would have killed or exposed himself a long time ago.

Unless he's just going mad very slowly, she thought. Something was nagging at her mind, but she couldn't make sense of it. *That might explain why he's tearing the Empire apart too.*

She scowled as tiredness overwhelmed her. There *had* to be a solution – and there *had* to be a way to make sense of what he was doing, even if it *was* seemingly impossible. She knew more about magic than anyone else, even the Witch-King himself. But her knowledge didn't cover Johan's power, or what the Witch-King was doing. It was immensely frustrating …

And, with that thought, she drifted off to sleep.

Chapter Eleven

Johan looked up as Elaine descended the stairs, the following morning, and felt his breath catch in his throat. Perhaps it was the sheer relief at seeing her alive, perhaps it was the fact she was wearing a dressing gown rather than a robe or travelling clothes, but he couldn't help thinking she'd never looked more attractive. He stared …

… And then caught himself and looked away, hastily.

"Go wash," Elaine said, her cheeks red. She'd sensed his emotions, of course. Johan half-wished the ground would swallow him up, leaving nothing behind. "I'll see you at breakfast."

Johan hurried past her and up the stairs, cursing himself under his breath. She was going to be angry at him – or, worse, make fun of him. The maids had always made fun of him when they thought he couldn't hear, knowing he lacked the magic to punish them. Jayne had been the only girl to show any real interest in him and that hadn't lasted past the moment his damned father had tried to arrange their marriage. She'd hated him …

He pushed the thought aside, bitterly, as he stepped into the bathroom and washed himself thoroughly. There hadn't been time to wash the previous night, not when he'd wanted – needed – to stay awake, just in case the rioters attacked the house. He'd heard bangs and crashes – and people shouting – outside, but no one had tried to breach the fragile wards. By the time the sun had finally risen, he'd only managed to snatch a few hours of sleep.

Donning a set of clothes that had been left for him by the Levellers, he hurried back downstairs to discover that Sarah and a couple of people he didn't recognise had arrived and were unloading a large hamper of food. Elaine and Sarah were talking quietly in soft voices, while Dread was speaking to a large man carrying a hammer under one arm and Daria was watching them all with quiet amusement. Johan cringed again at the realisation she would have smelt the sudden rush of arousal, even though he'd washed himself with warm soapy water. The werewolf was probably wondering why he hadn't tried to jump Elaine.

Because she's my mistress, he thought. It wasn't a convincing argument. *And because we don't have time.*

"We brought chicken," Sarah said, holding out a drumstick. "Better eat as much as you can, young man. We're going to be leaving after breakfast."

Johan nodded. "What happened?"

"Well, most of the City Fathers are dead or missing, so a handful of merchants managed to take control and start making preparations for war," Sarah told him. "Not everyone *believes* in the Emperor and his flying dragons, but they do know we've given more than enough cause for war to all the bordering states. I don't think that any of the foreigners are going to urge mercy when they get home."

"No, they won't," Dread agreed. "How bad was it?"

"Several hundred men and women humiliated, nineteen killed, thirty-seven raped and fifty-nine injured," Sarah said. "They'll be vowing bloody revenge as soon as they're out of the city."

"But Alfred is dead," Johan protested. "We killed him, didn't we?"

"As far as we know," Sarah agreed. "His magic died when the Firepowder exploded and no one's seen anything of him since the blast. But we never found a body."

"You wouldn't," Dread commented.

"Probably not," Sarah said. She ran her fingers through her long blonde hair. "The foreigners are heading home, carrying with them tales of horror. I imagine it won't be long before the first armies show up at our gates."

Johan swallowed. "But it wasn't *your* fault!"

"It won't matter," Dread pointed out. "Falcone's Nest controls a number of trading routes, so whoever manages to take the city – using whatever excuse best suits them – will have an advantage as the Empire slowly disintegrates. I imagine a couple of unleashed kings will have ideas about just *who* should take the city – and the deaths alone are more than enough cause for war."

"Quite," Sarah agreed. She cleared her throat as Johan tucked into the chicken. "Just about everyone who can afford it is leaving the city, so we've taken the liberty of assembling a set of coaches to travel to our next destination. We'll be leaving in a couple of hours, taking the magicians and a number of chemists with us. The remainder of our group will stay here and try to slow the Emperor down."

"Which won't be easy," Elaine said. "The bridges may be gone ..."

"But he can still fly," Sarah said. She scowled down at the table. "We may lose the battle, but we can at least delay him a little."

Sure, Johan thought. *Just as long as it takes a dragon to fly across the river and rain down fire on the defenders.*

"There are a handful of magicians remaining in the city," Sarah added. "They may have a chance to slow the Emperor down."

"I doubt it," Elaine said, tartly. "Dragons are tough."

Sarah gave Elaine a nasty look, then shrugged. "Be ready to leave in an hour," she said, firmly. "I don't expect this place to be spotless – if we survive, we'll deal with the mess – but make sure you take everything you brought with you."

"Understood," Dread said.

Johan finished eating the chicken, then took a slice of bread and sat down at the table. Elaine wasn't looking at him, either out of embarrassment or fear that she would betray something to her comrades. Johan seriously considered trying to touch her mind, but decided it would only upset her. She'd have to come to terms with her own feelings before she started to talk to him. They'd known the bond would be deeper than a normal bond, yet they'd also assumed they'd be able to cope with it at leisure. They hadn't realised they'd be fleeing for their lives from an invincible foe.

I could stay here too, he thought, remembering how the bridges had caught fire and melted into the Lug. *If I had him in eyeshot, I could deal with him ...*

It was a tempting thought. He *hated* Deferens, hated him for what he'd done to Elaine and Charity and Cass, hated him for having power and allowing it to turn him into a monster.

If the Emperor died, the Empire would stagger but it might recover in time to deal with the Witch-King. A new Grand Sorcerer could be chosen …

And that would betray the Levellers, he added, in the privacy of his own thoughts. *They'd be pushed back to square one.*

He shook his head, slowly. If he'd known about the Levellers before he'd developed his powers, he would have joined. Why not? He knew more about how power corrupted – and how the *lack* of power weakened – than Hawke, even though Hawke had watched helplessly as his daughter was humiliated and abused. And he also knew the Iron Dragons didn't use magic at all. He could have been a Leveller and never looked back to his roots. Even now, with enough power at his fingertips to make any normal magician fearful, he had no intention of betraying them. They deserved better.

Daria poked him with a fingernail. "A coin for your thoughts?"

"I was miles away," Johan said. "Just … just lost in my thoughts."

He looked at Daria, feeling an odd sense of detachment. He'd thought the werewolf was beautiful, when he'd first seen her; beautiful, muscular, strong and confident. It was strange to think that she and Elaine were friends, because they seemed to have nothing in common beyond magic. And yet, where he'd once wanted her, he now felt nothing but abstract admiration for her. The bond was drawing him towards Elaine.

"Try not to get stuck in them," Daria advised, deadpan. "It's hard to find your way out."

Johan smiled. "Really?"

"There was a magician who developed a spell to organise his own thoughts," Daria said, as she took a piece of chicken and began to dissect it with her teeth. Even in human form, they were sharp enough to suggest her true nature. "He eventually managed to lock himself inside a fantasy and the druids had to break him out before his body died. And then he took one look around at the real world and plunged straight back into his mind."

"At least he died happy," Johan said. How often had he dreamed of having the same powers as Jamal? Or Charity? He wouldn't have minded going back to childhood if it had meant growing up with magic. "There aren't many people who can say that."

Daria gave him a considering look. "How would you know?"

Johan had no answer, so he finished eating and helped Dread and Elaine to clear the table and pack the remains of the food back into the hamper. Sarah had slipped out while he wasn't looking, perhaps checking the route to the coachhouse or obtaining more supplies before they left the city for good. He couldn't help wondering how she felt, leaving her home behind; her father, at least, had looked a decent sort. Sarah had stayed with him when she could easily have found a husband and moved out.

He glanced at Elaine as they finished, but she was talking to Dread about the route to Ida. Johan sighed, then walked out of the room as Sarah reappeared and beckoned them out of the house. The roadside looked reassuringly normal, but he couldn't help noticing that a number of glass windows – a sign of wealth and power – had been smashed during the night. Anyone wealthy enough to afford glass for his windows could easily have paid to have them warded, yet some of the wards had started to fail. He had a feeling it boded ill for the future.

The Levellers wondered if the magic was going away, he thought, numbly. Elaine had rubbished the suggestion, but she might well have wanted to believe it was nonsense, rather than a very real possibility. *What if they're right?*

"Come on," Sarah said, once everyone was outside and the doors were locked. "There isn't much time."

The streets looked oddly deserted as they walked back towards the inn. A handful of slaves were clearing up the mess left behind by the rioters, but most of the population seemed to be staying indoors or working away from home. Johan listened, carefully, and heard the sound of construction work along the edge of the city, where the walls provided a limited form of protection. The citizens were working hard, he was sure, but it was useless. They were not going to be able to stop a dragon by building high walls.

They could charm the walls to repel fire, he thought. His parents had spent weeks doing just that, once the family moved into Conidian House. Jamal had got out of it, while Johan hadn't been able to help, but the other children had assisted as best they could. *It might give them a chance ...*

He shook his head as a line of archers appeared, carrying makeshift bows. Wooden arrows with metal tips wouldn't worry a dragon; hell, the beast might not even deem the archers worthy of killing. A couple of arrows looked to be enchanted – their tips replaced by crystals that glowed faintly, even in daylight – but would they be powerful enough to burn through Dragonhide? He had a nasty feeling they wouldn't be anything like capable of doing real harm to a dragon.

Two coaches stood outside the inn, harnessed to two horses apiece. A handful of guards – Johan hoped they were Levellers, rather than private guardsmen or mercenaries – stood next to them, their horses tied to a wooden post. They looked tough, Johan decided, but they also looked wary. Too much had happened in the last couple of days to allow anyone to relax.

Sarah spoke briefly to her father, then motioned to the coaches. Johan hesitated, then followed Elaine and Daria as they scrambled into the second coach. Dread followed them, looking around grimly. It wasn't hard to realise that they were trapped if a marauding dragon saw them from high overhead and swooped down to attack – and, with the windows covered by thick curtains, there would be no warning before the coach was incinerated. Elaine sat down on a hard wooden bench, then opened her pack and produced a book. Daria sat next to her before Johan could and closed her eyes, pretending to be asleep.

Johan looked at Dread, who shrugged and reached into *his* pack, producing a small chessboard and a set of wooden pieces. The thought of the stony-faced Inquisitor playing chess made Johan smile; he nodded, accepting the implicit offer. Dread set the chessboard up, then silently offered to let Johan play white. Johan accepted as the coach shook, then started to move, rocking violently from side to side.

"My father's coach had spells on it to compensate," he said, feeling sick. "Can we put some on *this* coach?"

"Not unless we want to be detected," Elaine said. Her voice was tart, but he was relieved to hear it. It was the first thing she'd said to him since breakfast. "They'll be looking for runaway magicians."

Johan nodded, reluctantly. "You can't hide the magic?"

"Not without making it useless," Elaine admitted. Her words brought a sense that she was keeping her emotions under firm control. "It would just be a waste of magic."

Johan couldn't help feeling envious. He didn't know how she could read, not when the coach was rocking backwards and forwards. It was hard enough to play chess. Johan hadn't played *that* often – the only person who'd play with him was his father – and he hadn't had much practice, but it was clear that Dread was *good*. Even spotting Johan a knight and a cleric, he still won several games in a row. But then, he would have needed to while away the time on stakeout *somehow*.

He looked up as the former Inquisitor checkmated him for the fifth time. "Where did you learn to play?"

"Thinking several steps ahead is supposed to be a useful skill for the Inquisition," Dread said, resetting the board. "You're not thinking like a player."

Johan scowled, stung. "I *do* know how to play!"

"You know how the pieces move," Dread said. "*However*, you're not giving any thought to how they *interact*. The sorceress" – he tapped the regal figure with one scarred finger – "is the most powerful piece on the board, but even she needs support to achieve checkmate. You can't checkmate me with just *her*."

"So I need a tower or *something* to keep your grand sorcerer from taking me," Johan said, carefully. "But she's still doing most of the work."

"Yes, she is," Dread agreed. He smiled as he removed his sorceress from the board. "Which is why so many players give up when they lose their sorceress."

Johan nodded and started to play again, thinking about each move before picking up the piece and pushing it forward.

"Tell me something," he said, in hopes of distracting

Dread. "Why do we have the grand sorcerer as the *least* capable piece, even though a *real* Grand Sorcerer would be powerful enough to defend himself."

Dread tapped his grand sorcerer thoughtfully. "The grand sorcerer doesn't represent a powerful magician, not here," he said. "He represents a chain of succession, just as kingship is more than the sum of whoever is lowering his despotic rump onto the throne at any one time. A checkmate doesn't *take* the grand sorcerer, Johan. It breaks the line of succession, so there won't be another grand sorcerer."

"And ends the game," Johan said. He stared down at the pieces for a long moment, then remembered his family. Jamal would have inherited, if their father had died; *his* children would have become the Prime Heirs. But now, he had no idea who was the Family Head; Jamal was powerless, Johan was gone, Charity was a slave ... "Who's in charge of House Conidian now?"

"I have no idea," Dread said. "Your younger siblings are too young for the role, I suppose."

"Jay is fourteen," Johan said.

"Then I imagine the Emperor has taken advantage of the situation to strip House Conidian of everything it has," Dread said. He tapped the chessboard meaningfully. "Is there anything you can do about it now?"

"No," Johan said. He moved a piece forward, then swore as Dread took advantage of his move to take one of the knights. "But it stings."

"I shouldn't worry about it," Dread advised. "Unless you intend to claim the position for yourself ..."

"No, thank you," Johan said. "I ..."

He broke off as the carriage shuddered to a stop. Moments later, someone rattled on the door.

"We're outside the city, near the woods," Sarah called. "You ready?"

"Yes," Daria said. She gave Elaine a tight hug, then winked at Johan. "Good luck, both of you. I'll see you in Ida!"

She stood as the door opened. Outside, Johan could see trees and a pair of guards, peering in at them curiously. Daria snapped into wolf-form – Elaine scooped up her robe –

and darted out of the coach, vanishing in the undergrowth. If there were other werewolves nearby, she'd be able to track them down before too long.

"Good luck," Elaine breathed, as the door slammed closed again. Her emotions were still under tight control, as if she were shutting him out. "All we can do now is hope we get to Ida in time."

"We will," Johan said, as reassuringly as he could. He glanced at Dread. "Your move."

Dread moved a piece forward, then smirked. "Checkmate."

Chapter Twelve

The town had offered no resistance. It hadn't been enough to save it.

Charity walked through the smouldering remains, feeling sick. The Emperor – bored, frustrated or angry – had unleashed the dragons on the town as soon as it came into view, then directed his soldiers to kill or capture the civilians. There hadn't been any magicians, as far as anyone had been able to tell; the men had been pressed into the army or simply enslaved, while the women had suffered a fate worse than death. Charity had almost been relieved when the screaming ended, even though she knew it meant their throats had been cut. At least their suffering was over.

The soldiers gave her a wide berth as she peered at what had once been a counting house, where the local tax gatherers had plied their trade. If there hadn't been a pair of golden scales lying on the ground, somehow untouched by the flames, she wouldn't have been able to tell it apart from any of the other buildings. She was surprised the scales hadn't been looted – the soldiers had taken everything that wasn't nailed down – but rumour had it that the tax gatherers had cursed their sign of office, just to make sure it wasn't stolen one dark night. If they weren't the least popular people in the world, Charity didn't want to meet the people who *were*.

The Emperor, she thought, numbly. The town had offered no resistance and yet it had been burnt to the ground, its population butchered after the soldiers had had their fun. If there were any survivors at all, they were the people who'd seen the army coming and fled into the countryside, hoping to remain hidden until it was gone. *After this, no one is going to want to bow the knee to him.*

She looked up as a shadow passed overhead. A dragon was flying in lazy circles around the town, its beady red eyes searching for trouble. Charity shook her head tiredly, half-wishing the soldiers would put an end to her life. The Emperor didn't need to be popular when he had dragons, dragons that answered to him and him alone. Anyone who dared stand in his way would be crisped before they managed to finish speaking the words of a formal challenge.

And even if he does duel someone, he's a formidable sorcerer, she thought. *And he's been storing power from his victims.*

A horseman cantered past from the south, pulling up outside the Emperor's tent. He'd set up a small camp, although it was clear he had no intention of staying in the town for longer than it took to strip the countryside of everything his army could use. Foraging parties were already prowling through the fields, removing corn, digging up potatoes and replenishing the army's stocks of water from the wells. By the time they finally moved on, Charity thought as she started walking back to the tent, it would look like a horde of locusts had passed through the countryside, consuming everything in their path.

She pushed the tent flap aside and stepped inside. General Vetch was standing beside the Emperor – a sign of great honour – while the rider was kneeling in front of him, his eyes staring firmly at the ground. Charity prostrated herself at once, hoping she wouldn't be told to leave. The Emperor's behaviour was increasingly unpredictable. There were times when he would gloat to her, if only because he *needed* to gloat to someone, and times when he treated her as little more than a slave. He'd even told her to go help the cooks once, when he'd been in a particularly foul mood.

"Your Supremacy," the rider said. "The bridges over the Lug have been destroyed."

Charity forced her face to remain impassive. The Emperor was *not* going to be pleased, particularly as General Vetch had warned him, several times, that delaying their advance would give the locals a chance to organise a defence. He'd even raised the spectre of the bridges being ruined before the army could force a crossing and occupy the city. The Emperor had dismissed his concerns, but now …

And what will he do, Charity asked herself, *when the General was right and he was wrong?*

She risked a glance at the Emperor. His face was as impassive as hers, one hand stroking his beard as he thought. General Vetch looked equally impassive; he'd been right, he *knew* he'd been right, but it was dangerous to be right when the Emperor was wrong. A single spell could blast him into ashes and he knew it. But the Emperor didn't seem *particularly* angry.

"I see," the Emperor said, finally. "And the city itself?"

"I am unsure, Your Supremacy," the rider said. His voice was clearly nervous. The bearer of bad news might well be *blamed*, even though it made no sense. "The other two scouts in the city were cut off, after the bridges were destroyed. They were unable to obtain a boat across the river before I had to withdraw."

The Emperor said nothing for several moments. Charity looked down at the ground, hoping he wouldn't lash out at his servants. Part of her wondered if she should hope he *would*. It would, perhaps, put an end to her misery. And yet, the thought of just giving up and ending her life was horrifying.

"There are plans to deal with the situation," he said, finally. "Speak to no one of this matter. You are dismissed."

The rider rose, bowed so deeply his nose almost touched the ground, then backed out of the tent as rapidly as he could. Charity didn't blame him. The Emperor might easily have decided to kill the rider, if only to conceal his own failure. Who knew *what* would have happened if the army had pushed forward faster?

"General," the Emperor said. His voice was remarkably calm. "The four lead regiments are to reassemble, then advance forward to the Lug. I and my dragons will accompany them. The remaining regiments are to complete foraging, then follow the lead regiments as fast as possible."

The General hesitated. "Your Supremacy," he said. "Moving the regiments across the Lug will be impossible without shipping. We could move westwards and attempt to secure a crossing higher up the river ..."

"Let me worry about that," the Emperor said, cutting him off. He cast a timekeeping charm in the air, then nodded to himself. "I want the lead regiments on the banks of the Lug in five hours."

Charity risked another glance and saw the General wince. Five hours … the soldiers would be lucky if they made it, even if they left their packs behind and force-marched down the road. The dragons could be there in bare minutes, if necessary; indeed, she was surprised the Emperor hadn't ordered the dragons to fly ahead of the army. Burning Falcone's Nest to the ground wouldn't take long at all.

"Yes, Your Supremacy," General Vetch said, finally. Charity didn't really blame him, not when the Emperor was clearly already in a foul temper. The soldiers would just have to march as hard as they could. "I'll see to it at once."

He bowed and left the tent. Charity remained, pressing her face into the ground. If the Emperor started to take it out on her … she could do nothing but take it. Instead, he started to mutter to himself, so quietly she couldn't make out any of the words, as if he'd forgotten she was even there. It wasn't until he stood up and walked into her that he snapped out of his trance and looked down at her.

"Rise," he ordered.

Charity sat upright, carefully keeping her eyes lowered. She'd seen a slave battered to death for daring to make eye contact with his master. The Emperor might have more use for her than fetching and carrying, but she suspected he didn't really care if she lived or died. She had nothing to offer him any longer, not even influence. Her slavery ensured that her stewardship of House Conidian was gone.

Not that any of the Great Houses matter any longer, she thought, morbidly. *The Emperor has dragons!*

"Tell me," the Emperor said. "What do you make of it?"

"Falcone's Nest knows you're coming," Charity said, shortly. If only she wasn't compelled to tell him the truth! "They took down the bridges to make it harder for you to get at them."

"But they're in for a surprise," the Emperor said.

Charity nodded slowly, following his logic. "They don't know about the dragons."

But how could they *not* know about the dragons? It had been three days since Knawel Haldane had been attacked and occupied, three days when messengers could have ridden on horseback in all directions or sorcerers transmitted messages to their friends, allies and contacts. By now, the entire world could have heard of the dragons ... unless, of course, they didn't believe it. And why would they? Everyone knew the last dragons had been wiped out centuries ago.

"That's not all," the Emperor said. He smiled, coldly. "You are to assemble a cartload of charged crystals, then ensure they accompany the lead regiments and myself. I have a plan to deal with the rebellious city."

"Yes, Your Supremacy," Charity said.

"Go," the Emperor ordered.

He was already muttering to himself again as Charity rose and stepped out of the tent, into the bright sunlight. The lead regiments were forming up, the soldiers grumbling quietly as General Vetch and his subordinates bullied them into formation. Charity felt a moment of pity for Falcone's Nest – the lead regiments were encouraged to commit as many atrocities as possible – and then hurried past them. No one would be so foolish as to touch her – she belonged to the Emperor – but she could feel their eyes lingering on her as she walked over to the sorcerers. An Inquisitor, standing outside the handful of tents, eyed her sharply. There was something damned and suffering in his eyes.

Charity shivered. She'd been forced to give her oath to the Emperor, but the Inquisitors had sworn loyalty to the Empire and the Golden Throne. None of them had really expected a *genuine* heir to arrive in the Golden City and claim their allegiance, let alone that he'd make a mockery of their true purpose. The Inquisitors had never been liked, but now they were actively feared. They'd become Dark Wizards in their own right.

"I need to speak to Roth," she said, curtly. There was no point in trying to commiserate with him, or anyone else. They were both slaves and nothing either of them could do would change it. "Where is he?"

The Inquisitor looked at her for a long moment. "In the North Tent," he said, finally. His voice was flat, utterly atonal. It was the voice of a man who had given up, yet was forced to live. "He's with two of the captives."

Charity thanked him, then walked to the North Tent and

braced herself before stepping through the hatch. Roth – the leader of the red-robed magicians – was a monster, a twisted sadist who enjoyed making people scream. Now, a young man lay on the table, his chest torn open to reveal his beating heart, while a young woman stood behind him, her eyelids cut away to force her to watch. Roth himself was poking inside the man with his wand, jabbing away at parts of his body just to see what happened. Charity had to swallow hard to keep from being sick. The Emperor had surrounded himself with monsters, some of them very inhuman, but Roth was the worst of the lot. Even the soldiers were kinder.

"My Lady Charity," Roth said. His face was covered in blood. "What can I do for your *master*."

"He wishes you to prepare a cartload of charged crystals," Charity said. She hadn't talked to Roth very often, but he'd missed no opportunity to rub her slavery in. The man had even had the nerve to ask the Emperor if he could have Charity, when he tired of her. "They're going to Falcone's Nest."

"Oh," Roth said. He wasn't fool enough to defy an order. The Emperor could kill him on the spot – or throw him to his pets. "I'd better deal with it then, hadn't I?"

He snapped his fingers. The young man gasped, then died; the young woman crumpled to the ground, her eyes already dead. Charity forced herself to keep her face impassive, although she suspected Roth had no trouble reading her disgust and horror in her eyes. The magician called for a pair of slaves, told them to clear up the mess and beckoned Charity to follow him as he walked out of the tent and into the next. This one was surrounded by a trio of magicians who cast a dozen detection spells before allowing Roth and Charity to enter.

She sucked in her breath as she saw the crystals. They were glowing with brilliant white light, each one storing the life energy and magic of countless magicians. Roth admired them for a long moment, then ordered a set of servants to start carrying crystals out to one of the carts. They obeyed, even though they weren't spellbound slaves. Charity had been told, in no uncertain terms, *not* to use magic anywhere near the crystals. The results would be disastrous.

And if it hadn't been an order, she thought bitterly, *I might have been able to defy it.*

The Emperor was standing there impatiently when the cart was finally moved over to where his personal guard was waiting, but he didn't seem inclined to berate her for it. Instead, he ordered her to sit beside him on a dragon and cling onto him as the beast rose through the air and headed south, towards Falcone's Nest. The land lay spread out below them as they flew, the blue ocean in the distance drawing her eye like a magnet. Johan had talked about becoming a sailor, once upon a time. How much misery might have been spared if her father had simply let him go?

We could have dealt with the blood issue, she told herself. *Jamal would remain Prime Heir, the rest of us would be married off and no one would ever know our parents had given birth to a Powerless.*

She pushed the thought aside as the dragon, surrounded by a flock of other dragons, dropped down towards the Lug. From high overhead, the river looked tranquil, but she'd overheard enough conversations between General Vetch and his staff to know it was regarded as unpleasantly treacherous. The remains of the bridges bore mute testament to the skill of the builders … and whatever force had battered them down. It looked, very much, as though the wooden and iron structures had melted to nothingness.

"The Watchtower was destroyed," the Emperor said, as he steered the dragon down towards a hill. "I wonder if the same method was used to destroy the bridge."

Charity had no idea. The remaining Inquisitors had been unable to determine how their citadel had been destroyed, even though it had been the most heavily protected building in the city. She'd even heard that forbidden protective spells had been worked into its defences, ones that were an instant death sentence if used elsewhere. But now … the Watchtower was nothing more than a ruin, its occupants dead and its records destroyed. She couldn't help thinking of the Empire. Perhaps the Watchtower's ruin was merely a prelude to the death of the Empire itself.

The Emperor climbed off the dragon as soon as it landed, his guards fanning out around him as he peered towards

Falcone's Nest. Charity stayed a step behind him, studying the distant city. Hundreds of people were gathered on the far side, staring at them. They had to have seen the dragons as they swooped over the bridges, then landed. And now ... why hadn't the Emperor launched an attack?

It was just over five hours later when the lead regiments – and the cart – arrived, led by General Vetch. Charity was unsurprised to see that he'd ridden a horse, rather than walking beside his men. The General had probably thought he needed to be alert when he arrived. His men took a short rest, drinking water and eating *cram* from their packs, as the Emperor started issuing orders to his magicians. Charity watched, feeling a crawling sense of imminent doom pulsating through her mind, as the crystals were carefully embedded in the ground. She'd seen rituals before, thanks to the Emperor, and the least of them had been hellish.

"It is my honour to serve my Emperor," one of the red-robed magicians said, as he took his place at the centre of the crystals. "I praise your glory and I ask merely for your blessing."

"You have it," the Emperor said.

He waved the watching magicians – and Charity – back as the ritual began. Magic – the collected magic of dozens of other magicians – built up rapidly, making her hair want to stand on end. The magician who'd started the ritual was chanting loudly, bellowing out words in a guttural language she didn't recognise. White light flared up from the crystals, then darted out over the water. The river started to bubble as the power built up ...

... And then the ground shook, violently.

Charity stared in disbelief as, piece by piece, a giant causeway rose up from beneath the waves. It was huge, easily twice the size of the roads that bound the Empire together, water flowing off into the Lug as the causeway grew larger. And then the white light faded, snapping out of existence to reveal burnt-out crystals and a dead sorcerer. Channelling so much magic had killed him.

"Advance," the Emperor ordered.

Chapter Thirteen

The dragons took off, breathing fire as they flew across the river and swooped down on the fleeing crowd. Flames flashed through the streets, incinerating hundreds of civilians as arrows flashed up to challenge the dragons. They ignored them until a handful started exploding, but the charms and hexes weren't enough to do more than tickle the dragons as they tore through the city. Charity could only close her eyes and say a silent prayer to the gods as the dragons wiped out the defences, piece by piece.

"Watch," the Emperor ordered.

Charity's eyes snapped open, just in time to see the lead regiments reach the end of the causeway and surge into the city. Resistance, if any had been planned, was utterly broken; the regiments secured the shoreline, then advanced through the burning streets, screaming a demand for surrender. The dragons rose higher, their eyes searching for more targets, as the civilians started to give up. Charity shivered as the Emperor started to walk forward, stepping over the causeway as calmly as if he were walking into his living room. She couldn't help noticing that the water behind the causeway was already starting to rise.

It'll flood, she thought. She'd never seen magic worked on so great a scale – there were legends of such feats, but they all dated back to the gods – and she had no idea how long the causeway would actually *last*. It felt solid under her feet, but it was hard to deny the sheer pressure of thousands of tons of water. *And when it floods, it'll break.*

"Put units at each of the gates, then hold," the Emperor ordered, as he reached the far side and halted. "Don't send troops into the rest of the city until they surrender."

"Yes, Your Supremacy," General Vetch said.

"And organise a bucket brigade," the Emperor added. "I want the fires doused as swiftly as possible."

Charity watched, absently, as half of the soldiers turned their attentions to putting out the fires, while the remainder waited for the enemy to either attack or surrender. The locals didn't seem prepared to do anything, but wait for the Emperor to make the first move. It struck her, suddenly, that they might already have wiped out whoever was in charge of the city, ensuring that *no one* could surrender. What would the Emperor do if there was no way to force the city to submit without destroying it?

General Vetch turned as a soldier ran up to him, then looked back at the Emperor. "There's some resistance in the merchant quarter," he reported. "A set of our lads went in there and didn't come out again."

"The dragons will burn it down," the Emperor said, coldly. "Or knock it down, which might save more of the city."

An hour passed slowly – very slowly – before a handful of men came into view, carrying a large white flag. The Emperor nodded to his men, who searched them thoroughly and removed their weapons before carting them forward and throwing them to the ground in front of the Emperor. They looked like merchants, Charity decided; their clothes had once been valuable, before they'd been brutally torn and covered in mud. And they'd carried short swords. They had to be reasonably prosperous men.

"Mercy," the leader said, grovelling in the mud. "I beg of you."

The Emperor looked down at him for a long moment. "Why did you destroy the bridges?"

There was a long pause. "We had no choice," the man pleaded, finally. "We ..."

"I am the Emperor," the Emperor said, cutting him off. "This city is now under my direct control. As payment for your sins against me, you will assemble makeshift bridges as quickly as possible so we can continue to move troops across the Lug. In addition, every magician within the city is to report to my camp and you, personally, will hand over your families as hostages for good behaviour. If these terms are refused, your city will be treated as hostile and sacked."

Charity watched the merchant grovel, feeling disgust mixed with pity. The city couldn't have stopped the army, even before the Emperor had revealed his secret weapon. There was no choice but surrender. And yet, part of her wished the city had been able to mount a better fight. It might have killed the Emperor and her.

"Every guardsman within the city will be inducted into my army," the Emperor continued. "All weapons not in the hands of active guardsmen are to be surrendered by the end of the day; anyone found possessing a weapon after midnight will have his hands cut off, just to illustrate the point. My troops will take possession of all strongpoints, military stores and slaves. Any resistance to any of these demands will result in the severest of punishments."

"Yes, Your Supremacy," the man said.

"And the people responsible for destroying the bridge will be handed over to me," the Emperor concluded. "I wish to ... *thank* ... them personally."

"They're dead," the man said, desperately. "The fires burnt them!"

"We shall see," the Emperor said. "Go gather your families. Their time as hostages has begun."

He watched the men shuffle off on hands and knees, then turned to General Vetch. "Inform the troops that I expect them to behave themselves," he ordered. "They are to treat the population with respect, as long as my orders are obeyed. Deploy one of the regiments to secure the strongpoints, then detail two more to gather as many ships and crews as they can, so we can start shipping the rest of the army over once the causeway collapses. Keep them busy."

"Yes, Your Supremacy," General Vetch said.

Charity found herself watching, helplessly, as the Emperor's troops slowly brought the city to heel. If the dragons hadn't been enough to squash resistance, the mere sight of the causeway – and the rapidly-growing lake behind it, was enough to convince even the most fanatical of secessionists to give up. Charity watched the lower half of the river start to dry up, wondering just what would happen when the dam finally broke. The waters were already lapping around the edge, pushing against the stone with immense force. Hell, it was already starting to flood the upper reaches of the city.

She smiled, despite herself, as the remains of a dozen sunken boats came into view. A handful of people were already splashing towards them, despite the presence of an army; a tentacle emerged from one of the larger wrecks, revealing that it had become the nesting place of a water monster, which was now hopelessly trapped. Below it, hundreds of crabs scuttled around in surprise, attacking stranded silvery fish. They'd both be scooped up within seconds and dumped into the pot, once the rest of the population started to explore the exposed riverbed. At least some good would come out of the whole affair …

"Your Supremacy," a soldier said. "We have captured a man bearing one of your sigils."

"Show him to me at once," the Emperor ordered.

Charity turned to watch as a dark-skinned man was pushed forward by the guards. The Emperor dismissed them with a wave, then peered down at the man as he fell to his knees and lowered his eyes. His face looked to have been badly beaten, although Charity had a feeling the wounds were two or three days old. How much her life had changed, part of her reflected helplessly, that she was now judging wounds by sight!

"Your Supremacy," the man said. "I beg for your indulgence. I would have returned to Your Supremacy …"

"I will decide when you have made your report," the Emperor said. It dawned on Charity that the man must be one of the Emperor's spies – and he thought he was in trouble, given the sheer scope of his grovelling. "What happened in this city?"

"Two days ago, they started rounding up foreigners," the man reported. "I was caught by one of their patrols and put in the stocks, along with every other foreigner in the city. They were going to kill us. And then there was an explosion, destroying the City House. A strange magic-user broke us out."

The Emperor leant forward. "And then?"

"I hid, waiting to see what would happen," the man continued. "The new government tried to organise a defence, unknowing the power of Your Supremacy. They sent messages everywhere before Your Supremacy arrived."

"I see," the Emperor said. "How many messages did they send?"

"My sources claim they sent horsemen in all directions," the man said. "Your Supremacy, most of my sources were caught up in the chaos and killed."

The Emperor eyed him for a long moment. "And how were the bridges destroyed?"

"They don't know, Your Supremacy," the man reported. "No one knows how it was done."

Just like the Watchtower, Charity thought.

"I see," the Emperor said, slowly. "Tell me about the magician who helped you escape."

The spy hesitated. "It could be a matter of honour ..."

"*Tell me*," the Emperor thundered.

"She was ... odd," the spy said. "I barely noticed her at first. She was short, slight, with long brown hair. They'd put her in stocks too, but left her clothed, which was strange. They exposed most of the women among the prisoners. But when I saw her eyes, they were *red*."

The Emperor leant forward. "It's *her*!"

Charity blinked, realising who he meant. Red eyes? The Head Librarian didn't have red eyes, did she? She'd seen them and they'd been a lovely brown ... but that could easily have been a glamour. There hadn't been any suggestion the Head Librarian was particularly powerful, apart from the fact she'd served on the Privy Council. *That* was no position for a lightweight. But red eyes suggested a brush with wild magic, at the very least. Her father had been a powerful magician and his eyes had been blue.

"We've been looking for her," he added. "What happened to her?"

"She ran off in the confusion," the spy said. "I didn't know to follow her!"

"She must have left the city by now," Charity offered, hoping to distract the Emperor. "She'd know we were coming, even if the City Fathers didn't."

The Emperor ignored her. "Was she alone?"

"I don't know, Your Supremacy," the spy said. "There were hundreds of foreigners in the stocks. Any of them could be with her and I wouldn't know."

"She would have seen the dragons," Charity said. "We waited for hours before attacking."

"We shall see," the Emperor said. His eyes closed in contemplation. "If she's moved past Falcone's Nest, she could have taken a number of possible roads ... but we know where she's going."

He looked at the spy. "Report to the druids, then hold yourself in readiness. I will have need of you."

"Yes, Your Supremacy," the spy said.

The Emperor looked at Charity for a long moment, then glared at the nearest guardsman. "I want you to find General Vetch and bring him here at once," he ordered. "And bring Roth too."

Charity shuddered inwardly as the guard hurried off, then turned as she heard a dull rumble from behind her. The causeway was finally breaking, releasing a flood of water that rocketed downstream towards the ocean. Dozens of boats, stranded on the riverbed, were smashed to flinders as the water slammed into them, throwing their occupants into the unforgiving waves. She saw a handful of people crossing the riverbed overwhelmed and washed away by the water, thrown down towards the sea. Somehow, she doubted they had a hope in hell of surviving.

The Emperor laughed, even though the wall of water had smashed many of the boats he'd hoped to use for himself.

"Let them talk about this," he said, as General Vetch approached. "It will show them not to trifle with my power."

Charity couldn't disagree. *No one* had performed such feats in living memory. She knew – as the outsiders wouldn't – that hundreds of magicians had died to cast the spell, but the prospect of killing his own people wouldn't slow the Emperor down for a second. The dragons were bad enough, yet this was worse. It wouldn't be long before the Emperor had the bright idea of triggering an earthquake and destroying an entire city. She just hoped he wouldn't ask *her* what he could do with the stored power.

"Your Supremacy," General Vetch said.

"The Head Librarian was here," the Emperor said. "You are to search the entire city from top to bottom. Anyone who stands in our way is to be killed. Inform the authorities of whom we seek and tell them that handing her over will spare the rest of the city from my men, then make contact with the underground and make them the same offer. No, anyone from the underground who finds her for us will be raised to lordship of the entire city."

General Vetch looked surprised. "She's one person, Your Supremacy," he said. "A woman and a weak magician. What can she do?"

"Everything," the Emperor hissed.

Charity stared at him. His voice sounded different.

There was a long pause. "You are to order the search," the Emperor said, in a more normal tone of voice. "I shall be in the tollhouse, studying the maps."

Charity followed him as he stalked into a tollhouse that had been turned into a temporary base of operations. None of the occupants had objected, not when they'd been evicted at sword-point. The Emperor's staff had already laid the maps on the table; one showing the city itself, one showing the surrounding countryside and one showing the entire continent, with the road network outlined in blue ink. Charity stood behind the Emperor as he reached for the final map, waiting for orders. She knew they'd come soon enough.

"She needs to get to Ida," the Emperor mused. He looked up at her. "And your *dear* brother is already on the prowl. Unless, of course, she's separated from her apprentice."

He didn't bother to wait for her to respond. "She could have gone five different ways," he mused, "but the only way to get up the mountains to Ida is through World's Gate – the town here, at the base of the mountains. More to the point, that's the route she'd know; she took it before, back when she first visited Ida. Our best hope to catch her would be to take World's Gate and set up a base there."

"Yes, Your Supremacy," Charity said.

"She *has* to pass through World's Gate," the Emperor repeated. "The only other option would be to climb the mountains, which would be madness. But ... putting a force in World's Gate would alert Ida to our presence."

Then attack Ida directly, Charity thought. The dragons could reach the tiny state within a day, perhaps less.

Whatever the reason behind the Emperor's strange obsession with Ida – and the Head Librarian – he could satisfy both goals easily. *Don't waste time bringing your army when all you need are a few scouts.*

The Emperor, thankfully, didn't ask for her opinion. Instead, he called one of the staffers over to him.

"Assemble a small unit of troops," he ordered. "They are to wear the Empire's livery, rather than mine. Once ready, they will be flown to World's Gate, with orders to be billeted on the town for the next two weeks. They are to be on their best behaviour."

"Yes, Your Supremacy," the staffer said.

Charity felt her heart sink. Ida had been under suspicion in the months prior to the Emperor's rise to power, although she'd never found out why. The Grand Sorceress had been running troops through the region every so often, threatening Ida … the whole affair had never made any sense to her. But they were used to seeing the Empire's troops moving through World's Gate, not *quite* occupying Ida, yet close enough to make the threat very clear. Johan and his mistress might walk straight into a trap.

They'd know about the Emperor, she thought. *They wouldn't be fooled by the pretence. But they'd have no choice. They'd have to work their way through World's Gate unless they try to climb the mountains directly …*

"The troops are to be accompanied by three Inquisitors," the Emperor continued. "Everyone who enters the town is to be checked for glamours, then interrogated under truth spells. When they show themselves, they are to be arrested at once; the Head Librarian is to be brought back here under heavy guard, while anyone with her" – he shot a nasty look at Charity – "is to be executed on the spot."

No, Charity thought.

She had little faith in Jamal's ability to track Johan, although – as he shared the same blood – a magician would be able to use Jamal to trace his brother. But an Inquisitor – *three* Inquisitors – was a different story. They'd set up a trap within the city …

"Charity, you are to take my orders to the Inquisitors, once they arrive," the Emperor said.

Charity hastily prostrated herself in front of him, hoping that it would be enough to hide her sudden smile. He'd wanted to rub her slavery in still further, but he'd made a mistake. A small one, perhaps, yet it was there. She would carry out his orders – she *had* to carry out his orders – but he'd left her a loophole. If she told the Inquisitors *exactly* what the Emperor had ordered, they'd do it ... and make the trap blindingly obvious. She would have skipped out the door if she hadn't known it would alarm him, or convince him to ask her just what had made her so happy ...

It was a loophole, she told herself again. Not much of one, perhaps, but it was there ...

... And just thinking about it gave her hope.

Chapter Fourteen

"The Gap," Johan said, as the small convoy rattled over the bridge. "I heard stories, but I never really believed them."

Elaine sighed, inwardly. Three days of travel had been awkward, to say the least. She hadn't thought of herself as attractive until she'd met Bee – and, after he'd dumped her, a string of unsuccessful dates had convinced her that Bee had been an exception. Daria might call her pretty, but no one else seemed to agree. She had thought that the curses of red eyes and political power, no matter how little she wanted it, would leave her an old maid for the rest of her life.

But Johan *was* attracted to her. He hadn't been able to hide the flurry of emotions that had passed through his mind, nor the embarrassment of *knowing* she knew how he felt. Elaine couldn't help being torn between embarrassment herself and the odd thought that she *liked* Johan, even though he was her apprentice. A relationship between them would be taboo – it would certainly cause comment – even though they weren't related in any way.

There's a reason we don't allow apprenticeship bonds between men and women, she thought, grimly. She'd gone through all the reasons when she'd reluctantly convinced herself that the bond was the safest course of action, allowing her to shut Johan down if necessary. And the Grand Sorceress had agreed, pointing out that no other magician could be trusted not to abuse such power. She had told herself that she could keep the relationship *professional* ...

... And I was wrong, she admitted, reluctantly.

It was a bitter thought. A bond between two men or two women wouldn't have pulled them together, unless the stronger of the two was homosexual, but she was too young to distance herself from Johan. They were compatible and the bond was mutating, drawing them together. She *knew* it was the bond, wearing down her resistance to such an improper relationship ... and yet, even *knowing* it wasn't entirely her own decision, she still found it hard to resist.

She forced the thought away, drawing on all her remaining mental discipline as she looked out at the Runnymede Gap. It *was* impressive, strikingly so; a long cleft in the ground that had only just avoided becoming a lake. The Empire's engineers had bridged it at a dozen crossing points, ensuring that travellers didn't have to climb down into the canyon and back up the other side to reach their destination. A handful of people lived at the bottom, Elaine recalled; they rarely had any contact with the rest of the world. And they liked it that way.

Magic could have created the Gap, she thought. *But no one knows for sure.*

She closed her eyes in silent contemplation. Her head was full of spells that hadn't been performed for centuries, spells to rend the ground like paper or freeze an entire lake to solid ice. One of them could easily have created the Gap, smashing anything that lay in its path and slaughtering hundreds of thousands of victims. She couldn't have hoped to cast them herself – the spells were so powerful that even a full-fledged Inquisitor would have found it impossible – but they were a constant temptation to her. If she found a way to rewrite them, she could turn the spells against Deferens and his army.

The carriage rattled onwards. She did her best to concentrate on her book, cursing the lost opportunity to pick up more books in Falcone's Nest; she'd read the book before and the text was still firmly fixed in her mind. But at least it kept her mind off Johan and the bond between them, even though she could still feel his presence in her mind. He kept glancing at her, then looking away. The bond was bad enough for Elaine, but she knew it would be worse for him.

His father never trained him in any of the mental disciplines, she thought, sourly. If she ever had a chance to meet Duncan Conidian, she silently promised herself, she could show him exactly what it had felt like to be his Powerless son. *He can't even begin to recognise where the bond stops and genuine feeling starts.*

"We're approaching an inn," Dread said. "We're going to

stop here."

Elaine looked up, out of the carriage. It wasn't dark yet. Indeed, it looked like midday. They were approaching a small hamlet, a handful of houses dominated by a single large inn. Elaine sniffed the air and grimaced. The air stank of too many horses in close proximity, suggesting the inn was actually a coachhouse. They could change their steeds here, if the innkeeper liked the look of their horses.

"It's not *that* late," Johan said. "I thought we could make it to World's Gate by nightfall."

"We probably could," Dread said, curtly. "However, I'd prefer not to walk blindly into World's Gate."

Elaine frowned. "We've been there before ..."

"That time, we didn't have an Emperor hunting us," Dread said. "If *I* was in charge of planning the pursuit, I'd leapfrog the hamlets and send troops directly to World's Gate. They know we *have* to pass through the town before heading up to Ida."

"Unless we want to climb the mountains," Elaine said. They'd scrambled out of Ida last time, she recalled, but it had almost killed them even in early summer. Now, the mountain peaks in the distance were covered in snow and the air was growing steadily colder. "Do you think the Emperor's taken precautions?"

"I'd be surprised if he hadn't," Dread said. "He knows where we're going, after all."

The carriage rattled to a halt outside the inn. Dread told them to stay where they were, then jumped down to have a brief chat with Sarah. The Levellers gathered around them, their faces darkening as Dread pointed out the danger. Elaine tried to listen to them, but the magicians had cast a spell that made it impossible to eavesdrop. Instead, she looked at the distant mountains, recalling their first visit to Ida. They'd been lucky to escape with their lives.

And we never knew what was hiding under the mountains, she thought. *If we'd known ... we'd both have died on the spot.*

"Daria hasn't returned," Johan said, softly. "Is she alright?"

"I hope so," Elaine said. "But you know it could take a

while."

There was no point in trying to hide her concern. She'd half-expected Daria to catch up with them by now, but there had been no sign of the werewolf. Had the Travellers decided to keep her from helping any further? It didn't seem likely, but the Emperor might have made a deal with them after learning Elaine had been helped by a werewolf. The offer of lands for themselves had to be very attractive after years on the road. What if they *had* agreed to help the Emperor?

"She'll be fine," Johan said. "She told me that werewolves can't deceive each other."

"That's true," Elaine said. There were times when she wondered if werewolves weren't better than the rest of the human race. They were seen as brutes, if not savage monsters, yet it was vanishingly rare to see an abused werewolf child or a werewolf rapist. "But if the pack believes that joining the Emperor is a good idea, it will be hard for any werewolf to resist long enough to escape."

It wasn't a pleasant thought. The downside of being a werewolf was pack loyalty – there was no such thing as a lone werewolf. Even Daria had needed to return to the camp every few months to renew herself. If the other werewolves had decided to submit to the Emperor, Daria would find it hard to convince them otherwise ... and she might be swept into the pack instead of being allowed to leave. Elaine knew that her friend might be lost within the pack forever.

Dread poked his head back into the carriage. "We're going to be staying here for the night – perhaps two nights – while a couple of horsemen go ahead," he said. "Get your bags and jump down. There's a set of rooms being prepared for us."

"They might even have better food," Johan said. "Or is that just a dream?"

"They have a captive market," Dread said, dryly. "What do you think?"

Elaine smiled in genuine amusement. One thing the orphanage had taught her was not to be fussy with food. There was no way the staff could afford anything more than cheap pieces of meat – if they were lucky – and stale vegetables. Johan, on the other hand, had grown up in one of the Great Houses. *He'd* been used to eating truly excellent food, even though he was the family embarrassment. No doubt he would have complained about the food if he'd gone to the Peerless School, like Millicent had done. Elaine had thought she was crazy until she'd started to eat with the Grand Sorceress.

She sobered as she remembered Light Spinner. The older woman had been formidable, but she'd also been decent. She hadn't deserved to die at Vlad Deferens' hands, after being forced to watch as the Empire fell into his lap. Elaine promised herself, as she walked into the inn, that Deferens would pay for all he'd done. He was a monster in human form.

And if he's a monster, she asked herself, *what's the Witch-King*?

"Johan and I will be sharing one room," Dread said. "You can share with Sarah."

"I need to talk to you afterwards, once we've settled in," she said. She did her best to ignore the flash of disappointment from Johan. There was no way they could share a room, not when the bond was pulling them together. "Can we talk in a private room?"

Dread nodded. "I'll see to it personally."

Somewhat to Elaine's surprise, the rooms were clean, the beds were comfortable and the food was quite good. Or maybe it shouldn't have been a surprise, she told herself, as she finished off a plate of roast lamb, boiled potatoes and gravy. The inn was in the midst of farmland and the farmers probably didn't have many other customers. Sarah chatted happily with the waitress, who turned out to be the owner's daughter, while Dread made the rounds of the handful of drinkers. By the time he returned, Elaine knew, he'd have drawn every last piece of gossip out of them.

Johan looked at her as the dinner came to an end. "I think we should talk."

Elaine tasted his emotions and shivered, inwardly. Johan was a mess; she'd known he was a mess, but now it was far harder to ignore or confront. He wanted to do what was right, yet he was tormented by his past and tempted by his power. She felt a stab of guilt that she knew he'd sense, but she couldn't go with him. The bond would overwhelm them both.

"Go upstairs," she said, finally. "I need to speak to Dread."

Johan looked doubtful. "Will you be safe here?"

"I think so," Elaine said. "I'll see you soon, promise."

She leant back in her chair and surveyed the room as she waited. A handful of locals were drinking steadily, while a number of guests were eating dinner or chatting loudly amongst themselves while waiting for the waitress. They looked like traders mostly, although there were two women who were definitely magicians, standing next to an older man carrying a sword slung over his shoulder. A bodyguard, Elaine reasoned; it was odd for a magician to require a bodyguard, but some mages preferred to have cold steel between themselves and minor threats. The bodyguard looked back at her, his gaze flickering over her face, then looked away. No doubt he didn't see her as a threat to his charges.

And he's right, Elaine thought. Idly, she wondered what the three of them were doing, then dismissed the thought. *We're not here to pick fights.*

"Elaine," Dread said. He held out a hand and helped her to her feet. "Shall we go?"

He led her up a flight of stairs, then into her bedroom. Sarah was missing; Elaine had a feeling that she was still talking to the waitress, perhaps offering to help in exchange for the latest news. Dread closed the door, moved his hand in a familiar pattern, then winced. He could still make the motions and say the words, but he no longer had the magic to make the spells work.

"It isn't easy to do *anything* without magic," Elaine said, as she cast the ward herself. "How are you coping?"

"We were taught not to rely on our magic," Dread said, quietly. He leant against the wall, watching her through cool grey eyes. "But it isn't easy."

Elaine nodded. For a magician – even her – magic was part of daily living. Why get a candle when you could create a light globe that would suit you perfectly? Why endure aches and pains when there was no shortage of spells that could smooth such minor irritations away? But for someone who could no longer use magic, the memory of what that had been like was a constant mocking torment. No wonder so many magicians went mad when they lost their powers. It was almost like losing an arm or a leg.

"I'm sorry," she said.

"Don't be," Dread said, harshly. "I will learn to cope without it."

He took a long breath, steadying himself. "What did you want to talk about?"

"The bond is pulling Johan and me together," Elaine said, flatly. "He's already fixated on me."

"He *was* glancing at you like a lovelorn loon," Dread agreed, after a moment. "You do realise that it was pretty much inevitable?"

Elaine grimaced. The *first* time they'd tried to form the bond it hadn't worked properly, leaving them unaware of the full effects. When she'd changed the ritual, it had worked … and, instead of having the time to cope as they'd drawn closer together, they'd been forced to flee the Golden City. Dread was right. It would only be a matter of time before they wound up sleeping together.

The bump on the head probably didn't help either, she thought, darkly.

She felt sick. Head wounds were feared by all magicians, because there were no spells that could repair a damaged mind. It *was* vaguely possible, if the victim trusted the caster completely, but it rarely worked very well. The knowledge in her head told her it only 'worked' by rewriting the victim's brain at will, leaving him at the mercy of the caster. It wouldn't be hard for the caster to reshape the victim into something altogether different.

"Not a good thing, normally," Dread added, drawing her out of her thoughts. "Here … who would know?"

"I agree with you," Elaine said. "Now … do I agree with you because you're right or because I *want* to agree with you?"

Dread met her eyes. "You tell me."

"I wish I knew," Elaine said.

"There is a *reason* such bonds are frowned upon," Dread said, curtly. "You two may find it hard to separate over the next few weeks, at least until the bond steadies itself. I don't think it would be easy to *break* the bond."

Elaine nodded, shortly. The bond lasted at least four years, binding master and apprentice together. It could be renewed afterwards if the participants chose, but she knew that was uncommon. Most apprentices wanted to strike out on their own after four years of learning …

… But then, most apprentices enjoyed a more balanced bond with their master.

"The thought of severing the link is … unthinkable," she said. It would be difficult, even with a full-fledged sorcerer to help. Neither of them *wanted* to lose the bond. "But how would we know if our feelings are *real*?"

"See if you keep them after four years," Dread said. He held up a hand before she could say something cutting. "For the moment, try to keep them under control. It isn't long until we reach Ida."

"True," Elaine agreed.

"I can speak to Johan, if you like," Dread said. "There're a few pieces of advice I could give him."

Elaine shook her head. "I think he'd hate it," she said. "You're not his father."

She scowled. What *would* Johan's father have said? She doubted it would be anything good, not when Johan was an embarrassment. He'd probably planned to sterilise Johan, just to make sure there were no more powerless children. She cursed inwardly as a thought struck her. *Had* he sterilised Johan? It would have been easy, with the right potion; Johan might not even *know* he was sterile. Or maybe he'd simply had his memory wiped afterwards …

I could check, she thought. *But what would I do if he is?*

"Then sleep, for the moment," Dread said. "The horsemen won't get back here until tomorrow."

"I will," Elaine said. She gave him a long look. "Thank you."

"You're welcome," Dread said. "Just … be careful. This could ruin your reputation if it gets out."

Elaine had to laugh. "The Emperor has branded me a traitor and a fugitive from justice," she pointed out. "I don't think it matters if they add warping an apprenticeship bond to the list."

"It might," Dread said. "Bonds are sacred, after all. You might not have deliberately intended to warp one, but that's what happened. All it takes is one idiot to start a rumour and your reputation will be mud. And if you have to convince magicians to follow you later …"

"I understand," Elaine said. "I'll keep it quiet."

"Very quiet," Dread said. "I don't know *what* Light Spinner was thinking."

"She wanted someone to keep Johan under control," Elaine told him, bluntly. "I don't think she dared risk anything weaker than an apprenticeship bond."

"And now you're dealing with the consequences," Dread said. "Watch yourself."

Chapter Fifteen

Johan didn't sleep well.

He'd always slept lightly, even as a child – Jamal had a habit of sneaking into Johan's room and enchanting his possessions – but this was different. He dreamed of Jamal and someone whispering to him and a face that blurred into Elaine. When he awoke, he was drenched in sweat and uncomfortably aware that he didn't feel quite right. He climbed out of bed, washed himself in the tiny bathroom and dressed, feeling unsteady. And yet, he didn't feel *ill*.

Sarah met him as he walked downstairs, wearing a leather jerkin with her long blonde hair running down the back. He couldn't help noticing that her trousers were tight around her rear, but this was nothing more than a dispassionate appraisal. She gave him an odd look as they reached the bottom of the stairs, then led him into the dining room. A handful of guests were sitting at various tables, eating breakfast. Dread and Elaine were sitting together – he felt a spurt of envy so strong it almost overpowered him – and talking in low voices. Sarah sat down next to Elaine and waved to the waitress. Reluctantly, Johan sat next to Dread.

Your dreams weren't pleasant, Elaine sent, through the bond. *Are you all right?*

No, Johan sent back. He hadn't thought she would have sensed his discontent. *I was dreaming of Jamal.*

Definitely a nightmare, Elaine agreed. *Make sure you eat plenty today.*

Before Johan could ask why, the waitress arrived and took their orders. Dread ordered a massive plate of bacon, eggs and fried potatoes, then insisted that everyone eat the same before leaving the inn. As soon as the waitress had gone, Sarah cast a privacy spell into the air, ensuring that no one else could overhear their words. Johan tensed. The horsemen might have made it back from World's Gate by now.

"There's a small army in World's Gate," Dread said, quietly. "It's led by a handful of Inquisitors and they're checking everyone who enters the town. They're not being remotely subtle about it."

Elaine smiled, although there was no amusement in her words. "They're trying to give us an opportunity to slip through, aren't they?"

"It looks that way," Dread agreed. "We certainly couldn't fail to spot the checkpoint well away from the town."

He reached into his pocket and produced one of the paper maps he'd obtained from the waitress, when they'd arrived at the inn. "Entering the town will be enough to get us all captured. They'd insist on removing the glamours and …"

He nodded at Elaine, who made a face. "My eyes will be enough to condemn me," she said, grimly. "I don't think there's anyone else walking around with red eyes."

Dread unfurled the map on the table. "We can't go through World's Gate," he said. "Or, at least, *we* can't go through the town. Sarah and the Levellers could, if we weren't accompanying them."

Johan shivered. "So how do we get to Ida?"

"We're going to have to climb," Dread said. He traced out a route on the map. "If we head north from here, we should be able to make the climb up this line here and reach the lower levels of Ida …"

"It will be treacherous," Elaine said. "The whole area is covered in snow."

"I've done mountain climbing as part of my training," Dread said. His grey eyes were very cold. "I don't think it will be easy, but I don't think we have any other choice."

"There's no way we can lure them out of World's Gate?" Johan asked. "I could make a diversion …"

"It would be far too revealing," Dread said. "These are trained Inquisitors who probably understand your weaknesses very well. I was able to knock you out, remember?"

Johan nodded, rubbing the back of his head. Dread had knocked him out before he'd realised the Inquisitor had been closing in on them. If he hadn't been tough enough to resist his oaths, just long enough, they would all have been shipped back to the Golden City. Or Elaine would have been, at least. Johan had a feeling *he* was considered too great a threat to be allowed to live.

"We'd need equipment," Elaine said. "Where do you intend to get it?"

"There's a climbing lodge here," Dread said, tapping the map. "The three of us take two of the horses to here, where we … *obtain* the equipment, hire a guide and set off up the mountain."

"If we *can* hire a guide," Elaine said. "I didn't see any the last time we were here."

"It wasn't a planned trip," Dread said. He looked at Sarah. "Can you and the other magicians make your way through World's Gate to Ida?"

"Unless they try to stop us," Sarah said. "Three Inquisitors and a large company of soldiers …"

She broke off as breakfast arrived. Johan tucked in, then caught a flicker of amusement from Elaine and looked up to see Dread eating at terrifying speed. Johan fought to keep a smile off his face as he looked back at his plate, cutting his way through the bacon and chewing it piece by piece. It wasn't as good as the meals he'd enjoyed in House Conidian, he considered, but in some ways it was definitely more flavourful. Elaine picked at her food, clearly nervous. The prospect of a long climb up the mountains didn't please her.

It can't be that bad, Johan sent. *We were up in the mountains last month.*

Those weren't real mountains, Elaine sent back. Her thoughts were tinged with worry. *Trust me, Johan. These mountains are going to be worse.*

Johan didn't believe her, not really. They finished their breakfast, paid the bill and headed outside, where they parted from Sarah. The Leveller gave them all a tight hug, even Dread; Dread gave her a letter for Queen Sacharissa, asking Sarah to pass it to the Queen if they didn't make it to Ida.

"The Queen – she was the Princess at the time – was quite taken with Dread," Elaine said, her thoughts tinged with amusement. "I think she even tried to lure him to Ida to be Prince Consort."

Johan gaped. "Really?"

"He didn't go, of course," Elaine added. "But if he had, things would be different."

"Mount up," Dread ordered, as he walked over to them. "It's time to go."

Johan was relieved – and yet disappointed – when Elaine chose to ride behind Dread, rather than him. He knew he was a good horseman, but it would have been incredibly distracting to have her behind him. The horse neighed loudly as he scrambled onto its back, then moved forward as he tugged on the reins. Dread moved up next to him, his face grim.

"If anyone asks, you're my children," he said, shortly. "And we're taking the long way home to Appal."

"Understood," Johan said.

He smiled inwardly as Dread cantered off. The story wasn't particularly convincing; Dread might have looked in his early forties, but Elaine didn't really look young enough to be his daughter, although Johan had to admit it was theoretically possible. On the other hand, people aged quickly in the mountains. Elaine might be taken for someone five years younger if the watchers expected her to look older than she was. But she certainly didn't have the rough hands of someone used to working the fields.

Let's hope we don't get caught, he thought. *Maybe we should stick with the other story.*

It grew colder, rapidly, as they galloped towards the mountains. Johan couldn't help feeling intimidated as they grew larger, their peaks fading in and out of visibility as nasty-looking clouds formed high overhead. Snowflakes started to fall, rapidly turning to water as they settled on the horse's coat; Johan wished, suddenly, that he could use charms to warm himself, without running the risk of accidentally cooking the poor animal. The road, thankfully, was made for bad weather. It grew harder to ride the horses when they turned off the stone road and headed up a muddy half-frozen track. The mist, slowly rolling down from the mountains, was making it very hard to see.

Dread slowed his horse, then glanced back at Johan. "Have you ever ridden in these conditions before?"

Johan shook his head. He'd never been allowed to go

outside the family's lands, back when they'd lived outside the Golden City. But there *had* been plenty of room to canter about, enjoying the solitude and – relative – safety from his siblings. He'd loved the horses back there ... he fought down a sudden stab of homesickness, then looked down at the muddy track. It was almost invisible in the gloom.

"We may have to get off and walk," Dread said, shortly. "I ..."

He broke off as a set of buildings loomed out of the mist. One of them was a general store; the others, made from stone, seemed designed for cold weather. Dread pulled the horses to a stop, then jumped down and helped Elaine to climb off the horse. Johan followed, holding the horse's reins in his hands. Frost had started to form on the poor animal's hair.

"Stay here," Dread ordered. "I'll speak to the owner."

He walked inside, shaking the snow and water from his clothes. Johan looked at Elaine, who looked frozen, even though she would have cast warming charms to keep herself from getting too cold. She looked terrified, her face pale and wan; Johan took her in his arms and hugged her tightly, realising slowly that she was half-asleep. She'd used a charm to make herself sleep, despite the risks. It had probably been the only way she could cope with the ride.

"You'll be fine," he whispered, feeling a dull flicker of emotion in response. The cold must have dulled his mind too or he would have sensed that something was wrong. "It's probably going to get colder."

Dread returned. "I've spoken to the owner," he said. "He'll give us climbing gear and clothes in exchange for the horses."

Johan nodded – he was too tired to speak – and helped Elaine into the general store. The owner eyed them both in some concern, but said nothing. Johan guessed he didn't really believe the cover story, yet felt no obligation to pry. The mountainfolk, from what Dread had said, had as little to do with the Empire as possible. He sat down next to Elaine, then accepted a mug of hot chocolate gratefully. Elaine needed to be helped to drink the warm liquid.

"Get changed into these clothes," the owner advised,

passing Johan a large set of furs. "My wife will be down in a moment if the lady wants assistance."

Johan was too wet to care about undressing in front of a stranger – or his wife. His clothes were soaked through; it was a relief to get out of them, dry himself with a warm towel and then get into the furs. Someone had charmed them to help repel water, he realised, as he grew warmer rapidly. Elaine was helped into the next room and emerged, ten minutes later, wrapped up in so many furs she was barely recognisable. But at least she looked reassuringly normal.

"I'm sorry," she said, quietly. "I should have known better than to use charms ..."

The owner's wife – a hefty woman with a motherly face – brayed like a mule. "If you get trapped up there, get undressed and snuggle," she said, loudly. "It will keep the cold away."

Johan blushed, brightly. Elaine looked as if she would sooner be somewhere – anywhere – else. The owner laughed, said something to his wife in a language Johan didn't recognise, then proffered a large bag of tools. Dread took it, glanced inside, tested a handful and then nodded curtly. The owner opened the door and looked outside.

"The storm is subsiding," he said. "If you are determined to go, then you should leave in twenty minutes. But I would really advise you to take the road."

Dread shook his head. "We have to go this way," he said. "There isn't time."

Johan frowned as the owner and his wife exchanged glances. *They* had to think the three of them were committing suicide, if the mountains were as bad as everyone said. And yet, they weren't trying to *stop* them, merely urging them to take the safer route. Johan half-considered trying to talk Dread into waiting until the snow cleared, then dismissed the thought. It might not be long before the enemy started sending patrols around the mountain, even though very few people would dare the climb to Ida. And besides, *here* the snow would lie for months.

"The guide will meet you at the black rock," the owner said. "And *don't* lose the charmed needle. It will always point to Ida."

Dread nodded and looked out of the door. The snow had stopped falling, leaving the tiny village buried under a layer of white. A handful of other villagers could be seen in the distance, clearing the snow away from their homes. Johan puzzled over it for a long moment, then decided that the weight of the snow might eventually crush the buildings, if given enough time to build up. Dread waved goodbye to the owner and led the way out into the cold. Johan looked at Elaine, then followed him. Elaine brought up the rear.

"Don't use any charms past this point," Dread warned, as they reached the edge of the village and peered up towards Ida. The mountains loomed above them, threateningly. "You can't afford to blur your thoughts."

"I understand," Elaine said, quietly.

Johan reached for her gloved hand and held it gently as they walked towards the black rock, standing right at the base of the mountain. The guide was waiting for them, his face oddly perplexed. He exchanged a few words with Dread, then turned to start walking up towards Ida. Johan kept hold of Elaine's hand as they slowly walked away from the village, then looked back. The village had already vanished in the mist.

He sensed Elaine's trepidation as the path slowly became more treacherous. The world seemed to blur to white; it was hard, very hard, to spot anything resembling a landmark. Snow lay everywhere, covering the path; the guide slowed, poking at the ground with a stick before daring to keep moving forward. Johan looked up into the clouds, then down; a slope led down the mountainside and vanished into the mist. He honestly couldn't understand how *anyone* lived near the mountains. They were beautiful, but how could *anyone* eke out an existence when they were trapped by snow four months out of twelve?

The air grew thinner, making it harder to breathe. It was a relief when the guide called a halt, insisting they take a few moments to catch their breath and eat a handful of dried fruit and nuts. Elaine looked dreadfully tired and Johan didn't feel much better. He'd been wrong; they hadn't even started the most dangerous part of the climb and he already wished they'd tried to sneak past the Inquisitors instead. It was hard, so hard, to force himself to start again when the guide ordered them to resume the climb. Part of him – and part of Elaine – just wanted to sit down and wait for the cold to take him.

I will not let this beat me, he thought, trying to push the thought at Elaine. His mind seemed to be slowing down. The cold was slowly leaching through the furs, despite the charms. *I will not let this stop me from reaching Ida.*

The air turned savage, suddenly; a cold blast of wind threw sleet and ice into their faces, forcing them to duck. Johan covered his eyes and waited until the blizzard had come to a halt, then staggered onwards, still clutching Elaine's hand. Behind them, the mist was rising, as if it was crawling up the mountainside. Johan felt a shiver running down his spine, then a wave of sickness that almost knocked him to his knees. Elaine gave him a sharp look, visible even through the furs; Johan gathered himself, unsure what had happened. It felt as if someone had just walked over his grave …

There was a flicker of light. Johan blinked in surprise – someone had cast a spell – and then swallowed in horror as a low rumble echoed through the air. An avalanche of snow was breaking loose and falling down the mountainside towards them, building up speed as it moved faster and faster. The guide shouted a curse and then lunged forward, running towards a rock that might provide shelter. Johan yanked Elaine forward as they ran, Dread catching her other hand and pulling her under cover. And then a second spell slammed into the ground under their feet, separating them.

"Get down," Dread shouted. "Someone's hunting us!"

Johan turned, too late. The impact had thrown him behind the rock, but Elaine was still in the open, without any form of protection. He felt a shock through the bond, a confused series of impressions that threatened to drag him into the maelstrom. And then snow fell all around them, the rock shuddering slightly as it threatened to roll down the mountainside, crushing them below its weight. Johan panicked; the rock shattered, the blast smashing through the snow and clearing the air.

But, when he pulled himself to his feet, there was no sign of Elaine. The guide's body lay on the ground, shattered and broken, but where was Elaine?

"Johan!"

Johan froze, utterly unable to move. It wasn't magic, it was fear. The voice … was a voice he'd never expected to hear again. It couldn't be Jamal, part of his mind insisted; Jamal had fled after losing his powers. But the voice was so familiar he couldn't deny it. His elder brother had tracked him down and …

No, he thought. Jamal was powerless. He couldn't torment Johan any longer. *This isn't fair …*

Chapter Sixteen

The flash of magic came too quickly for Elaine to shout a warning, even as it triggered an avalanche. She was fairly sure her thoughts weren't actually slowing down, but it certainly *felt* as though she was unable to think quickly as Johan and Dread pulled her forward. The cold was wearing away at her, leaving her almost defenceless ... she didn't even have a chance to raise a ward before the second spell slammed into the ground, hurling her back under the tidal wave of snow.

It hit, throwing her down the mountainside. She tried, desperately, to summon the magic to save herself, but nothing seemed to work. Her thoughts felt sluggish, as if something was influencing them, as if something was slowly draining her very life. A wave of magic caught her, yanking her out of the snow and throwing her down. She hit a patch of soft snow and lay there, stunned. Someone had targeted her specifically, someone ...

She opened her eyes, unsure of just when she'd actually closed them. The avalanche had stopped, thankfully, but there was no sign of Dread, Johan or the guide. She stared up the mountainside for a long moment, wondering just how far she'd fallen, and then twisted her head as she heard someone running towards her. A woman wearing furs dropped to her knees next to Elaine, then threw back her hood to reveal long brown hair, brown eyes and a smile that was oddly familiar. And yet, Elaine couldn't place her ...

"Help," she croaked. She had no idea if the woman was friend or enemy, she knew she was dead if she didn't get help. "Please ..."

"Shut up," the woman ordered. She tore off her gloves, then pulled Elaine's hood free, allowing the cold to sting her bare cheeks. "Just relax and this won't hurt."

Elaine felt icy fingers touching her forehead. "What ...?"

"I said, shut up," the woman ordered. Her fingers seemed to bore straight into Elaine's skull, burning through her mind. "Everything you have will become mine …"

Pain flared through Elaine's mind as her thoughts were ransacked, ruthlessly. It was a violation … an *impossible* violation. And yet, Kane had done the same … and Kane had been her father. The woman … it dawned on her, suddenly, that the woman had to be her *mother*, the woman who'd given birth to her at Kane's command and then left her at the orphanage for years. No one who wasn't a direct blood relation could have cast the spell to drag the collected knowledge of the Great Library out of her mind …

The sense of betrayal was overwhelming. Kane had said her mother had been a whore – Elaine had always assumed her magic had come from Kane, who'd been a magician himself – but it was clear now that her mother had been a magician too. No, *was* a magician; a magician working for the Witch-King. She tried to struggle, but the weight holding her down was too strong. A direct blood relation could have influenced her thoughts from a distance, even if she'd rendered herself untraceable. No *wonder* she'd been so tired!

A whore, she thought, numbly. *It would have been so much better if she'd just been a whore.*

She moaned in pain as the fingers retreated, then she felt another spell inching its way into her mind. It was hard, so hard, to muster any defence, but she tried. The spell seemed to hesitate, almost as if it were a living thing, and then it thrust forward again. This time, her mind snapped under the impact …

… And darkness swallowed her into its maw.

***

Jamal hadn't changed much, as far as Johan could tell, save for a single nasty scar on his face and a wild madness in his eyes. He stood, perfectly balanced on the snow, wearing a set of magician's robes that seemed hideously out of place. A wand sat at his belt, while he held a short sword in one hand and a charmed shield in the other. Johan had to fight the urge to cringe back as Jamal studied him, remembering how he'd been jinxed, hexed and cursed repeatedly. He knew Jamal no longer had the power to hurt him, but he didn't really *believe* it.

"You're looking well," Jamal said, finally. He took a step forward, casually. "I do believe a life on the run suits you."

Johan found his voice. "How did you track us down?"

Jamal smirked. "You're minutes from death and *that's* your first question?"

He shrugged, keeping his eyes fixed on Johan. "We share the same blood, remember? I found it easy to follow you."

"No, you didn't," Johan said. He reached out for Elaine, but felt nothing. She couldn't be dead ... and yet there was nothing coming down the link. "You don't have any magic left. Someone else was with you."

Jamal flushed. "The Emperor wants you dead," he said, tightly. "He even sent someone to deal with your slutty friend. Does it feel *better* when you are bonded to your partner?"

Johan clenched his fists. Jamal was working for Deferens? Somehow, he wasn't surprised. Jamal had always been ambitious; he'd searched for a good marriage, a good apprenticeship ... anything else that could help him crawl up the social ladder. Working for the Emperor might even prove a way to regain some of his former life, even if he no longer had any magic. It wasn't likely that anyone else would be willing to help.

He found his voice. "You're a monster ..."

"You're the one who broke father," Jamal reminded him. "You took his magic, remember?"

"He let you free," Johan snapped. "Why didn't he keep a tight leash on you when you were in deep shit? The oath he swore could have killed him – or the Inquisitors would, if they decided he'd evaded his sworn word!"

"He loved me," Jamal said.

"And you broke his heart," Johan said.

Jamal shrugged. "I would have made House Conidian great," he said. "Father knew that, I think."

"You would have destroyed us," Johan said. He had a feeling he wouldn't have lasted, once Jamal had taken the helm. A Powerless was nothing more than an embarrassment. No one would have given a damn if Johan's father had killed him. Or if his brother killed him after becoming Patriarch. "House Conidian would not have survived."

"I would have been great," Jamal sneered. The contempt in his voice was striking. "Look at you! You steal power, somehow, and yet … here you are, apprenticed to a *mere* librarian. And a young bitch, at that!"

He leered in a manner that was all too familiar, a reminder of the days when Jamal had been able to have anyone he wanted while Johan was always alone. "Tell me; do you feel your cock sliding into her when you take her?"

"Shut up," Johan snapped. The mockery was more than he could take, but he had to keep control of himself. "You're not worthy to talk about her!"

"Do you feel your fingers on her breasts?" Jamal asked. His face twisted into a snarl. "Do you taste your …"

"Shut up!" Johan shouted. How *dare* his brother speak so unpleasantly of *Elaine*? "I'll kill you!"

"I'd be careful what you shout here," Jamal sneered. He jerked a hand, indicating the mountainside. "Even the slightest scream could trigger another avalanche."

He stepped forward, lifting his sword. "And no, you won't kill me," he said. "You have *never* been able to lift a hand to me."

"Because you always made sure I couldn't," Johan said. His legs felt as if they were rooted to the spot as Jamal approached, cold ice holding him firmly in place. "You never gave me a fighting chance."

"You never deserved one," Jamal told him, smoothly. "You were nothing more than a filthy dirty *powerless* mundane. How could you *possibly* have come from our father's loins? How could our father, the greatest sorcerer outside the Golden City, have sired a powerless child? When all of the rest of us have plenty of magic? And how could our mother have given birth to it?"

He met Johan's eyes. "I know! Three years after I was born, our parents found a baby on the doorstep, wrapped in swaddling clothes and wailing piteously. And, because they needed someone for us to practice on, they took the baby into their house and called it their son, even though it had no magic. They didn't care about the child! No *wonder* father quietly encouraged me to test my spells on you. You weren't his son!"

"That's a lie," Johan said, frantically. He knew there were plenty of tests to confirm the parentage of children, if there was even the tiniest fraction of doubt. Given his ... *condition*, those tests would definitely have been used. "I would have been tested ..."

"Why bother?" Jamal asked. His voice lightened, slightly. "He *knew* you weren't his son and you weren't going to inherit, so why bother testing you?"

Johan stared at him. Could it be true? His parents had had all sorts of arguments about him as he'd grown older, his father even hinting that his mother had done something appalling and brought upon herself the punishment of the gods. And yet, his father had never even *hinted* to Johan that he might not be his son. Duncan Conidian had been horrified to have sired a powerless child, but he'd never given Johan up for adoption ...

He laughed, suddenly. "You've overplayed your hand," he said, taking a step backwards. He no longer felt scared, merely angry. "If that were true, if I was no relation to you, how could you have found me?"

Jamal smiled, then lunged forward. Johan jumped back, focusing his mind; Jamal lashed out with his sword, which became a snake in his hand. It turned with a nasty hiss; Jamal dropped it at once, then threw himself forward. Johan imagined a wall between them; Jamal ran headlong into an invisible force and fell to the ground, blood leaking from a nasty gash in his forehead.

"I took your power," Johan said, feeling the magic growing stronger as hatred roared through his mind. "And now you're going to suffer ..."

Jamal turned, staring up at him. "Please ..."

"You never listened when I begged," Johan shouted, ignoring the danger. He envisaged something picking Jamal up and throwing him away; Jamal screamed as he was wrenched from the ground and hurled into the distance. He hit the ground hard enough to break bones. "You never treated me as anything other than your toy!"

He strode over to where his brother had fallen. Somehow, despite everything, he was sure his brother wasn't dead … but that was good. The hatred burning through him demanded that Jamal die at his bare hands. Cold rage powered him as he peered down at the broken body, one leg twisted so badly that it was clearly shattered. Blood pooled on the snow, mocking him. Jamal's life was slowly leaking away. He gathered himself, ready to kick Jamal to death …

"Careful," a quiet voice said. "You can give into the darkness that way."

Johan stared down at Jamal, suddenly shocked. "I …"

He turned. Dread was standing behind him, leaning on a climbing pole. The Inquisitor looked battered, but alive. Johan looked at him, feeling the rage slowly draining out of his mind. All that was left was bitter horror … and fear. He still couldn't feel Elaine. Her mind was gone.

"If you kill him, like that, you'll lose yourself," Dread warned. His voice was very calm, as if he were quite willing to accept whatever decision Johan made. "Madness will overcome you."

Johan looked back at Jamal, who was staring up at them. His brother had always been a bully … and a coward, too. Jamal had always tormented those with less magic or wealth than himself, but he'd never tried to fight anyone stronger. He'd certainly failed to stand up to the Inquisitors when they'd arrested him for attacking mundanes. Now …

"He's a danger," Johan said, numbly. He'd never considered that anyone could use his blood to track him down, although in hindsight it was obvious. Deferens had Charity under his control, after all. Misogynist prick he might be, but Deferens should have had no problems using Charity's blood in a similar spell. "We can't leave him alive."

"You can't kill him," Dread said, grimly. He seemed to come to a decision. "I need you to find Elaine."

Johan nodded, reluctantly. The bond seemed broken, as if she was gone … and yet, his feelings for her hadn't changed. He knew little about bonds – Elaine had made him read a book on them, but the book hadn't covered their situation – yet it seemed to him that his feelings should have snapped back to normal, if the bond had shattered completely. No, she had to be alive, just … unconscious. It was turning into a habit.

He closed his eyes and concentrated as hard as he could, trying to feel the thin remains of the bond. It *was* there, but faint; terrifyingly faint. Gritting his teeth, he started to walk in a circle, trying to track down where the bond was strongest. Unsurprisingly, it felt as though Elaine had fallen down the side of the mountain.

"Jamal Conidian," Dread said, quietly. Johan stopped to listen, even though he had the feeling he didn't want to hear. "By the power vested in me, I find you guilty of crimes against the Empire, including assault, misuse of magic, breach of your parole and horrendous abuse of innocent victims. I sentence you to death."

Johan stumbled away, but he couldn't help hearing a final crack. The bond led him down the mountainside; he picked a path down as quickly as he could, trying to ignore his conflicted feelings. He'd *hated* Jamal. He would have been quite happy if he'd never seen his brother again. And yet … there was a part of him that regretted Jamal's death. His brother shouldn't have had to die at Dread's hands.

"You killed him," he said, as Dread caught up with him. He wasn't surprised to see that the former Inquisitor wasn't carrying a body. There was no point in trying to bury Jamal, not in the snow. Johan wouldn't have cared if the mountain lizards tore Jamal apart to feed their young. "Why?"

"You were right," Dread said. "He had to die. I killed him so you wouldn't have to."

Johan looked down at the ground, unsure if he should be relieved or angry. Dread had taken the decision from him, choosing to assert his authority … if, of course, he still *had* any authority. Did an Inquisitor still bear the burden of his office without magic? Johan had a feeling the answer was no, but he doubted anyone would care to tell Dread that. Magic or not, Dread was still formidable.

The bond pulsed, suddenly. Johan ran down the mountainside, suddenly heedless of the danger, and let out a sigh of relief as he saw Elaine's body lying on the ground. A woman was kneeling next to her, her fingertips on Elaine's forehead. She looked up when she heard Johan running towards her, her face twisted into an odd scowl. Her brown hair reminded Johan of Elaine ...

There was a flash of light. When it faded, the woman was gone.

Johan ignored it as he knelt down next to Elaine. Her hood had been torn back, allowing her hair to spill out onto the ground. Gritting his teeth, Johan pulled it back into place, then touched her bare skin. She was still breathing, he thought, but she was very cold. Her lips were so pale as to be almost translucent.

"Help me," Johan said, as Dread came up behind him. "What do we do?"

"I'm not sure," Dread said. He poked Elaine's body in several places, trying to elicit a reaction. "Her magic must have protected her, because she isn't frozen to death ..."

He paused. "Can you still feel her emotions?"

"I can't feel anything, apart from the bond itself," Johan said. Was Elaine dying? What had that woman *done* to her? Who *was* she? "It's like her mind isn't there any longer."

"Then you have to find it," Dread said, flatly. "Touch the side of her head, then plunge into her mind and find her before her body dies."

Johan hesitated. "But ..."

"Do it," Dread said. "Unless you *want* her to die."

Johan pulled back Elaine's hood and stared down at her face. She looked ... fragile, somehow, almost like a living doll. If anything, her face had grown paler ...

"I don't know how," he said, touching her skin lightly. It didn't feel *human*. "I don't know how to do it."

"Close your eyes," Dread said. "Feel the bond; it should form around your fingertips. All you have to do is travel through the bond and into her mind. It should be possible, even given your ... unusual magic. Make sure you leave a trail behind you so you can find your way back out."

Johan closed his eyes. Elaine's presence was there, but weak; he concentrated on his fingertips and realised, suddenly, that there was a way to walk right into her mind. It felt wrong to even think about it, but merely finding the way was enough to send him flying down the link. His body seemed to fall away from him as he left it behind …

Shit, he thought. What if he *couldn't* get out? He concentrated, envisaging leaving a trail behind him as he moved onwards into the darkness, then started to search for Elaine. Her presence seemed to be everywhere, yet nowhere. *Where are you?*

But there was no answer.

Chapter Seventeen

Elaine opened her eyes.

She was standing in the middle of a room – she assumed. There was a lantern, a table, two comfortable chairs, a pair of cups and a pot of warm liquid, but there were no walls. The pool of light shed by the lantern was surrounded by darkness, a darkness so deep that she didn't dare stare into it despite the sense that there were *things* out there, watching her. No matter what she did, she couldn't touch Johan's mind. She was alone …

"Greetings," a voice said. She'd been wrong. A man was sitting in one of the chairs, reaching for the pot of warm liquid. "What would you like to drink?"

Elaine stared. The man was … *heroic*. She couldn't think of any other word to describe him; he was tall, handsome and muscular, wearing a suit of charmed armour with a sword slung over his shoulder. His hands were so solid that she doubted he could pick up a china cup without breaking it, yet he held the pot so gently he didn't even spill a drop. Elaine recognised him, but she suspected she was the only living being who *would*. No one else remembered Valiant, the man who'd become the Witch-King.

"You!"

"Me," the Witch-King agreed. He waved a hand at the table. "Please, sit. We have much to discuss."

Elaine hesitated, then sat down facing him. Up close, there was something subtly *wrong* about his features, as if they were slightly out of focus. Or, perhaps, a glamour that wasn't perfectly tuned, imperfect enough to reveal that it *was* a glamour. The more she looked at him, the more she saw *something* hiding under his appearance, something she couldn't quite perceive. It was utterly inhuman.

"Is that what you *really* look like?"

The Witch-King smiled. "Is that your first question?"

Elaine shrugged. She'd never really thought of the Witch-King as *human*, or anything other than a distant presence pulling the strings. A lich, if the knowledge in her head was accurate, would look like a walking skeleton, barely even humanoid. Hell, if his body was crippled, he would find it very hard to repair. But the person facing her certainly *looked* alive and well.

"For the moment," she said, looking down at the table. It *felt* real. "Are you going to give me straight answers to anything else?"

"Maybe," the Witch-King said. He lifted his cup and took a sip. "There's nothing here that can harm you, young lady. I give you my word on it."

Oddly, Elaine believed him. "Where am I?"

The Witch-King smiled. "This is the centre of your mind," he said. "You're trapped here until your body dies."

Elaine stared at him. "That woman … that woman was my mother, wasn't she?"

"She couldn't be anyone else," the Witch-King said. "I held her in reserve until she was needed, then placed her back on the game board."

"I never considered the possibility," Elaine admitted, more to herself than to him. "It never crossed my mind that my mother would have been a magician …"

"There's a lot magicians don't understand about magic," the Witch-King said. "But then, you know that better than I."

Elaine nodded, slowly. Kane had been a powerful sorcerer; logically, she should have inherited at least the *potential* for power from him even if her mother had been a mundane whore. But two magicians … it was vanishingly rare for them to produce a low-power child, let alone a Powerless. Had something been *done* to her, while she'd been in the womb or just afterwards, to ensure her magic never flourished? Or had they simply been poor choices?

"You did something to me," she accused. "Something that weakened my magic."

"It would be more accurate to say I matched your parents in the reasonable belief they would produce a weak magician," the Witch-King said. "There isn't anyone, with the possible exception of you, who understands just how the different ... *strands* of power and potential weave together. Most of the magic they had cancelled itself out when you were conceived, ensuring you wouldn't have *that* much talent."

He took another sip of his drink. "You weren't the only prospect, of course," he added, after a moment. "Merely the one who was gently steered towards the Great Library, so you'd be in place to receive the spell that turned you into the Bookworm."

"Into a living repository of knowledge," Elaine said.

"Quite," the Witch-King agreed. "I needed to know what had been developed in the years since I was entombed."

Elaine shook her head, slowly. "And Johan? Did you create him too?"

"No," the Witch-King said. "House Conidian is an *old* house. Johan was merely the lucky one who had the greatest power of all woven into his strands. But then, I was not expecting Duncan Conidian to let him live. He *looked* like a terrible embarrassment."

Elaine's eyes narrowed. "*You're* responsible for the Powerless being purged?"

"Of course," the Witch-King said. "Magic runs in their strands ... and the longer it takes to develop, the more powerful it is."

"That's the complete opposite of what I was told," Elaine said. "I ..."

"Yes," the Witch-King said. "It wouldn't do to have more rivals to *me*, would it?"

He placed his cup down on the table, gently. "You already know that some magicians have bursts of wild magic, when they're shocked or frightened or think they're about to die," he said. "Such bursts are often far more powerful – and chaotic – than the more focused spells you're taught in the Peerless School, which is why magicians are normally trained to keep their thoughts and emotions under tight control. The first burst of wild magic is celebrated because it marks the child as a magician, right?"

"Right," Elaine said.

"However, what the families *don't* realise is that the spells they've been taught are designed to help a child develop his or her magic *early*," the Witch-King continued. "They're expected to develop their potential as soon as possible, which ironically cripples their ability to use wild magic. And someone who is *resistant* to the spells, someone with the potential for truly great power, is often believed to lack power completely. The Great Houses, in the name of killing off embarrassments to their bloodlines, are wiping out the handful of magicians who could match me."

Elaine closed her eyes, trying to think. Johan had shown traces of magic, the first time she'd met him, but the traces had been ... *odd*. Had the spells she'd used been designed to track high magic rather than wild magic? Or had they been crafted, somehow, to dampen any traces of wild magic? It wasn't impossible ...

"Johan didn't register as a magician," she said, slowly.

"Of course not," the Witch-King agreed. "One could just as easily undress a girl, then proclaim she isn't a boy because she lacks a penis. If one lacks the *concept* of girls, one might even conclude that *that* 'boy' is a freak of nature, rather than something natural."

"You *hid* it from us," she accused.

"Oh, it wasn't *just* me," the Witch-King said. "You're the only person alive who really knows what the wars were like, back when I was Valiant. The Emperor wanted – really wanted – to make sure they never happened again. And they haven't, not really. There were no more wild magicians ... well, until Johan.

"I crafted spells to help the weak, to show them how to use their potential to the fullest – just like you, although you did a better job. And those spells weakened their ability to use wild magic ..."

"That's how you do it," Elaine said, as the pieces of the puzzle fell into place. "Those spells of yours, the ones in your book. They open gaps in the user's mental defences."

The Witch-King nodded. "There are always magicians willing to seek ways to enhance their power, willing to use even dangerous or forbidden spells," he said. "And when they cast them, they open a gateway for me."

Elaine fought hard to steady herself. How many magicians over the centuries had wanted to enhance their powers? And how many of them had slowly opened their minds to the Witch-King? She'd checked for compulsion spells, but she'd never realised that the corruption was so insidious, that it opened the victim's mind willingly. It would be next to impossible to detect; hell, the victim might not have any idea of what was happening to him.

"It isn't even *one* spell," she said, feeling growing horror. She *knew* the spells, but she hadn't realised just how they went together. "They cast several of them and the combined effects open their minds."

"Correct," the Witch-King said. "Your existence poses a curious threat to my plans. You lack the power to use the spells, yet you have the knowledge to take the spells apart, rework them and – perhaps – realise their hidden purpose. Your lack of power renders you very hard to see."

And that's why you got blindsided by the Levellers, Elaine thought, coldly. In hindsight, it was far too obvious. *Most of them are mundanes. Sarah and her friends don't have that much more power than me. You concentrated on magicians powerful enough to be useful and unstable enough to risk using dangerous spells. It never occurred to you that mundanes and low-power magicians could pose a threat.*

She gritted her teeth, forcing the thought back into a corner of her mind. The Witch-King might not have a direct link to her mind, but he clearly had her trapped. Maybe, just maybe, he could read her thoughts …

"You're the one responsible for my lack of power," Elaine said, trying to distract him. "It must have galled you to know that *I* had the knowledge."

"Not really," the Witch-King said, dispassionately. "You lacked the ability to *use* the knowledge effectively."

"That isn't true," Elaine said. "I reworked a handful of spells …"

"There are limits to your abilities," the Witch-King said. "Indeed, were it not for your dead Inquisitor friend, you would be mine by now. I could have dissected your knowledge at leisure."

But Dread isn't dead, Elaine thought. Or *was* he dead? She'd lost sight of him when the snow had slammed into her. *When he lost his powers, did the Witch-King lose track of him and think he's dead?*

She clung to that thought. Dread was tough, tough enough to defy his oaths, tough enough to survive a life without magic. He'd help her, surely … but could he help her without magic?

"Deferens," Elaine said. "He's one of yours, isn't he?"

"As you know," the Witch-King agreed. "There's quite an interesting story there. I took the Emperor's last surviving child and then built up a society around him, one carefully controlled to ensure the bloodline survived intact. Over the centuries, the priest-kings I founded crafted a civilisation that was practically based around action, brute force and instantaneous action. The children of the Golden Bloodline were not trained to *think* or to evaluate their society, let alone realise its weaknesses. They were using my spells before they started to grow manly beards."

There was a hint of a sneer in his voice. "It's astonishing what someone will come to accept as natural, if you start early enough," he added. "Deferens is perfectly balanced between a thrusting desire to win, to force everyone else to submit, and a single-mindedness that makes it easy for me to steer him in the right direction. His obsession with you is merely a means to *my* end."

Elaine shuddered. "You *made* him obsessed with me."

"Hardly," the Witch-King said. "Deferens was raised to value strength and determination – to him, a woman who submits is worthless. An odd contradiction; his sisters were raised as little more than brood mares, their marriages arranged to suit his family, yet he values strong and independent women. He may not even realise this himself."

"I imagine not," Elaine sneered. "He chafed under Light Spinner."

"It's not in his nature to permanently accept anyone superior to him," the Witch-King said, dryly. "No amount of thrashings from his father curbed his rebellious and violent nature, let alone kept him from eventually ending his father's life. Light Spinner would have been forced to kill him when he challenged her. There couldn't be any permanent truce between them. But, despite that, he admires strong women. He views you as a potential partner, even though he has a far more powerful woman in his thrall."

"Creepy," Elaine said. She'd grown up knowing that she was unlikely to snare a powerful magician, even after becoming the Bookworm. And yet the thought of Deferens taking an interest in her was thoroughly unpleasant. "I won't let him have me."

"It does not matter," the Witch-King said. "You will die here."

Elaine looked around. The darkness seemed to be slipping closer.

"I won't die here," she said.

"There's no way out," the Witch-King said, surprisingly gently. "Elaine, your body is already dying. The cold will kill you if the injuries don't. There may be nothing here that can actually harm you, not even me, but it doesn't matter. Your body is dying."

Elaine looked at him. "Then why are you here?"

"I won't die when you die," the Witch-King said, before she could even formulate the thought. "It has been a long time since I spoke to anyone on even terms."

"You've been trapped in the darkness for a thousand years," Elaine said. "I think you're insane."

"I can't go mad," the Witch-King said. "There were spells I used to ensure I wouldn't lose my mind."

Elaine wondered, just for a moment, if that were actually true. Anyone willing to turn himself into a lich, trapping his mind and soul in a dead body, had to be already halfway to madness. And the Witch-King had been in that state for a thousand years. Maybe he'd ensured he couldn't collapse completely into madness, but she wouldn't have bet on him being sane.

"Tell me something, seeing as I'm about to die," she said. "Why? Why *do* this to yourself?"

"They called us gods," the Witch-King said. "We *were* the gods you worship."

Elaine recoiled in shock. She had never been particularly religious, but the words he spoke were blasphemy. Everyone knew the gods were above the mortals, looking down from on high and helping those who praised them, or did their work. And yet, she had never seen any evidence the gods existed, while she knew – all too well – that there were some magicians so powerful they might well be gods.

"The wars were over *which* set of us would rule," the Witch-King said. "Some of us developed ways to raise the dead and draw on their power. They would have killed everyone for their magic. We stopped them. *I* stopped them. But the Emperor decided that magicians would no longer seek worship. We would no longer hold ourselves above the mortal mundanes."

It wasn't true. It couldn't be true. And yet ... the strongest of mundanes was powerless against even the weakest of magicians. It wouldn't be hard to use magic to draw life from a mundane, extending a magician's life while turning a mortal to dust; it wouldn't be hard to work most of the miracles attributed to the gods with magic, even the provision of good or bad luck. What if it were *true*? What if the magicians of that age had been like Johan, but blessed with supportive families who were prepared to wait for their power to develop?

Johan's magic is strange, she thought. The tales of the gods had made them out to be capricious, willing to help or torment humans on a whim. *But it can't be godly ...*

"You did all this because you wanted *worship*?" she asked. "That's *it*?"

"The Emperor wanted to destroy our past," the Witch-King said. "He created the Black Vault, but many books were to be destroyed rather than saved. I couldn't let him do it. It would have destroyed our society."

"And so you waged war on him," Elaine said. "You wanted to take the throne for yourself."

"I would have preserved everything we were," the Witch-King said. "And I will restore the glories of the past, when I rise again."

He leant back in his chair. "There isn't much time left," he added, darkly. "I will be sorry to lose you."

"You won't get my knowledge," Elaine said.

"I already have it," the Witch-King said. "Your mother took it, remember? Your knowledge is mine."

Elaine sighed, feeling cold ice starting to crawl through her mind. "Who *was* she?"

"A runaway," the Witch-King said. "One of Deferens' distant cousins. She had magic and didn't see why *she* should be nothing more than a pampered brood mare. Her father, who was not a very nice man, carelessly locked her in his study, where she found one of my books. The rest is history."

"I'm related to Deferens?" Elaine asked. It wasn't a pleasant thought. "Really?"

"Only vaguely," the Witch-King said. "He neither knows nor cares."

"And he doesn't know you'll keep using him as a tool until he goes mad," Elaine snapped. It was suddenly very hard to speak. The ice was crawling into her mouth. "Your tools *always* go mad."

"They do," the Witch-King confirmed. "But I get some use out of them first."

He leant forward as the table dissolved into nothingness. "Time is up, Elaine," he said, softly. He placed a gentle kiss on her forehead. "Goodnight."

Elaine stared back at him, mulishly, as her vision started to blur. "I ..."

"Elaine," Johan shouted. His voice echoed through the darkness. "Where *are* you?"

"Impossible," the Witch-King said.

Elaine shook herself free. "I'm here," she shouted. If the Witch-King was shocked, perhaps there was a chance after all. "Johan!"

Chapter Eighteen

Johan hadn't been sure what to expect when he plunged into Elaine's mind, but perhaps it shouldn't have surprised him that it was a library. There were bookshelves everywhere, crammed with books; everywhere he looked, there were books, piled on tables, dumped on the floor or holding up the roof. And yet, the whole scene looked as though a tornado had torn through the building and scattered all the books. If they represented parts of Elaine's mind, the darker part of his mind wondered, what did it mean if they were out of place.

He plunged onwards, feeling as though he was navigating through an immense labyrinth that shifted around him as he moved. The line he was feeding out behind him glowed, but everything else was wrapped in shadow. *Things* seemed to be moving at the corner of his eye, mocking him; no matter how quickly he turned to look, he never saw them directly. A faint smell hung in the air, a musty smell that reminded him of the day Jamal had dumped his prized adventure stories in a puddle, just to watch him scream. The books had died … and Elaine, he realised numbly, was dying too.

"Elaine," he shouted. His voice seemed to vanish in the shadows. There wasn't even an answering echo. "Where *are* you!"

There was no response. He forced himself to move onwards, even though the bookshelves seemed to be growing closer. They would trap him, if he stayed too long; it would be easy, so easy, just to snap back to his own body. He was *sure* that merely turning back would be enough to zap along the line and return home. But he was damned if he were leaving without her.

"Elaine," he repeated. "Where are you?"

"Johan," Elaine called.

Johan blinked. The bookshelves retreated as her voice echoed through her mind. Gathering himself, he swam after her before he could think better of it. Her mind seemed to twist around him – dark shadows closed in on him threateningly – but he refused to let go of the tentative contact. The shadows grew teeth and claws; he briefly considered trying to summon light, then dismissed the thought. A normal magician might be able to fight a mental battle without actually doing real harm, but if he tried to make light he might well injure or kill both of them. He did his best to ignore the menacing shapes and discovered that, as long as he showed no fear, they didn't try to close with him.

"Johan," Elaine shouted, again.

Johan plunged into the darkness and fell ... and found himself in a tiny room, illuminated by a single lantern. Elaine was sitting on a chair, her arms wrapped around herself, while a handsome man was looming over her, his face contorted into a mixture of surprise, amusement and anger. Johan hated him on sight, although there was something about him that felt oddly familiar.

"Get away from her," he growled.

"Her body is already dying," the man said, calmly. Johan was *sure*, somehow, that he wasn't a representation of Elaine's thoughts, or an aspect of her personality. "You really don't have much time to save yourself."

Johan lunged forward. The man reached out, his arm transforming into a claw that snapped right through Johan's neck. His head fell off and landed on the dark floor, his vision spinning madly until he came to a stop. There was no blood; his body stood there, as if losing his head was somehow normal. Johan stared up at him, shocked. He should have been in terrible pain, but instead he felt as if he were in two places at once.

"Not real," Elaine croaked. "I ..."

"Be silent," the man ordered. He cast a glance at Elaine and a gag appeared over her mouth, cutting off her words. "I am surprised your friend chose to wander into your mind, but you can die together."

Not real, Johan thought. If nothing here was *real*, then his head hadn't been cut off and ... he forced his body forward, fists slamming into the stranger. The stranger seemed amused; his arms became swords, which he used to hack through Johan's body. Pieces of flesh landed everywhere, yet there was still no pain. *If nothing in here is real …*

He concentrated. His vision blurred, just for a second, and then his body was intact again, staring at the stranger. Elaine looked … *weaker*, somehow; her skin so pale it was almost translucent. This was *her* mind and when she died, they'd die with her. But the stranger … Johan looked at him, trying to understand who he was and why he was remaining within her mind.

"There's no way you can learn how to defeat me in time," the stranger said. Oddly, Johan had the impression he was quite sincere. "Go back to your own body."

"Go back to yours," Johan snarled. Where had the stranger even come from? No one else had touched Elaine, apart from the strange woman. Was he looking at her? Or was it something else? He wished, suddenly, that he'd spent more time looking at books about mental magic, rather than wishing to be a great sorcerer. "Who are you?"

The stranger bowed politely. "Valiant," he said. "And the King of Witches."

"You can't be," Johan said. "Who *are* you?"

"He's telling the truth," Elaine said. The gag was gone, as if it had never been. "I'm going to die. Get out of here."

Johan shook his head. "I'm not leaving you!"

"Sweet," the Witch-King said. "But quite futile. You cannot save her body, or her mind."

He glanced at Elaine. "Time is up," he said. "You fought the good fight. But now it is over."

"I won't let her die," Johan insisted.

"You may not be able to save yourself," the Witch-King observed. "Your magic is not designed to repair damaged bodies, even if you knew how to use it. The longer you stay here, the greater the chance you will die with her."

Johan looked at Elaine, who stared back at him. She was the one person who'd been nice to him. He was *damned* if he was leaving her. And yet, what could he do? He could reshape his body, just like the Witch-King, and fight him … but he had a feeling it was futile. The Witch-King wouldn't be hurt, any more than Johan had been hurt. They could tear each other apart until Elaine finally died …

And then it struck him.

He reached for the link they shared and plunged down it into the very core of her being, touching her mind and sharing his life. Elaine started violently, then stood upright as their thoughts blurred together. White light blazed through her mind, revealing the link the Witch-King had forged between his network of magic and Elaine; they shoved, together, and the Witch-King went tumbling out of her mind. It was *her* mind, s/he realised; there was no way he could keep her from controlling it, once she realised she could.

His power danced around him as he tumbled back through the link; Elaine drawing on it, almost casually, to heal herself. Knowledge spun around him as he slammed back into his own body, falling over backwards as a flash of wild magic shoved him away. Dread caught him as Elaine's body glowed with light, then fell back and hit the ground. Johan shook himself free and ran towards her. The snow was melting …

"Elaine," he breathed.

Elaine opened her eyes. "Johan …"

He leant forward and kissed her, feeling her lips pulsing against his. The world seemed to vanish around them as her arms came up and held him tightly. She was all that mattered to him and he knew, now, that he was all that mattered to her. He wanted to tear off his furs and hold her close …

Dread cleared his throat. "There's a time and a place," he said, gruffly. "Look around you."

Johan opened his eyes, then swore. The ice was still melting. Their furs were soaked – it was suddenly very hard to stand up and help Elaine to her feet – but that wasn't the real danger. It was easy to see that the melting snow might cause another avalanche. Elaine smiled at him, her face flushed with a mixture of happiness and embarrassment; her eyes made a silent promise that there would be time for the two of them later, when they were alone. He kept hold of her hand as they scrambled away from the melting snow and resumed the long trek towards Ida.

"That woman teleported," Dread said, once they were clear of the water. "I thought that was impossible."

"It is, unless you work the calculations very precisely," Elaine said. She hadn't let go of Johan's hand either. "You'd need to know *exactly* where you were in relation to the place you intend to appear. And you'd have to avoid any protective wards on the way ... I wouldn't do it unless I was desperate."

She scowled, suddenly. "The Witch-King might have given her an unexpected advantage," she added, after a moment. "He could have done the calculations for her, using the bond between them to place her location."

Dread's eyes widened. "Who *was* she?"

"My mother," Elaine said.

Johan listened, squeezing her hand gently, as Elaine explained the full story. He'd tried to love his mother, even though she'd often pretended he didn't exist; the thought of discovering that his mother had tried to *kill* him was horrific. The idea that his magic had merely been waiting to finally explode, on the other hand ... how many other children had been killed because they hadn't shown signs of magic before their twelfth birthday? And the thought of his magic *always* being different wasn't reassuring either. Was he doomed to be an outcast forever?

"He was laying plans for centuries," Dread said, when Elaine had finished. "By all the gods, we were playing right into his hands when we thought we were fighting him."

"Back when we first went to Ida," Elaine said, "you questioned me about magicians who'd become more powerful. They tended to go mad. Was that because of the power or because they had contact with the Witch-King's mind?"

"There's no way to know," Dread said. "You'll have to go through the spells, line by line, and see what he did to them."

Johan shook his head slowly. "If he's that powerful," he said, "why did he wait until now?"

"I don't know," Elaine said. "It couldn't have taken him a thousand years to produce either Deferens or myself."

"The Empire was stronger then," Dread pointed out. "And more people knew the dangers of allowing *anyone* to sit on the throne. A thousand years after the wars and the various kingdoms might start to demand independence from the

Grand Sorcerers."

"Or the Empire itself would become corrupt," Johan said. "It allowed people like Jamal to flourish."

"You may be right," Elaine said. "If the Witch-King was trying to ensure that no one like you survived long enough to develop magic, he would have needed centuries to make sure that everyone got the message."

"But he didn't expect the Levellers," Dread said. "Or either of you."

Johan frowned. Something was missing, he was sure. But what?

The Witch-King had deliberately set out to ensure that wild magicians were killed before their powers developed. *That* much was obvious ... and he'd been so successful that Elaine, someone with the collected magical knowledge of the Empire in her head, hadn't recognised him for what he was. Or had he been aiming for something else? If the spells intended to test for magic helped everyone who *could* develop magic before they turned twelve, what did they really do to them?

Gave them high magic at the price of not being able to control wild magic, he thought. *But what did that do to them?*

It seemed a puzzle. No matter how he looked at it, he couldn't see any weaknesses ... apart, perhaps, from an inability to deal with a wild magician. His power had been impossible for Elaine to counter, while he'd burnt through wards as if they were made of paper. And yet, the other magicians seemed so much more versatile. They could do all sorts of spells that Johan, for all his power, had been unable to duplicate. Potions, too, were beyond him. If using high magic was a curse, it was a very odd one.

"We'll keep working on the problem," Dread said, as they kept walking up the path. "Right now, reaching Ida is still our priority."

Johan smiled at Elaine, who was *still* holding his hand, then slipped back into his own thoughts. Raw power versus the ability to control it, to make the most of what one had ... it was hard, perhaps, for him to choose. But if magicians were identified as magicians before they turned twelve ...

"Elaine," he said, slowly. "What do students actually *learn* at the Peerless School?"

"Magic," Elaine said.

Johan shook his head. "I mean ... when you went, what happened?"

Elaine gave him an odd look. "They tested all the children at the orphanage," she said, after a moment. "If someone had manifested wild magic beforehand, they were taken away at once and adopted by magical families. Someone like me ... I was given a scholarship to the Peerless School, but expected to stay in the orphanage until I was old enough to live on my own. There wasn't much hope of being adopted."

"You're lovely," Johan said. "Why didn't anyone want you?"

"The older the child, the less likely anyone would want to adopt," Elaine said. There was a hint of bitter pain in her mind. "Older orphaned children tend to have problems in adapting to a new home, even if the parents are kind and loving. Magic ... doesn't make it any easier, even if they go to a family *used* to magic. And I didn't have the power to make it worthwhile."

Johan felt her pain and winced. His family hadn't wanted him either, but at least he'd *had* a family. Elaine ... had no one. Her father and mother had abandoned her as soon as she was born, then come back into her life to exploit her. Even her *birth* had been the result of cool calculation rather than a loving marriage.

"So you went to the school," he said, slowly. "What happened?"

Elaine took a moment to gather her thoughts. "We were tested, again, once we passed through the gates, then assigned wands and dorms," she said. "The first five years of schooling covered everything from potions to divination, although we were expected to study government and the social graces in our own time."

Johan fought down a smile. Elaine had probably *hated* trying to learn how to comport herself in public, or in a Great House. His mother had drilled a few lessons into his head, although she'd given up when it had become clear that Johan wasn't likely to be leaving the house anytime soon. They'd been bad enough for him, but for Elaine they had to have been naked torture. She was too shy and retiring to like the thought of attending social gatherings.

"Sixth and seventh years were more focused around potential careers," Elaine continued, after a moment. "We spent a lot of time practicing spells … I failed several courses because I couldn't build up the power to cast the spells time and time again. I was very lucky to scrape through with a pass, thanks to my theoretical work. The practical exams were disasters."

Johan blinked. "You couldn't pass?"

"I couldn't cast some of the spells," Elaine said. "Like I said, I was very lucky to scrape through."

"I see," Johan said. He had the odd feeling he was missing something important. "And then you went straight into the library?"

Elaine smiled, wistfully. "I'd always liked old books."

Johan turned to Dread. "What did *you* do?"

"I was apprenticed to an Inquisitor and put to work," Dread said, shortly. "I had the opposite problem. My theoretical work was never up to standard."

"I can't imagine you having problems with anything," Elaine teased, lightly.

"But I did," Dread said. "It always struck me as tedious."

Johan contemplated the issue as hours passed and they walked further up the path. He was missing something, but what? What was nagging at the back of his mind?

"Ho," a voice called. "We see you!"

"Stay still," Dread ordered, tightly. "They *may* be friendly."

Johan looked up. Five men, wearing bright red and yellow uniforms, were advancing down the path towards them. They looked far too obvious against the white snow, which might have been the point. They'd certainly be hard to miss.

"This path is closed," one said. "Why are you here?"

"We're here to see the Queen," Dread said, producing the dead skull-ring and holding it out to the soldier. "Please can you escort us to her?"

The soldier looked at the ring for a long moment. "Do you expect us to just take you into her throne room?"

"No," Dread said, in tones of heavy patience. "I expect you to take us up to Ida and hold us until the Queen is informed of our presence, whereupon she will order you to bring us to her."

"Very well," the soldier said, after a moment. "Come with us."

Johan couldn't help noticing that they kept a sharp eye on their uninvited guests, their hands always near the pommels of their swords. They might not be precisely *unfriendly*, but they weren't taking chances either. He did his best to ignore them, concentrating instead on the feel of Elaine's hand against his. She felt surprisingly warm.

"She'll remember Dread," Elaine reassured him, quietly. "I think she'll want to meet with us."

"I hope so," Johan muttered back. "The soldiers don't look *that* welcoming."

Chapter Nineteen

Elaine took a moment to consider her own feelings as they were escorted up the rest of the path and through the walls of Ida. Johan … Johan had risked *everything*, including his life, to save her, even though he'd had no idea how to fight a mental battle. Elaine knew, all too well, that it could easily have been disastrous, if they hadn't already been linked together by the bond. She would have died, despite his presence; only combining her knowledge with his power had saved them both. And now …

She held his arm tightly, recalling the kiss that they'd shared. It was enough to warm her, she thought, despite the cold. Ida had been cold when she had visited months ago, but now it was colder; ice and snow lay everywhere, despite the best efforts of the tiny kingdom's population. She felt Johan's amazement as they were escorted through the paved streets, passing hundreds of stone houses, before they were finally led into the castle. The population seemed happy enough, as far as she could tell, but there was a faint undertone of nervousness in the air. Had they *realised* there was an occupying army in World's Gate?

They know they're under suspicion, Elaine reminded herself. *Even if they don't know why, even if they don't understand what happened to the Crown Prince, they know the Grand Sorceress suspected them of something.*

She kept that thought to herself as the soldiers led them through a stone gate and into the keep. A trio of guards met them and there was a brief exchange of words, before their escorts marched them through a set of doors and into a comfortable but sparse waiting room. It was clearly intended to be secure, she noted; a handful of locking spells crawled over the door as soon as it was closed. They weren't exactly *prisoners*, but they weren't exactly honoured guests either.

Johan gave her a sharp look. "What now?"

"We wait," Dread said. "The Queen will decide the next step."

Elaine nodded, then sat down on one of the chairs and carefully removed her outer layer of furs. The water had frozen, unsurprisingly; she cast a handful of spells to remove the ice and dry the furs, then pulled them back around her. There was literally nothing else to wear until the Queen saw them. She helped Johan with *his* clothes, then offered the same to Dread. He shook his head, then resumed pacing the small room. Elaine watched him for a moment, holding Johan's hand tightly. If Dread was wrong, if the Queen wasn't pleased to see them, they'd be trapped in the midst of a hostile kingdom.

The door opened thirty minutes later, revealing a middle-aged man wearing a green suit and black hat. "The Queen will see you in the small audience chamber," he said. "I have been commanded to escort you there."

"It will be our pleasure," Dread said. He turned and led the way towards the door. "Which way is it from here?"

Elaine followed him through a maze of lit corridors. She hadn't had much time for sightseeing last time she'd been in Ida, but she had to admire the sheer determination of the builders. Ida was easily the strangest state she knew, a tiny little kingdom protected by towering mountains. Even with her suspicion that the Witch-King had something to do with it, she had to admire the achievement.

"Your Majesty" their escort said, as they stepped through a purple curtain. "I present to you our guests."

Elaine smiled as she curtseyed in front of Queen Sacharissa. The queen had cut her long red hair, somewhat to Elaine's surprise, but otherwise she hadn't changed *that* much from the girl who'd escaped her kingdom, only to return and become its Queen. Sacharissa gave Dread a welcoming smile that promised much, if he was prepared to abandon his oaths, then swept her gaze over Elaine and Johan.

"I've heard disturbing rumours," Sacharissa said. "It is *very* good to see you again."

"Thank you, Your Majesty," Dread said. His voice was curiously flat. He was no longer an Inquisitor and no longer had his duty. "We have much to tell you."

"Start with the army in World's Gate," Sacharissa said.

Dread nodded, then started to explain. Sacharissa listened carefully as he explained that Deferens had taken over the Empire, then set off with a colossal army to level Ida and take *something* from the catacombs under the kingdom. They'd already agreed not to mention the Witch-King to Queen Sacharissa, just in case she was already one of his pawns. She didn't have any magic, as far as Elaine knew, but one of the magicians in her kingdom could easily have put her under his spell.

Or Trebuchet could have done it, Elaine thought. Trebuchet had been King Hildebrand's Court Wizard, but he'd almost certainly been working for the Witch-King. Sacharissa hadn't been considered a serious candidate for the throne, yet the Witch-King knew not to overlook her merely because she was younger than her brother. *But if she had been under a spell, why would she have helped us escape Ida the first time?*

"So he has dragons and magicians and an army and he's coming *here*," Sacharissa said, finally. "Why? What do we have that's so important?"

"Deferens is a small man, Your Majesty," Elaine said. She recalled the Witch-King's words and shuddered. "Your brother competed against him, seven months ago. It would not be out of character for him to want revenge."

"But you said he wanted something hidden here," Sacharissa said. "What? Is it something we can turn against him?"

"I doubt it, Your Majesty," Dread said. "It's something from the distant past that cannot be used without risking utter disaster. We dare not talk about it now."

Sacharissa gave him a long look. Elaine wondered just what she thought she'd see. Dread was easily twenty years older than Sacharissa, with decades of experience in concealing his thoughts and feelings. But Sacharissa had grown up in a Royal Court, watching the courtiers try to manipulate her father into doing their bidding. Sacharissa would hardly be blind to nuances that Elaine knew *she* had no hope of seeing.

"He's coming," Dread said. "He'll overwhelm your kingdom and put it to the sword."

"I understand," Sacharissa said. She took a long breath. "You had people coming up from World's Gate, didn't you?"

Elaine smiled, before she could stop herself. They'd made it?

"Yes," Dread said. "What happened to them?"

"They took up residence in one of the inns," Sacharissa said. "I shall have messengers sent to bring them here."

"You must," Dread said. "Your Majesty, your kingdom is not going to be shown mercy."

"I've heard rumours of what happened to Falcone's Nest," Sacharissa said. "This kingdom is not an easy place to attack."

"You're not facing a normal foe," Dread said. "He has dragons."

"Then we shall prepare our defences," Sacharissa said. She gave him another long look. "You can speak with me, privately. Your companions will be escorted to rooms of their own, where they can wash and change their clothes. We will discuss our defence plans at dinner."

"Gather your magicians," Elaine said, as the Queen clapped her hands to summon a servant. "I have spells they need to learn."

"It will be done," Sacharissa said. "And I hope to talk to you soon, Elaine. It has been too long."

Elaine nodded, then allowed the servant to lead Johan and her out of the room. Sacharissa must have recognised them from the description, because the servant led them directly to a room that had already been prepared for her. Johan would have the room next to hers ... she shook her head, gently. The thought of being apart for longer than a few moments was horrific. They'd only grown closer when they'd merged their minds.

"There are clothes in the dresser," the servant said. "The Queen hosts Evensong Dinner at seven. Will you require an escort?"

"Yes, please," Elaine said.

She stopped, unsure of herself. Was it customary to tip servants in Ida? The servant withdrew before she could decide to offer one of the remaining coins in her pouch to him, closing the door so lightly she barely heard a sound. And Johan was right next to her ... she could feel his pulsing desire, merging with her own. It made it hard, so hard, to think clearly.

"You risked everything to save me," she breathed, as she turned to face him. Had she always thought of him as stunningly handsome or was it just the bond, adjusting her feelings to make sure they were compatible? "You could have died in my mind."

"I couldn't let you go," Johan said. He seemed to be quivering, torn between the impulse to take her in his arms and fear – however irrational – of rejection. "I don't think I could live without you."

Elaine met his eyes. He meant it. He meant every word. The bond had drawn them so close together that neither of them could live without the other. And the way his power had merged with her knowledge ... was this how it had been, before the first set of necromantic wars? A wild magician mated to a high magician?

"I know," she breathed.

It was suddenly very easy to take a step forward and bring her lips against his. He kissed her back, hard; his hands started to work on her furs, tearing them away from her bare skin. It felt different from the time Bee had touched her, taking her virginity ... and yet, it felt perfect, as if each successive kiss was making her more and more excited. She pulled him towards the bed as he stumbled out of his clothes, then fell backwards onto the soft blanket ...

... And then there was no room for anything, but each other.

***

Johan watched Elaine sleeping, her naked body streaked with sweat. He felt ... odd. He'd never slept with anyone, not even one of the maids, before now. He knew *she* hadn't been a virgin – he'd seen some of her memories when he touched her mind – and yet it didn't bother him. All that mattered was that she was his now ...

He'd watched Jamal's courtship technique with a mixture

of envy and disgust. Envy, because it seemed to work; disgust, because there was a fine line between Jamal's technique and outright rape. But then, Jamal *was* a powerful magician. It was unlikely there was *anything* he could do to the household maids that would get him punished, by either his parents or the Inquisition. Everyone knew the maids were there to be used.

But he couldn't have acted like Jamal, not really. It wasn't just that he didn't have the power, it was that he *knew* what it was like to be helpless. Instead, he'd tried to be nice and sweet and it had never been enough until now. He'd hated being a virgin, yet now ... now it had paid off, in the best possible way. He could feel Elaine's presence in his mind as easily as he'd felt her body pressed against his. And her experience had made it better for both of them.

Jamal is dead, he reminded himself. *And I am alive.*

He felt oddly at ease with Jamal's death, even though part of him still wished he'd been the one to kill his brother. But if Dread had been right ... killing Jamal himself would have been giving in to madness, to anger and rage and outright hatred. No, Dread *had* been right. He knew that killing Jamal would have been revenge, not justice. But where did revenge stop?

Cass tried to tell me, he thought. *But would I have listened if she'd told me before she died?*

Elaine shifted in her sleep, her bare breasts pushing against his skin. Johan lay back, cuddling up to her. There couldn't be anything wrong with their relationship, no matter what society would say. The bond had only made it stronger – and given them the ability to combine their strengths into one. Even the Witch-King had been surprised, although he'd known countless magicians like Johan. Could it be that he hadn't expected the bond? Could it be he'd created the taboo to *prevent* other magicians from forming their own partnerships? It made a certain degree of sense.

He felt the bond shift gently as Elaine opened her eyes. "Johan," she said, huskily. "What time is it?"

Johan hesitated. They'd made love ... how many times? He'd always thought that he'd remember everything, but that could have been nothing more than Jamal's bragging to his cronies. He looked at the grandfather clock and blinked in surprise. Six in the afternoon? Really?

"Six," he said. He reached down and started to play with one of her breasts. "I ..."

"We have to get up," Elaine said. She swung her legs over the side of the bed and stood, tottering slightly. There were faint marks on her back and buttocks where he'd held her too tightly. "We're due for dinner at seven."

"We could skip it," Johan said, mischievously. "I'm sure the Queen wouldn't mind if we stayed away from her plans to seduce Dread."

Elaine turned and gave him a long look – he had no difficulty in seeing that she was tempted – before shaking her head firmly. "We can't afford to give offence," she said, as she walked towards the washroom. "The Queen might be willing to cut us some slack, but some of her noblemen will see it as a deliberate insult."

"So I left a Great House where failing to bow as you enter is a declaration of war and entered a castle where failing to attend dinner is a deliberate insult," Johan said. He stood and looked at himself in the mirror. Elaine had left marks on him too. "The more things change ..."

He raised his voice as she walked into the washroom. "When this is over, where do you want to go?"

"Somewhere nicely isolated," Elaine said. "But maybe not *too* isolated."

"Just the two of us on an island somewhere," Johan said, following her inside. "It wouldn't be bad, would it?"

Elaine gave him a tired smile. "Do you know how to assist in a birth?"

"No," Johan said, reluctantly.

"Or catch a rabbit, or grow crops, or anything else we might need to survive," Elaine added, dryly. She turned on the shower, then stepped under the water. Johan shivered in sympathy as lukewarm water cascaded down from high overhead. "We couldn't survive on our own and you know it."

"I suppose," Johan said, reluctantly. He stepped into the shower, then held her as the water washed them both clean. "But it would be nice to be away from *everything*."

He gave her a kiss as he climbed out of the shower and walked back into the room, where he found the clothes the servant had left for him. Magic must have been involved, he guessed, because the outfit fitted surprisingly well. The dark trousers and shirt made him look like a combination of magician and soldier. In some ways, he decided, as Elaine emerged from the shower behind him, it was perfect.

"It suits you," Elaine said. She seemed oddly self-conscious about dressing in front of him, despite the bond; he turned away to give her what privacy he could. "But you'll probably need something else for the descent into the catacombs."

Johan shivered, despite the warm room. "Do you think we can get to him before it's too late?"

"I don't know," Elaine said. There was a pause as she searched for a piece of clothing and pulled it on. "Clearly, there's some reason there *has* to be an army occupying Ida before he rises from the catacombs, but what? Unless he thinks Ida alone can offer meaningful resistance."

"If it was that easy," Johan said, "why would he ever emerge at all?"

"Good question," Elaine said. "And I have no answer."

She paused, her breath catching in her throat. "You may turn around now," she said, softly. "I'm ready."

Johan swung around, unable to avoid sensing her nervousness, her fear that he would reject her. Elaine was wearing a long green dress that swirled around the stone floor, hiding her shoes from his gaze. It covered everything below the neck, hinting at her curves rather than revealing them, but it drew his attention anyway. He couldn't keep himself from staring as she turned, the dress fanning out around her to reveal that she was wearing flat leather shoes.

"I'd prefer to wear something I could run in," Elaine said, her cheeks colouring as she sensed his amusement. "I'd prefer not to wear a dress at all, but I wasn't given trousers and I don't have time to change yours."

"You could ask for a pair," Johan said. He hadn't seen any maids within the castle, but he was sure a crowned queen would have dozens of female attendants. Charity had had nine and she'd kept them all hopping. "Or don't women wear trousers here?"

"I can't recall," Elaine said. She stood on tiptoes, gave him a gentle kiss and then turned towards the door, just as the clock struck seven. Someone knocked as soon as the clock had finished chiming. "Shall we go?"

"If we must," Johan said. He reached out and took her hand, then hesitated. "Should we be so close here? Won't the Queen object to … you know, us?"

Elaine laughed. "They'll know what we've been doing," she said. She held up a mirror, winking at him. "That grin on your face gives it away."

"Oh," Johan said.

"I wouldn't worry about it," Elaine added. Her face twisted into a tart smile. "The kingdom has too many other things to worry about right now."

Chapter Twenty

The Runnymede Gap had lasted for thousands of years, ever since *something* had rent the ground and created a parting in the very earth itself. Over the years, the Empire had bridged the Gap in a dozen places and a number of towns had been built at the bottom, isolated from the rest of the world.

It took the Emperor's magicians twenty minutes to shatter both walls, collapsing the Gap into nothingness.

Charity watched, feeling nothing but numb horror, as magic tore through the stone. A dull rumble echoed through the air as the canyon shattered, great chunks of rock falling free and plunging into the Gap. Homes and farms at the bottom were smashed to rubble before the inhabitants knew what had happened, their lives snuffed out by the Emperor's sorcerers. She turned, just in time to see the red-robed sorcerer collapse into dust, his work completed. The Gap had been closed. There would be no need to use *any* of the bridges to move the army on to Ida.

"Send the scouts forward," the Emperor ordered, coolly. "Once the dust has settled, start moving the first regiments over the Gap and onwards to Ida."

"At once, Your Supremacy," General Vetch said.

The Emperor took one last look at the remains of the once-great landmark, then turned and strode back to his tent. Charity knew she should follow him, but she hadn't been given any specific orders and so she remained where she was, watching as the scouts spurred their horses forward and over the debris. It looked like a giant bowl now, dust rising up as the horses picked their way through the broken rock, but they seemed to have no trouble finding their footing. And, this time, it didn't look as though the makeshift embankment would collapse any time soon.

She closed her eyes in pain. Was there *anything* that could slow the army down, let alone stop it? The Emperor had bridged the Lug and closed the Gap by sheer force of magic, unleashing the collected might of countless magicians. How could the mountains of Ida stand in his way, when he could summon earthquakes to smash them to rubble? He'd storm through the remains of the tiny kingdom and put its population to the sword, throwing its queen to the soldiers. Charity shuddered to think about what would happen to *her*.

A low roar echoed through the air; she opened her eyes and looked up, just in time to see a dragon flying overhead, heading towards Ida. By now, according to the reports, the entire continent knew about the dragons … and what the Emperor's troops had done to every town and city that had crossed their path. It made no sense! Charity could understand crushing rebellious states – the Emperor would have to crack a great many skulls to secure his power – but why butcher entire populations that were no threat, that were prepared to submit at once without a fight? It was almost as if the Emperor was *determined* to push the entire world into revolt.

And with his dragons, he might well win a global war, she thought, numbly. The carnage would be horrific, of course, but the Emperor would have a decisive advantage. And yet, why was he making it impossible for potential allies to bend the knee to him? They'd fight if they knew they were going to be butchered, even if it *was* futile. They might take a few of the Emperor's men with him. *What is he doing?*

Charity shook her head tiredly, wondering if she could force herself to the edge of the Gap – or what remained of it – and jump over the side. She didn't want to watch as the army marched onwards, looting, raping and burning its way through anything in its path. But her body quivered at the thought, reminding her that her oaths prevented suicide – or any form of self-harm. She couldn't even put herself in danger on the off-chance it might kill her. There was no way to escape the trap.

Another flight of dragons swooped overhead, their riders catcalling cheerfully as they flew over the marching soldiers. Charity watched them go, feeling a sudden flicker of envy, then turned and made her way back towards the tent. The first regiments were already on their way, crossing the Gap and heading on towards the nearest town. Behind them, the conscripts from a dozen towns and cities were following, their faces pale and wan. Several dozen had been crucified in the last couple of days for trying to desert, while others had been stripped and whipped around the camp for failing to meet the army's exacting standards. Charity had a feeling that none of the young men would ever see their homelands again, although they were luckier than their womenfolk. Charity knew, all too well, what the army had done to them.

He's being cruel for the sake of being cruel, she thought, as she reached the tent and opened the flap. She understood the need to make examples, sometimes – her father had been happy to punish his subordinates who didn't meet their commitments – but the Emperor was being pointlessly nasty. It made no sense. *Does he want to push them into rebellion or merely crush all that remains of the previous Empire?*

It was a chilling thought. The army had rounded up and sacrificed countless magicians, slowly destroying magical society even as it tormented mundane society. And the Emperor held the Peerless School, as well as hundreds of children from the strongest magical bloodlines. Given enough time, he could make sure that magician training remained firmly in his hands; male magicians would swear loyalty to his bloodline, female magicians would be enslaved and turned into brood mares. Did the Emperor intend to provoke a civil war so he could use it to reshape the entire world?

She heard a muttering sound ahead of her and tensed, then pressed onwards. The Emperor was seated in his wooden chair, muttering to himself. Charity recognised a handful of words from one of the oldest languages in the world – it was said to predate the Empire – but she couldn't pull them together into a coherent whole. Her father had tried to make sure that Jamal and Charity learnt enough to get by – some really interesting books were written in ancient languages – but neither of them had mastered more than the basics. It hadn't seemed important at the time.

"Your Supremacy," she said, bowing. "I …"

The Emperor looked up. His face was different, somehow. Everything was the same, yet there was a definite sense that he wasn't quite the same person. Charity shivered – these attacks were becoming more and more frequent – and then she froze as his eyes locked on hers, holding her spellbound. His eyes narrowed, as if he wasn't sure who she was, even though he'd been the one to enslave her. And then his eyes looked down at the map.

"Ida," he said, clearly. And yet his voice was wrong, as if he'd forgotten how to talk. "We must get to Ida."

"The scouts are already on their way, Your Supremacy," Charity said, carefully. "They will reach World's Gate and link up with the forces there by nightfall."

"Good," the Emperor said. "But it is already too late."

He shuddered, suddenly. Charity wondered if she should call a druid, even though she was sure the Emperor would refuse to show any weakness to anyone. His entire body twitched – for a moment, she was sure he was going to be sick – and then he looked up. His face had returned to normal.

"Charity," he said. He sounded normal again, as if nothing had happened. "What news of the scouts?"

"They're on the way to Ida, Your Supremacy," Charity said. But she'd already told him once, hadn't she? It didn't seem like the kind of news he'd want her to repeat time and time again. "They should be in World's Gate by nightfall."

"And the Head Librarian should be in their hands," the Emperor said, his face twisting into an ugly leer. Charity felt another stab of pity for the Head Librarian and hoped – prayed – that she remained out of the Emperor's clutches. "And then we will put Ida to the sword."

But you said it was too late, Charity thought.

She kept that thought to herself. There was no way to know what was wrong with the Emperor, but as long as he didn't ask her specifically she didn't have to tell him. If he'd forgotten … it suggested brain problems, perhaps caused by overuse of dark magic. Who knew? Maybe she could take advantage of it. A mental collapse might well lead to his death, which would free her from her oaths. She could run before the army realised its commander was dead.

The tent flap rustled. Charity turned, just in time to see Moeder, the older woman who'd gone with Jamal to capture the Head Librarian. She looked ... *pleased*, although there was no sign of either Jamal or the Head Librarian. Charity felt her heart sink as the woman bowed curtly to the Emperor, clearly unwilling to submit herself to him. She *had* to have completed her mission.

"Your Supremacy," Moeder said. "I must report that the Head Librarian escaped and Jamal is apparently dead."

Charity staggered, shocked. Her brother was *dead*? He'd been awful to her – and everyone else – and yet he'd been her brother! She stared down at her hands, feeling the weight of Jamal's dagger in her belt. How could he be dead?

"Dead," the Emperor said. His face darkened rapidly. "How do you know?"

"I forged a blood-link," the woman said, coldly. "He died."

The Emperor glowered at her. "Explain."

Charity listened as Moeder outlined the entire story. The team had gone to World's Gate, expecting to trap their prey when they walked through the town to Ida. Instead, the Inquisitors had made their presence alarmingly obvious and the blood-tie between Jamal and Johan had showed the latter heading *away* from World's Gate. They'd gone in pursuit; Jamal had stayed behind to deal with Johan, while Moeder had gone after the Head Librarian and knocked her out. And then Johan had prevented Moeder from taking the Head Librarian when she'd escaped.

"You failed," the Emperor growled.

"Only partly," Moeder said.

She stood defiantly, as if she hadn't failed at all. Charity felt her heart slowly climbing into her mouth. The Emperor didn't tolerate failure. Moeder was likely to wind up being tortured to death, or drained of her magic and thrown to the soldiers, or simply fitted with a slave collar and enslaved. And yet ... the Emperor's face shifted, again, as he clapped his hands to summon the guards.

"Take this woman to a tent and guard her," he ordered. His voice was different too. "She is to be treated as a honoured guest, but not allowed to leave."

Charity gaped as Moeder was pulled out of the tent by the guards. She was to be treated as a honoured guest, even though she'd failed? It made no sense!

"They escaped the trap at World's Gate," the Emperor mused. "How?"

Charity fought – desperately – to keep her mouth closed, but the oath compelled her to answer truthfully. "The Inquisitors made the trap obvious," she said, damning herself to the deepest darkest hells. "Johan and his friends saw it before it could close and walked elsewhere."

"So my tools are not as loyal as they should be," the Emperor said. He didn't seem to realise that Charity had noticed the loophole too, but maybe it was just as well. His low opinion of women might have saved her life. "They shall be punished."

He stood. "We ride," he ordered. "We will be at Ida soon enough and storm the mountains before the kingdom can organise a defence."

"Yes, Your Supremacy," Charity said.

The Emperor strode out of the tent and issued orders. Moments later, the remainder of the camp was hastily dismantled by the soldiers and loaded onto carts. The slaves followed, carrying vast quantities of material; the magicians brought up the rear, watching carefully as the carts carrying their supplies crossed the remains of the Gap. Charity watched an uncomplaining Moeder shoved into one of the luxury carts, trying to understand just why she was staying so calm. Didn't she know she was doomed?

She mounted up behind the Emperor as he climbed onto a dragon and then ordered the giant beast into the air. It was colder now, Charity noted; the distant mountains covered with ice and snow. Perhaps Moeder and Jamal couldn't be blamed for failing to realise how treacherous the landscape could be … she closed her eyes as it grew colder, trying to come to terms with her feelings. Jamal would have happily abandoned her to slavery, if the Emperor had kept his word, but she couldn't have abandoned him.

If everything had remained normal, she asked herself, *what would I have done with him?*

Jamal would have hated the thought of relying on charity – she smirked at the unintentional pun – and remaining cooped up inside the house, just as Johan had. But there wouldn't really have been a choice, would there? The blood ties were still there, even if Jamal was powerless and Johan was ... whatever he was. Someone who wanted to curse their entire family could have used Jamal's blood as a weapon, although the nasty part of her mind pointed out that anyone with a grudge probably had it *because* of Jamal. Why bother cursing the whole family when there was a perfect opportunity to exact revenge on Jamal?

But it no longer mattered. Jamal was dead.

She opened her eyes as the dragon swooped down and landed in front of a small town. The population looked to have fled, or decided it was safer to remain indoors when dark deeds were afoot. A handful of soldiers were waiting at the gates, bowing in salute as the Emperor climbed off the dragon and strode towards the buildings. Charity followed, shivering helplessly as she stepped outside the dragon's magical field. The cold would have worn through robes, let alone the wisps of material the Emperor had ordered her to wear. She had a nasty feeling that if she stopped, the cold would kill her.

"Your Supremacy," the sergeant said. He pointed a finger through the gates towards a large building. "We have secured that inn as a base of operations."

"Good," the Emperor said. "Have the lead Inquisitor brought to me."

He stepped through the gates and into the town. Snow lay everywhere, glinting under the light from the windows. Charity would have found it charming if she hadn't feared what the Emperor would do; instead, she kept her eyes down as she followed the Emperor through the door and into the inn. It was warm enough to start unfreezing her toes; she cursed under her breath as the Emperor looked around, then sat down on a comfortable chair and motioned for her to kneel beside him. The stone was hard and cold under her bare skin.

"Your Supremacy," a voice said. Charity looked up to see an Inquisitor, a dark-skinned man wearing a long black cloak and carrying an iron-tipped staff. The skull-ring on his finger glowed with red light. "You wished to see me?"

"Yes," the Emperor said. "Why did you set up the

checkpoint outside the gates?"

There was a long chilling pause as the Inquisitor fought his oaths. "I wished to make sure the fugitives would have a chance to see us," he said, finally. Blood started to trickle from his nose as the oaths reasserted themselves. "And they slipped through the net."

"So it would seem," the Emperor said. "Why did you defy my orders?"

"Your orders were not broken," the Inquisitor said. "They were merely ... subverted."

"I see," the Emperor said, very slowly. "You carried out my orders to the letter, but made use of a loophole to subvert them. Well done. *Very* well done."

His gaze sharpened. "Kill yourself."

The Inquisitor shuddered, more blood flowing from his nose. Slowly, inch by inch, his hand reached for a dagger and drew it from his belt. The blade glinted under the candlelight as he struggled to throw it away, to break his oaths; Charity found herself unable to move her gaze as he lifted the knife to his throat, holding it right at the very edge of his skin. A tiny pinprick of blood appeared at the very tip of the blade, trickling down to touch his hand. And then the knife practically leapt forward and slashed his throat wide open.

Charity shuddered as the Inquisitor stumbled, then fell to the floor. The knife crashed down and bounced off the stone, coming to rest near the Emperor. He looked ... *pleased,* although there was something about his expression that chilled her to the bone. Did he almost ... *admire* the Inquisitor?

"Give him a hero's funeral," the Emperor ordered. "Once the rest of the army arrives, we will lay plans for the assault."

The guards hurried out, taking the body with them. Charity watched them go, then turned to stare at the Emperor. A thin smile curled over his lips as he contemplated the bloodstained floor.

"A brave man," he said, although she wasn't sure if he were speaking to himself or to her. "A shame he had to die."

"Yes, Your Supremacy," Charity said.

"Strong magic and a strong mind," the Emperor added.

"He could have been great if he had served me."

Or overthrown you, Charity thought.

"You will clear up the blood," the Emperor ordered. Charity shuddered. Did he know she'd seen the loophole too? Or was it just one more way to humiliate her? "I want the floor spotless by the time the generals arrive."

Charity bowed her head. "Yes, Your Supremacy."

Chapter Twenty-One

Elaine hadn't been sure what to expect from the Queen's private dining room. She'd only ever attended a handful of formal dinners, all in the Imperial Palace, at Light Spinner's behest and she'd left as soon as she decently could. *They* had taken place in a large ballroom, easily big enough to accommodate hundreds of guests; she'd felt so badly out of place that she'd spent the whole dinner staring at her plate. But Sacharissa's private dining room was small, comfortable and had barely enough room for her guests. She stepped inside, smiled wanly at Dread's knowing expression, and took her seat. Johan sat next to her, his emotions under tight control. Sarah, Brian and a handful of Levellers she didn't know were already sitting around the table.

"This is a Council of War," Sacharissa said, once three aristocrats had entered the room and joined the small gathering. "Colonel Tarpon, commander of the Royal Guard; Duke Agues, Master of the Road and Lord Appleton, Master of Magic."

Elaine gave the final nobleman a long look. It wasn't uncommon for the mundane aristocracy to produce magicians – Sacharissa's brother had been a powerful magician before his untimely death – but it was rare to allow one so close to the throne. The Court Wizard should have quietly steered Appleton somewhere else, perhaps urging him to leave Ida altogether and threatening him if he refused to go. But he was still here ... she concentrated, probing his magic field gently and decided Appleton wasn't *that* powerful. He'd probably gained the job through nepotism.

Which is par for the course, she thought. *How else do aristocrats get jobs?*

She frowned, inwardly. Appleton looked more of a thinker than a doer, although he *did* have a wand at his belt. His face was so bland she would have thought it was a glamour if she hadn't been skilled at sensing them. Beside him, Colonel Tarpon looked almost as tough as Dread – his face was scarred and he had an eyepatch covering one eye – while Duke Agues looked alarmingly fat and happy. She forced herself to remember that fat didn't always mean evil, even though the orphanage supervisors had been heavily overweight and thoroughly nasty. It wouldn't have bothered her so much if the orphans hadn't had to struggle for food.

"There's no proof the Emperor means us harm," the Duke said. "Your Majesty's father is dead now, along with his crimes."

"The Emperor has burnt his way through several cities which are – forgive me – far more valuable to him than Ida," Dread said, curtly. "You've heard the rumours."

"Rumours grow in the telling," the Duke pointed out.

"But not the stories from World's Gate," Colonel Tarpon said. "Your Grace; there's an army taking up position at the bottom of the mountain. I dare not assume it's friendly."

"There isn't room for doubt," Sacharissa agreed, calmly. "They're intent on destroying our kingdom."

"Then we surrender," the Duke said.

"They're crushing *everyone* in their path," Dread said. "You could bend the knee to them and they might still kill you."

Elaine nodded when Sacharissa turned to look at her. She had a feeling that at least *some* of the aristocracy thought they could make a deal with Deferens, even though such a deal would be hideously one-sided at best. And, with the Witch-King under Ida, she was *convinced* that Deferens would agree to whatever he had to so he could take control of the kingdom, then lay waste to Ida with fire and sword. The aristocrats might be the last to die, but they *would* die.

"Then we may as well fight," Sacharissa said. She waited until the servants had placed bowls of steaming hot soup in front of each of them, then smiled. "*Can* we fight?"

Colonel Tarpon looked straight at her. "Your Majesty," he said. "If it was a normal army, I would believe we could hold it off. They would have immense difficulty getting anything larger than a few companies of men up the road to Ida. But they have *dragons*! And *very* powerful magic. The reports say they bridged the Lug."

"Not for long," Sarah snapped.

"Long enough to take the city," Colonel Tarpon said. He didn't seem to be offended by her tone. "We couldn't survive if they used such a powerful spell to break our wards."

Elaine closed her eyes, allowing knowledge to bubble to the surface. "The ritual in question is very fragile," she said. And it would certainly kill the caster. Deferens might even be running out of sorcerers willing to die for him. "I don't believe Falcone's Nest had enough sorcerers who could manage to deflect it, but it is certainly *possible*."

Dread looked at her. "Can you?"

"Of course she can," Johan said. He squeezed Elaine's hand under the table. "Elaine is a genius."

"True," Sarah agreed, as Elaine flushed. "Some of her spells are works of art."

She looked at Appleton. "How many magicians are there in Ida?"

"Only fifty-seven," Appleton said, "assuming you count hedge wizards and a handful of very minor sorcerers. Ida has never been a popular place for sorcerers."

Elaine wasn't surprised. The Witch-King might have influenced any who had been fool enough to enter the kingdom, but he didn't really need to bother. Any sorcerer with real power would probably be ambitious and Ida, trapped in the mountains, was hardly large enough to suit a fully-fledged sorcerer. They'd go to the Peerless School and never look back. Hell, Sacharissa's brother was the only sorcerer she knew who'd stayed in Ida.

"They can learn some of my spells," she said, bluntly. "Sarah and the others already know enough of them to start teaching the basics."

"Of course," Brian agreed.

"We can also show your people how to make Firepowder," Brian added. "However, unless we can find the right materials, it won't be easy. We *can* produce everything from scratch, but it will take longer than we have."

Sacharissa frowned. "How long?"

"Months," Brian said. "But we can make it very quickly if

we have the materials."

"We will see that you have everything you need," Sacharissa said. She looked at Dread. "If we *can* turn back the army, we will. What then?"

Dread sighed. "Let the army batter itself to death against the walls," he said. "The Empire will not long endure him once his dragons and magicians are gone."

Elaine sucked in her breath. "You're talking about ending the Empire."

"Yes," Dread said. "I do not believe we can rebuild any longer."

He looked down at his bowl of soup. "The Grand Sorceress is dead; the Inquisition is gravely weakened; the Great Houses have been broken; countless magicians are dead; the trade links that bind the Empire together have been shattered ... and there's a madman on the Golden Throne. Even if Deferens dies tomorrow, the damage he has done is beyond repair. It might be better to have the Empire shatter than attempt to rebuild it."

"There will be war," Elaine said, very quietly.

"Good," Sarah said. "Let the aristocrats kill each other."

Sacharissa cleared her throat. Sarah's face darkened, but she said nothing.

"It would be the end of life as we know it," Johan said.

Elaine kept her face impassive, although she knew Johan could sense her doubt and concern – and her fear for the future. A world without the Empire? How long would it be before the magical society cracked and broke too, if it wasn't already broken beyond repair? She had no doubt that there *would* be war, as kings and princes sought to claim power for themselves; it wouldn't be long before the Peerless School and the remains of the Golden City became prizes to be won. And how long would it be before the kingdoms started experimenting with forbidden spells?

"Yes, it would," she said, finally. "But I submit to you that allowing the Emperor to win will be even worse."

The Duke eyed her darkly. "And how do you know that?"

"Vlad Deferens comes from a society where the strong rule the weak – or, at least, that's how he would put it," Elaine said. She *had* done a little research after all, back when

Daria and she had been betting on who would be the next Grand Sorcerer. "There is no permanent stability, Your Grace. Sons kill fathers as soon as they think they can get away with it – and it is accepted, because a son who kills his father is clearly stronger. Magicians, too, compete for power and place; women are turned into broodmares and slaves, forced to serve men and have no will of their own."

She took a breath. "The only way to get any stability is to become an eunuch," she added, knowing it would make the men quail. "Eunuchs have some freedom because there's no prospect of them siring a line for themselves, but they're still regarded as weaklings. Would you like to live there? I believe Deferens intends to impose a similar system on the entire world."

Colonel Tarpon frowned. "Why?"

"Because he *believes* in his society," Elaine said. "He thinks his rule is justified because he is strong, because he can do anything and get away with it. He's even willing to accept the possibility of someone killing him because that would put an even *stronger* leader on the throne. Extending his society is practically a religious duty because the more people who are part of it, the more strong leaders will rise to the top."

"He's not interested in a line of succession," Sacharissa said, coldly.

"No," Elaine said. "The prize of Empire will go to the strong."

"And if that's done on a far greater scale," Dread added, "there will be civil war."

"We will resist," Sacharissa said.

She must, Johan said, mentally. His thoughts were shaded with remembered pain. *She'll get the same treatment as Charity, if she survives.*

She will, Elaine agreed. The thought of Sacharissa being broken by Deferens was horrific, but it had to be faced. *Deferens won't allow her to survive her kingdom. He may even kill her to make sure the royal line comes to an end.*

"So we hold," Sacharissa said. She looked at the Colonel. "You have assembled the militia?"

"Yes, Your Majesty," Colonel Tarpon said. "The enemy

will field a great many more soldiers, I fear, but we will have some advantages. I've already deployed scouts to watch the road from World's Gate. So far, there's been no attempt to push up towards Ida, but that won't last. They're just waiting for the rest of their army to arrive."

"Expect them to cover the snow in their dead bodies, if necessary," Dread said. "They've been conscripting young men from every town and city they passed. I imagine they'll use the ill-trained levies for the first assault, then put in their better-trained troops."

"They could not have trained for our weather," Tarpon assured him.

"Don't count on it," Elaine said. "They're bound to have known they'd have to take Ida."

"They were planning the invasion from the moment Deferens took the throne, perhaps before," Dread agreed. "I don't think they'll have failed to stockpile cold weather gear while making their plans."

"You would have seen the plans," Sacharissa said.

"They didn't cover the dragons," Dread said. "The first draft was to take World's Gate, then thrust up the road. There weren't many other options, short of bringing in Alpine troops from another mountain state. But the dragons can leapfrog over the defences …"

"If the creatures can endure the cold," Tarpon mused.

"They're not *normal* creatures," Elaine warned. The spells to summon dragons were very clear in her mind. "Don't expect them to be deterred by a little snowfall."

"The snows here are quite something," the Duke assured her.

"So are the dragons," Dread said, curtly. "If we start training the magicians after dinner … how long will it take them to master the spells?"

"Perhaps a few hours," Elaine said. She sensed a flicker of irritation from Johan and nodded in rueful agreement. There was a part of her that wanted to forget everything and climb back into bed with him. "I can also work on rites to deal with the magic rituals, assuming Deferens tries to use them."

"It's one of his advantages," Dread said. "There's also the other problem …"

Sacharissa held up a hand. "We'll talk about that later," she said. A set of servants appeared, removed the bowls and brought in steaming plates of roast meat. "Let us talk about something else over dinner."

Elaine wasn't sure that was a good idea, but Dread didn't seem to mind. It *was* an interesting conversation; Sacharissa chatted to Sarah about the Levellers, while Tarpon and Brian talked military tactics involving Firepowder. Johan listened, fascinated; Elaine recalled he'd always been interested in non-magical ways to do things, even though he'd developed greater powers than anyone had expected. By the time the dinner finally came to an end, she was surprised to find that she'd actually enjoyed herself.

She thought of the army, massing slowly at World's Gate, and shivered. The soldiers wouldn't show any mercy, if they broke through the walls. Ida wasn't a populous state – she had a vague idea there weren't more than around thirty thousand people in the entire kingdom – but they were all dead if Deferens won. She still had no idea why he was so determined to clear the way for the Witch-King ...

Maybe someone needs to open the lock for him, she thought. It seemed unlikely – the whole plan could have failed, leaving the Witch-King trapped forever – but she had to admit it was a possibility. *Or is he reluctant to emerge into a hostile population?*

"I've taken the liberty of assembling the magicians in the lower ballroom," Appleton said, when Sacharissa formally brought the dinner to an end. "Do you wish to start teaching them now?"

"Yes," Elaine said, rising. "Sarah?"

"We're coming," Sarah said. "We can use the spells now, can't we?"

"If the dragons arrive, give them your best shot," Elaine said, firmly. She looked at Appleton, who was eying Sarah with undisguised curiosity. It wasn't hard to realise that he was wondering why a young magician would join the Levellers. "Do you have any magicians who are used to working as a pair?"

"Four," Appleton said. "Do you want them to meet with you separately?"

"Yes, please," Elaine said. "I need to teach them how to deal with a ritual."

The ballroom was larger than she'd been dreading, crammed with fifty magicians who looked askance at her and her companions. Johan sat to the rear as Elaine briefly explained her spells, demonstrated a couple to show how they worked, then watched as Brian, Sarah and the others started to teach the spells. Brian, despite his earlier complaining, was a natural teacher, she decided; he had more success with his students than did anyone else.

"He's good at appearing confident," Johan said, when she explained it to him. "It helps them believe his words."

Elaine nodded, then allowed Appleton to lead her into the next room. Four magicians sat there, waiting for her. Two of them were elderly women; the other two were young men, who sat too close together to be anything but lovers. They'd have to be, Elaine knew; it wasn't *easy* to work together and it required a considerable degree of trust and acceptance that was rarely found outside a relationship. In some ways, they were bonded just as closely as Johan and herself.

But they set out to form a bond, she thought, as she introduced herself. *No one would make a fuss about them!*

"The Emperor has succeeded in concentrating the magic of countless magicians, then redirecting it to a single purpose," she said, pushing the thought aside. "This ritual is dangerous because it kills the caster, making it hard for them to do more than very basic tasks. If the reports from Falcone's Nest are accurate, the causeway didn't have any way to control the water or let it flow normally, ensuring its eventual destruction."

"Stupid design," one of the men commented.

"Indeed," Elaine said. "However, even getting as far as they did was extremely lucky. A single enemy sorcerer could have disrupted the entire spell."

"Causing a backlash," one of the elderly women said. Her voice was warm, but there was an edge in it that bothered Elaine. "That's what you want us to do."

"Yes," Elaine said. "I want to mess up the ritual before the spell can take shape."

She outlined the spells she wanted to use, then went

through them with the four magicians while Johan watched from behind. They were quick learners; the elderly women, in particular, were well used to the concept of conserving their power. Elaine wondered, absently, just why they'd stayed in Ida – it wasn't as if anyone would disapprove of them – but knew she didn't dare ask. She didn't have time for an argument.

"Good work, young lady," they twittered, when she'd finished. They seemed to speak in unison half the time, as if they were a single mind in two bodies. "We can use this, if necessary. Go get some rest."

Elaine smiled, then left the room. Johan looked relieved as they made their way back to their bedroom, although she could sense a strange mixture of apprehension and fear filtering through his thoughts. He knew the enemy was unlikely to give them much time – if any – before launching an attack. They could die tomorrow.

She kissed him as soon as the door was closed, then pushed him towards the bed. Johan kissed her in return, his arms roaming over her back and down towards her rear. Sex would drive away their fears …

… But they came back afterwards, as they lay together on the bed. They could die tomorrow and the Witch-King could rise, unimpeded …

It was a long time before she could sleep.

Chapter Twenty-Two

Charity felt unclean as she followed the Emperor out of the inn, even though she'd washed herself thoroughly after manually cleaning the floor of every last stain of blood. The oath – the damned oath – had kept her focused on the task, forcing her to keep going even though the innkeeper's daughter had offered to take over. It had been hours before she'd been able to convince herself she was done, then go to her bedroom and scrub herself clean. Even so, she felt as if there was blood on her hands.

I could have closed the loophole, she thought. The cold air gripped her as soon as she left the building; she crossed her arms under her breasts to keep from shivering. *I could have made the orders so specific they had to be obeyed.*

The Emperor ignored her shivering as he walked through the gates and reviewed his troops, standing to attention as best they could. Great fires were burning everywhere, warming the air; the men, wearing armour and furs, looked grimly determined to fight to the last for their Emperor. Charity had no idea if the Queen of Ida was scared, but she knew damn well that *she* was scared. The human wolves looking at her were only constrained by the certainty that she belonged to the Emperor. He'd issued strict orders against looting or rape in World's Gate and he'd *still* had to hang a number of men for disobeying his commands.

I suppose that's what you get if you encourage them to commit atrocities, she thought, as the Emperor turned to peer towards Ida. *You get men who are incapable of holding their baser impulses in check.*

She sucked in her breath as she looked towards Ida. The mountain kingdom was barely visible in the clouds, the grey buildings blending into the rock until she wasn't sure where one ended and the other began. She couldn't help feeling dizzy as her eyes picked out the road, slowly making its way up towards Ida. It looked too thin to be safe; there were no barriers between the narrow road and a plunge to certain death. A gust of wind would be enough to send a carriage plummeting off the edge and into its grave. The Emperor didn't seem intimidated, though; he merely lifted his hand and a flight of dragons rose into the air, their riders lifting their swords in salute.

"Your Supremacy," General Vetch said. Charity turned to see him walking towards them, carrying a sword in one hand. "Your forces stand ready to attack."

The Emperor smiled. "Then let the attack begin!"

***

Johan could feel Elaine's fear as they hurried through breakfast, then met Dread and followed him out of the castle, down towards the walls. The stones felt reassuringly solid to the touch, but Elaine was terrifyingly aware of just how easy it would be for the Emperor's magic to break them. Her fear was infecting Johan's own thoughts, he knew, as he scrambled onto the wall; he tried to remember the previous night instead, recalling just what they'd done together. He felt sore in delicate places and she didn't feel much better.

"Don't worry," he said, as they peered out over the battlements. The walls plunged down for hundreds of metres, vanishing somewhere in the mists. He wouldn't have placed money on anything, even a dragon, surviving such a fall. "They're not going to winkle us out of here."

"They're already trying," Elaine said. She had her eyes closed as she reached out with her magic, tasting the air. "The dragons are on their way."

Johan frowned, then stared as the first dragon broke through the clouds and came into view. He'd seen them wheeling over the Golden City – a pang in his chest reminded him that they'd killed Inquisitor Cass – but it was the first time he'd seen them at close range. They were stunning; monstrous beasts, covered in green, gold and red scales, breathing fire as they swooped over the city. He couldn't help but feel a stab of envy as he saw the riders, even though he knew the price Deferens had paid to bring the dragons into the world. They could fly high over the world, so high that none of the magicians and kings and merchants *mattered* any longer.

"Hold the line," Colonel Tarpon shouted, loudly. "There's nowhere to go, lads, so you may as well stand your ground."

The lead dragon roared, its neck spinning madly like a wild thing and leaving a coil of fire in the air. Johan peered at the riders, wondering if Charity or Deferens was among them, but they all looked to be male and young. The other dragons echoed it, breathing more plumes of fire into the air. Johan wondered just what they were doing – they could have attacked by now – and then frowned as he saw the troops advancing up the road from World's Gate. The dragons were trying to distract them.

"Time's up," Elaine breathed, as the dragons flocked together and lanced towards the walls, breathing out powerful streams of flame. She raised her voice, then the wand she'd picked up from Appleton. "Now!"

Johan braced himself as she cast the spell, just as the dragons washed fire over the stone walls and buildings beyond. He grabbed hold of her, calling on his power to shield them both, as her spell struck the lead dragon. For a horrific moment, he thought it had failed ... and then green light flared around the creature, attacking the magic holding it in the air. The rider let out a scream of panic as the dragon flipped over and plunged down, hitting the wall and then sliding over the edge to certain death. Johan hoped, in a moment of bitter vindictiveness, that the rider had fallen with the beast.

"You got it," he said, as his power faded.

"Good," Elaine said. "What about the others?"

Johan looked around. The walls were scorched, but intact; the buildings looked to have survived the flames, although he could see several small fires where something more flammable than stone had been caught by the dragons. A dead dragon was stuck on top of the wall, while two more had fallen in the city itself. One of the riders looked to have landed on his head and died; the others had been hauled off their mounts and beaten half to death before superior officers had intervened and dragged the captives to the cells. They'd be interrogated, later, on just what the Emperor had in mind.

"I think we surprised them," he said. The remaining dragons had veered back, their riders staring in disbelief at the remains of their fellows. "They weren't expecting to lose."

Elaine smiled, tiredly. "They haven't lost yet."

***

Charity pressed her lips tightly closed when the first dragon plummeted from the sky, wrapped in a haze of green-yellow magic. It struck the ground, let out a final blast of fire and died. The rider was crushed under its enormous bulk. Five more dragons died in quick succession, one managing to land on the walls before the magic holding it together vanished, leaving it nothing more than a dead carcass. Two more followed their comrades into death before the riders jerked back, evading a handful of pursuing spells.

"They killed my dragons," the Emperor said. He sounded shocked, as if he couldn't imagine something powerful enough to kill a dragon. Light Spinner had done it, but she'd had the collected raw magic of the Golden City at her disposal. Ida ... shouldn't have had *any* sorcerers of her calibre. "They killed my dragons!"

"Yes, Your Supremacy," Charity said, heedless of the dangers. He could beat her, or humiliate her, or even kill her, but she'd never forget what she'd seen. "They killed your dragons."

The Emperor clenched his fists. "Send in the archers," he ordered, tightly. "And order the advancing columns to pick up the pace!"

"Yes, Your Supremacy," General Vetch said.

Charity turned her gaze back towards Ida ... and the circling dragons. Knawel Haldane and Falcone's Nest had been made of wood; their walls had been stone, but everything from their guardhouses to residencies had been made of wood. The dragons hadn't had any difficulty barbecuing everything in sight, laying waste to entire cities. But Ida was made of stone, stone that had probably been charmed to repel fire. There was very little for the dragons to burn.

Save for the people, she thought, as the secondary columns started their advance. *They could still die when fire roasts them to a crisp.*

But the Emperor had been knocked back on his heels. She took heart from that, if nothing else. There *were* spells that could be turned against dragon …

"And order Roth to select a new martyr," the Emperor ordered. "If they think they can fight me, they can burn."

***

"Arrows," someone shouted. "Duck!"

Elaine ducked down as a flight of arrows shot over the wall, one of them striking a soldier who hadn't been quick enough to take cover. He staggered, then fell off the battlements and down into the city. Johan landed next to her, using his magic to shield them both. He felt torn between excitement and fear …

"Cast protective wards," she called, lifting her wand. It would drain her badly, but there was no choice. The archers could force the defenders to keep their heads down until the dragons and infantry reached the walls. "Don't let them keep us down."

"I can help," Johan muttered, as she carefully stood up. An arrow smashed into the ward and shattered to splinters. "They're down there, aren't they?"

Elaine nodded as two more arrows struck her protections. The archers had taken up position in the open, as if they expected Ida not to have any archers of their own. *That* was a mistake, Elaine was sure; she'd seen the archers training earlier, near the murder holes. She eyed the enemy archers carefully, then looked up at the dragons. They were still keeping their distance, even as the infantry advanced. It wouldn't be long before they reached Ida, despite the cold wind. And then they'd try to storm the gates.

"Fire," Tarpon shouted.

A dozen archers fired as one, hurling a stream of arrows towards the enemy archers. Nine fell at once; the remainder hastily took cover, such as it was. Elaine felt a glimmer of sympathy as the remaining archers were picked off, then frowned as she saw a trio of red-robed men hurrying along the road. The sorcerers might not have her finesse, but they definitely had the power to shield the enemy troops.

"Now," Brian ordered.

A deafening explosion echoed out; moments later, Elaine saw an avalanche that dwarfed the earlier one falling down towards the enemy troops. They didn't have a *hope* of escaping, she realised numbly; they were too far from the walls and too far from safety to get clear of the snowfall before it was too late. The tidal wave of snow overwhelmed them, blotting them out of existence and sending their mangled remains falling over the cliff. A handful of archers had taken up position again, protected by the sorcerers, but even they weren't good enough to stop the avalanche. They died within seconds.

"Got them," Johan shouted. "They're gone!"

"But we can't play that trick twice," Elaine said. She tried to think like Deferens, but ran into the problem that she was *rational*. In *his* place, she wouldn't have launched the offensive at all, because she wouldn't want to lose so many men. Deferens, on the other hand, believed that all resistance to his rule had to be brutally crushed. "They'll start a second assault once they know what to expect."

She looked back at the dragons. They were still firmly out of range, at least to her; she briefly considered asking Johan to attack them, then dismissed the thought. She had a feeling they'd need his power before too long. Silence fell over the battlefield, broken only by the cawing of the birds as they swept over the field, picking at half-frozen corpses before they froze completely. She peered down towards World's Gate, wondering just what was going through the Emperor's mind. What would he do now?

Dread appeared, keeping low as he ran around the battlements. "Grab something to eat," he ordered, passing them both a roll of bread. "You don't know when they're going to attack again."

"Maybe we taught them better," Johan said.

"I don't think so," Dread said. He peered over the battlements carefully, his face darkening as he took in the scene. "The Emperor cannot leave without teaching us a lesson. He'd lose too much face."

"It could destroy him," Elaine pointed out.

"It's his mentality," Dread said. "The whole concept of simply recognising that some mountains are too difficult to climb is beyond him."

Johan snickered. "You mean he can't resist the temptation to stick it into a tempting orifice."

"Johan," Elaine said, although she found it hard to keep herself from smiling. "That's terrible!"

"But accurate," Dread said. "Right now, he's regrouping and considering his next step."

***

"Your Supremacy," General Vetch said. He looked as though he expected to be executed for his failure. "The advance columns have been wiped out."

Charity drew in her breath, waiting for the Emperor's reaction. His face had darkened steadily since the dragons had been forced back, although he hadn't exploded with rage at her or anyone else. Instead, he'd just sent additional orders to Roth and settled back to watch the archers as they fired arrows into the city.

"So I see," the Emperor said. He took a long moment to survey the remains of the battlefield. "But they cannot keep triggering avalanches, can they?"

"They have already damaged our morale," General Vetch said. "The conscripts are uneasy."

"Make examples of anyone who dares defy my will openly," the Emperor ordered. He turned to face the General. "Assemble the second-rank sorcerers to accompany the infantry and the archers; they are to protect the advancing men from arrows. The first-rank sorcerers are to mount the dragons and protect *them*. I want them held in reserve for when we use the ritual."

The General blinked. "Your Supremacy?"

"They're casting spells that interfere with magical fields," the Emperor said. He smiled, rubbing his hands together with glee. "A dragon is a hugely magical creature, General. They simply cannot exist without magic. However, we have magicians too. One of them should be able to shield the dragon from the spells that would otherwise destroy it."

He leant back, holding his hands behind his back. "The

battle is not yet over, General," he added. "It has barely begun."

Charity winced, inwardly. The Emperor was right. He didn't care about losses; he only cared about winning and losing. The battle wasn't over until he *said* it was over.

Keep fighting, she thought. She tried to think of another loophole she could exploit, but nothing came to mind. *Don't let him win!*

***

"They're forming up new lines," Dread observed. "They're definitely planning something."

Elaine nodded in agreement. "How's the Queen coping?"

"I had to ... *convince* her not to put herself on the front line," Dread said. "She was insistent on showing herself to her people, but if she happened to be killed ... well, the defence line would fall apart."

He shrugged. "Ida couldn't really hope for a better leader in the times to come."

Elaine allowed herself a smile. "Did she try to seduce you?"

Dread gave her a hard look. "Does it matter?"

"You're not an Inquisitor any longer," Elaine said, after a moment. Dread's stern gaze was still unnerving, even though he no longer had any magic. "And she *does* need a strong right arm."

"I haven't looked beyond the war," Dread said, quietly. "If I die today, or before the Witch-King is defeated, it won't matter what hopes and dreams I might have had. Afterwards ... I may look around for other options."

"Marry her," Elaine urged.

Johan looked from one to the other, shaking his head. "There's an enemy force on the other side of the walls and you two are talking about *romance*?"

"Better to have something to distract yourself," Dread said, bluntly. "Battles like this are rare – or were, I should say. They used to be long hours of boredom and fear, broken only by moments of screaming terror."

"Oh," Johan said. He looked down at the stone ground. "I think you should marry her."

Dread sighed. "You *do* realise there's a good chance I won't survive?"

Elaine gave him a long look. Everything that gave Dread's life meaning – the Grand Sorcerer, the Empire, the Inquisition, his magic – was gone. He'd dedicated himself to service long before Elaine was born ...

... And now he couldn't serve *anyone*.

"Don't seek your own death," she said, firmly. "I want you to live."

"I was seriously tempted to put you in jail," Dread said. Elaine remembered how they'd first met and coloured. She'd lied to his face, a criminal offence. "Are you *sure*?"

"You did your duty," Elaine said. She reached out and gave him a hug. "We'd be dead already if it wasn't for you."

"I know," Dread said. He hadn't returned her hug. She wasn't surprised. The thought of Dread showing any real affection was hard to comprehend. "But there will be time to decide what to do afterwards once we win."

"Yeah," Johan said. "I ..."

"Quiet," Elaine hissed. Something was pricking at the edge of her mind. A sense of magic; too far away to be pinpointed, too close to be ignored. It should have been impossible. Even the Watchtower or the Imperial Palace hadn't been noticeable at long range. "I ..."

She sucked in her breath, feeling a surge of horror. "They're working a ritual," she snapped, bracing herself frantically. She'd never felt anything like the sensation, but it couldn't be anything else. "They're about to attack!"

Chapter Twenty-Three

"Now," the Emperor ordered.

Charity braced herself as the sorcerer's chanting grew louder, slowly reaching a crescendo as magic flared around his form. His robe caught fire as blue light flashed over his hands, dancing through the runes he'd drawn on the ground and gliding rapidly towards Ida. He let out a scream as the flames grew hotter, but held himself together. Charity couldn't help being impressed at his determination, even though she knew it spelt the end of the battle. He'd die, but his death would tip the scales in the Emperor's favour.

"Let Ida fall," the Emperor said, as the magic picked up speed. The ground started to shake violently. "Let them all die."

***

"Get the counterspells up," Elaine ordered, running towards the two elderly women. "Hurry!"

"The spells are in place, dear," one of the women said. She sounded calm, even though there was a very good chance she and her partner were about to die. "We're ready."

Elaine nodded, then turned to look as a wave of blue light raced towards Ida. The magic was so strong that she wouldn't have been surprised if the mundanes could sense it, even though a baseline sensitivity to magic was the first requirement for actually being a magician. It looked irresistible, although she knew better. The structures taking place within the light could be broken easily, given the right impetus.

"Now," she ordered.

The elderly women joined hands, then started to mutter a spell in unison. They couldn't hope to match the blue wave of power, but they didn't have to. All they really had to do was disrupt it, ensuring that the Emperor's servant couldn't keep it under control. Elaine braced herself as their magic reached past her and lanced into the blue light, causing wave after wave of feedback. She ducked down low as blue light exploded, then flickered out of existence.

"By all the gods," Johan breathed.

Elaine rose to her feet and peered over the battlements. The snow was gone. So were the advancing forces, simply blinked out of existence. The road looked badly damaged; the craggy cliff face below the walls looked ... *smoother,* somehow. What had the Emperor's men been trying to do? Level the walls? Bring Ida down to ground level? Or simply trigger an earthquake that would devastate the city?

She turned back to the two magicians and winced. They were dead, their hands still interlinked and identical smiles on their faces. She cursed herself under her breath – she could at least have watched them die for their kingdom – and then closed their eyes, as gently as she could. They'd died because of her, but at least their deaths had not been in vain.

"I'll see they get a proper burial," Colonel Tarpon said. "My Lady, it will not be long until they resume the offensive."

"We will be ready," Sarah said, coming up behind him. "Did they stop the spell?"

"I think so," Elaine said. She didn't really doubt it, but how much stored magic did the Emperor have? He'd rounded up every magician he could get his hands on and drained their power for his spells. "But the Emperor isn't out of tricks."

"Neither are we," Johan assured her.

"We only have one other joined pair," Elaine said. The elderly women had volunteered to go first, pointing out that they'd had long and happy lives. It didn't make her feel any less guilty for sending them to their deaths. "I don't know how many magicians he has who are willing to give their lives for him."

***

Everything went wrong with terrifying speed. The chanting stopped, a half-second before the magician threw up his arms and screamed, his body catching fire and burning to ash.

Charity had only moments to realise that something *was* wrong before the blue light recoiled, lancing back towards the camp like a hunting flame. The Emperor bit off a stunned oath, then threw himself to the ground as the blue light exploded; Charity followed, feeling her head spin as the magic flashed over her. For a moment, she honestly believed someone had kicked her in the head. She'd always been sensitive to magic, but this was something far outside her experience.

"They did something to the spell," the Emperor snarled. "Get up!"

Charity obeyed, helplessly. A dozen red-robed magicians were lying on the ground, clutching their heads, while even the Inquisitors looked stunned. The magical blowback must not have been strong enough to change them – she glanced down at her body to make sure nothing had changed without her knowledge – but it had definitely been enough to hurt every magician within range. In the distance, the dragons were roaring in pain, breathing long plumes of fire into the sky. They'd have sensed the blast too.

They did it, she thought. She couldn't imagine *what* could have stopped the ritual in its tracks – a greater ritual, perhaps – but it hardly mattered. All that mattered was that the ritual had been stopped and the magic of countless magicians had been wasted. The Emperor would not be pleased, but she found it hard to care. *They saved their kingdom!*

"Your Supremacy," General Vetch said. "The troops are in some disarray."

The Emperor glared at him. "Assemble the main regiments for an assault," he ordered, sharply. "We'll use the vines."

Charity kept her face impassive. The spell's backlash had melted the snow and damaged the road. It had only succeeded in making it *harder* for the troops to get to Ida, let alone scramble over the walls. The dragons were the Emperor's trump card and they'd been beaten, unless he was right about his magicians being able to deal with the counterspells and keep the dragons in the air.

"The dragons will provide cover," the Emperor added, after a moment. "The magicians will shield them."

"The magicians are in pain," the General warned. "Your

Supremacy ..."

"We cannot lose this battle," the Emperor hissed. "Assemble the troops!"

Charity watched with bated breath. General Vetch was from the same homeland as the Emperor. He could remove a failed leader, if he had the nerve ... but did he have the magic he'd need to break through the Emperor's protections? If he'd taken Jamal's knife ... Charity briefly considered trying to give it to him, but she knew her oaths wouldn't let her. She couldn't kill her master or assist anyone else to kill him.

"Yes, Your Supremacy," General Vetch said, finally.

He bowed, then headed off to the camp.

***

"They're forming up again," Dread said, lying on the battlements and peering towards World's Gate with a telescope. "I don't think the Emperor has given up."

"He can't give up," Elaine said. She sat next to Johan, taking what time she could to gather herself before the next attack. "It would cost him everything."

"He could lose his army storming Ida," Dread pointed out. "The dragons were unstoppable until now. He might no longer be Emperor when this is finished, but just another warlord."

"Assuming the spells get out," Elaine said. One of the Queen's magicians – a mountaineer – had insisted on slipping out of the kingdom, heading down to the nearest friendly town. He'd make sure that knowledge of the spells spread widely, ensuring that dragons would no longer be able to run riot through the Empire. "He's still got plenty of advantages."

"He's also being an idiot," Dread observed. He was still peering through his telescope, his eyes narrowing as he took in the sight. "They're going to lose hundreds of men just reaching the walls."

Elaine pulled herself to her feet and walked over to the battlements. "The dragons are coming back," she noted. "They must have prepared counterspells for the counterspells."

Johan gave her a mischievous look. "Can you write

counterspells for the counterspells for the counterspells?"

"Shut up," Elaine said, without heat. "I'm not sure what they're going to do …"

She closed her eyes, thinking hard. How would *she* do it? The counterspells would have to blend into the magical field surrounding the dragon or it would run the risk of accidentally knocking the dragon out of the air anyway. She doubted the Emperor would reward a sorcerer who scored an own goal. But the dragons were surrounded by chaotic waves of magic, ensuring that the spells would have to be carefully watched by a magician capable of adjusting them at a moment's notice.

"Hit them several times," she said, finally. "It might work."

"Try and devise something better than *might*," Dread ordered. He cursed under his breath as the dragons closed in, howling their fury to the skies. "Here they come."

Elaine ducked down as the dragons flashed overhead, breathing flames down on the city. Most of the counterspells worked, but not enough to keep them from bathing parts of the wall in lethal fire. She snapped off a spell at one of the dragons, only to see it flash out of existence as the sorcerer on top countered it. They were risking their lives pushing their magic so far from themselves, she noted absently, but they didn't have much choice. Losing the dragon would mean a long fall and a very hard landing.

"Tell the archers to aim at the riders," she shouted, as she sent off another spell. This time, the dragon flipped over and crashed into a stone building, shattering it to rubble. The dragon survived long enough to breathe flame into the next building – Elaine saw tongues of flame blasting out of every door and window – before the spell completed its work and the dragon died. "They're not capable of protecting themselves."

Another dragon swooped overhead, breathing fire. Johan grabbed her, his power surrounding them both as flames billowed over the walls. She looked around as the beast headed onwards, trying to see Dread; she thought, for a horrified moment, that he was dead before he emerged from a stone nook, coughing frantically. The walls around them were scorched and pitted; the dragon turned, clearly ready for another run, just as a spread of arrows slammed into its hide. Most of them shattered uselessly, but one struck the rider and sent him falling to his death. The dragon died moments later as Sarah scored a direct hit with her spell.

"Climbers," Tarpon shouted, as the last dragons retreated. "Man the walls!"

Elaine turned, just in time to see a green shoot rise up over the battlements. It was so out of place that she found it hard to comprehend what it was, before memories rose up from the back of her mind. Climbing vines had been used as siege weapons during the necromantic wars, growing so rapidly that infantrymen could scramble up the green branches while the roots dug under the walls, weakening them until the point they collapsed. She'd never thought that Deferens might use them, but if he'd brought back the dragons …

She shook her head as the first soldier appeared on the edge of the walls. The dragons were a major accomplishment, even if they'd cost hundreds of lives apiece. Compared to them, the climbing vines were nothing more than magically-altered plants. It wouldn't be hard for a twelve-year-old, a new student at the Peerless School, to make them, assuming they could find the right ingredients. Hell, for all she knew, Deferens *had* set schoolchildren to making weapons of war.

Dread lunged forward, raising his staff. The soldier had no time to react before Dread slammed the iron tip into his crotch, sending him doubling over in pain. Elaine sensed a flicker of sympathy from Johan as the soldier screamed, just before Dread slammed his staff into his head. It had probably been a mercy, part of her mind noted, as several more soldiers appeared on the walls. They were followed by an entire line of man-sized insects that had been turned into weapons of war.

"Get back," Dread shouted, as soldiers rushed to repel the incursion. "Let us handle it."

"Let me help," Johan hissed, as Elaine stumbled backwards. "I can take them down …"

"Not now," Elaine said. She had an idea, but they'd need to get into a better location before they tried it. "Let the soldiers handle the invaders."

She pointed her wand at a pair of enemy soldiers and used a light spell to send them falling back out of the battlements and out of sight, then led the way down to the ladders into the city. Flames were rising up from a dozen places, marking spots where the dragons had found something flammable; hundreds of grey stone buildings were scorched and pitted, their inhabitants desperately trying to use buckets of water to quell the fires consuming the remains of their belongings. The castle had been scorched badly, but seemed to have survived intact.

They sent the children there to keep them safe, she thought, as she hurried towards one of the watchtowers. *If the dragons managed to breathe fire into the castle, they might have burnt up the oxygen.*

She pushed the thought aside – there was nothing she could do about it – and slipped into the watchtower. A pair of women wearing leather armour and carrying swords blocked her path, then stepped aside when she held up the medallion the Queen had given her. Elaine had to smile – she'd never heard of women fighting as common soldiers until she'd returned to Ida – and then ran up the stairs. The watchtower was carefully placed to allow the occupants to stare down at the road leading up to the kingdom. She cast a protective ward, then started to try to make sense of the battle.

"They're coming faster now," Johan said.

Elaine followed his gaze. It was hard to separate the common soldiers, to work out who was on what side, but the officers were easy to recognise. The Emperor's officers wore red cloaks and carried the battle standards of the Empire, while Ida's men wore green and carried no standards. Behind the infantry, there were a handful of crawling monsters: giant caterpillars, oversized spiders and deadly ants. The Emperor clearly hadn't stopped at dragons when he'd started uncorking the deadly threats of the past. She felt a shiver running down her spine as she saw one of the spiders climbing over the walls, then sighed in relief as Brian hit it with a spell. It collapsed instantly as its magical field vanished.

They're too large to live without magic, she thought. *Just like the dragons.*

She looked at Johan. If she was right, they should be able to channel his magic through the bond and control it. If she was wrong …

"I'm ready," Johan said. He turned to look at her, his trust shining through the link. "Are you?"

"I think so," Elaine said. She took his hands and closed her eyes. "Concentrate on fire …"

****

Charity watched helplessly as the Emperor's troops advanced forward, scrambling up the creepers and throwing themselves over the walls. Hundreds had died, but the Emperor had thousands in reserve, backed up by his army of creepy-crawly monsters. Inch by inch, they were pushing the defenders off the walls and securing control of the battlements, which made it easier to rush new troops forward. The Emperor, it seemed, was finally winning.

A dragon swooped low over the city, breathing fire over the defenders. The Emperor's troops raised a cheer as the dragon retreated, then lunged forward into the empty space and summoned reinforcements. A handful of arrows flashed down from deeper within the city, but it wasn't enough to stop the advance. *Nothing* could stop it. Charity closed her eyes in pain. Johan and his friends would die as Ida fell to the Emperor, its population butchered and sole city destroyed. There could be no escape.

"They will burn," the Emperor breathed. "They will *all* bow before me."

Charity *felt* it suddenly, a tingling in the air that made her hair stand on end. She flashed back, her head spinning, to the moment Johan had turned her into a rat, to the moment her thoughts had come to an abrupt halt as *everything* changed. The ground seemed to shudder beneath her feet; she closed her eyes, fighting for balance, then looked up as brilliant light flared over the walls. Flames flashed into existence, burning the creeper to ash and incinerating the advancing soldiers.

They're not normal flames, she thought, stunned. There were magicians who could unleash the very fires of hell, but none of them could *control* the flames. Here … the flames seemed to be advancing under intelligence guidance. *That's magic*!

"Get another ritual ready," the Emperor barked. His voice was hard, but Charity thought she could hear cold desperation in his tone. "Those flames have to be snuffed!"

"Yes, Your Supremacy," General Vetch said.

"No," the Emperor said, before the General could summon the magicians. His voice was different. "Pull back the remaining troops."

Charity blinked. She'd expected anything, but an order to retreat. "Your Supremacy?"

"Pull back the remaining troops," the Emperor repeated, as the flames grew brighter. Charity was sure she could see *shapes* within the blaze, flaming humanoids walking through the air and incinerating everyone they touched. The sight chilled her to the bone. "We will hold position here and keep Ida under siege."

"Yes, Your Supremacy," General Vetch said. He sounded relieved, too relieved to question the change in his master. "I shall see to it at once."

The Emperor turned to look towards the flames. "This is only the beginning," he said, so quietly that Charity was the only one who heard. "There will be time to revenge myself on Ida later."

His face shifted again. "We will hold the line here."

"Yes, Your Supremacy," Charity said. Was he mad? But his madness had produced a reasonable decision. "Ida *did* take a battering."

"Yes, it did," the Emperor agreed. "We will regroup and prepare another offensive."

Chapter Twenty-Four

"They're cheering for you," Elaine said, as she led Johan back towards the castle. A handful of soldiers had surrounded them, providing a honour guard. "They think you won the war."

Johan nodded, feeling a confused mix of emotions. He'd *wanted* fame, once upon a time, but he hadn't realised that fame would bring notoriety. He could have been a great warrior or a mighty builder if his family had given him the chance … now, he was a magician and his magic had been used to incinerate hundreds of people. It was worse, far worse, than the moment he'd destroyed the bridges, even though the flames had been under Elaine's control. How many people had died at his hands?

Elaine squeezed his hand. "There was no choice," she said, quietly. "You were the secret weapon."

Dread met them at the castle's entrance. Johan smelt burning wood – the gates had been destroyed by the dragons – as they walked inside, heading towards the throne room. The Queen had commanded the battle from her War Room, he knew, although he had a feeling she hadn't issued many commands. Colonel Tarpon – and Dread – had been the officers on the spot. But her survival meant the kingdom's survival.

No wonder she wants Dread, Johan thought numbly. *Even without magic, he's formidable.*

"Welcome back," Sacharissa said, once the doors were closed. "And I thank you."

"It isn't the end," Dread warned. "The Emperor is unlikely to tolerate our survival for long."

Sacharissa bowed her head in mute acknowledgement. Johan couldn't help feeling a flicker of pity, understanding – finally – some of the pressures that had driven his father. House Conidian needed to survive, whatever the cost. But

Duncan Conidian had allowed his oldest son to become a bully ... he hoped, inwardly, that Sacharissa would make sure her children didn't turn into monsters, no matter who she married. Dread would probably make sure of it personally.

"I know," Sacharissa said. She looked at Elaine. "Are you sure you and Johan want to go alone?"

Johan sensed Elaine's hesitation. She was the most capable magician in Ida – he felt another stab of guilt for stealing Dread's powers – and she was bonded to him, but she might find herself badly outmatched if she ran into trouble. And yet, he understood why she wanted to handle it alone. A large search party tramping through the catacombs might trigger hidden defences or even awaken the Witch-King ahead of time ... and mundane soldiers would be little more than targets to the lich.

"I don't think I have a choice," Elaine said. "There isn't anyone who can come with us."

"Then go, with my blessing," Sacharissa said. She clapped her hands together, summoning a tall man wearing a green uniform. "Carlos will show you to the entrance."

Johan blinked in surprise – he had expected more of a fight – but he knew that Sacharissa believed they were searching for an ancient artefact, rather than a lich. She probably assumed she'd have the chance to take a look at it once it was hauled up to the surface – and find out if there was a way to turn it against her enemies. Johan knew she'd be disappointed, but kept that thought to himself. The fewer people who knew what they were hunting, the better.

"Take my staff," Dread urged. "It has some protective charms built in."

"I don't know how to use it," Elaine said. She gave the ex-Inquisitor a long look. Johan didn't need to bond to know she wished Dread could come with them too. "Take care of the surface, all right?"

Dread nodded. Elaine bowed to him, curtseyed to the Queen and then allowed Carlos to lead them out of the room. Johan hastily bowed himself – he had no idea how much reverence was due to a queen, but he liked and respected Sacharissa – and followed Elaine as Carlos led her down a long flight of stairs into a set of underground chambers. One of them, brightly lit by magical orbs, was crammed with young children and a handful of expectant mothers, who stared at them openly as they passed. Johan had no idea if the children gathered here were *every* last child in Ida, but he hoped – prayed – they survived the next assault. Vlad Deferens was unlikely to leave them in peace for long.

"This is the gate to the catacombs," he said, after they had walked down another winding set of stairs. Johan couldn't help wondering if they were actually below World's Gate. "Beyond this point, no one may go without permission."

"We have permission," Elaine said. Johan caught the tension in her voice, although he doubted Carlos would be able to hear it. "Open the doors."

Carlos nodded curtly, then pressed his hand against a giant stone door. There must have been magic in them, Johan decided, for they opened the moment he touched them. Inside, there was nothing but a long, dark passageway leading downwards. The air smelt stale, as if it had been centuries since the doors had been opened. He felt an odd thrill as he stepped forward, mingled with fear. They could be lost under Ida forever, if they weren't careful.

He looked at Carlos, trying to keep the concern out of his voice. "Is there a map?"

Carlos laughed. "Of course not," he said sarcastically. "The catacombs are meant to be *safe*!"

"Thank you," Elaine said, tartly. "Wait for us here."

She took Johan's hand as she walked forward, through the doors. Johan heard Carlos snicker behind them – he made a mental note to extract painful and humiliating revenge later – as the doors closed, plunging them into darkness. Elaine cast a light spell, then looked around carefully. Johan did the same, taking in the stone walls and the hundreds of carvings someone had carefully etched out on the stone. The darkness fell back, inviting them to walk onwards; in the distance, he could hear the sound of water dripping to the ground.

"There was an agreement between Ida and the Empire, made sometime after the Second Necromantic War," Elaine said, very quietly. "The Kings of Ida and their people wanted the right to bury their bodies, rather than burn them to ash. They agreed that the bodies could be stored in the crypt below Ida, as long as they were held within a pocket dimension that could be collapsed at a moment's notice."

Johan nodded, slowly. It was vanishingly rare for dead bodies *not* to be burnt, not when the remains of a living person could be used in all manner of dark spells. If Jamal had been able to track him down, just through the blood-tie, another sorcerer could do the same – or worse – with a sample of Jamal's blood. His father had worried, endlessly, about what would happen if Johan had fallen into enemy hands. Even death wouldn't keep him from being used against his family.

"Because the bodies might come back to life," he said, carefully. "Would they have a link to the living?"

"I'm not sure," Elaine said. "If someone had your father's body, they might be able to curse you, but I don't know if they'd succeed if they had your *grandfather's* body. Or your great-grandfather's body."

Johan scowled. "Because I'm only a fourth of him," he said. The gods knew his parents had dug back through the family tree, trying to find an answer to the question of why Johan had apparently been born without magic. "There would be too many other potential relatives."

"Correct," Elaine agreed. "Unless, of course, someone wanted to curse your entire family."

They reached the bottom of the passageway and looked around as it opened into a wide chamber. Elaine tossed a second light globe into the air; Johan looked around as it revealed a hundred broken statues, lying on the ground where they'd fallen. The only intact one was of a bearded man with a grim expression, carrying a sword in a manner that was better for showing off than actual fighting. Johan couldn't help thinking he looked tough, then frowned as he sensed a flicker of dismay from Elaine.

"There are traces of magic leading further down into the catacombs," she said. "I think they're heading towards the pocket dimension."

Johan gave her a puzzled look. "Can't we just collapse it?"

"If we can," Elaine said. She closed her eyes for a long moment. "If the Witch-King is in the dimension, we can try to crush him by collapsing the dimensional walls around his body …”

"Except he might have taken precautions against us doing that," Johan finished, as her voice trailed off. "Or he isn't in the dimension in the first place."

"It's a possibility," Elaine agreed. She waved her wand in the air, casting a handful of tracing spells. "The magic is flowing this way, so …"

The air grew warmer as they made their way deeper under the mountain. Johan looked around, taking in the growing number of statues and – below them – the coffins that housed the remains of Ida's dead. They'd have decayed by now, he was sure, although there were plenty of spells that could have preserved a dead body from the moment of death. He briefly considered opening a coffin, then rejected the idea. The dead should be allowed to stay dead.

"The agreement puzzled me at the time," Elaine added, as they passed a line of weeping angel statues. "There was no logical reason for the Empire to allow Ida such freedom, not when undead plagues can be devastating. Hell, Dark Wizards would be making a run to Ida just to stock up on components from dead bodies. But if the whole agreement was meant to hide something …"

"Like the Witch-King," Johan said. "But Ida was never overrun by his forces."

"Valiant could have been playing both sides of the war," Elaine said. "The books aren't very clear on just how many people knew that Valiant had betrayed the Emperor. They may never have drawn the connection between Valiant and the Witch-King. If Ida thought it was doing a service for the great hero …"

She shook her head. "Or they might just have been spellbound, like Deferens' distant ancestors," she added. "They were encouraged to develop an insular culture that kept itself as aloof as possible from the rest of the world."

"Except that both Hilarion and Kane came from Ida," Johan pointed out. "He must have intended to bring Ida's isolation to an end eventually."

"We wouldn't take them seriously," Elaine said. "I don't think *anyone* took Hilarion to be a serious contender for Grand Sorcerer, not at first."

She shook her head. "We may never know," she concluded. "All we can do is try to deal with the Witch-King before it's too late."

Johan nodded and followed her through another series of twisting corridors. It felt odd to him, as if something was gently trying to push them away; he couldn't help thinking of the first set of wards that had protected his family's original home. They convinced people that there was nothing there; mundanes would turn around and walk away, ignorant of the hidden building behind the walls. Even magicians would have problems getting through the first line of defence, unless they were truly determined to break in. *They* tended to be met by heavier defences once they crossed the walls.

"The magic traces are actually making it harder for the wards to push us away," Elaine said, when he mentioned that out loud. She sounded more than a little disturbed. "There's an elegance here I haven't seen since I started crafting my own protections."

"The Witch-King knows more about magic than most," Johan reminded her. "He might be able to duplicate some of your work."

"Or create it first," Elaine said. She turned a corner and came face to face with a stone door, blocking their path. "The traces go through here."

"I could blast down the door," Johan suggested.

"It might provoke a reaction," Elaine said. She held her wand out, testing the door carefully for unpleasant surprises. "There's a nasty set of hexes buried within the stone. I'll have to remove them one by one."

Johan looked around. The faint sense that the wards were pushing him away was growing stronger; somehow, no matter how much he tried to ignore it, he had the feeling that someone was watching them. He peered at the statues, leaning against the wall, and shuddered. They were too perfect to be real.

There was a flash of light, then the door opened, revealing a giant chamber. A faint light pulsed down from high overhead, illuminating a giant coffin positioned right at the heart of the cave, surrounded by hundreds of runes. Johan hadn't seen anything so elaborate, even when he'd walked into the Great Library and seen some of the defences. The scent of magic in the air was almost overpowering …

"Stay where you are," Elaine snapped. Johan started. He'd begun to walk forward without quite realising what he was doing. "You don't know what other traps there are in here."

Johan flushed in embarrassment. He'd been the victim of enough pranks to *know* the dangers and yet the magic had influenced him, pulling him into the chamber. Elaine gave his hand a gentle squeeze, then leant forward, waving her wand in the air. The runes seemed to glow brighter for a second; the magic field flickered, then steadied itself.

"Interesting," Elaine mused.

"That's not quite the word I would have used to describe it," Johan said.

Elaine nodded, one hand stroking her chin. "The pocket dimension must be directly above us," she said, slowly. "Anyone carrying out a check wouldn't have detected anything *below* such a concentration of strong magic, assuming they even bothered to look. The runes aren't just for preservation, Johan; they're for concealment. I don't think anyone, even an Inquisitor, could have found this place without help."

Johan frowned, feeling cold ice trickling down his spine. "So how did *we* find it?"

"We were looking for it," Elaine hazarded. He sensed her doubt and shared it. The Witch-King might have deliberately let them come to him, rather than push them away. "Unless his protections have been fading over the last few decades."

She waved her wand again. "It should be safe to walk closer," she added, "but don't stand on any of the runes. I think you'd regret it."

Johan nodded, then froze as he heard a creaking sound behind him. He turned and peered into the darkness, but saw nothing. The expression on the nearest statue looked faintly mocking … had it *changed*? He shared a glance with Elaine, tasting her concern. If he'd paid more attention to the statues …

"The magic is shifting," Elaine said, very quietly. "It's growing stronger."

The creaking sound echoed, again. Johan stared at the

statue, suddenly convinced it was alive and watching them. It shivered, suddenly; its arms rose and stretched, as if it were waking up from a long sleep. Elaine bit out a curse and pulled him back, into the chamber, as more statues came to life. Their angelic faces were twisted with bitter hatred as they turned to face the intruders. Johan reached for his magic, trying to focus his mind. They were trapped …

"Don't step on the runes," Elaine reminded him. She pointed her wand at the closest statue, but seemed unwilling to try anything. "The magic is changing, pouring downwards …"

She sucked in her breath, sharply. "The pocket dimension," she hissed. "It's practically *built* from raw magic. The Witch-King is sucking the power down into his tomb."

Johan whirled around. Raw magic was flickering over the coffin, dancing pulses of blue light that reminded him of the wave of magic Deferens had unleashed on Ida. He gritted his teeth as the runes started to glow brighter than ever before, shaping the magic that would return the Witch-King to life. Elaine threw a spell at the nearest statue, a blasting curse that should have smashed it to atoms, but the spell came apart long before it touched the stone. Inch by inch, the statues advanced, pushing them deeper into the chamber.

"The runes are breaking up spells," Elaine said, sharply. "Take my hand …"

A statue lunged forward and grabbed her. Johan let out a yell and jumped for her, only to be caught by another statue and dragged backwards. A cold hand grabbed his neck and lifted him into the air, turning him around so he could see the glowing coffin. Elaine managed to work a spell, but all that happened was that the air shimmered faintly before the magic was absorbed into the Witch-King's runes. Johan reached for his power, then stopped. It was hard to control it without Elaine.

He kicked out at the statue, to no avail. Elaine was struggling frantically, but the statue held her firmly. Her wand dropped from her hand and hit the ground; a statue, moving with surprising speed, picked the wand up and snapped it. Elaine kept struggling until her captor froze, holding her firmly in place. Johan's captor locked solid seconds later.

A cracking sound echoed through the chamber. Inch by inch, the coffin was starting to open as the magic poured forward. Cold fear ran through Johan's mind as he realised they'd failed, that they'd made a deadly mistake. They should have blasted the coffin the moment they'd recognised what it was, although he suspected the runes would have kept it safe. But it was too late. The Witch-King was rising …

… And he was going to deal with them personally.

He reached for Elaine's mind, trying to touch her one final time. But the bond refused to work properly. He could sense her presence, but no more.

"I'm sorry," he called, as *something* started to rise out of the coffin. "I love you!"

Chapter Twenty-Five

Elaine was utterly petrified as the Witch-King rose from the grave.

She felt her body locked by fear, her eyes unable to look away. She'd expected a decaying body, one animated by the sheer force of the Witch-King's will, but instead there was a glowing skeleton, wrapped in blue fire. Raw magic, she realised numbly; the Witch-King had drawn on the magic of the pocket dimension and used it to reanimate his body. He climbed out of the coffin slowly, moving with a slowness that convinced her that he had indeed been immobile for nearly a thousand years.

He's learning to reuse his body, she thought, frantically. *This* wasn't the handsome man who'd talked to her as she lingered on the verge of death, but something utterly inhuman. And yet, she knew him to *be* human. *But he will spend the rest of existence trapped in that monstrous shape.*

The Witch-King stretched out his arms. Elaine felt the statue's grip on her loosen, before it crumbled into dust and she fell to the ground. Johan let out a curse as he hit the stone floor; his captor had collapsed too, along with the others. Elaine looked at the remains of her wand, then started to stand upright. The Witch-King paid her no mind as she started to inch over towards Johan. Did he recognise the danger? Or was he so confident that he could handle the two of them united?

The bonds weren't so developed in his time, Elaine thought. They'd come later, along with many other forms of high magic. *He may not know half the magic I know, even if I can't use it.*

She froze as the Witch-King turned his head to look at her. Blue fire flared where his eyes should have been, mocking her. His bony hand reached out towards her, wrapped in blue fire, then pulled back as he gained more control. Elaine had to look away as the light grew brighter, stumbling backwards in horror and dismay. The Witch-King took a step forward, then another. She thought, for a moment, that he was taunting her, giving her the illusion that she could escape, before realising that he was still relearning how to use his body. The ground shook – she sensed a final flare of magic, high overhead – and then settled as the glowing runes started to wink out, one by one.

"Elaine," Johan shouted. She turned to see him running towards her, his clothes covered in dust. "Take my hand!"

Elaine reached out and grabbed hold as he pulled her backwards to the gate. Touching Johan felt immensely reassuring, even though she knew they'd made a deadly mistake. The Witch-King eyed them both through glowing blue eyes, then advanced forward. Elaine reached for her magic and threw a curse at the Witch-King, followed by a prank spell that had caught many more powerful magicians than herself off-guard. Both spells struck the Witch-King and vanished in the fire surrounding him.

His mouth lolled open, then closed slowly. Elaine stared, then allowed Johan to pull her through the gate as the Witch-King made a strangled sound. He was learning how to *talk* too; it wouldn't be long, she was sure, before he could start giving orders in person. Darkness fell over them like a shroud as they pelted up the corridor, but an eerie blue light followed them as the Witch-King walked after them. He didn't seem to be *hurrying*, she realised numbly; he hadn't even tried to stop them. They simply weren't important to him.

"Link our minds again," Johan insisted. "We can stop him together."

Elaine nodded, even though her mind was gibbering on the verge of panic. She knew, all too well, just what could happen to both of them. They'd lost, she thought; the Witch-King was free, walking slowly back to Ida. She could collapse the tunnels around him, but he had more than enough magic to burn himself free. Blue light flickered around them as the Witch-King walked into view, advancing with more confidence as he relearnt the skills. It wouldn't be long before he could speak too.

She held Johan's hand, then reached out and touched his mind. He touched her back, his fear merging with his determination to make up for their mistake by stopping the Witch-King; power surged around them both and lashed out towards the advancing lich. Light flared around him, the passageway melting as the magic pulsed though it, but the Witch-King was untouched.

He made a coughing sound. It took Elaine a heartbeat to realise he was *laughing*.

"Your magic is like mine," he said. His voice was so harsh that it was hard to make out the words, but Elaine thought she got the gist. "Do you really believe *I* could be beaten as easily as your pathetic stunted brother?"

Elaine felt Johan's shock as the magic faded away. He'd been able to do almost anything he'd put his mind to, once his powers had appeared. She'd seen him burn through invulnerable wards, turn someone into a *real* rat, steal a magician's magic, burn bridges to ash and raise a firestorm that had defeated the first attack on Ida. And yet the Witch-King had shrugged off his attack as if it were nothing. No, *less* than nothing.

The Witch-King didn't strike back. He just kept walking forward, driving them back as his magic pulsed on the air. Elaine saw statues falling apart as he drained the magic from them, coffins exploding as his gaze fell on them; she feared he would raise an army of undead before realising that he was drawing power from the preservation spells. Johan was on the verge of panic; Elaine bit her lip, grabbed his hand and summoned his power again, directing it at the ceiling. The roof melted, burying the Witch-King in molten rock. She hoped – prayed – it would be enough to stop him, but it exploded outwards seconds later. He kept walking forward, untouched.

"There has to be something we can do," Johan said.

"Maybe," Elaine said.

She'd never tried using the bond to analyse magic before, but she couldn't think of anything else. Looking at the Witch-King with her normal sensitivity was like looking into a brilliant sun. But when she merged her powers with Johan, she saw the magic that bound the Witch-King together, a complex array of spells in perfect working order. She'd never seen anything as clever, not even when she'd started rebuilding the defences of the Great Library. The Witch-King had the advantage of perfect spellwork as well as ancient power.

And yet … something was nagging at her mind.

"You will all fall before me," the Witch-King informed her, calmly. "You have failed."

Johan pulled his hand free, his hatred surging forward. Elaine barely had a second to brace herself before he lashed out with his power, his hatred sizzling on the air. The Witch-King seemed unmoved, but the tunnels started to shake violently, rocks and dust dropping from the low roof. Elaine swore as Johan threw more and more power into the attack, then tried to grab hold of him. The Witch-King did … *something* and she felt herself hurled away and straight into a stone wall. Dust was falling from overhead in a steady stream; she could feel tiny earthquakes shaking the ground. He was on the verge of bringing the whole tunnel system down around their ears!

Johan, she thought, trying to pick herself up. Her legs weren't functioning quite right; it took her several seconds to realise that they'd been cursed, cursed in a manner no one had seen for nearly nine hundred years. No one else would have a hope of breaking the curse. It was so dangerously subtle that even *she* had problems handling it.

Johan turned … and then the Witch-King knocked him back down the tunnels and out of sight. Elaine cringed as he turned his gaze on her, blue fire burning brightly in his eyes; she expected nothing but death. She was a threat to him, a threat he couldn't allow to remain in place; she cancelled the curse and staggered to her feet, hoping she'd have a chance to make her escape. But there was so much dust falling from above – the ground was still shaking – that she could barely breathe, let alone see. She was trapped …

The Witch-King waved a hand, dismissively. Elaine braced herself for death – or a curse that made the earlier curse look harmless – but nothing happened. Instead, he turned away and walked down the corridor, dismissing her. Elaine stared after him, then tried to sense Johan through the mental link. But he'd unleashed so much power that all she could sense were flashes of emotion, blindingly powerful. There was no way she could reach him. And then a handful of rocks fell behind Johan, cutting her off from the passageway.

She looked up. The roof was slowly starting to collapse.

Gritting her teeth, she turned and limped up the corridor, trying to call out to Johan as she moved. She hated the thought of leaving him – she had no idea what would happen to her if he died, given how closely they were linked – but she couldn't stay where she was. Johan's mind seemed confused, twisted between life and death, hatred and rage. She called to him again and again, but there was no response. And then she heard something cracking overhead …

Elaine forced herself to run as rocks fell, hammering down all around her. But it was far too late. Something struck the back of her head and she plunged into darkness.

***

Johan *knew* he'd made a mistake the moment he tried to draw on his hatred. He wanted the Witch-King dead – deader – but he hadn't understood, not really, that the Witch-King was actually more like him than Elaine. Given years of proper training – and centuries of planning, alone in the darkness – the Witch-King *had* to be capable of fighting him on equal terms. No, not *equal* terms; superior terms.

He struggled to rein in his anger as it spiralled out of control, slashing into the stone and hacking it apart. It was sheer damn luck the catacombs hadn't collapsed completely; vaguely, he remembered Elaine saying something about the mountains being solid stone, incredibly hard to mine. Dust swarmed through the air; he coughed, clearing his throat, as he saw blue light approaching him. The Witch-King seemed unstoppable.

He called Jamal a stunted magician, Johan thought, clenching his fists. It was possible the Witch-King meant that Jamal had lost his powers, but Johan had a nasty feeling he didn't. If the Witch-King regarded Jamal as stunted, even when he'd had his magic, it suggested all sorts of nasty things about the Witch-King's own powers. *But Dread stopped me with a rock to the head.*

"You have no idea how to use your powers," the Witch-King said. He stopped, standing a bare metre from Johan. The blue fire surrounding him didn't seem to warm the air. "I can teach you."

Johan felt a flicker of temptation, which he ruthlessly squashed. Elaine … was, at best, knocked out, somewhere on the other side of the rock fall. The Witch-King might have killed her … he suspected, intellectually, that if she died he'd die too, but he didn't know for sure. It wasn't something he wanted to test, either. The Witch-King had hurt Elaine badly, steering her life so he could use her as nothing more than a tool, and he was *damned* if he was betraying her.

"I wouldn't trust your lessons," he snarled, finally.

"Your appearance is odd," the Witch-King said. "I believed I had taken steps to ensure that *all* wild magicians died before they could use their powers."

"My father refused to kill me," Johan said.

"Indeed," the Witch-King said. "A most perplexing decision."

Johan stared at him. "You'd kill your own son?"

He knew the answer as soon as he'd framed the question. The Witch-King had buried himself for a thousand years, using mental influence to shape and change the society he'd left behind, just so he could rise into glory. *Of course* he'd kill his son. There couldn't be anyone related to him left! Even if there were blood descendents, the Witch-King wouldn't feel any particular loyalty to them.

"Your existence made your family vulnerable," the Witch-King stated. He turned his head from side to side slowly, studying Johan. "Your father should have disposed of you."

"I think you underestimate the love a father has for his son," Johan snapped.

"Your father allowed you to be tormented for seventeen years," the Witch-King pointed out, smoothly. "One or more of those pranks could easily have killed you, if there had been a tiny mistake. That isn't love, or concern. That's the sign of a man unable to take the hard decisions."

Johan swallowed. He didn't want to believe it, yet he had a

nasty feeling the Witch-King was right. His father hadn't killed him, but he hadn't done anything to stop Jamal either, at least until Jamal had finally managed to get into real trouble. Even then, he hadn't managed to do anything *effective*. Jamal had remained the same bullying asshole he'd always been right up until the day he'd died. Maybe their father hadn't dealt with the problems Johan's existence had caused, but he hadn't dealt with Jamal either. Johan's blood ran cold as he wondered, grimly, if his father had hoped there *would* be an accident.

I could have died, he thought. He started to shake as he remembered all the near-disasters, all the times he could have lost his powerless life. *And father's hands would have been clean.*

The thought chilled him to the bone. Jamal's idea of fun had been downright terrifying, but the younger siblings had been worse. Not out of malice, although he'd hated spending time as a doll or a pet, but out of sheer ignorance. They could have done something fatal without ever realising what had happened. Hell, their father could have wiped their memories of the accident and told them that Johan had fled the house for good. None of them would miss him enough to start looking for him.

"He should have killed you," the Witch-King said.

"But he didn't," Johan said. He reached for Elaine again, but felt nothing. Was she dead? Or was the Witch-King interfering with the bond? It had surprised him the first time, after all. He wouldn't let it be used against him again. "I'm still alive."

"*That* is a matter of opinion," the Witch-King said. He held out one flaming hand. Johan leant backwards, unwilling to risk touching the raw magic. Even *he* knew it could be very dangerous. "Swear your oath to me and I will teach you how to use your powers properly."

"No," Johan said.

"You will almost certainly kill yourself," the Witch-King said, dispassionately. He didn't seem particularly concerned, although Johan had the odd sense that it was a genuine offer. But then, if he swore an oath, he would be trapped. "Don't you want to live?"

"Not with you," Johan hissed. *Elaine*? What had happened to Elaine? "What did you do to her?"

The Witch-King shrugged. "Does it matter?"

"Yes," Johan said. Rage flared through him; he drew on his power and threw it at the Witch-King, trying to wipe him from existence. The power grew stronger and stronger, but the Witch-King remained unmoved. His survival only made Johan madder; he gathered everything he could and pushed it at his enemy. "I want you dead!"

The Witch-King made a gesture with one hand. Johan had only a moment to recognise the spell before a strange calm descended on his mind. His rage was literally snuffed out of existence. It was a calming spell, he recognised numbly; he'd had similar spells cast on him more than once, when he'd been a child. But this one was so strong he literally felt nothing beyond a dull sense of his own existence.

"It is far too late for that," the Witch-King said. He turned his gaze towards a tunnel leading away from Ida. "Come with me."

"No," Johan said. It was hard to remember *why* he shouldn't listen to the Witch-King – the numbness was seeping into his thoughts – but he forced himself to think of Elaine. And yet, the more he thought about her, the harder it was to remember why he should care. "I won't …"

The Witch-King crooked a finger. Johan felt himself picked off the ground and pulled along behind the ancient sorcerer as he walked onwards, through a tunnel that actually went further and further under the ground. He tried to break free, but it was impossible to care about what was happening, even though he *knew* he would be killed. The tunnel widened suddenly, revealing a rapidly darkening sky … was it really night-time already? It had been midday when they'd descended into the catacombs …

"It has been so long," the Witch-King said, pausing to look up at the sky. "I have missed it."

He turned his head slowly, looking up towards Ida. Johan felt himself rolled over; the city was illuminated by glowing lights, but the fires looked to be gone. Part of his mind noted that Deferens might be sending more soldiers to attack at night, yet it was hard to remember why that was important.

The Witch-King gazed at the city for a long moment, his skull-like face unreadable.

"They have forgotten me," he said. In the distance, Johan could hear a group of soldiers approaching. It didn't feel like a problem, even though cold logic suggested otherwise. "But now they will remember."

He turned to Johan and reached out with one flaming fingertip. There was a pulse of magic as he touched Johan's forehead …

… And Johan blacked out.

Chapter Twenty-Six

Charity had expected the Emperor to be furious.

She'd braced herself for his temper, even though he'd never struck her; she'd braced herself for blows or humiliation or even death. But instead, the Emperor merely called off the attack, ordered General Vetch to prepare a second offensive once reinforcements arrived and returned to his tent to meditate. Charity looked in on him an hour later and found him sitting on his chair, staring at nothing and mumbling to himself. She closed the flap as quietly as possible and slipped away. He couldn't give her any orders if she wasn't there to hear them.

It was hard for her to be sure – she'd never had to care about the opinions of her inferiors before – but morale in the camp seemed to be low. Thousands of men were dead, the previously-invulnerable dragons had been crippled and Ida still stood above World's Gate, mocking them. Charity had no idea what had caused the firestorm that had slaughtered the advancing troops and nor did anyone else, judging by their whispered comments. The general consensus seemed to be that an angry god had reached down and blotted the advancing forces from existence.

She caught sight of a black-robed Inquisitor standing at the edge of the camp and wandered over to him. He turned to face her as she approached, something damned and suffering in his eyes. Charity understood; he'd sworn oaths that bound him to the Emperor, in the certain knowledge there was *no* Emperor. But now there *was* an Emperor and the oath-sworn had to obey him or die. It would be hard for any of them to summon the drive to force their oaths to kill them. Charity knew *she* didn't have the determination to push the oath to break her.

"Night is falling," the Inquisitor said. A low rumble echoed through the ground, then faded away into nothingness. "Night is falling and something is wrong."

Charity gave him a sharp look. Earthquakes? Was Roth trying to trigger an earthquake? No, the Emperor would have had to order it and the Emperor had remained in his tent. It had to be something else, but what? Even if the Queen of Ida was prepared to countenance her sorcerers being sacrificed to power a spell – and if the sorcerers were willing to be sacrificed – they couldn't have enough sorcerers to make a difference. Another tremor ran through the ground and she shuddered. In the distance, birds were spiralling upwards, shocked from their perches. A handful of tiny animals appeared from nowhere and ran into the distance, squeaking in shock. Something was *definitely* wrong.

"I'm sorry," she said, quietly. She'd surrendered to the Emperor, but the Inquisitor had sworn his oaths in good faith. "It wasn't your fault."

The Inquisitor gave her a look that made her take a step backwards, just as the ground shook again. He blamed himself, she saw; he hated what he'd become, what the Emperor had made of him ... and yet he could do nothing. The Emperor would never release him from his oaths, if only because he'd try to *kill* the Emperor the moment he was free. All he could do was follow orders, search for loopholes and pray that someone killed him before it was too late.

But it's already too late, Charity thought. She'd been spared some of the darker tasks, but she'd done enough to ensure her damnation once she died. Taking the children from the Peerless School for the first sacrifice had been quite bad enough. The gods would spit on her in horror, then discard her into the deepest darkest hell-pit they could find. *There's no way out for us.*

The ground shook, one final time. Charity blinked in surprise as she saw a flash of blue light to the west, where the mountains rose steeply into the darkening sky. There were patrols out there, watching and waiting in case the defenders tried to mount a counterattack, but nothing else ... surely, no one would be experimenting with raw magic so far from the camp? It wouldn't be safe ...

Because the locals hate us, she thought, bitterly. Most of the population had either fled to Ida or vanished into the mountains, but enough remained to keep their homes firmly barred shut against all intruders. She wouldn't put it past them to sneak out at night and cut the throats of a few unwary soldiers. *They'll never forgive us for what we've done.*

There was another flash of blue light, then nothing. The Inquisitor stirred, his eyes narrowing in concern, as Charity heard booted feet striding up behind her. She turned, then fell on her knees as she saw the Emperor, wearing a long golden cloak that concealed his red garments and bare legs. Maybe he honestly didn't feel the cold, she thought. He wasn't wearing *that* much more than her.

The Emperor didn't look at her or the Inquisitor. Instead, he just waited; his hands resting firmly by his side. Roth appeared moments later, flanked by Moeder; the older woman looked tired, as if she'd been drugged. There was nothing at all in her eyes.

"Fetch the crystals," the Emperor ordered, curtly. He jabbed a finger at the frost-covered ground in front of him. "Place them all here."

"Yes, Your Supremacy," Roth said.

He bowed and hurried back towards his tent. Charity could hear him barking orders to the slaves, who started to unload the remaining crystals from the carts and carry them over to the Emperor. Charity frowned as the small pile of glowing crystals grew larger and larger, wondering just what was going through the Emperor's mind. Was he planning to turn the stockpiled magic against Ida? Or force Charity or the Inquisitor to channel the power? Or did he have something else in mind. She tasted the raw magic brushing against her mind and fought down the impulse to turn and run. She'd heard enough stories about people who'd had close encounters with raw magic to know it wasn't safe to remain near such a high concentration for long.

But this isn't a natural concentration, she thought. Powerful magicians came from regions contaminated with wild magic ... but so did all sorts of abominations. Werewolves, vampires, mermaids, trolls, goblins ... creatures that, at best, would never be considered fully human. *Surely the Emperor wouldn't be standing so close if there was any real danger.*

She glanced up as she saw another flicker of blue light, then froze as a handful of figures emerged from the darkness. Five soldiers and … she heard Roth's stunned curse as the sixth figure came into view, a glowing skeleton wrapped in blue fire. The sheer *presence* would have sent her to her knees, if she hadn't been kneeling already. No one, not even her father or Light Spinner, had such a presence. Enough magic to burn the camp to ash pulsed on the air, centred on the glowing figure. She knew, without a doubt, that resistance was futile.

It took her a moment to see the final figure, floating helplessly in the air behind the glowing skeleton. Charity peered into the darkness and flinched in surprise as she recognised Johan: bruised, battered, unconscious and very clearly a prisoner. The Emperor, the only person who hadn't fallen to his knees, took a step forward and bowed once, as if to an equal. There was a long pause, pregnant with menace, and then the skeleton bowed back.

"The crystals are yours," the Emperor said. His voice was twisted, as if he were fighting a compulsion curse. Charity looked from one to the other, trying to understand what was happening. The Emperor didn't seem happy. "Take them."

The glowing skeleton nodded, then made a gesture with one hand. Johan dropped to the ground and lay still. Charity started forward instinctively, then froze as the skeleton looked directly at her. She could see blue fire flaring around its eyes, as if its skin had been replaced by raw magic. The force of its gaze held her utterly immobile …

… And then it turned and walked towards the crystals. Charity slumped, forcing herself to watch as the skeleton picked up the first crystal. There was a brilliant flash of white light; the crystal flickered, then died. The skeleton had absorbed the magic … one by one, it consumed the other crystals, the blue fire growing brighter and brighter. Charity couldn't move as the last of the crystals died; the skeleton seemed to hesitate, just long enough to worry her, then turned and beckoned to Moeder. The woman stumbled forwards and knelt before the skeleton.

Charity's eyes narrowed. *What is she doing …?*

Moeder bowed her head. The skeleton touched her hair

lightly with one glowing hand. Blue fire flared over Moeder's body, although it didn't seem to be hurting her. Charity watched, torn between awe and horror, as long seconds passed, trying to work out what was happening between them. And then Moeder fell forward and hit the ground, breaking the connection; the blue fire surrounding her flickered and died. The skeleton looked at the Emperor for a long moment, then turned and walked away from the camp. Charity thought it would turn towards Ida, but instead it seemed to be heading south, back the way the army had come.

"By all the gods," Roth breathed. "Your Supremacy?"

Charity looked at the Emperor. He was frozen, seemingly unable to move. She felt a moment of hope that he might be completely gone, then shuddered inwardly as his entire body jerked. He took one look at the dead crystals, then turned to peer down at Johan. The Emperor's eyes seemed to almost look *past* him for a long moment before they focused on Johan's face.

"Charity," the Emperor said. He sounded ... odd, as if he still wasn't quite himself. "Johan is our prisoner. You will take him to your tent, secure him and feed him Amanda's Draught every two hours."

"Yes, Your Supremacy," Charity said. She hesitated. "May I use magic?"

"If you must," the Emperor said. "Roth; you will take Moeder to her tent and leave her there, under guard. Should she recover, she is not to leave."

He paused, a cold smile flickering across his face. "General Vetch?"

"Yes, Your Supremacy?"

"You are to rally the troops and prepare for a final assault on Ida, to be launched as the dawn breaks," the Emperor said. "We have been visited by a god. Our mission is blessed. Make sure the troops *know* what happened."

He looked at the soldiers who'd escorted the god – Charity had some trouble believing the skeleton was a god, but she was unable to deny the sheer sense of power that had surrounded the entity – and smiled at them.

"You are promoted up one rank," the Emperor said. "You

are to tell everyone you know what you saw and make them understand what it means. A god has come from the heavens to assist us. We cannot fail."

The soldiers bowed in unison. "Yes, Your Supremacy."

Charity sighed as her oaths forced her over to Johan. Up close, he didn't look as badly injured as she'd thought, but she cast a pair of diagnostic spells anyway. She wasn't quite sure why he was stunned; it looked like spell damage, yet she didn't recognise the spell or see any easy way to counter it. Gritting her teeth, she cast a levitation spell of her own and lifted Johan up into the air, carrying him over to her tent. The troops were already talking in low voices as she walked past them, rumours already spreading wildly out of control. It sounded as though the Emperor had been personally blessed by a senior god.

She shook her head in dismay. There were hundreds of thousands of gods, ranging from the household gods that protected families to the greater gods who laid down the law for their believers and punished wrongdoers. The Empire had recognised most of the gods, but there was no reason why someone couldn't worship whatever they wanted. They were all *real*, after all, even if only a handful of people worshiped a particular god. But now ...

What does it mean, she asked herself, *if a real god is walking the earth?*

The Emperor had said the entity was a god, but if the Emperor had told her it was a sunny day she would have dressed for the rain. She simply didn't *trust* the Emperor; he'd enslaved her, humiliated her and was in the process of tearing his empire apart. And that meant the creature *wasn't* a god. But if it wasn't a god, what *was* it?

She laid Johan down on the bed and hesitated. The Emperor had told her to secure him, but what did that mean? Chains? Or merely tie his hands and feet to the bed? She knew a hundred spells that could keep him docile and enslaved ... except those spells might no longer work. He'd developed an odd kind of magic, after all. She looked down at him for a long moment, then looked around for something she could use to tie his hands to the headboard. It might not be enough to immobilise him completely, but it would be a good faith attempt to carry out the Emperor's commands.

The tent opened, revealing a grim-faced Inquisitor. "I have chains for you," he said. His face was impassive, but Charity saw horror in his eyes. He'd either seen the entity or heard the rumours running through the camp. "The Emperor has commanded that he is to be as close to immobile as possible, without the use of magic."

"Thank you," Charity said, sourly.

She stepped back and watched as the Inquisitor chained Johan up, spreading his arms and legs until he could barely twitch. Charity sighed – the Emperor clearly thought that Johan needed to be able to move to work magic – and then started to pick through the small stockpile of potions ingredients she'd been allowed to bring with her. Amanda's Draught was not actually hard to brew, but she couldn't help feeling nervous as she put the ingredients together and waited for the potion to boil. It always took longer when she wasn't at ease with herself.

"Make sure it's cool enough to drink before you force it down his throat," the Inquisitor warned. "The Emperor will want to talk to him later."

"Of course," Charity said. She doubted she could have hurt Johan, even if she hadn't been ordered to look after him. He was her brother, after all. "What *was* that … that *thing*?"

The Inquisitor turned to look at her. "What sort of *god* requires a source of magic?"

Charity stared down at the bubbling liquid. Gods didn't need *anything*, although she had heard whispers about sects that claimed the gods were actually dependent on humanity rather than the other way round. They tended to keep their heads down in civilised cities. But the Inquisitor was right. What sort of god needed magic?

"I don't know," she said. Her own family traced its bloodline back to the gods, but she couldn't help wondering if that was a lie. It wasn't as if the records were *that* good, past five or six hundred years. And besides, if magicians came from the gods, how did one explain mundane-born magicians? Were they the children of gods? "But if it needs magic, is it actually a god?"

"Quite," the Inquisitor said, bitterly. "But it doesn't matter.

All that matters, right now, is that the entire camp *believes* that it's a god."

He bowed and retreated. Charity watched him go, then tested the potion, decided it was cool enough to drink safely and poured a small amount into a beaker. It had been years since she'd had to force-feed anyone potion – they'd been taught how to do it at school, but she hadn't gone into healing – yet it was simple enough. She used a very minor spell to trigger the swallow reflex as she poured the warm liquid into his mouth.

Johan gasped once, then shuddered. Charity winced in sympathy. Amanda's Draught deadened emotion, *all* emotion. It wasn't addictive, technically, but it tended to be difficult to stop using it, once the drinker had grown accustomed to life without feeling. And the Emperor had ordered her to make sure he drank it every two hours. Coming off it was not going to be easy. She might have to leave him chained up until he got over the emotional breakdown, if he ever did.

"I'm sorry," she whispered. She half-hoped he'd throw up, but his stomach seemed to accept the draught. He was used to drinking potions, just like everyone else. She even remembered him trying to make them, when they'd been younger. "I don't have a choice."

She braced herself, then started to probe at the stunning spell. The Emperor hadn't said she couldn't wake him up, after all. It was hard to see just how the spell worked – she had never seen anything like it, even in the family's private library – but a shock *should* break the spell and wake Johan. Or so she hoped ... she pushed her fears aside and jabbed him with a stinging hex. Her cheeks burnt with embarrassment as she remembered using hexes on him before, as a joke; she hoped, despite herself, that the potion had worked. If Johan had truly killed Jamal ...

He might kill me too, she thought. In some ways, it would be a relief. After being a slave, she understood perfectly how Johan had felt while he was growing up. *And I would deserve it for everything I did to him.*

Johan twitched once and opened his eyes.

"Elaine?"

"No," Charity said, softly. Elaine? The Head Librarian? "It's Charity, Johan. You're a prisoner in the Emperor's camp."

Chapter Twenty-Seven

"Elaine?"

Elaine barely heard the voice. She hurt. Every last part of her hurt. It was hard, so hard, to think straight; her mind hazed in and out of awareness, leaving her wondering if she was imagining the voice. And then she felt something hot touching her cheek, snapping her awake. She was surrounded by bright lights ...

"Elaine, it's Daria," the voice said. "Can you hear me?"

"... Yes," Elaine managed. Her throat hurt badly. "Where ..."

"You have to lie still," Daria warned. "You're in *terrible* shape."

Elaine shuddered, trying to recall what had happened. The Witch-King had slapped her aside, rocks had been falling ... she must have been caught in the rock-fall and crushed. Except ... she was still alive, if barely. One of the more complex protections she'd woven into her skin must have saved her life. And Daria ...

"You found me," she breathed.

"Not easily," Daria said. Her voice was very grim. "Elaine, I need to get you out of here ..."

"Cast a freeze spell, the strongest you can," Elaine ordered. It would hurt badly, but she couldn't think of anything else that Daria could do. "Freeze me, then get me up to the druids."

Daria hesitated. "Are you sure?"

"Yes," Elaine said, flatly. "Do it."

She wanted to scream as the spell took effect. The pain grew stronger, hacking away at her mind, but she forced herself to push it to one side. Her body shook violently as Daria pulled her out of the rocks and levitated her down the corridor. It crossed her mind that she might already be doomed – she'd probably lost a great deal of blood – but the freeze spell should keep any further damage from occurring until the druids managed to go to work. The real problem was her sanity; the freeze spell made it impossible for her to do anything about the pain. People had been known to go mad when the spell had been used to torture them.

Her eyesight seemed blurred, as if the world was slowly fading into darkness. Daria would have far better night vision than her, she recalled, but it needed *some* source of light ... sparks seemed to flash across her eyes as they moved further up the tunnels, Daria pulling her along as hard as she dared. By the time they passed through the stone doors and hurried up to the palace, Elaine was fighting desperately to keep herself conscious. Her thoughts were threatening to blur into madness.

"By all the gods," a voice said. "How is she still alive?"

"Magic," Daria said. Elaine felt a table underneath her back, then caught sight of a dark figure looming over her. "Elaine, I'm going to have to release the spell ..."

"Wait," the voice ordered. "Let me prepare a second spell first ..."

Elaine braced herself ...

... And opened her eyes, feeling sore.

"Elaine," Daria said. She was standing next to Elaine's bed, looking down at her with anxious eyes. "How are you feeling?"

"Sore," Elaine said. "What ... what happened?"

"You survived being half-buried in rocks," the unfamiliar voice said. A man wearing the long white robes of a druid came into view, one hand burnishing a golden wand. "You should have died in the catacombs."

"I know," Elaine said. She forced herself to sit upright and realised she was naked. She had always been pale, but now it looked as though half her skin had been cut off and regrown rapidly. It would be weeks before she stopped looking like a pink and white patchwork. "We failed. He's free."

He must have believed I was dead, she thought, numbly. The rocks should have been enough to smash her flat. If one of her protections hadn't held her in suspension, they *would* have been. *But he's on the loose now.*

She reached out for Johan and felt, again, the sense of

presence … and nothing else. "Johan?"

"I didn't find him," Daria said. "The passageway below where I found you was blocked completely, Elaine."

"I'm not surprised," Elaine said. If she could still feel Johan, he wasn't dead. But the Witch-King might have a use for him, if he'd kept Johan alive. Unless Johan was trapped beneath the rocks too. His magic might have protected him from death. "What happened to you?"

"I met up with the Travellers and convinced them to come with me to Ida," Daria said, bluntly. "When we got there, the army was blocking the way, so I sneaked forward once the army fell back and headed up to Ida. Nearly got myself skewered by an arrow before I managed to make myself known to Dread. He sent me down to look for you."

"He's not going to be pleased with me," Elaine muttered. She shook her head – it couldn't be helped – and swung her legs over the side of the bed. "Help me up?"

"I would advise you to stay in bed," the druid said. "It took me five hours to repair all the damage, young lady."

Elaine looked down at her naked body. There were no scars, but when she drew on her magic she could feel just how much work he'd done. Her bones had practically been rebuilt, her muscles regrown … her skin itched, badly. Her protections must have made it easier for him, she reasoned. And yet she'd still come to the brink of death.

"There isn't time," she said. The Witch-King was on the loose, Johan was missing and Deferens was still out there, perched at the foot of the mountain. "I need to see Dread."

Daria smiled. "You are going to dress first, I take it?"

Elaine nodded. The druid passed her a set of clothes, a comfortable shirt and trousers that looked to have been hastily cleaned. She wondered if they came from one of the dead – Ida wasn't the kind of place where possessions were buried with dead bodies – then decided she didn't want to know. All that mattered, right now, was that they fitted. She glanced at herself in the mirror and nodded to herself. She looked decent.

Daria held her arm to steady her as she made her way from the room. "I see you and Johan have been busy," she said. "How was it?"

Elaine flushed. "Very good, thank you," she said, crossly. Daria had had hundreds of boyfriends; Elaine had had only one, before Johan. "Do I still smell of him?"

"And the happy smell of two bodies coupling," Daria said. She helped Elaine up a long flight of stairs and into the war room. "We'll find him again, I promise."

"I hope so," Elaine said. Dread and Sacharissa were leaning over a map, one showing the lands around Ida. "We failed."

"So I gathered," Dread said. He didn't sound angry, thankfully. "And you're lucky to be alive."

Elaine nodded as she stumbled into a chair. It might have been wrong to sit in the Queen's presence, but her legs felt as if they were on the verge of buckling. Sacharissa gave her a concerned look, her eyes deeply worried. Dread, next to her, looked tired. Too tired.

"The army is still down there," Dread said, softly. "I have a feeling they're going to launch a final attack as soon as dawn rises. Once that happens ..."

Elaine nodded. Ida's defences had been badly weakened, while Johan was missing; a second attack, using the same techniques, might just break through the walls and open the city to invasion. Once the walls fell, Ida was doomed. Deferens could just keep feeding troops into the city until the population was exterminated. But what was the Witch-King doing?

"He's free," she said, and outlined what had happened in the catacombs. "What is he doing?"

"Unknown," Dread said. "He may have displaced Deferens or he may have headed somewhere else."

Elaine looked down at her hands. If the Witch-King assumed she was dead ... she shook her head. She probably didn't matter any longer. The one chance to stop the Witch-King before he rose from the catacombs had been lost. For all she knew, the Witch-King and Deferens intended to raise the siege and go ... where? What did the Witch-King actually *want*?

He thinks of himself as a god, she thought, coldly. *Would he try to force people to worship him?*

"He's too powerful to be stopped easily," she mused.

Something was nagging at her mind, something she was missing. "I think he combines both wild and high magic ..."

She broke off as it struck her. "My mother," she said. "What happened to her?"

Daria gave her an odd look. "Your mother?"

"We don't know," Dread said. "She vanished after attacking you ..."

"... And stealing the knowledge from my mind," Elaine finished. "I know more about high magic than the Witch-King – I must; I have a thousand years of knowledge on him."

"True," Dread agreed, after a moment. "Even if his agents kept him abreast of magical research, it couldn't be as comprehensive as your knowledge."

"So he took the knowledge from my mother," Elaine said, slowly. "But then ... what does he want it *for*?"

"Power," Daria said. "You were teaching people how to cast spells with reduced power. I'm sure he'd find that knowledge useful, even if he has more raw power than a bad-tempered Inquisitor."

"Perhaps," Elaine said. It wasn't something she could have taught a powerful magician, not when showing off was half of the reason they used such powerful spells. And yet, she had the odd feeling that Daria had put her finger on the core of the problem. Did the Witch-King have a reason to want to conserve power? "I ..."

It hurt to laugh, but Elaine found herself snickering as the pieces slowly fell into place. No *wonder* Deferens had launched an assault on Ida. No *wonder* he'd been so obsessed with capturing her and bringing his army to the mountain state. No *wonder* the Witch-King had waited so long before emerging. It all made a horrific kind of sense.

Dread cleared his throat. "Is there a *reason* you're sniggering like a girl?"

"She *is* a girl," Sacharissa pointed out, elbowing him.

Elaine gathered herself. "I'll have to run through the numbers," she said, "but I think the Witch-King needs an influx of power to keep himself alive. He's practically *made* of raw magic."

"Hellfire," Dread swore. "He's not a true lich?"

"I don't think so," Elaine said. "But then, no lich has ever been recorded to last over a thousand years."

She took a long breath. "If he runs out of magic, he comes apart at the seams," she added, carefully. "Deferens came here so quickly, sacrificing hundreds of magicians along the way, to build up the magical reserves the Witch-King would need to sustain himself. He wants the knowledge I have to reduce his power consumption to extend his life."

Dread frowned. "But if he needs magic to live …"

"If he manages to drop down a level or two," Elaine interrupted him, "he could probably survive for centuries simply by absorbing magic from a handful of sacrifices."

"Or convincing people to give him magic willingly," Daria offered. "There are ways to share magic, aren't there?"

Elaine nodded. It wouldn't be hard, either; she could easily see several different rituals that could be adapted to fuel the Witch-King. He'd have to start a breeding program for magic-users, but it wouldn't be hard. Deferens had already wiped out or subverted most of the institutions that might try to stop him.

He wanted to trigger the breakup of the Empire, she thought, numbly. *Get the kings free of their bonds, then encourage them to start fighting their neighbours and scrabbling for real power. And in the meantime, the Witch-King rebuilds his power and then moves out to put the Empire back together on his terms …*

"We have to find Johan," she said. A thought had occurred to her, but she'd need Johan to help. "I can still sense him."

"It's not going to remain dark for long," Daria warned. "If Johan is outside the tunnels, Elaine, he may well be a prisoner."

The Witch-King might find a use for him, Elaine thought. Taking over another body wouldn't be easy, but it could be done as a last resort. *And he already knows how to adapt Johan's power to use high magic.*

"We have to find him," she said, firmly. She couldn't sense Johan beyond a vague awareness of his existence, but she could overcome that problem. "I can triangulate his position, I think."

Dread and Sacharissa exchanged glances. "It would be

risky," Dread said. "You might be captured – *again*."

Elaine rubbed her forehead. *Everyone* seemed to want to capture her – but then, the knowledge in her head was literally priceless.

"There's no choice," she said, finally. "If Deferens launches a final assault on Ida, Your Majesty, can Ida survive?"

"Probably not," Sacharissa admitted. Her face darkened, slightly. "Our defences are almost broken."

"Then finding Johan may be the only hope you have," Elaine said. She stood, balancing herself carefully. "How long until dawn?"

Daria frowned. "Two hours, at best."

"Then we need to start now," Elaine said. She gave Daria a wink. "Coming?"

"I should come too," Dread said. "If nothing else, I can divert their attention while you make a run for it."

"Stay here," Daria advised. Her nose twitched, meaningfully. "Take some personal time."

Sacharissa blushed. Dread looked … *uncomfortable*. Elaine had to fight to keep her amusement from showing on her face.

"There's a war on," Dread said, finally.

"Then you might die tomorrow," Daria said. She held out an arm to Elaine. "We'll see you later."

She helped Elaine out of the room and down towards the walls. Elaine shuddered at the sight of scorched buildings, dead bodies and an entire dragon being dissected by the local butchers, then forced herself to concentrate on Johan. Her lover was down towards the edge of the mountains … she changed position and tried again, mentally linking the lines together. Johan, unless she was very much mistaken, was in the enemy camp. He had to be a prisoner.

"He's in the camp," she said, grimly. "How do we get past the guards?"

"I had a look at them on my way up," Daria said. "They didn't *look* very skilful … we could probably slip by them if we were invisible, provided someone jiggered the wards."

Elaine smiled. "I can do that," she said. "Let's go."

The walk down to the camp was nightmarish, even with a

werewolf helping her. Elaine nearly lost her footing a dozen times, something that would have meant certain death if she fell over the cliff and down onto the jagged rocks below. Dead bodies lay everywhere; a handful of dead dragons could be seen at the bottom, their scales glinting oddly in the moonlight. When the battle was finally over, Elaine suspected, the bodies would be cut up and sold. Entire fortunes would be made by the person who took possession of their hides.

"All right," Daria said, as they finally reached World's Gate. "The camp is just beyond."

Elaine cast invisibility spells over them both and then walked forward until she sensed the first ward protecting the camp. It wasn't as solid as she would have expected if Inquisitors had been involved in constructing it, but they might have taken advantage of another loophole in their orders. She touched it gingerly with her magic, carefully opened a gap and slipped through. A handful of patrolling soldiers came into view; she froze, careful not to move, as they walked past, their weapons clearly visible. If Deferens had any sense at all, they'd be trained to watch for invisible opponents.

Pity it isn't snowing, she thought. *That would have covered our tracks nicely.*

The soldiers walked into the distance, towards a mass of red and gold tents. Elaine closed her eyes, sensing Johan's presence, then swore under her breath as she opened them and saw the Inquisitors outside the tents. They *knew* how to fight magicians. It would be impossible to sneak past them without some kind of diversion, but what? They'd be trained not to panic when something went badly wrong.

Daria slipped up next to her. "I could shift into wolf form and attack ..."

"They'd kill you," Elaine whispered back. She concentrated, trying to reach Johan, but there was no response. Was he stunned? Or had his mind been wiped? If the Witch-King planned to take Johan's body for himself, he wouldn't want to deal with the previous occupant. "I think we need to look for a way to divert attention."

She slipped away from the tents and into the darkness,

trusting Daria's nose to allow her friend to stick with her. Hundreds of soldiers were kneeling on the ground, listening to a sermon from one of their own; he was ranting about a god he'd seen in person. Elaine remembered the Witch-King's appearance and shuddered. It was clear the Witch-King had come to the camp, taking the magic Deferens had collected and abandoning Johan. And he probably *would* be taken for a god if anyone saw him.

A pair of Inquisitors appeared, walking past the kneeling soldiers. Elaine didn't recognise either of them, but she could tell they were both feeling helpless. They'd seen the very worst of magics unleashed, magics they were sworn to stop and yet they could do nothing. She felt a flicker of sympathy ...

I could let them capture me, she thought. *They'd take me to Deferens ...*

And then what? Her thoughts answered. She knew Deferens too well to believe she could talk him into abandoning the Witch-King. *He wouldn't listen to a word you said. And even if he did, could he do anything? The Witch-King spent years turning him into a tool.*

She looked up at the mountains. Dawn was slowly starting to break.

Chapter Twenty-Eight

Johan opened his eyes. "Elaine?"

"No," his sister said. "It's Charity, Johan. You're a prisoner in the Emperor's camp."

Johan felt … no emotions. His body wasn't numb, as far as he could tell; he could feel iron manacles cutting into his wrists and ankles. But he felt nothing; no fear, no alarm … not even a hint of pleasure at meeting his sister again. He closed his eyes, trying to summon the magic, then cursed under his breath as he realised it was impossible. No matter how he tried, he couldn't make himself angry.

"Amanda's Draught," Charity said, apologetically. "The Emperor's orders."

"Oh," Johan said. He knew he should be angry, but it was impossible to muster any real concern. Deferens had drugged him to keep him unemotional. It was just a fact. "Do I have to be chained up?"

"The Emperor ordered it," Charity said. "I can't free you."

Johan nodded, then took a long look at his sister. She was wearing a faint wisp of silk over her breasts and another over her hips, barely covering her genitals. He couldn't help thinking of the pleasure slaves he'd seen, during his rare excursions outside the family home. And Charity was a slave … he knew he should be outraged, or even angry at her personally, but he still felt nothing.

"I see," he said. He reached out for Elaine, but there was nothing coming through the link, save for a vague sense that she was still alive. What had happened to her? "What happened?"

"An … *entity* brought you to the camp," Charity said. "The Emperor ordered me to look after you. I healed you up and then woke you."

"Once you drugged me," Johan said. The entity had to be the Witch-King. He couldn't think of anything – *anyone* –

else it could be. "And the Emperor himself?"

"Ordered another attack on Ida, to be launched at dawn," Charity said. She touched the knife at her belt gingerly. "There's barely a couple of hours left before the sun rises over the mountains."

Johan grimaced. If he hadn't allowed himself to get captured … it was hard to force himself to care, even though he wanted to curse himself with the vilest words he knew. *He* had been the only thing that had protected Ida from death and destruction and now he was in the enemy's camp, his powers neutered. He gritted his teeth and tried to summon a spark of anger, but felt nothing. Even if he managed to break free – he inspected what little he could see of the bed, only to discover it looked quite unbreakable – he still wouldn't be able to use magic.

"It's pointless," he said. If the Witch-King was free, Ida was no longer important. "Why is he doing it?"

"I don't know," Charity said. "He's odd, Johan. I don't understand him. Every so often, it's like a different person is talking through him."

Johan frowned. "One is," he said. "That entity you saw was the Witch-King. The Emperor is just another of his pawns."

Charity looked down at him in flat disbelief. "The Witch-King?"

"He's the power behind all the recent disasters," Johan told her. A thought occurred to him and he played with it, carefully considering just how to phrase his words. "Charity, there are times when he just shoves the Emperor right out of his body and takes over."

"But he's still issuing orders," Charity said.

"Yes, but they're not *his* orders," Johan said. He managed to lift his head, slightly. "As long as someone else is speaking through his mouth, the Emperor is effectively dead. He's certainly not in his right mind."

Charity's mouth opened and closed for a long moment. "Are you saying there are times when the Emperor isn't the Emperor?"

"Yes," Johan said. Would she see the implications? He didn't dare try to speak any plainer, not when she had to rationalise it for herself. Oaths were dangerous things. The only person he'd known who had managed to forsake one and survive was Dread and he'd had help. And it had still cost him his magic. "It's not him all the time. His mind is elsewhere."

"I see," Charity said. She touched her knife – Jamal's knife, Johan noted – again. "Can you swear to that?"

"I can swear that everything I've said is literally true," Johan told her. He wasn't sure if the oath would work. He'd tried to swear oaths as a teenager, in the hopes it would reveal some spark of power, but nothing had ever happened. Now ... he wasn't sure *what* would happen, if anything would. "Charity ..."

"I see," Charity said. She looked down at the ground, her body shaking slightly. "Johan, what happened to Jamal?"

"Dead," Johan said. "His body is somewhere in the mountains."

"Glad to hear it," Charity said. She was still playing with the knife. "Johan, what *happened* to us?"

Johan sighed. "The family?"

Charity nodded. Johan took a moment to organise his thoughts. The Witch-King had had a point, he suspected; their father had always been reluctant to make hard decisions. And yet ...

"Father was a failure as a father," he said, bluntly. "What happened to him?"

"I have no idea," Charity said.

Johan lifted his head, again. "Jamal is dead, I'm a prisoner, you're a slave ... the others? What happened to the others?"

"At the Peerless School," Charity said. "The Emperor left it alone."

"They're probably not going to be safe for long," Johan said. If the Witch-King needed sources of magic, the children at the Peerless School would make tempting targets; powerful enough to be useful, too young to defend themselves. "Where did the Witch-King go?"

"I don't know," Charity said. "Johan ..."

"The world is at risk," Johan said. He had a feeling he was going to need *days* to purge his system of the drug, even if he somehow managed to convince Charity to stop feeding it to him. "Charity, we have to stop him."

Charity looked back at him. "How?"

Johan closed his eyes in pain. They'd lost their best chance to stop the Witch-King when he'd been separated from Elaine … and that had been his fault. The Witch-King was staggeringly powerful – and, if he had Elaine's knowledge, he'd be able to use it too. Johan wasn't sure how that worked – he hadn't been able to use high magic, when he'd tried – but the Witch-King clearly had a solution. He was a terrifyingly intelligent enemy.

"I don't know," he said, opening his eyes. "But if that army overruns Ida, there will be no hope of stopping him."

"I see," Charity said, quietly.

Johan leant back on the bed. "What's happening to the rest of the world?"

"Falling apart," Charity said. "Kingdoms are declaring themselves independent everywhere."

"It doesn't suit Vlad Deferens," Johan said. "What is he doing about it? He should be giving orders to bring the kingdoms to heel. But instead, he's fixated on Ida. The *Witch-King* issued those orders."

He pushed his advantage. "Why would the Emperor cut his own throat? He wouldn't. It's just like Lord Gresham!"

Charity's face paled. She would know the story, of course; it had been quite a scandal before they'd moved to the Golden City. Lord Gresham had been crippled, thanks to a very nasty curse, but he'd managed to literally possess the body of his oldest son. It had only been through sheer luck that anyone had noticed, as far as Johan could recall; the Inquisitors, if he'd heard correctly, had discovered that Lord Gresham had swapped minds with his son, leaving the young man trapped in an elderly – and crippled – body. Jamal, of course, had found the story hilarious. Johan had wondered if their father had intended to do the same with Jamal …

But the important part of the story was that the victim's mind hadn't been in his body.

Charity stared down at him for a long moment, then turned and left the tent.

Johan scowled, pulling on the chains. They remained resolutely unbroken. The manacles cut into his wrists when he pulled too hard; he considered, briefly, trying to break his wrists into powder, before deciding it was unlikely to work very well. And even if it did, he would be trapped, in the heart of the enemy's camp, with neither hands nor magic. The only thing he could do was wait …

… And hope that Charity took the bait.

***

Charity wasn't sure *what* to think.

Her oaths bound her to the Emperor. She was his, body if not in soul; he could order her to do anything and she would have to obey. And yet, she *knew* the Emperor wasn't always himself. There had been times when she'd thought she'd seen another personality, someone else peeking out from his eyes …

… And if that were true, where *was* the Emperor?

Some of his decisions made sense, but others didn't … and he was not a particularly stupid man. Charity was *sure* he was *too* obsessed with Ida – and the Head Librarian – but not enough to throw away his Empire. He'd taken a major risk just claiming it for himself. The Golden Throne would have killed him if he hadn't shared the Royal Bloodline. And yet, he was practically destroying it. Just attacking Ida one final time would bleed his army white, even if he won. He might destroy Ida and her entire population and wind up losing the war.

But if Johan was right, the person who issued those orders wasn't the Emperor.

She stood outside the tent, thinking hard. Lord Gresham had proved it was possible to swap minds; he'd done it for years before he'd been detected. It had been years since she'd heard the story, but she was sure it had been erratic behaviour that had finally tipped off the authorities. The old man hadn't been prepared for the hormones of youth, if she recalled correctly. It was quite possible that the Witch-King was swapping minds with the Emperor every time he wanted a specific order given to the army …

And yet, the Emperor just seemed to take it in his stride.

But he could be under a spell, she thought. The most dangerous compulsion spells didn't *force* someone to follow orders, they encouraged someone to come up with good ideas for doing something. *He might just accept the change when he returns to his own body.*

Her thoughts hardened. *And if he isn't in his body …*

She touched the knife at her belt, then started to walk towards the Emperor's tent. It looked as if he were holding a staff meeting, outlining his plans for invading and occupying Ida; she saw a dozen guards outside, including three Inquisitors. She walked past them – they knew she was harmless – and into the tent, where she saw the Emperor holding court with General Vetch, Roth, an Inquisitor and several officers she didn't know.

"I want the castle stormed as soon as we're through the gates," the Emperor said, peering down at the maps of Ida. Charity had a feeling it wouldn't be easy to reach the castle – Ida was practically *designed* to stand off an invading army – but she knew the Emperor would just keep pouring men into the breach until it was all over. "The Queen is to be captured alive."

Poor bitch, Charity thought. The Emperor wouldn't allow her to live, certainly not as a free woman; she'd probably wind up enslaved, if she wasn't killed out of hand. *She needs to keep some poison – or a dagger – on hand at all times.*

"Your Supremacy," General Vetch said. "It would be easier to clear the houses first, then turn on the castle. It is not designed to withstand a long siege."

The Emperor's face shifted. "The inhabitants of the castle must be killed, save for the Queen," he ordered. "There is no time to waste on civilians."

Charity shivered. Now that Johan had pointed it out, it was easy to see the shift in personality. The Emperor was a bumptious combative man, someone who enjoyed humiliating her just for his own amusement; the other personality was cold, dispassionate, and even less concerned about casualties. She'd wondered if the Emperor had a split personality, but now she knew the truth. Someone else was swapping minds with him on a regular basis.

"The civilians will have time to rebuild their defences," General Vetch warned. "The castle won't last indefinitely …"

"They will surrender once their Queen is a prisoner," the Emperor snarled. "The castle is to be attacked first."

There was a long pause. "Your Supremacy," one of the other officers said. "The reports from Falcone's Nest claim that the pontoon bridges have been destroyed."

The Emperor's face shifted again. "Have them repaired!"

The officer looked nervous. "Your Supremacy," he said. "The garrison in Falcone's Nest doesn't have the manpower to force the locals to rebuild the bridges. Our reinforcements will be delayed, quite sharply."

If there are any, Charity thought. The Empire hadn't had a sizable land force for generations; it hadn't *needed* one. Deferens had built up a private army in his homeland, but it wasn't large enough to dominate the entire continent. The dragons should have tipped the scales in his favour, yet three-quarters of them were dead. *We might be alone out here.*

"Then order the garrison to burn Falcone's Nest to the ground," the Emperor snarled, slipping back to normal. "The city is to be completely destroyed!"

"They don't have any dragons," the officer insisted. "Can we send back a flock of dragons ..."

"They're needed for the assault on Ida," the Emperor said. "We do not have dragons to spare."

Because you need raw magic to summon them and you gave it all to the Witch-King, Charity thought, nastily. *Right now, you simply don't have enough magicians to generate enough power even if you threw them all under the knife.*

Another officer leant forward. "Your Supremacy, our situation is precarious," he insisted, smoothly. "Our logistics are very poor ..."

"Then strip World's Gate of every last morsel of food," the Emperor ordered.

The officer rose to his feet. "There isn't enough food in the town to feed the entire army, even with the recent losses," he insisted. "We can send out foraging parties, but the farmers will have already hidden their crops. Even if we succeed in finding corn and livestock, it will run out quickly. We need to fall back before the army starts to starve."

"Don't burden me with logistical problems," the Emperor snarled.

"The army will *die* if we stay here," the officer said. Charity admired his bravery, even though she had a feeling it was about to prove fatal. "Your Supremacy, we are already on short rations."

The Emperor's face shifted. "That will no longer matter after tomorrow."

Charity felt her blood run cold. *That* was not the Emperor.

"Your Supremacy," the officer said.

The Emperor lifted a hand. "Do you feel ready to challenge me?"

"No, Your Supremacy," the officer said, hastily. "But …"

"*Die*," the Emperor snarled.

Charity's hair stood on end as the Emperor cast a spell at the officer. He shrank rapidly, his body warping and twisting into a snail. Charity fought down the urge to vomit as the Emperor stood, walked over to the snail and stamped on it, hard. Several other officers turned pale and looked away. Charity half-expected the snail to return to a crushed human body, yet it stayed inhuman. She'd known the Emperor was powerful – he'd been a contender for Grand Sorcerer – but *that* powerful?

"The final attack will be launched in thirty minutes," the Emperor said, as he returned to his seat. "Once Ida has been destroyed and the population butchered, we will return to Falcone's Nest and punish those who dared interfere with our plans. Am I understood?"

"Yes, Your Supremacy," General Vetch said, hastily.

"Good," the Emperor said. "You are to prepare the troops. They are to be told – yet again – that we have the blessing of a god. You will make them understand that this assault will be decisive, that the destruction of Ida is an offering to our god."

"Yes, Your Supremacy," General Vetch said.

The Emperor rose. "Our god is with us," he announced. "Charity; come here."

Charity obeyed, helplessly. But at least she was closer to him.

"The god has already given us mastery over the Golden City and the Great Houses," the Emperor said. He reached out and stroked Charity's hair. "Now, we will take mastery over the kingdoms and secure our hold on the Empire."

"Your Supremacy," General Vetch said. "There will be much hard fighting to come."

"We have a god on our side," the Emperor insisted. He thumped the table to make his point, shaking the entire tent. "Victory will be ours."

"There's no need to attack Ida," General Vetch said. His face was frantic. Charity knew he was worried, yet he didn't dare oppose the Emperor. "We could win Ida, we could destroy Ida, and lose everything."

The Emperor's face shifted, becoming someone else. "Ida must be destroyed ..."

Charity braced herself, pulled Jamal's blade from her belt and shoved it right into the Emperor's chest. He'd *known* she was under his control. The thought of her striking him had never crossed his mind. He gasped, then staggered; the blade, charmed to cut through all defences as long as it was wielded by a Conidian, was instantly lethal. His face shifted back, too late; he collapsed to the floor, blood leaking from his wound.

"The Emperor is dead," General Vetch said. *He* hadn't seen it coming either. "I ..."

Charity ducked – too late – as Roth hurled a spell at her. She screamed in pain as the spell burnt through her protections, slicing into her body ...

... And then Roth exploded into bloody chunks as the Inquisitor cursed him from behind.

Chapter Twenty-Nine

Elaine and Daria were midway back to the tents when all hell broke loose.

The Emperor's tent exploded into fire, an Inquisitor standing in the middle of the blaze with flames lapping around his hands. Elaine had a moment to see the Emperor's body lying on the ground before she threw herself down; the Inquisitor shouted something in battle language and fired off a series of curses towards the red-robed magicians. The Inquisitors outside Johan's tent joined in seconds later, hurling their own spells into the battle.

"Stay down," Elaine hissed. Soldiers were running in all directions; some heading towards the magicians, others fleeing into the breaking dawn. The Emperor was dead; the Emperor was dead and all oaths to him were null and void. His magicians were powerful, but did they stand a chance against the Inquisitors? "We have to get to Johan!"

She pushed herself as low as she could, despite the cold, and crawled towards the tent. The battle was growing louder; five Inquisitors had banded together, magic shimmering around them as they strode towards their enemies. She felt a flicker of envy for the power they wielded so casually and forced herself to remember the cost as she reached the tent and opened the flap. Johan was lying on the bed, his arms and legs spread out and chained to the railings. He lifted his head as the flap opened, his eyes narrowing, but showed no other reaction.

"It's me," Elaine hissed. She dispelled the invisibility spell and stood up. "What happened?"

Johan smiled, but it looked twisted, as if he'd forgotten how to smile naturally. "Amanda's Draught," he said, as Elaine tried a spell to free his hands. Hot sparks flared around the manacles, stinging Johan's hands. "The Inquisitors provided the chains."

Elaine nodded, recalling the spells the Inquisitors used. The chains would be charmed to make any attempt to break them doomed to failure, perhaps even to kill the person they held if they were overwhelmed with stronger magic. She placed her hand on the lock for a long moment and muttered a charm so old she had a feeling even the Inquisitors didn't know it any longer. The charm faded away into nothingness; she worked a second spell and opened the locks, releasing Johan. He gave her a tight hug as he sat upright, but there was no real feeling in it. It would be hours, perhaps days, before he recovered the ability to *feel*.

"Don't worry about it," Elaine said. "You'll be better soon."

"I told Charity that the Witch-King swapped minds with Deferens whenever he wanted to issue orders," Johan said, as he lay down on the ground. "Did she believe me?"

"Someone must have killed the Emperor," Elaine said. Charity? It was possible, at least; Deferens would never have regarded her as a true threat. And if she genuinely *believed* that she was striking at the Witch-King, rather than Deferens, her oaths wouldn't have stopped her. "The Inquisitors are free."

"Good," Daria said. She sniffed the air as thunder cracked outside. "The battle is growing nastier."

"They might think we were to blame," Johan said, grimly. A spell burnt through the tent over their heads and vanished through the other side of the canvas. "What if *they* try to kill us?"

Elaine groaned. The Emperor was dead ... and yet, they were still in a mess. She briefly considered trying to sneak out of the tent, but it would run the risk of being caught up in the fighting. The gods alone knew what the Inquisitors would think. They'd know her as a Privy Councillor, she knew, but they swore their oaths to the Emperor and the Grand Sorcerer. The only person who might be able to talk to them on even terms was Dread.

The tent shook violently, then tore open. Three black-clad Inquisitors strode through the gash in the canvas, their eyes flashing with deadly fire. Elaine looked up at them and carefully held out her hands to reveal they were empty, hoping that both Johan and Daria would have the sense not to do anything that looked threatening. The Inquisitors had been through hell, forced to watch as Deferens made a mockery of their duties. They wouldn't be in a good mood.

"Lady Elaine," the lead Inquisitor said. His eyes flashed over her face for a long moment, silently confirming her identity. "What are you doing here?"

"Trying to free my apprentice," Elaine said, as he motioned her to her feet. "The Emperor is dead, right?"

"Correct," the Inquisitor said.

"And she's a Privy Councillor," Daria said, sharply. "That puts her in charge, doesn't it?"

The Inquisitor frowned. "There is *nothing* about this that is regular," he said, after a moment of thought. "Technically, I think we would have to find the next Grand Sorcerer."

"But in the interim between Grand Sorcerers, the Privy Council is in charge," Daria pressed, her voice hardening. She'd been betting on the outcome, Elaine recalled suddenly. "And as Elaine is the last one standing, that puts her in charge."

The Inquisitor smiled. "For the moment," he said, bowing his head. "Lady Elaine, I am Inquisitor Dolman. I am at your service."

Elaine breathed a sigh of relief as she tried to think what to do. She'd planned to sneak Johan out of the camp ... not take command. Hell, she *hated* being in command. Vane had served as her spokeswoman in the Great Library because she'd disliked facing the population. But she didn't have any choice.

"I need to know what's going on," she said, as the other Inquisitors bowed and left the tent, heading for the sound of battle. "What happened?"

Dolman tilted his head slightly, silently communicating with his fellows. "The Emperor was stabbed by Charity Conidian, who is currently in the Royal Tent under guard. We were free at once and attacked the red-robes before they could react to the sudden change. Most of them are dead now; the remainder have rallied the loyalists and retreated towards the Runnymede Gap. The conscripts are either in confusion or running into the countryside. We have secured the dragon pens and the twelve remaining dragons, but their riders are dead."

Elaine nodded, slowly. "Send a messenger to Ida," she ordered, after a moment. "Inform Dread that ..."

Dolman caught her arm. "Dread survived?"

"Sort of," Elaine said, carefully. She wasn't sure how the Inquisitors would react to a powerless Dread. "Inform him that the Emperor is dead and request he come down at once to take command of the remains of the army."

"Yes, My Lady," Dolman said.

"I can take the message," Daria volunteered. "They'd be more likely to listen to me than a stranger anyway."

"Good point," Elaine said, after a moment. She looked at Dolman. "The Witch-King came to this camp, I assume. What happened to him?"

"The skeleton, I assume," Dolman said. "He's no god, is he?"

"No," Elaine said. "Just a monster."

"He walked off towards the Gap," Dolman said. "We don't know where he went afterwards."

Elaine had a nasty suspicion she knew the answer, but there was nothing that could be done about it, at least not now. "I need to speak to Charity," she said. "Please escort me to her tent."

The camp looked as if a firestorm had struck it, she saw as they stepped out of the tent. A dozen tents were flaming ruins; hundreds of bodies lay everywhere, mainly red-robed magicians or personal guardsmen. Elaine winced as she saw a couple of dead Inquisitors, then frowned as she looked towards the soldiers. The conscripts, mostly terrified young men, were being watched carefully by the Inquisitors. They looked as though they expected to be marched to their own executions at any moment.

We'll have to do something about them, Elaine thought, grimly. *But what?*

She looked at Dolman, who seemed unperturbed by the violence. "What happened to the cities?"

"The Emperor looted them for men and materials he needed for the army," the Inquisitor said, flatly. "It will be a long time before any of them recover."

If they ever do, Elaine thought, as they reached the tent. *The Witch-King may have his own ideas about how to deal with them.*

Dolman paused, reaching for the flap. "Do you want messages announcing the Emperor's death sent to the other kingdoms, My Lady? It might delay civil war."

Elaine looked at Johan, who shrugged. It *might* delay civil war, but it wouldn't heal the damage Vlad Deferens had done to the Empire. His army had made itself supremely unpopular; by now, she couldn't really blame any of the kingdoms for declaring independence and building up armies of their own. How could *she* hold it together when someone as powerful as Light Spinner had failed in far more favourable circumstances?

And the Witch-King will already know Deferens is dead, she thought. There was no logical reason to keep it a secret from everyone else. Besides, she had a feeling that rumours were already spreading, just to keep the pot boiling. *We might as well try.*

"Send a message announcing the Emperor's death," she ordered, finally. "And tell them that the Privy Council" – it sounded better than claiming authority in her own name – "will endeavour to repair the damage he did to the Empire."

"Of course, My Lady," Dolman said.

"I'll go back to Ida," Daria said. She glanced at Dolman and smiled. "If Dolman will grant me an escort to the edge of the camp ..."

"It will be my honour, My Lady," Dolman said, gravely.

Elaine smiled as she stepped into the tent. Charity was sitting on the ground, her hands clasped in her lap and her eyes fixed on the body in front of her. A grim-faced Inquisitor was standing behind her, although it wasn't clear from his pose if Charity was a prisoner or merely under his protection. Elaine nodded to him and then turned her attention to the body. Even in death, Vlad Deferens *reeked* of perverted masculinity. The red shirt he wore was stained with his own blood; his legs, strong and muscular, carried the scars of countless nasty skirmishes as he'd fought his way to the top.

She closed her eyes for a long moment. Deferens had been

a jerk from the very moment they'd first met, a woman-hating monster who had seemed a serious contender for the post of Grand Sorcerer. And yet, Deferens had been shaped by the Witch-King from birth. His thoughts had been steered down pathways the Witch-King had determined, his career moulded to suit the Witch-King's purposes. Had he ever really had a chance? How much of what he'd achieved had been his own work and how much had been the Witch-King, covertly steering matters from his tomb?

"Deferens may still be out there somewhere," Charity said.

Elaine jumped. Charity sounded cold; no, dead and cold. She might be powerful, but she'd probably never killed *anyone* by her own hand. The girl Elaine remembered from their first meeting had been easy to hate, the daughter of a Great House born with strong magic and stronger connections. But now ... Charity had been a slave, her obedience compelled by powerful oaths that would have forced her to do anything Deferens had commanded. Elaine knew, all too well, just what Deferens would have made her do. She couldn't find it in her to hate Charity any longer.

"I killed the other mind," Charity said, in her broken voice. "He's still out there somewhere."

Elaine rather doubted it. Deferens had been pushed into a corner of his own mind by the Witch-King, not forced to trade bodies with him. The Witch-King hadn't been a cripple, after all; Deferens had been his tool, not his replacement body. But Charity needed to feel otherwise, if only to keep her oaths from killing her. She'd broken them rather spectacularly, after all.

"Maybe," she said. She shot Johan a look, cursing Amanda's Draught under her breath. It would have been easier, far easier, to warn him not to suggest that Deferens might be permanently dead. "Don't worry about it, really."

"I did so much for him," Charity said. Tears were sliding down her face and staining the wisps of silk she wore. "Don't you know how much I did?"

"You swore your oaths," Elaine said, quietly. It was a point of law that no one could be blamed for anything they did under oath, although Charity would likely be shunned for the rest of her life. "You shouldn't blame yourself for him."

"No, you shouldn't," Johan agreed. He knelt down next to Charity and wrapped his arms around her. "You need a proper night's sleep ... well, a proper *day's* sleep. Once you're feeling better, we can find a way to deal with the other threat."

Elaine nodded in agreement. "Take Lady Charity back to her tent and make sure she gets a proper rest," she ordered, addressing the Inquisitor. "Charity, try to wash, change into something a little less comfortable and sleep. We won't leave without you."

Johan looked up at Elaine. "Should I go with her?"

"If you think it will help," Elaine said. She had her doubts – it wouldn't be too long before Johan started coming off the Draught – but she understood why he'd want to be there. Charity and Johan would need time to repair their relationship. "Once you start feeling things again, come straight back here. You'll need help getting through the after-effects without an emotional breakdown."

"I will," Johan promised.

Elaine watched them leave and then looked around the Royal Tent. Vlad Deferens hadn't travelled in style, she had to admit; he'd made certain to bring a solid bedstead rather than one of the fancy beds from the Imperial Palace. She knelt beside him and, resisting the urge to be sick, ran her hands through his pockets. There was nothing, apart from a notebook, a handful of pens and a tiny wand, contaminated with dark magic. She took the blanket from the bed and used it to pick up the wand, placing it on the far side of the tent, before turning her attention to the notebook. It looked blank, but a simple revealing spell turned up a list of enemies and people who were going to be purged, once the Emperor had completed the destruction of Ida.

If we didn't have a civil war already, she thought morbidly, *we'd be bound to have one after everyone on this list was targeted for extermination.*

She dropped the notebook into her pocket and started to search the Emperor's trunks. Two of them contained clothes – Vlad Deferens' trademark red kilt and red shirt; she couldn't help grimacing at the realisation he'd worn nothing under the kilt – while the third contained a number of books.

Most of them looked to be guidebooks to the Empire, but several of them were clearly magic and one of them was yet another copy of the Witch-King's personal spellbook. No doubt Deferens had used the spells often, developing his magic while tightening the Witch-King's grip on his mind.

Idiot, she thought, as she placed the book on the bed and stood. But she couldn't blame him really, nor any of the Witch-King's other victims. There weren't any others who could have spotted the hidden commands worked into the spells, let alone edited the spells to remove them. Hell, they'd need a completely comprehensive grasp of magic to even realise there *was* a problem. *No wonder the Witch-King was so keen to capture me.*

She pushed the thought aside as she looked down at the body. Dread had told her that Deferens had been *obsessed* with her, after she'd escaped an unbreakable spell and fled an inescapable prison. It wasn't a pleasant thought. She had a feeling Deferens had regarded her as a challenge, someone whom he *had* to break; if he'd caught her again, she knew it wouldn't have been anything like as pleasant as the *first* time. And yet, in the end, he'd been killed by someone he'd regarded as beneath him.

"A fitting end," Elaine said, quietly. "And precisely what you deserved."

Gritting her teeth, she cast a preservation charm over the body as the flap opened, revealing Inquisitor Dolman. They'd probably need to show the body to anyone who thought the Emperor was still alive, before dumping it in the Lug and letting the water take it down to the ocean. Or, perhaps, giving it a honourable funeral. Deferens *had* been an Emperor, after all, the rightful heir to the throne.

"My Lady," Dolman said. "How may I be of service?"

Elaine sighed, inwardly. She knew how to manage a library, not an army. The Great Library had been relatively easy, particularly with Vane doing all the talking. But here …?

"Do whatever you have to do to prepare the army to march," she said, finally. "Do you think it will stay together?"

"I would not care to hazard a guess, My Lady," Dolman

said. "The Sergeants were very good at breaking down previous loyalties, but most of them have fled. I suspect that most of the conscripts will want to return to their homes, even though they won't be welcome."

Elaine frowned. "They won't?"

"The Emperor was quite happy to let the conscripts loot, rape and pillage their former homes," Dolman said. "It broke the ties they had to their homelands."

"I see," Elaine said. "You might want to make that clear to them."

"I will," Dolman said. "If you would care for a word of advice, My Lady ...?"

Elaine nodded, harshly.

"You can offer considerable rewards to anyone who stays with the army, including resettlement well away from their former homes," Dolman said. "But it would be a mistake to *force* anyone to stay. You don't have a solid core of decent officers."

"Then offer those rewards," Elaine said, tiredly. "And when Dread arrives, hand command of the army to him."

Chapter Thirty

Johan hadn't seen anything of the camp when the Witch-King had handed him over to Deferens, who had dumped him on Charity. Now, as he followed his sister through the frozen grounds towards her tent, he couldn't help thinking that it looked a ghastly mess. A handful of dragons sat in their pens, watched by a couple of Inquisitors, while dead bodies lay everywhere. He wondered, absently, if they'd resort to feeding the corpses to the dragons, solving two problems at once. Sooner or later, the dragons would need to feed ...

He pushed the thought to one side as Charity led him into her tent, leaving the Inquisitor outside. She'd always liked luxury – he'd sneaked into her room in Conidian House several times when they'd been younger – but the tent was bare, with hardly anything beyond a bed, a small trunk of clothes and a pair of spare wands. She sat down as he closed the flap, placing her head in her hands. Johan sat down next to her and placed an arm over her shoulder, trying to give what support he could. It wasn't easy.

Charity had always been ... if not *nice* then decent. Sometimes. She had hexed him more than once, but she'd never been as thoroughly unpleasant as Jamal. Indeed, there had even been times when she'd helped him to flee the house for a few short hours, despite their father's orders. Maybe she'd felt a prisoner too, despite her magic. She'd been raised knowing that everything in her life, from her studies at the Peerless School to her husband, would be determined by their father.

"I'm sorry," he said, unsure what to say. If it had been Jamal, he would have rubbed it in as much as possible, but Charity ... she hadn't deserved to be broken. "I'm sorry ..."

"Not your fault," Charity said. She leant against him for a long moment, then stood and opened one of her trunks. "Look the other way for a moment, please."

Johan nodded and turned to stare at the canvas as Charity opened one of the boxes and rummaged through it for something a little more concealing. It normally took hours for her to be ready for anything, but this time she was ready in seconds. The dress she'd pulled over her shoulders was as enveloping as a set of school robes, concealing everything below her neckline. Johan eyed the discarded harem outfit, wondering – absently – just what Elaine would look like in something similar, then pushed the thought aside. Clearly, the Draught was still effective.

"That feels better," Charity said. She picked up one of the wands – Johan cringed back instinctively – and snapped it into place. "But I feel dirty."

"Elaine said you should wash, then sleep," Johan said. He paused as a thought struck him. "Did ... did he *touch* you?"

Charity shook her head. "Never," she said. "He just enjoyed having me at his beck and call."

Johan frowned in bemusement. He'd always assumed that Deferens would be just like Jamal, having his way with everything young, female and vulnerable that crossed his path. The idea of Deferens *not* taking advantage of Charity was puzzling. She'd been his slave; he could do anything to her, if he wanted. And yet he hadn't touched her.

Perhaps he'd been more interested in men, he thought. And yet it *did* make a certain kind of sense. If one had been raised to detest women, why would one want to have *sex* with women? Surely the whole affair would seem disgusting? He shook his head, snorting rudely at the thought. *Deferens was a right piece of shit.*

"At least you got his body," Johan said. He wasn't sure if *Charity* believed that any longer, but he wouldn't try to convince her otherwise. "And you freed yourself."

"I don't think I'll ever be free," Charity admitted. She sat on the bed, looking down at her knees. "Do you remember being young and happy?"

"No," Johan said, tartly.

Charity flinched at his tone. "I used to think that happiness could be found at the end of life," she said, softly. "And now I find out that it's at the wrong end."

Johan shook his head. "You were young, beautiful,

wealthy and powerful," he said. "Do you think your maids would have agreed with you? Or the whores on the streets? Or scholarship pupils at the Peerless School? Or ..."

"You've made your point," Charity said.

"You went through hell," Johan told her. "But you freed yourself. And now you can resume your position as Head of House Conidian."

"Hah," Charity said. "Do you think anyone will *accept* me after I was enslaved?"

"People *have* been enslaved for short periods of time and then released, once they worked out their sentence," Johan reminded her. "Besides, who else *is* there?"

"You," Charity said. "You're old enough to become the Conidian."

"No, thank you," Johan said. He didn't *want* to spend the rest of his life slowly becoming his father. Besides, he had the feeling that Elaine wouldn't want to stay in the Golden City ... if, of course, the Witch-King was defeated. "You're the only one who can take it."

"I don't want it," Charity said.

"Nor do I," Johan countered. "Hold the position long enough for Jay to turn nineteen, then hand it over to him. By then, you may have recovered your poise."

"Everyone will remember me in *that*," Charity said, kicking the harem outfit. "They'll spend the rest of their lives making fun of me."

"Ignore them," Johan said. "At least you're not running around without a single spark of magic to defend yourself."

He shrugged. "Besides, I don't think there's *anyone* in the Golden City who doesn't have a secret shame of their own, not now," he added. "You were a slave. What about the assholes who went along with Deferens *willingly*?"

Charity smiled, wanly. "That's true," she agreed. "But ..."

"Sleep," Johan said. He felt a sudden flicker of concern, reminding him that the Draught was slowly wearing off. "I'll stay with you until you're deeply asleep, if I can."

"You don't have long," Charity said, as she lay down and covered herself with the blanket. "I think you have only minutes, at best."

Johan nodded. The concern was growing stronger; he was

suddenly very – very – aware that Elaine wasn't far from him, her presence in his mind suddenly sparking with emotion. He forced himself to remain calm as his sister closed her eyes, muttering a sleeping charm just loudly enough to be heard. Her body shivered one final time, then started to breathe normally. Johan stared down at her for a long moment before standing and walking out of the tent. Outside, the Inquisitor was still waiting.

"Please make sure she isn't disturbed," he said, quietly. Elaine might be able to boss Inquisitors around, but he suspected *he* had no such authority. "She needs her rest."

"She will have it," the Inquisitor assured him.

"Thank you," Johan said. He felt another quiver of emotion; a flash of rage that suddenly became an urge to sit down and cry like a baby. "I ..."

"Go to your friend," the Inquisitor ordered. "You'll need help."

Johan nodded and hurried towards the Royal Tent, turning as he heard a loud roar behind him. The dragons were devouring the remains of human bodies, as he'd expected; teams of slaves, still held in bondage by their collars, were carting the bodies over to the pens and throwing them to the giant beasts. It struck Johan that giving the dragons a taste for human flesh was probably a bad idea, but he knew enough about their creation – and the legends that had been passed down through the ages – to be sure that it probably wouldn't matter. The sorcerers who'd first called them into the world had wanted weapons of war, creatures that would rend and tear their way through entire armies, and they'd succeeded beyond their wildest dreams.

He felt another stab of envy as he saw the harness on the back of one of the dragons, a green-scaled brute happily chomping its way through the remains of a red-robed sorcerer. It would be fantastic, he was sure, to mount a dragon and fly high over the country, staring down at the tiny people below. He almost turned and walked towards the pen before catching himself; the slaves were being very careful, but the dragons were snapping and snarling at them as if they preferred live prey. They probably did. If *he'd* been designing weapons of war, he'd want them to go after the fleeing armies too.

The thought made him feel a surge of absolute terror. It was all he could do to keep going, staggering onwards, until he reached the tent. Elaine was inside, sitting at a table and talking to Dread and Dolman, maps spread open in front of her. Johan felt a surge of jealousy – how *dare* she talk to any other man – that almost sent him stumbling forward, fists at the ready. It took everything he had to catch himself ...

"Handle the army," Elaine ordered, as the two Inquisitors rose to their feet. "Give us some privacy."

"Yes, My Lady," Dolman said.

Johan forced himself to stand still as the men slipped past him and out of the tent. His skin was prickling, as if someone had hit him with an itching hex; Jamal had to have done it ... no, Jamal was dead. Wasn't he? His mind warred with itself as he forced himself to remember that Jamal *was* actually dead. But what about the body? There hadn't been time to go back and bury it ... could Jamal have recovered and walked off? It didn't seem possible ...

"You need to listen to me," Elaine said. She was standing right in front of him, her eyes flickering between brown and red as his mind fought the glamour. "You're coming off a powerful drug. I need you to listen to me."

Johan reached for her as his entire body shuddered. He wanted her, he hated her, he loved her, he loathed her ... somehow, he forced himself to grip her hands as the string of emotions roared through his mind. His legs buckled and he sat down hard on the frozen ground; Elaine pulled him closer and hugged him as he shuddered once again. Her calmness was reassuring, despite the confusion shimmering through his mind. And then he remembered Jamal and started to cry helplessly.

"It's all right," Elaine breathed. She grunted as he gripped her hands tighter – he felt a stab of pain through the bond – but didn't try to pull back. "Just keep focusing on me."

Guilt flared through Johan's mind. He'd hurt her! He knew he was strong; he'd squeezed her hands tight enough to hurt. How could he? How could he hurt the woman who'd taken care of him, who'd been the first person to show any concern or consideration for him, who'd opened her heart to him … he let go of her hands and pushed her away, trying to stumble to his feet. He could get out of the tent and start running into the mountains, where he could die well away from everyone else. He'd hurt her! He deserved nothing less.

"Sit down," Elaine said, gently. "Please."

"I hurt you," Johan pleaded, as she caught his hands again. "Let me go!"

"You're not in your right mind," Elaine said. "I don't blame you for anything you do while you're recovering …"

Johan shuddered as she pulled him close and hugged him. He wanted to run and, at the same time, he wanted to grab her and rip off her clothes. Elaine held him tightly as he fought for balance between the two conflicting urges, her voice whispering sweet nothings in his ears as she rocked him forwards and backwards. His body shuddered one final time and …

… He found himself lying on the bed, staring up at nothing.

"Elaine?"

"I'm here," Elaine said. She was sitting beside the bed, one hand holding a mug of water, but he could feel her presence in his mind. "How are you now?"

"I'm not sure," Johan admitted, reluctantly. She passed him the water and he drank greedily, feeling dehydrated. "What happened to me?"

"You were drugged to keep your magic under control," Elaine said. "Quite clever, really; I suspect the Witch-King must have suggested it. When the drug left your body, you were hit with withdrawal symptoms. I kept you here until you finally collapsed."

Johan frowned, looking down at his shirt. Someone had cleaned it using magic – it had to be Elaine – but the faint stench of vomit still hung in his nostrils. His skin felt cold and clammy, his shirt and trousers soaked with sweat. He tried to sit up, but a wave of dizziness overcame him and he had to lie back down. Elaine took the empty mug of water, refilled it from a jug at the head of the bed and passed it back to him. Johan had to drink several more mugs, one by one, until he felt refreshed.

"My clothes ..."

"I had to clean them," Elaine said. Her lips twitched in sudden amusement. "I'm afraid they were rather messy."

"I don't want to think about it," Johan said. A memory surfaced from the confused thoughts occupying his mind; he'd hurt her, hadn't he? He glanced at her wrists and saw nasty bruises against her pale skin. "I ..."

She followed his gaze. "You weren't in your right mind," she said. He had a vague memory of her saying that sometime before, but it wasn't clear. "I don't blame you for your actions while you were coming off the drug."

Johan flinched. What had he done?

"I blame myself," he said. "Elaine ..."

"Don't," Elaine ordered. She poked him with a long finger. "Does your sister blame herself?"

"I think she does, yeah," Johan said. "But I wasn't under a spell ..."

"But you were drugged," Elaine said. She rose to her feet, revealing that she'd changed her clothes while he'd been sleeping. Had he thrown up on her shirt? Or had he done something worse? "Johan ... you are not to blame yourself, do you understand? Or I'll turn you into something unpleasant."

Johan had to smile, despite the guilt. Not knowing what – if anything – had happened was worse than being caught trying to sneak into his brother's room. He *loved* Elaine; he didn't want to hurt her, even by accident. But he knew she wouldn't tell him what had happened, merely keep the memories to herself. She didn't want to burden him with *real* guilt.

"I'll try," he mumbled. He wasn't sure if Elaine could make good on her threat, but he didn't want to find out the hard way. "How ... how long was I out?"

"Several hours," Elaine said. "I didn't dare use any potions, so I had to wait for you to sweat the rest of the poisons out of your body."

She walked over to a corner, where a large washtub had been placed; Johan watched as she pointed her finger into the water and muttered a spell. Steam started to rise from the washtub, revealing that someone had filled it with water.

Johan eyed her with some concern as she turned back to face him, her face twisting into a smile.

"It would probably be better to use a stripping spell," she said, as she held out a hand and helped him to stand up. His legs felt a little stronger now, but he still had to fight to remain upright. He doubted he could undress manually even with her help. "I'm sorry ..."

Johan shrugged as his clothes fell into dust. Jamal had thought the spell a hoot, often bragging of the times he'd used it on unsuspecting girls at the Peerless School. He'd used it on Johan too, although it was less entertaining for Jamal than some of the other spells he'd been fond of casting. Johan sensed Elaine's wry amusement as she helped him over to the tub and used magic to levitate him up and over the water. Seconds later, she dropped him into the tub and started to scrub his back with a cloth.

"I thought you were in command," Johan said. The combination of her touch and the warm water was exciting, too exciting. "Shouldn't you be issuing orders or something?"

"Dread's in command," Elaine said. She looked oddly embarrassed, lowering her eyes. "I don't *like* command."

"But you're the sole remaining Privy Councillor," Johan objected.

Elaine looked away. "I hated the post," she said. "I'd have been happy with the Great Library. Light Spinner ... *insisted* ... that I also take a seat on the council. I think she meant it as a consolation prize for being stuck in the Golden City."

"I'm sorry," Johan said. He could taste her deep regret, mingled with a strange kind of shame. It took him a moment to work out that Elaine *thought* she should be a commanding personality, even though she wasn't. "But can Dread issue orders?"

"They remember him and respect him, even without magic," Elaine said. "Now the Emperor is dead, they're free to go back to their original oaths. They wiped out the red-robes at considerable speed, Johan. I never really appreciated how good they were ..."

Johan sighed as she finished washing his back and helped

him to his feet. "Do you think we have time …?"

Elaine smiled. She didn't need to do more than taste his emotions to know what he was *really* asking.

"We'll make time," she said, as she undid her shirt. Johan felt a surge of lust as her breasts bobbled free, then a matching surge from her. "The world can wait."

Chapter Thirty-One

It took all of Elaine's courage to walk out of the tent, once they were both clean and dressed, but somehow she made it. Dread had understood, thankfully, that she'd wanted to take care of Johan personally – she was the safest choice, if his magic had started to flare out of control – yet she was sure he understood why she wanted it. Elaine knew she just wasn't cut out to issue orders to men stronger, both physically and magically, than herself. It was a mystery to her how Queen Sacharissa managed it.

She's a Queen, born to a King, she thought. *She had command taught to her from the day she spoke her very first word.*

Johan followed her. He was trying to look innocent, but she rather doubted that anyone would believe they'd been doing anything other than making love.

Elaine smiled at the thought as she paused long enough to look towards Ida. The sun was slowly sinking below the mountains, casting long shadows over the camp. It looked as though they'd lost a day, she decided; she hoped – prayed – that the Witch-King hadn't made good use of the time. If he'd headed south after dumping Johan, chances were that he was retracing the army's steps to the Golden City.

He could have taken one of the dragons, she thought. *But balancing the different kinds of magic might have taxed even him.*

She sighed and walked into the command tent. Dread and Dolman had set up a large table and covered it with maps, while Sarah, Tarpon and a couple of men Elaine didn't recognise were sitting on the far side. They rose as she entered, Sarah's face twisting with bitter amusement. Leveller that she was, the idea that Elaine had a *right* to take command had to hurt. And yet, there wasn't any choice. Elaine took the seat at the head of the table, then waved for everyone else to sit down. Johan sat next to her, his eyes grim. There was no sign of Charity – or Daria – at all.

She'll need to sleep it off, Elaine thought. Charity had been enslaved ... held in bondage by her own oaths, rather than a slave collar. It would take years for her to leave the ghosts of her past behind. *But at least she'll have some help, if we survive.*

It took her a moment to clear her throat for attention. "Gentlemen and lady," she said. She'd never chaired a meeting, not even at the Great Library. "What's happening with the army?"

Dread smiled at her, rather wanly. "Right now, we have around five thousand infantrymen and twelve dragons," he said. "Between the ... combat losses and the deserters, the army has been quite badly weakened; we're *very* short of senior officers, even though Queen Sacharissa has loaned us a number of experienced men. Morale is appallingly low; there's a strong feeling that the Witch-King is a god among *some* men, while others just want to go home. I have a feeling that we're going to find it difficult to get *any* effective fighting out of them."

"They'd just be targets if they had to fight the Witch-King," Elaine said. "Where *is* he, anyway?"

"Good question," Sarah said. "We've been attempting to divine his location, as he's the single most powerful concentration of magic in the world. He's actually broadcasting flares of magical interference, but we believe he's slowly walking towards Falcone's Nest."

Elaine frowned. "Walking speed?"

"More or less," Sarah said. "He doesn't seem to be in any hurry."

"Perhaps he can't move any faster," Johan suggested.

"It may not matter," Dread said. "Yes, maybe he can't move any faster than a normal soldier carrying a heavy pack. But as long as he's drawing on magic to power himself, he can just *keep* walking when the soldier gives up and collapses. He could make it back to the Golden City long before any of us."

"That isn't true," Johan said. "We have dragons."

Brian gave him a sharp look. "Can we fly them?"

"Yes," Dolman said. "The control spells are lodged in their harnesses, allowing anyone to actually *fly* the dragons once they're mounted up. But I don't think the Witch-King will have any problems casting the same spells you used to defend Ida and knocking the dragons out of the sky."

"He didn't see the spells in action," Sarah objected.

"It's unlikely to matter," Elaine said. "If he took the knowledge from … from my mother, he won't have any difficulty crafting similar spells for himself."

"You're smart," Johan objected.

"So is he," Dread said, before Elaine could muster a response. "Someone who turned himself into a near-lich and laid plans that matured over generations – and brought the Empire down in flames – can hardly be called an idiot."

Except he nearly lost everything, Elaine thought. *If we'd managed to get to his coffin before Deferens arrived, he would have been unable to find a source of magic potent enough to keep him alive, once he rose.*

"I threw everything I had at him," Johan said. "He's immune to my power. We hit him with Elaine's spells and even buried him under falling rocks and he just kept coming."

"He's not all-powerful," Dolman said, firmly. "There would be no point in having this meeting if he could just snap his fingers and blot us from existence."

He's not all-powerful, Elaine agreed, mentally.

She reached into her pocket, produced a notebook – the one she'd taken from Deferens' dead body – and started to scribble down calculations. The Witch-King had managed to combine both wild and high magic to create his new body; that, at least, was obvious. Indeed, his body was very definitely made of raw magic. But he clearly needed to refuel regularly or he'd simply wind down and stop, his body dissolving into dust. The more she thought about it, the more she was sure they were missing something obvious.

He's going back to the Golden City, she thought, recalling the earlier discussion. They'd agreed the Witch-King needed a source of power. *There, he can find the Peerless School and the Great Library …*

She sucked in her breath. "Deferens … what did Deferens

leave behind, when he left the Golden City?"

"He left the city under martial law," Dolman said. "There were a couple of thousand troops on the streets and a handful of magicians, but not enough to force the defences of the Great Houses or the Peerless School."

Elaine frowned, looking down at her calculations. "And the Great Library?"

"Remains locked, unless the wardcrafters managed to break through the defences after the army left," Dolman supplied. "I don't think the Great Houses *wanted* to take up arms against the Emperor, not after his dragons made an example of House Lakeside."

Ouch, Elaine thought. She sensed Johan's sudden concern through the bond. They'd left his younger siblings at House Lakeside before leaving the Golden City. *They may not want to fight Deferens, but the Witch-King would be worse.*

"The Golden City remains the single strongest concentration of magicians in the world," she said, after a moment. "If my calculations are correct" – she knew there was no way to test them – "the Witch-King should be able to make himself effectively immortal by sacrificing the remaining children at the Peerless School. He'd achieve a level of magic, ebbing and flowing around his intellect, that would never actually fade."

She took a breath. "He would, to all intents and purposes, make himself a *genuine* god."

"So we have to stop him from reaching the Peerless School," Dread said. "How?"

"Force him to expend magic," Sarah said. "The more he uses to defend himself, the less he will have to keep himself alive."

"He's got a *lot* of magic," Dread warned. "Even if we managed to catch him, he'd have enough power to just keep walking, burning his way through all resistance, until he reached the Golden City."

"He could probably walk over the Peaks if he couldn't get into the tunnels," Johan added, darkly. "I don't think he'd be deterred by wild magic."

"He'd just see it as a source of power," Elaine mused. Had the weather-control spells been *meant* to feed the Witch-

King? Light Spinner had prevented that, at least, when she'd used the remainder of the spells to kill a dragon. "Unless he had problems absorbing wild magic …"

She looked back down at her calculations. "There *is* a possibility," she said. "But we'd need to get back to the Golden City ahead of him."

"Use the dragons," Dolman said. "Leave the army here and leapfrog over the Witch-King."

"There's still an occupation force there," Dread said, quietly. "*And* the hidden defences of the city itself."

Elaine blinked. "Hidden defences?"

"They're normally only discussed with the Grand Sorcerer," Dread explained. "We are sworn to secrecy on pain of" – he looked at his hands – "magic loss."

"Except that the defences require a Grand Sorcerer – or an Emperor," Dolman said. He took a harsh breath, then let it out slowly as it became clear the secret was already out. "There isn't an Emperor in residence."

"There will be," Dread said, darkly. "Deferens presumably had relatives who share his bloodline. The Witch-King might be waiting for one of them to reach the Golden City and take the Golden Throne."

But there could be one there already, Elaine thought, grimly. *And if that happens, Dolman will switch sides again. He'll have to.*

She sensed the sudden burst of amusement from Johan, an instant before he threw back his head and started to laugh. Everyone stared at him as he giggled helplessly. Elaine opened her mouth and closed it again, realising there was no point in trying to calm him down. He was just *too* amused for anything short of a kick to work …

Dread didn't seem to agree. "And what's so funny?"

"Deferens got the Golden Throne because he was related to the original bloodline," Johan said. He shot Elaine an unreadable look before continuing. "Does the Throne automatically accept children or does it merely wait for someone else with the right bloodline?"

Elaine hesitated, skimming through the knowledge buried in her mind. "It would go for an adult with the right bloodline," she said, after a moment. "The sitting Emperor would designate a heir, but whoever got to the Golden Throne after the Emperor's death would be the next Emperor, backed up by the Inquisitors."

Johan looked right at her. "You're related to Deferens," he said. "Why can't *you* take the Golden Throne?"

Elaine stared at him in shock. The Witch-King had had no reason to lie; he'd *known* she was dying, he'd merely wanted to speak with her before she passed on. It made a certain kind of sense, too; if the original plan had worked, she could have been held in reserve at Ida until the Witch-King emerged, then used to shut down the defences and take the city. And yet, what if she wasn't close *enough* to the bloodline? The Golden Throne might have *barely* considered Deferens a viable candidate.

She closed her eyes, trying to gauge how the throne would react. There was no way to know what criteria the original Emperors might have used; there had been candidates who'd died when they sat on the throne, but she didn't know anything about them. Later, the Privy Council had checked each candidate *thoroughly* before allowing them to take the throne. Deferens had been the first person in a thousand years to sit on the throne and *not* die horribly. It could work, if she was close enough to qualify …

… Or it could end very badly. The last unsuccessful candidate had taken hours to die.

"It might work," Dread mused, as Elaine opened her eyes. "But Elaine might not share the bloodline."

"She's related to Deferens," Johan insisted.

"Yes," Dread said, patiently. "If we assume the Witch-King was telling the truth, then she is – but tell me, on which side of the family? For all we know, Elaine and Deferens were close relatives even though she doesn't carry a droplet of the bloodline."

"There *is* a test," Dolman said. He tapped the table, thoughtfully. "We take the dragons and head straight back to the Golden City, perhaps taking the time to warn everyone along the way about the Witch-King. If we get into the city, we take Elaine straight to the palace …"

"Apart from the minor detail that there's an occupying army," Brian injected.

Dolman ignored him. "We get Elaine into the palace and test her blood," he said. "There's an ... artefact within the palace that glows if it's worn by anyone of the bloodline. If she *does* qualify as a potential candidate, she takes the throne and control of the defences. They'd slow the Witch-King down, if nothing else, buying us time to get the students away from him."

"He might attack the wards directly," Elaine said. She wasn't sure she wanted to *think* about the prospects of becoming Empress. It had been *quite* bad enough serving on the Privy Council. "I suspect he can drain power from them directly or simply burn through them. Johan didn't have any trouble seriously damaging the wards in the Great Library."

"I don't see any other option," Dolman said. "The longer we delay, the greater the chance that someone else will be plonked down on the Golden Throne."

"Then we leave tonight," Dread said.

Elaine swallowed. She didn't *want* to be Empress ... and, if Johan was wrong, they'd be in the middle of the Golden City, surrounded by an army of occupation. There was the *other* idea nagging at her mind, but she needed time to sit down and think about it properly. She had a feeling she wasn't going to *get* that time.

Everyone wants to be Emperor, Johan sent.

Not me, Elaine sent back. *I'd be a prisoner of the Golden Throne.*

She knew he'd sense her reluctance – but, at the same time, she understood what he meant. There wasn't any other choice. The Witch-King wouldn't have gambled everything on Vlad Deferens surviving to adulthood, not when half the men in his homeland died before they turned eighteen. There would be another heir waiting in the wings, perhaps far closer to the Golden City than themselves.

But then, his homeland is weeks away even on Iron Dragons, she thought, numbly. *And Deferens might not have wanted a potential rival so close. Could there be a heir a week from the Golden City? Or ...*

She shook her head. There was no way to know.

"Very well," she said, trying to sound commanding. "We will take the dragons and fly tonight. The remainder of the army can be sent home, if they wish, or allowed to go wherever they please. They're nothing more than targets to the Witch-King."

"Of course, My Lady," Dolman said. "With your permission, I'll ready the remaining Inquisitors and other magicians. We should be ready to depart within the hour."

"Have Charity come too," Johan said. "She might be able to convince the Great Houses to assist us."

"Do it," Elaine said.

She looked down at the table as the meeting slowly broke up, refusing to meet their eyes. Sarah and the Levellers had to be horrified; they'd watched the death of an Emperor, only to discover that they might be about to see the rise of an Empress. And yet, what other choice did they have? The Inquisitors had to see her as a better mistress than any of the Witch-King's puppets and *they'd* be in a race against time. Failing to put Elaine on the Golden Throne quickly enough to pre-empt the Witch-King would see them reduced to slaves again, slaves who would be perfectly placed to betray their former allies. They didn't see any choice either.

Dread patted her shoulder, gently. "You can abdicate once it's over," he said. "Or even leave the task of ruling to the Privy Council."

Elaine sighed. She had never wanted anything but the Great Library. Now ... she'd have to sit on the throne and rule ... or die, if it rejected her. Dolman was right; there *was* a test, but was it precise enough to be *definite*? It was a lot easier to say that someone was not related to the bloodline than close enough to pass the test, yet not close enough to sit on the throne.

"I will," she said, tiredly. She'd have to have children ... the idea of having children wasn't *bad*, but she'd never wanted them before. And then they'd be prisoners of the throne too. If they abandoned the throne, one of their distant relatives would take it in their place. "If we survive, if we make it work, we have to change the system. This cannot be allowed to happen again."

"It won't," Dread said. He turned towards the flap, then stopped. "For what it's worth, you know enough to prevent the same mistakes from being repeated."

"I'm sorry," Johan said, once Dread had left. "I just saw it …"

"I didn't," Elaine said, miserably. She felt a flicker of grim amusement as a thought struck her. "You do realise that makes you the Prince Consort?"

Johan blinked. "What?"

"The bond makes us married, by some rules," Elaine said. She smiled at his shock. "You're not going to be Emperor, just Prince Consort."

Johan stared at her, then smiled gently. "We're married?"

"By some laws," Elaine said. "I'm afraid it wasn't a big wedding …"

"Big enough," Johan said, firmly. "Besides, we can have a proper ceremony afterwards."

"If we survive," Elaine said. She met his eyes. "Dread was right, you know. We don't know *precisely* how I'm related to Deferens. It's quite possible I don't share the same bloodline – or enough of it to register. If the test fails, the whole plan falls through …"

She took a breath, then reached for him. "And if that happens," she added slowly, "there's only one last card to play."

Chapter Thirty-Two

"You don't have to watch me, you know," Charity said. "I'm not going to kill myself."

"That's good to hear," Daria said. She'd been sitting by the bedside when Charity awoke, then stayed with her despite polite requests and outright threats. "But your brother does want a friendly eye kept on you."

"Thanks," Charity said, sourly. She looked down at her dress and rose to her feet. "My brother should know I can take care of myself."

Daria met her eyes. "You were a slave for several weeks," she said. "Like it or not, you will be feeling the after-effects for many years to come. I strongly suggest you allow me to stay with you for at least a few hours."

"Fine," Charity said. She pulled her cloak over her head, then followed Daria as she led the way out of the tent. "Where are we going?"

"The Golden City," Daria said. A wild-eyed man was waiting for her, his features oddly *canine*. "One moment."

A werewolf, Charity thought. And if the man was a werewolf … she looked at Daria's hands and saw, even in the twilight, a thin layer of hairs. Daria was a werewolf too. But compared to the Witch-King, and the Emperor, Daria was harmless. *At least she can only tear my throat out if she gets mad at me.*

Daria spoke briefly to the man, who listened to her and then bowed his head. That was odd, from what Charity remembered; Daria should have had problems trying to give orders to an older male werewolf. But the werewolf turned and headed into the gloom, while Daria beckoned Charity to follow her towards the dragon pens. A handful of black-clad Inquisitors were already there, eying the dragons grimly. Charity felt another flicker of fear as one of the dragons peered at her, as if it were gauging her value as a food source.

She told herself, firmly, that she wasn't large enough to make a real snack.

"We're going to be flying back to the Golden City," Daria said. She smiled, nervously. "I'm a little scared of heights."

Charity blinked. "A *werewolf* is scared of heights?"

"I'm not scared of the fall," Daria said. If she was surprised at being recognised as a werewolf, she kept it to herself. "I'm just scared of the landing."

"It isn't that bad," Charity said. It occurred to her that Daria might be trying to draw her out of her shell, but it was hard to care. "You just keep a tight grip on the reins and pray the spells keeping the beast under control don't fail."

Daria bared her teeth. "And what if they do?"

"You die, I assume," Charity said. She'd seen the dragons flexing their necks. They wouldn't have any trouble snapping back and biting a rider right off the saddle. "There's no point in worrying about it."

She looked up as she saw a pair of light globes approaching, heralding the arrival of the Head Librarian and Johan. They were standing surprisingly close together, their hands almost touching; Charity realised, in a sudden flicker of insight, that they were lovers. It was a shock, at first; she wasn't *that* much older than him, but he was a Conidian while the Head Librarian had no family. And then Charity caught herself, bitterly. *Elaine* was a Privy Councillor, the sole remaining Privy Councillor, while Johan had abandoned his family and discarded his name.

Father would have been pleased, she thought. *He was always looking for new ways to gain influence over the other councillors.*

"Johan," Charity said. There was no point in discussing the matter now, not when they might not live past the next few days. They could talk about a formal marriage contract and ceremony later. "When are we going?"

"Now," Johan said. He looked past her at the lead dragon, his eyes shining with excitement as he imagined soaring above the earth. "How easy are they to fly?"

"Just think of them as oversized horses," Charity said, dully. She hadn't been allowed to control a dragon personally, but she'd watched and learnt. "Pull the reins up to steer the dragon into the air; push down on the saddle to make the dragon breathe fire. Don't let the beast collide with another dragon or they'll start fighting. Try not to cast spells while you're in the air, unless they're perfectly attuned to the dragon's magic field."

"Great," Johan said. He was smiling openly in a manner she remembered from when they'd lived in an isolated house, well away from anyone who might notice his lack of magic and remember. "This should be fun."

Charity exchanged glances with the Head Librarian. It was clear *she* didn't think it was going to be fun. Nor did a handful of the Inquisitors.

"Mount up," Dread ordered. Charity smiled as she recognised him. She'd thought he was dead, after he'd failed to return from his mission. "It's time to go."

"Very well," Charity said. She started to walk towards a dragon and was unsurprised when Daria followed her. "What did you say to your friend?"

Daria smirked. "They're going to run ahead of the Witch-King and try to find ways to slow him down," she said. "It may not work, but we have to try."

Charity puzzled over it for a long moment and finally nodded. In wolf-form, a pack of werewolves could travel far quicker than any human. They could catch up with the Witch-King, she was sure, but what could they do then? If Johan was right, neither magic nor physical weapons could touch him.

Maybe they can destroy bridges in his path, she thought, after a moment. The blue fire she'd seen was raw magic, not *real* fire, but maybe it could be quenched. *Or they could slow him down just by attacking and forcing him to waste energy.*

She shook her head. "They're going to die."

Daria lowered her eyes. "Too many of them are going to die," she said. "But they do understand the dangers."

Charity nodded as they reached the dragon, which eyed them unpleasantly but didn't try to stop them scrambling onto its back. Daria sat behind Charity as she picked up the reins, feeling magic crackling through them. If the control spells failed while they were midway to the Golden City ... she pushed the thought aside, bitterly. There was no choice but to take the risk and hope for the best.

"Let's go," Daria said.

***

"Your mother was still stunned," Dread said, quietly. "She's deep in a healing trance. The druid thinks it will be days before she recovers enough to open her eyes and he had *no* idea what she will be like."

Elaine nodded, tiredly. *Kane* – her father – had drained her of magical knowledge, leaving Elaine exhausted and wrecked. As far as she knew, *Kane* himself hadn't suffered any ill-effects, although he'd gone mad shortly afterwards. One of the spells he'd worked must have pushed him over the edge, if the Witch-King hadn't given him a shove. Kane had been aimed right at the heart of the Golden City, after all. No doubt her mother – Moeder, according to Dolman – hadn't taken the transfer of knowledge any better, even though she was clearly a stronger magician.

"She can be taken up to Ida," she said, finally. "If she recovers …"

She looked down at the ground, unsure what to say. She'd spent eighteen years wondering just who her parents had been and why they'd abandoned her at the orphanage. And then she'd believed Kane when he'd told her that her mother had been a whore. There hadn't been any reason to *disbelieve* him. Now …

It would be nice to know a woman strong enough to escape her people, she thought, wistfully. She'd always envied the girls who had mothers, older women who could help steer them through adolescence. *But if she's still working for the Witch-King …*

"If she recovers, and we win, I can talk to her," she said, finally. "Or would you advise against it?"

"If we win, she should be harmless," Dread said. He considered it for a long moment. "Or *relatively* harmless, at least. She'll still be a powerful magician."

Elaine nodded. It was odd; normally, the children of powerful magicians were powerful themselves. *She* should have been a fair match for Millicent, at the very least. But if her parents had both used forbidden rites to enhance their powers – guided by the Witch-King – their natural talent could still be quite low. Or maybe the Witch-King had done something to them to ensure Elaine would be born with only a low level of magic. She'd be capable of absorbing the knowledge of the Great Library, but not powerful enough to actually *use* it.

Shows how much he knew, she thought, darkly. *He never realised I could start breaking spells down into their components and rebuilding them.*

"It can wait," she said. She'd like to talk to her mother, just once, but unless they stopped the Witch-King the world was doomed anyway. "Let's go."

She had no trouble sensing Johan's excitement as he clambered onto the dragon and held out a hand to help her up. It wasn't easy to follow him, Elaine discovered; Dread had to give her a boost before she swung her legs over the saddle and wrapped her arms around Johan. The dragon felt uncomfortably warm, its scaly body quivering with raw magic; she shuddered, despite herself, as she recalled the price for summoning dragons into the mortal world. How many children – and grown magicians – had died to power Deferens' crude lust for dragons?

And the Grand Sorcerers were right to bury the knowledge of how to create the spells, she thought, as Johan gripped the reins. No matter how she looked at the spell, she couldn't see a way to break it down and rewrite it to take less power. There might be ways to ensure that *only* a handful of children had to die, but it was hardly any more moral. *Once the war is over, the knowledge will die with me.*

"Let's go," Johan said.

The dragon flapped its wings and rose into the air, leaving the campsite behind at terrifying speed. Elaine held Johan tightly as she looked down, seeing a handful of tiny lights below where Ida and World's Gate lay; she looked to the south, towards the Golden City, and saw nothing but darkness. The armies had devastated the surrounding countryside, she'd been told, yet she hadn't really understood what that *meant*. Now, as darkness hung over the land, she knew what it cloaked. Farms destroyed, towns burnt, men conscripted, women raped, children butchered … in a mere handful of weeks, Deferens had utterly destroyed the Empire's reputation. No matter what happened, Elaine couldn't imagine being able to pull it back together.

She closed her eyes as the dragon flew onwards, leaving Ida behind. Johan was enjoying himself, his childlike delight shining through his mind; Elaine was happy for him, really she was, but she would be happier still when they were back on the ground. She could hear the dragon's wings thrusting against the air, a dull heartbeat that tried to lure her to sleep. But it was impossible to forget that she was perched on the back of a dragon, a dragon that could turn on them at any moment.

Deferens might have rigged the spells to fail after his death, she thought, morbidly. There had been no time to test them, not when they'd been in a hurry. *It would be just the sort of thing he'd do.*

Or would he? He'd believed that the strongest deserved to rule – and anyone who killed him was stronger by definition. Elaine smiled at the thought; clearly, he hadn't seen either Charity or Johan coming. Why would he want to sabotage his successor? Kill a challenger, yes, but actively ruin the Empire the challenger should inherit? Elaine hoped – prayed – that she was right, that the spells weren't rigged. If they were, they'd probably fail when they were a thousand feet or more above the land …

"That's Falcone's Nest," Johan said, quietly. "*Look.*"

Elaine opened her eyes, then peered past him. The city was wreathed in flames, burning steadily; it looked as though the entire city was slowly burning to the ground. She stared, unable to tell if the Witch-King was fighting his way through the city or if one of the nearby kingdoms had attacked the city, just to avenge the treatment of foreigners within Falcone's Nest. Her shoulders ached, remembering the pillory and just how badly the foreigners had been mistreated. She wouldn't offer decent odds on Falcone's Nest surviving the next couple of years without losing its independence, now Deferens was dead. The Empire had effectively died with him.

"I can't see who's doing the fighting," Johan said. "The

Witch-King?"

"There's no way to know," Elaine said. She had a feeling the Witch-King would have preferred to avoid a battle that would have drained his magic, but there was no way to be *sure.* "Someone might have waited until Deferens was dead and then attacked the city."

Johan turned his head to look at her. "They'll be in for a surprise when you become Empress ..."

"If I do," Elaine reminded him. "And if we survive the next few days."

She shook her head. She'd be Empress with nothing more than nine Inquisitors at her command, if the Golden Throne didn't kill her. The Watchtower was gone, the Great Houses were broken ... the gods alone knew what had happened to the Peerless School. Her reign might come to a sudden end as every kingdom on the continent sent troops and sorcerers to burn the Golden City to the ground, putting aside their differences to make sure that no one would hold supreme power ever again. No, whatever happened, the Empire was doomed. All she could really hope to do was set something else up in its place.

If they let me, she thought. *They'd be more likely to insist on destroying the last remains of the royal bloodline.*

The thought sent chills down her spine as the dragons banked to avoid Falcone's Nest. The fighters, whoever they were, might know the spells that could bring dragons down. Elaine wouldn't have cared to bet against it, particularly since Ida had started to share them as widely as possible. In hindsight, that might have been a mistake. But she'd had no way to know that *they* would need to use dragons, let alone obtain them for themselves. They could have sacrificed every last man, woman and child in Ida and they wouldn't have garnered the power to summon *one* dragon.

"Dread wanted us to land to the north of the Golden City," Johan said, as the Seven Peaks slowly came into view. They looked odd against the brightening sky; it took Elaine a moment to remember that the Watchtower was missing. "The soldiers will have guards on all the tunnels."

Elaine looked up into the sky. It looked to be early morning, by her count; they'd flown over three hundred miles overnight. The soldiers might not have guards on the mountains themselves – unless they were mad enough to attempt to climb – but they'd definitely have people at the tunnels, watching for the Emperor's return. Getting over the mountains would be easy, on the dragons, but getting over them without being seen would be rather harder. She knew hundreds of invisibility, concealment and misdirection spells, yet none of them would be effective on a dragon. Their magic field would overwhelm *any* such spells she tried to cast herself.

"Take us down," she said, quietly.

The dragons landed neatly in a muddy field, one that looked to have been used as a campsite during the army's emergence from the Golden City. Elaine felt a stab of pity as she dismounted from the dragon. The people who lived outside the Seven Peaks were rarely important; hell, one could buy a large house outside the city for less than half of what it cost to rent a small apartment in the city itself. Light Spinner had talked about trying to end the stigma of living outside the city, pointing out that the Golden City was bursting at the seams, but …

She shook her head, wearily. Deferens had probably reduced the city's population quite sharply, either by driving them out or conscripting them into his army. She wondered, briefly, what had happened to the remaining Levellers – and some of her staff – as the dragons clumped together. Dread and Dolman had intended to spend the trip planning the next step of the journey.

"They'll probably have seen us landing," Dread said. "It won't take them long to realise we're not the Emperor."

"We could pose as his people," Daria suggested.

"They wouldn't be fooled," Dread said. "If most of the dragons swoop over the city and start hunting for targets, the remainder can drop Elaine, Johan and Dolman off near the Great Library, where they can break into the secret passageways. I can tell you where to find them."

"There *are* other passageways," Charity said.

"But not ones we know to be intact," Dolman said. He looked at Charity. "Can you fight?"

"I can hurl spells," Charity said. "But if I'm on a

dragon …”

"Just keep them away from the dragon's scales and you should be fine," Elaine said. "Stick to short bursts of magic, like curses and hexes; the dragon should be able to adapt to random flickers of magic."

"The defenders used a spell that killed the dragons," Charity objected.

"It isn't the same," Sarah said, briskly. "Is it?"

"No," Elaine said. "Simple spells should be fine."

She took a breath, feeling cold. If they failed to reach the Golden Throne, they were dead …

… And if they succeeded, she would be trapped.

"Let's go," she said, quietly.

Chapter Thirty-Three

"I'll take the dragon's reins," Brian said, firmly. "You'll need to jump off when the time comes."

"Understood," Johan said. He'd enjoyed flying with Elaine, but they didn't have time to argue. Besides, Brian was right. "He's a responsive beast."

Brian gave him a sharp look. "How do you know he's a *he*?"

Johan was stuck. "I don't know," he said, as he shifted backwards. "Elaine?"

"I think the only way to tell would be during mating season," Elaine said. She hadn't enjoyed the flight very much, unlike him. "Dragons have sexual organs, but they're retracted most of the time."

"Poor bastards," Brian commented. He pulled on the reins and the dragon leapt into the air, followed by the rest of the flight. "Do you think there's any danger in flying over the mountains?"

"Fine time to mention that," Johan sneered.

"Probably not," Elaine said, as the dragon rose higher. "Charity and Deferens flew from the Golden City without any problems."

Johan hoped she was right. The air was growing colder and colder, despite the steady warmth from the dragon. Lightning was flickering around the Seven Peaks; it looked, very much, as though clouds were forming around the mountains, but somehow refraining from actually covering the city itself. The air went very cold and wet for a long moment as the dragon flew through the cloud and burst into bright sunlight. Below them, the Golden City was spread out in all its glory.

He sensed a flicker of dismay from Elaine and winced in sympathy. There were no bells tolling to greet the dawn, no cries of praise from the hundreds of temples scattered over the city, not even crowds of people flocking to work or going to pray before returning home for breakfast. A hundred buildings looked to be in ruins, including several temples and guildhouses; the handful of people on the streets looked to be soldiers, while the population remained indoors. The Peerless School, at least, looked untouched, but it was surrounded by red-robed sorcerers and soldiers; the Imperial Palace, likewise, was heavily defended.

It isn't what it used to be, he thought, as the dragon roared a challenge. Several of the sorcerers were aiming wands at them, although they seemed reluctant to actually start casting spells. *The city that never sleeps is now dead.*

"I'm sorry," he muttered. Elaine had lived in the Golden City all her life. It had to hurt to see broken buildings and shattered lives. "We'll rebuild, if we win."

"I hope so," Elaine said.

Dolman whistled. The other dragons lunged forward, breathing fire as they rocketed towards the Peerless School. Flame flared around the wards – for a moment, Johan wondered if they would actually burn *through* the school's protections – billowing out over the guards, who scattered and fled ahead of the fire. The sorcerers started to throw curses back at the dragons, which were completely ineffective. Johan sneered to himself as the dragons swooped around for a second attack, Sarah and the other magicians hurling hexes towards the ground. The Emperor's goons clearly didn't know how to cast spells that actually *worked* on dragons.

"They're combining their magic," Dolman observed. The Inquisitor sounded completely unemotional. "It's not a bad move, if they can't kill the dragons directly. They can try to force them away."

Johan sensed another pulse of tension from Elaine before she spoke. "Take us down," she ordered. "But not too close to the Great Library."

"Of course," Brian said. "Your wish is my command."

Johan smiled as Brian pulled on the reins, steering the dragon over the city and hurtling towards a guardpost positioned at one end of a dark tunnel. Johan had a sudden flash of *déjà vu* before the dragon opened its mouth and blew fire over the guardpost, wiping out the guards before they could start to run. A red-robed sorcerer popped up from nowhere, waving his arms in the air as he began a chant; Dolman snapped off a spell and the sorcerer collapsed.

Brian looked back at him. "What was *that*?"

"Killing spell," Dolman said. "It isn't taught to anyone outside the Inquisition."

Elaine probably knows it, Johan thought. He kept that thought to himself. If Jamal had had such a spell, he would probably have used it early and often. *How many other spells are known only to a handful of magicians?*

The dragon settled to the ground. Elaine stumbled off, her mind scintillating with relief at being down on solid ground once again; Johan patted the dragon as he jumped down beside her and looked around. They'd passed through once before, he was sure; they'd fled the Golden City through a darkened tunnel. But the Iron Dragons he remembered seeing *near* the tunnel had been destroyed, reduced to pieces of torn and scorched metal. Even the prototype that had been placed on display was gone. No doubt the Emperor – and his patron – hadn't wanted to remind people that it was possible to do things without magic.

"Let's move," Dolman said, once he'd cast a spell to make them look like mundane citizens, rather than magicians. "We don't want to be caught on the streets."

Johan nodded in agreement. Overhead, the dragons were wheeling back into the sky, blowing gouts of fire into the air. The Golden City's buildings were heavily warded against fire, Johan knew, but anyone unlucky enough to be caught in the open was dead. If they were lucky, most of the enemy sorcerers and soldiers would have hidden inside the buildings, cowering as the dragons searched for new prey. It should give them time to make their way to the Great Library.

The air blew hot and cold as they hurried onwards, splashing through wet streets and piles of slush. It had been a hard winter, made worse by the breakdown in the weather control spells; Johan had a feeling it would be hard, if not impossible, to repair the damage and keep the Golden City warm all year round. Perhaps no one would try, if they had any sense at all. It had only made life harder for the civilians when the spells had been badly damaged by Kane.

He reached out to grip Elaine's hands as her emotions became more morbid. The Golden City had never quite been the paradise it had been called, but it *had* been a strange and wonderful place to live. Now, the once-great markets, where one could buy goods from all around the world, were closed; countless homes and boarding houses were bolted up, wary eyes peeked from covered windows as they hurried past. Johan had heard enough of what had happened in the other cities Deferens had occupied to know what might have happened in the Golden City. Elaine had to be having similar thoughts.

"I went to the gardens once," Elaine said, quietly. "They were … pleasant."

Johan followed her gaze. The gardens were almost unrecognisable. Trees that had once reached high over the city had been cut down, presumably for firewood, while the grass where children had played had been used as campsites for the soldiers and slaves. The pond looked empty; the soldiers, he guessed, had caught the exotic fish and eaten them to make a change from their rations. Some of the more interesting fish were poisonous, if he recalled correctly. Deferens was unlikely to give a damn if a few of his soldiers ate something lethal and died horribly.

He sucked in his breath as he caught sight of the construction at the far end of the once-proud gardens. A gallows, large enough to take over twenty victims, with nineteen bodies dangling from ropes. Behind the gallows, the street was crammed with crosses, each one displaying a body nailed firmly to the wood. Johan had seen horror – he'd experienced horror – but this was something else. Deferens had hunted down and crucified everyone who'd dared defy him.

"We asked the Levellers to help us," he whispered, staring at the dead bodies. None of them looked familiar, but that meant nothing. They'd died weeks ago. "Are they all dead now?"

"The Emperor purged hundreds of people," Dolman said. There was a hint of bitter guilt in his voice. "Merchants, scholars; everyone who disagreed with his point of view. The executions took *days* to complete."

And probably only caught a handful of Levellers, Johan thought, bitterly. He recalled Hawke – and Mildred, his young daughter – and shuddered in disgust. Had he signed their death warrants by taking Elaine and Daria to meet the Levellers? *Or maybe they made it out of the city in time.*

"You couldn't do anything to stop it," Dolman added, looking at Elaine. "The Emperor would have killed you if you'd stayed in the city."

"I know," Elaine said. She looked pale. "We need to move."

They hurried down the street, towards the Great Library. The streets looked torn and broken; Johan smiled, recalling the spells Elaine had used to cover their flight from the Great Library after they'd snatched her out of the Imperial Palace. A dragon wheeled overhead, the rider – Charity, perhaps – launching a couple of curses towards the Peerless School. Johan smiled, despite himself, at the thought. Charity had loved the school, but at the same time she'd probably fantasised about burning it to the ground …

"Halt," a voice bellowed.

Johan jumped and swore under his breath as seven soldiers ran towards them, carrying clubs rather than swords. They looked fearful, but nasty; their expressions shifted unpleasantly as they saw Elaine. Johan silently cursed Dolman for not making Elaine look like a man, then felt a surge of anger as he looked back at them.

"You are ordered to remain off the streets unless you have urgent business," the leader sneered. He hadn't taken his eyes off Elaine. "What business do you have here?"

"The Emperor ordered us to test the defences," Dolman lied, smoothly. Johan could feel *magic* seeping into his words. "You did well, thank you."

"And *you* are a liar," the leader said. "We are *protected* against such magics."

"Then die," Johan hissed. He knew what they had in mind for Elaine and it made him angry, *very* angry. "Burn!"

The leader took a step forward, then screamed as his entire body caught fire. His companions started to stumble backwards, but it was already too late. They died too, their armour melting as the blaze grew hotter. Johan felt sick, his anger calming, as he breathed in the stench of burning flesh. The unnatural flames died within seconds, but it was far too late for the guards. They were dead the moment his fires had struck them.

Breathe, Elaine sent.

"They probably wouldn't have had time to report us," Dolman said, "but we'd better hurry."

Johan nodded, taking one last look at the charred bodies before he followed the Inquisitor through the streets. The Great Library was rising up ahead of them, surrounded by a handful of guards and sorcerers. Dolman pressed the side of his head, silently communicating with his fellows; seconds later, a dragon swooped down and blasted the surrounding area with a great gout of fire. Johan flinched back from the heat – it was odd that he hadn't been burnt by his own fire – and then stared at the remains of the street. It was scorched and broken, water bubbling up from places where the pipes had been melted by the blaze. No wonder so many people had been scared of the dragons.

The Great Library itself was wrapped in glowing light as the wards fought to repel the flames and keep the library safe. Elaine squeezed his hand one final time, let go of him and ran across the square and up to the wards. They glowed brighter as she touched them, ignoring the shouts from a handful of advancing sorcerers and soldiers. Johan reached for his anger and directed it at the sorcerers, creating a gust of wind that picked the men up and hurled them towards the mountains. A dragon roared as it snapped one of them out of the air; others, deprived of their chance to feed, howled their disapproval.

"Shit," Dolman said, quietly.

Johan turned, just in time to see a block of ice forming around a dragon. The creature blew fire madly, but the spell summoning and freezing the water was too strong. Its wings were covered in ice; seconds later, it plummeted downwards and slammed into a building with staggering force. He hoped the riders were safe, but the ice might well have frozen them to death within seconds.

"They're trying to swat the dragons out of the air," Dolman said. "It isn't a bad tactic, either."

Johan nodded and looked at Elaine. She was still touching the wards ...

***

Elaine hadn't been entirely sure what to expect when she reached out with her mind and made contact with the Great Library's wards. In theory, they should have recognised her as their mistress; in practice, it was quite possible that Vlad Deferens had done something that would force them to recognise him – or Vane – instead. But as she grappled with the wards, it became clear that the wardcrafters had been unable to break into the library and so they'd settled for wrapping additional wards around the building, preventing her from returning home.

Nasty, she thought. She'd never been particularly good with wards and protections, at least until she'd become the Bookworm; the wardcrafters had done a very good job. In hindsight, she should have asked Johan to burn the wards down, despite the risks. *Very nasty*.

The wards howled as she plunged her mind forward. It was impossible to pull back and escape without being fried; her only hope was to head onwards and trust she could untangle the wards before it was too late. Powerful incants rose up around her, pushing at her mind; she shoved them back, hastily summoning new incants of her own. The wards seemed torn in two about her, as if half of them were prepared to bow the knee to her and the other half insistent that she be removed from the connection by force. It was almost as if the wardcrafters were determined that *no one* should be allowed to gain entry ...

It hit her in a moment of insight as she found the weak spot and brought pressure to bear on it. The wardcrafters had found loopholes in their own orders, just like Charity and the Inquisitors. They'd *wanted* to keep everyone out, including Vlad Deferens. She smiled, despite the growing pressure on her mind; Deferens hadn't known it, but he'd had a lot more enemies than anyone had realised. Gritting her teeth, she pushed again ... and felt the outside wards snap out of existence.

They must have wanted to hide the evidence, she thought, as she made contact with her old wards. Apart from her – and perhaps an Inquisitor – no one would have been able to tell there was any sabotage at all. It might even have *killed* the Emperor if he'd tried to make contact with the wards himself. Deferens had been powerful, but he didn't have Elaine's knowledge or a wardcrafter's years of training. *And if it took the Emperor down too, the risks would definitely have been worth it.*

Her own wards opened up around her, reminding her of just what she'd lost when she'd fled the Golden City. The urge to just bask in their touch, to allow her awareness to drift through the library, was almost overpowering. But there wasn't *time* to enjoy herself. She pulled back, after opening a gash in the wards, and called to Johan and Dolman. Johan ran over to her at once; Dolman launched a series of curses before running to join them, the wards snapping back into place to shield them. Elaine smiled, despite her sudden tiredness, as curses started bouncing off the wards. Nothing short of Johan's power would break through the wards …

And the Witch-King is a wild magician too, she thought, suddenly sober. *He might be able to break in himself.*

She cleared her throat. "Stay in contact with the walls," she ordered, as she started to walk towards the door. "You *don't* want them to consider you an enemy."

The wards snapped and crackled around them, unsure quite what to make of either Johan or Dolman. She suspected the wards remembered Johan from his first visit – or, perhaps, that they remembered something far older. There hadn't been anything about wild magicians in the library, not even in the Black Vault, yet whoever designed the Great Library had presumably known the dangers. She recalled just how many spells had been layered over the building, over the centuries; had one of them, long ago, been designed to repel wild magicians? And yet, Johan had destroyed some of the wards quite by accident …

Maybe he couldn't enter without permission, she thought, as they reached the doors. They were locked, but a simple spell was enough to open them. *Or maybe they assumed there would be no more wild magicians.*

"The dragons are pulling back," Dolman said, "but the red-robes are erecting wards and coming this way. I think they suspect we intend to turn the Great Library against them."

"Good," Johan said. "The more who try to break through the wards here, the fewer there are at the palace."

Elaine nodded, feeling her stomach clench. It was quite possible they could be walking into an ambush … and equally possible they would make it through to the palace, where she would be tested …

… And, in truth, she wasn't sure what result she wanted.

The door opened. "Come on," she said. She had no idea where the Witch-King was, but assuming he walked at a steady pace he'd be at the Golden City within a week, perhaps less. "There isn't much time left."

Chapter Thirty-Four

I'm home, Elaine thought.

The Great Library felt ... *welcoming*, even though it was cold and dark. She closed her eyes, reaching out to touch the wards and ordering the lanterns to come to life. The atmosphere still felt odd, even to her, as they walked through the mirrors and down into the basement, where the staff had been working on sorting the latest books before she'd ordered them all to leave. She felt as if she'd come full circle when she saw a pile of books, recalling a similar pile that had turned her into the Bookworm. One of her staff might have been the *next* person to encounter a charmed book.

I made sure they wouldn't, she thought, grimly. *I altered the wards to make it impossible for a second such book to enter the library.*

Johan touched her arm. She jumped. "Elaine?"

"I'm just ... stressed," Elaine said. She led them further down into the basement, mentally feeling out the complex pattern of the wards. The first secret passage might have been discovered, but there were two more within the building. "I'm sorry."

"Don't be," Dolman said, as they stopped in front of a large portrait of a previous librarian and peered at it. "Just get us to the palace."

Elaine nodded as she reached out to touch the portrait in the right place. The old librarian had been famous for absolutely nothing, beyond harassing his staff and appointing his cronies to positions of power; somehow, Elaine wasn't surprised that he'd managed to spend several thousand crowns on his own portrait, even though he hadn't been able to find the money to fund much-needed renovations. His successor had dumped the portrait into the basement, used it to hide one of the secret passageways and probably forgot it even existed. Elaine couldn't remember seeing it in all her days as a librarian.

She pushed the hidden switch and the painting opened, revealing a set of stairs leading down into the darkness. Dolman offered to go first, but Elaine shook her head and took the lead, generating a ball of light to illuminate her path. Halfway down, a set of wards started to spark ominously, ready to trap the three intruders below the city for the rest of their lives if they failed to satisfy them. Elaine gritted her teeth, pushed forward the codes she'd learnt when she'd taken office, and waited. Moments later, the wards withdrew to allow them to pass through without a fight.

"Another tunnel," Johan said, slowly. "How many *are* there?"

"Hundreds," Dolman said. "The entire city is honeycombed with tunnels."

Elaine nodded in agreement. There were maps in her head, maps of tunnels that had been built by the Grand Sorcerers and Great Houses, maps of tunnels and catacombs and hidden places that had been forgotten by everyone else. Even Light Spinner, she suspected, had never really known the full extent of the tunnel system. The gods alone knew how many youngsters had stumbled in and found themselves trapped, when they triggered a ward or hidden safeguard …

She walked onwards, feeling other wards pick and pry at her mind as she passed. She *was* a Privy Councillor, she *was* a trusted associate of the last Grand Sorcerer … and yet, she wasn't sure if Deferens might have managed to revoke her access rights. He hadn't managed to block her from the Great Library, but she'd been Head Librarian. What if she couldn't break into the Imperial Palace …?

"Here," she said, as they came to a solid stone wall. "If it lets us through, we will be in the lower levels of the palace."

"I'm ready," Dolman said.

Elaine looked at him and pushed her hand against the stone wall. The wards peered at her – she felt suddenly naked under their emotionless scrutiny – and parted; the wall shuddered, then slowly moved aside to reveal a colossal chamber. It was deserted, but bedrolls lay everywhere, suggesting the soldiers had used it as their barracks. Elaine glanced at Dolman, who slipped past her and over to the far wall, tapping at it with his wand. A second hidden passageway opened, revealing a flight of stairs. Elaine braced herself against an attack of claustrophobia and followed him up the stairs, Johan bringing up the rear. The door closed silently seconds later.

"They left this passage here," Johan said, his mind tinged with disbelief. "Why?"

"The palace isn't just the residence of the Grand Sorcerer – or the Emperor," Dolman pointed out, dryly. "There are – or were – thousands of civil servants who live and work in the building. The Grand Sorcerer often had meetings he didn't want anyone else to know about, so he used the passageways to sneak from room to room. No one but he and the Inquisitors knew they were there."

"And no one else could gain access," Elaine added.

"No," Dolman said. He hesitated, uncomfortably. "I think I'm *technically* supposed to wipe your memory after you exit the tunnels."

"Bad idea," Elaine said, quickly. Her protections would make it impossible; she honestly wasn't sure what a memory wipe would do to Johan. "Let's see what happens when we do the test first."

She tasted Johan's apprehension as they finally reached a hidden door and peered through a concealed eyehole, looking into an empty room. Dolman opened the door and stepped out, wand raised; no one moved to challenge them as Elaine followed him and looked around with interest. A chair sat in the exact centre of the room, manacles hanging down from the arms and legs; she shivered as she realised that she was meant to be restrained, while he tested her blood.

"You can't chain her down," Johan said, urgently. "What if we're attacked?"

"I won't," Dolman said. "That's for idiots who think we're joking when we promise mandatory sentencing for anyone stupid enough to try to fool us."

Elaine shivered. "Do you have any oath-bound obligations?"

"No," Dolman said. He gave her a thin smile as he opened a drawer and rummaged through it. "You don't have to sit down, if you would rather not. We just prefer to keep the tricksters to a minimum."

He withdrew a small iron crown, studded with red gems. Elaine felt her heart skip a beat as she recognised it, although she was perhaps the only person outside the Inquisition who *would*. It glowed if worn by someone who shared the royal bloodline ... all of a sudden, she wasn't sure she wanted to know. Certainty would push her onwards, either force her to enact the rest of the plan or flee the Golden City. And Dolman ...

He's putting his life in my hands, she thought, numbly.

It was suddenly hard to take a breath. She wasn't sure *she* could have done *that*, not with her experience of being under compulsion spells. Dolman would be *hers*, if she took the throne. She knew she was better than Vlad Deferens, but did *Dolman* know it? Or was he prepared to take the risk of her turning into a monster, if it was the price of stopping the Witch-King?

"Once you kneel down, I will place this on your head," Dolman said. "If you're part of the bloodline, the gems will start to glow. Are you ready?"

Elaine hesitated, then slowly knelt in front of him. Johan stood behind her, his emotions spinning through a confusing maze. She hadn't been joking when she'd told him there was a good chance they were already married, thanks to the bond. He'd see his life circumscribed as Prince Consort, as long as she stayed on the throne. All she had to do was say no ... hell, it wasn't as if she was facing the penalties for deliberately lying. She had every reason to think she *was* related to Deferens.

"Do it," she ordered.

Dolman slowly lowered the crown onto her head. She closed her eyes as it touched her hair, trying to withstand the urge to tear it away from her. It was heavier than she'd expected, pressing down on her scalp. She felt a tingle passing through her body, magic flickering over her ...

"Your Supremacy," Dolman said, tonelessly.

Elaine opened her eyes and looked up. Her head was surrounded by red light.

Red for blood, she thought, numbly.

She suddenly felt faint; she would have fallen over if Johan hadn't caught her, his strong hands holding her tightly. It was hard not to feel a sense of irony when she remembered her past life: an orphan, a poor scholarship student, a lowly librarian with barely enough magic to make an impression ...

"It worked," Johan said. Elaine shot him a nasty look for stating the obvious. "Now what do we do?"

Dolman carefully took the crown from Elaine's head and placed it back in the drawer. "We slip down to the Throne Room and take the Golden Throne," he said. He tapped his wand against the hidden entrance, opening it up. "Come, Your Supremacy."

Your Supremacy, Elaine thought. She hadn't realised just how strongly she'd hoped Johan had been wrong until she'd discovered he was right. *Once I sit on the throne, my life as I knew it will be over.*

She shuddered as she followed them back into the passageways. Light Spinner had wanted power; Vlad Deferens had wanted power ... but she wasn't like either of them. Deferens had been a ruthless bastard, a monster who'd enslaved Charity, Dread and thousands of others; Light Spinner had been kinder, yet no less ruthless. And the previous Grand Sorcerer, a man who'd ruled so long that even *she'd* forgotten his name ...

No one questioned his orders, she thought, bitterly. *But they'll question mine.*

She would almost have welcomed an enemy presence in the Throne Room, but it was as dark and silent as the grave. The Golden Throne sat in the exact centre of the giant chamber, glowing faintly as they stepped out of the hidden passageway. Elaine could practically *taste* the magic surrounding it, great strata of power surging down into infinity. For the first time, she believed – truly believed – the Witch-King's claim that mundanes had worshiped wild magicians as gods. The people who'd built the Golden Throne, and primed it to continue absorbing magic for centuries, had been far more powerful than any living magician, even the Witch-King himself.

Light Spinner was trapped here, she thought, as she took a step forward. The throne was surrounded by an aura that drew her in and repelled her in equal measure. *And Deferens was the last to sit on the throne.*

"Hurry," Dolman ordered, as the sound of running footsteps echoed through the chamber. "I think they've worked out what we're doing."

Elaine took another step forward, unable to think of anything but the throne. Even Johan receded to the back of her mind. It seemed to be taunting her, promising power and pain in equal measure. She'd wondered why successive Grand Sorcerers hadn't destroyed the Golden Throne – they lost everything if a true heir sat down – but she understood now. The Golden Throne was linked to *everything*, from the wards surrounding the Imperial Palace to the defences worked into the Seven Peaks. Destroying the Golden Throne would have crippled the entire city.

But the Witch-King would see it as a source of power, she thought, as she took another step forward. *He'd find a way to drain it into himself.*

"Elaine," Johan said. "I think you need to sit, now."

Elaine barely heard him as she reached out to touch the throne. Magic glittered around her fingertips, a final warning; if she didn't satisfy the throne, she'd be dead before a second had passed. How many had died, over the years, gambling that they had some of the bloodline in them? And how many had been *allowed* to die just to convince the population that there wasn't a secret test first? She ran her fingers over the throne, then turned. The light was so bright that it was hard for her to see anything beyond the dais, but she could hear the sound of fighting.

She sat.

The Golden Throne reached up and surrounded her. Magic flared brighter than ever, ripping through her mind. She wanted to scream, but she couldn't move; the throne was slowly tearing her apart, as casually as a sadistic young child would tear the wings off a fly. And yet ... there was something about it that was almost *welcoming*. Had Vlad Deferens left a surprise for anyone who sat after him? But Deferens was dead. No one had taken the throne since then ...

She felt the throne scrutinising every last atom of her body, then open up around her. It felt like touching the Great

Library's wards, only far – far – worse. And yet, the more her mind expanded, the more she understood what she was seeing. No wonder Deferens had had no trouble besting Light Spinner. The sheer power of the wards surrounding the Imperial Palace meant he'd had problems *only* turning her to stone. Disintegrating her and everyone else within the palace would have been far easier.

Her awareness snapped back to the Throne Room. Dolman was being pushed back, despite his power, by a dozen red-robed sorcerers. Johan was trying to raise a shield, but he couldn't produce enough control to do it without damaging the magic surrounding the Golden Throne and harming Elaine. Elaine concentrated, testing the hundreds of thousands of spells that made up the wards, and sent a single command. The wards lashed out and the red-robed sorcerers froze solid.

Deferens must have been far more used to having vast levels of power at his command, she thought, coldly. *He never even tried to be subtle with what he had.*

She sent her awareness running through the Imperial Palace, freezing every last sorcerer, soldier, servant and slave. A quick twist to the spell would ensure they never even *knew* they were frozen. Time would stop for them until the Inquisitors had a chance to sort them all out, then free the innocent and punish the guilty. Her awareness twisted again as the Imperial Palace noted the dragons; she told it, quite firmly, to leave the dragons alone. As far as she knew, Deferens had been the only person to produce Dragons and the last of them had been captured, after his death.

The Great Library isn't quite linked to the Imperial Palace, she noted, puzzled. She'd assumed it would be, although in hindsight she should have realised that they weren't, if only because Deferens had been unable to break into the Great Library. *And neither is the Peerless School.*

The answer rose into her mind from the throne. Both buildings had come into their own *after* the wars, after the Witch-King had been defeated. By then, the Golden Throne had been empty; no more heirs remained, save for the handful the Witch-King had kept in hiding. The Grand Sorcerers might even have been relieved. No, they *had* been relieved. Aristocracy was a poor way of determining who would hold ultimate power. So too, perhaps, was a magic-based meritocracy.

But it does cut down on succession disputes, she thought, as she opened her eyes. *No one doubts who is the next in line to the throne.*

"Your Supremacy," Dolman said.

He prostrated himself below her. Elaine blushed in embarrassed shock, understanding what he meant. He was *hers* now, bound as solidly to her as he'd been to the Emperor …

"Elaine," Johan said. She tasted *his* sudden embarrassment at *her* embarrassment. "Um … Your *Supremacy*?"

"Show the proper respect," Dolman growled.

"Let him talk freely," Elaine said. Her lips twitched. "And please, talk freely too. I don't want people bowing to me."

"Too late," Johan said.

"Call the others down," Elaine ordered. She wasn't normally so assertive. Was the throne pushing at her, gently moulding her into an Empress? "The remaining troops in the city are to surrender, if they want to; if not, we have to kill them before they can make a break for it."

"Of course, Your Supremacy," Dolman said.

"And please stop calling me that," Elaine insisted. "My name is *Elaine*!"

"Elaine the First," Johan said. Elaine glared daggers at him. "It's true!"

"I know," Elaine said, sourly. She could sense his amusement. "But you don't have to rub it in."

It was nearly an hour before Dread, Sarah, Charity and Daria were shown into the Imperial Palace. Dread prostrated himself at once – Elaine couldn't help feeling even *more* embarrassed at *Dread* prostrating himself – while the others hesitated. Charity moved to go to her knees, then stopped herself; Daria and Sarah were less inclined to bend the knee to anyone. Elaine understood; indeed, after everything she'd been through, she was more than willing to forgive Charity refusing to make *any* submission at all.

"The city is reasonably secure," Dread said. "But there's probably still quite a few enemy troops hiding out."

Johan frowned as he looked at Elaine. "You can't find them?"

"They're not in the palace," Elaine said. She groaned, inwardly; she was Empress with nine Inquisitors to her name, but very little else. "Charity, please can you speak to the Administrator? We're going to need his assistance and that of his staff."

"And the older students too, I'll wager," Dread said. "They may not be fully-trained, but they'd be able to help."

Elaine nodded. "And then see how many of the Great Houses are left," she added. That might be a mistake – the Great Houses hadn't liked having the *first* Emperor – but there was no choice. Their magic was needed. "I don't know how long we have before the Witch-King arrives, but I don't think it will be very long at all."

"I can see if we can make contact with the remaining Levellers," Sarah offered. "I don't know if Hawke survived, but if he did …"

"Find him," Elaine said. An idea was bubbling through her mind, now she'd seen the Golden Throne, but it would require some fancy timing. "We're going to need everyone we can get."

Chapter Thirty-Five

"It's reasonably safe out there," Dolman said, as Charity followed him out of the Imperial Palace. "But Her Supremacy insists I accompany you."

Charity nodded, too tired to argue. She wasn't sure what time zone she was in, let alone when she should be trying to get a nap, but there was work to do. She'd heard stories of people having problems when taking express coaches across the continent, yet it had never seemed a real issue to her. Flying on a dragon, on the other hand, left her feeling as if it were still the middle of the night, even though it was early morning.

The streets seemed quieter somehow as she walked towards the Peerless School, although she knew there were holdouts hidden within the city. She couldn't help glancing around, expecting an attack at any moment; the sense of being watched by inhuman eyes grew stronger the closer she walked to the school. It was quite possible the Administrator was watching her through early-warning wards, waiting to see what she'd do when she tapped on the wards and asked for admittance. He almost certainly knew what had happened to the *last* set of children she'd taken from the school.

Guilt burnt in her heart as she reached the edge of the wards and pressed her fingers against them, requesting entry. The Emperor had ordered and she'd obeyed, collecting three dozen children from the Peerless School and leading them to be sacrificed like lambs to the slaughter. Magic flickered around her fingertips; she found herself hoping, only half in jest, that the wards would repel her with lethal force. It would save her from her own helpless guilt. But the wards opened slowly, allowing her to walk to the gates. She glanced at Dolman, taking comfort in his presence, as she began the long walk. The giant stone doors opened up in front of her …

And the Administrator was standing in the hall, waiting for her.

She sucked in her breath sharply as his gaze flickered over her. This time, he wore the black and gold battle robes as if he had a right to wear them, his hand clutching a staff charged with deadly spells. She felt a flicker of hope as she realised he'd readied himself to fight, even though it would have been useless against the Emperor. Vlad Deferens would have knocked him aside if the Administrator had tried to stand up to him. But then, the bureaucrat could hardly deny what had happened any longer. She couldn't help wondering if he'd already drawn up plans to evacuate the school.

"Cast a truth spell," she said, harshly. *"Please."*

The Administrator frowned and waved his hand in the air. A faint golden glow appeared, humming faintly as it settled around Charity. A lie would turn the gold to red, she recalled; only a handful of sorcerers could trick such a spell and it was almost impossible to do it without being noticed. The Administrator would have access to her records, if he'd bothered to look them up after their first meeting. He'd know she couldn't hope to fool the spell for more than a few seconds.

"The Emperor is dead, long live the Empress," she said. The gold continued to glow, untroubled by deceit or falsehood. "Lady Elaine, the last surviving member of the Privy Council, has taken the Golden Throne. However, the Witch-King is heading towards the city and intends to take its resources for himself."

The Administrator's eyes went wide. He'd know, of course, that someone else had taken the Golden Throne – every powerful sorcerer within fifty miles would know – but he wouldn't know who, or why. He might well have assumed that Deferens' son had stabbed his father in the back and taken the throne. It was the sort of thing Deferens would have encouraged, if he'd believed his own words; he'd always insisted the strong should overtake the weak, after all. The thought made her smile. No doubt Deferens would have died sooner rather than later even without her.

"The Empress commands you to assemble your staff and

upper-level pupils who are ready to fight," she continued, without giving the Administrator a chance to speak. "Lower-level pupils are to be readied for immediate evacuation. Every magician in the city who is not going to join the defence has to leave, as soon as possible."

"I see," the Administrator said. He stared at the glow for a long moment, as if he couldn't quite believe either his eyes or ears. "I have only three hundred upper-level pupils."

The Great Houses must have started pulling their heirs out as soon as the Emperor turned his back, Charity thought. It was hard to blame them for trying, although they'd been taking a ghastly risk. Deferens would not have rewarded anyone for trying to escape his clutches. *But if three hundred are all we have, they will have to do.*

Dolman took a step forward. "And lower-level pupils?"

"Only two hundred," the Administrator said. "Mainly mundane-born."

Charity frowned. "Why?"

"The Great Houses sent fewer students after the ... near-disaster last year," the Administrator said. "It was a matter to be discussed by the Privy Council, before the Emperor took the Golden Throne."

"I see," Charity said. Elaine hadn't mentioned anything about it to her, although *that* meant nothing. She had the very distant impression that Elaine would have been happier having as little to do with the council as possible. "Have them readied to leave, then assemble the other pupils. They may be needed to reinforce the Inquisitors."

The Administrator looked alarmed. "My students are not trained combat magicians ..."

"They will have to do," Charity said, fighting down the urge to yawn. "The Inquisitor" – she nodded at Dolman – "will sort through their skills, then assign them to where they can be most useful. In the meantime ..."

She took a breath. "In the meantime, sir, is the rest of my family here?"

The Administrator looked at her for a long moment before nodding. Charity let out a sigh of relief; she'd known she'd have to ask, but at the same time she'd been terrified of the answer. Johan had sent the younger children to Lady

Lakeside and she'd sold what remained of her soul to keep them safe, yet she'd feared the Emperor would have decided to hurt them on a whim. It wasn't as if she had any way to force him to keep his side of the bargain.

"Please can I see them," she said. Her voice cracked noticeably, but she found it hard to care. "It's been so long."

The Administrator bowed gravely. "If you wait in the antechamber, I will have them sent to you," he said. "And then I will assemble the younger pupils. I assume they will be escorted through the mountains?"

"Yes," Dolman said, flatly. "Provisions will be made to send them to the nearest harbour."

Or the nearest harbour that's safe, Charity thought. *Falcone's Nest would be the closest and the whole city was in flames, only yesterday.*

She allowed the Administrator to show her into a small room, then waited; taking a seat while Dolman leant against the wall, his dark eyes missing nothing. Part of her just wanted to run, to hide from her siblings; part of her knew she'd failed them badly and just wanted to see them again before the end. The Peerless School felt oddly quiet – classes couldn't be in session, she thought – as if half the pupils had vanished. Or were they cowering in their dorms, after she'd taken students from the school? Did they *know* she was coming?

And if it had been this quiet back when I was a pupil, she reminded herself, *I'd have thought someone was planning something.*

The door opened, revealing her younger siblings. Charity stood and practically threw herself at them, wrapping the four children in a giant hug. Jay and Jolie looked pale – they were old enough to understand *something* of what was going on – while Chanel and Chime seemed alarmingly nervous. They'd been in House Lakeside when the Emperor had unleashed a dragon on Lady Lakeside and her family.

"I'm sorry," she said, through tears. "I ..."

"They said you're a slave," Jay said. He rubbed the side of his face, which was displaying a nasty bruise. "Is that true?"

"It was," Charity said. She knew she'd never live it down. A brief period of enslavement would have been quite bad enough, but she'd believed she'd belong to the Emperor for the rest of her life. "I ... I got better."

Jolie frowned. "What happened?"

"I killed the Emperor," Charity said.

She said the words slowly, finally allowing herself to accept that she'd cheated her oaths and survived. Nothing happened. She smiled in open relief – she'd shied away from considering the fact that she might have been wrong – and hugged her siblings tighter. Jay pulled back hastily – he thought himself too old to be hugged by his older sister – but the others hugged her back.

"Jamal is dead," she added, after a moment. She might as well get all the bad news out at once. "Johan ... is alive, but occupied."

She didn't miss the flicker of fear that crossed their faces. Johan had stolen Jamal's magic, after all; it was quite possible he'd want to do the same to them. They understood, instinctively, that magic was the only thing that made them special. Without it ... Jamal had ended up enslaved, while no one knew what had happened to their father. Johan had plenty of reasons to want revenge ...

"I don't think he'll want to hurt you," she said, finally. The hell of it was that she would have cheerfully accepted the loss of her magic, like Dread, if it had freed her from her oaths. It probably would have done if she'd had a chance. "But right now the four of you are going to be leaving the city."

Jay shook his head. "As the Conidian ..."

He broke off, looking confused. Technically, he *was* the Conidian, although he was still underage. The Empress would have to appoint a regent, someone who could run the family's affairs before he reached his majority; Charity wondered, absently, if Dolman would be interested in the post. If he wasn't ... it was quite possible that the Empress would pick someone who would loot the family bare before it was too late. The Empress's lover had every reason to want to hurt the family ...

"It may not matter in a week," she said, firmly. Most of the family's wealth still lay in their estates to the south, well away from the Golden City. The rest would probably have to be abandoned; it struck her, suddenly, that she wasn't sure if

Conidian House was still standing. "Jay, I expect you to look after your younger siblings ..."

"I will," Jay promised. He scowled at her. "But am I the Conidian?"

"You're the person with the best claim to the title," Charity said. "Jamal is dead, Johan doesn't want it, I don't want it either ..."

She shrugged. "But you have to understand that things have changed," she warned. "The title may be meaningless soon enough."

"I'll make it mean something again," Jay said, stiffly.

"You'll be taken out of the city," Charity said. "If the Empress allows it, I will have you sent directly to the estate. You can stay there until ... until everything is settled. There are enough wards there to keep you safe from almost any reasonable threat. If not, you'll board a ship and head off to a distant land. You should be safe there."

Unless the Witch-King really does become a god, she thought. The idea of a *real* god walking the lands was chilling. *He might be able to reach for them wherever they are*.

She spoke a silent prayer to the household gods, then looked at her siblings. Jay looked alarmingly like a younger version of their father, although his hair was jet black instead of grey. But then, the Conidian had had troubles even before the move to the Golden City. Jolie took after their mother instead, with golden hair and a smile that was so charming that it would have fathers preparing death hexes to protect their daughters in the next few years. Chanel too had her mother's looks, while Chime took too much after their father ... they'd be fine, she told herself, if they survived the war. Brains, beauty and whatever they could salvage from the estate.

"I expect you to go straight to the estate, or the ship," she said, looking each of them in the eye, one by one. "Do *not* attempt to stay here or go elsewhere."

"The Conidian cannot run," Jay protested.

Chime elbowed him, sharply. "Charity ... we don't want to leave you."

"You don't have a choice," Charity said. She loved her

siblings, but she didn't really want to spend too long with them. They were innocents and she ... was a wreck. "The family line must survive, whatever else happens."

She closed her eyes in pain. Their father would have lifted an eyebrow and his children would have scrambled to obey, Jamal would have used force or the threat of force. She ... didn't have the presence of her father, nor the willingness to cast compulsion hexes to make sure the children behaved. Besides, repeated compulsion spells could have an unpleasant effect on one's intelligence. She had a feeling that some of Johan's worse moments came from long-term spell damage.

"I understand," Jolie said. He took Jay's arm. "We'll get to the estate, Charity."

"I hope I'll see you again," Charity said. She hugged each of them, individually. "And if you don't see me again, remember I love you."

Chime looked doubtful. "Does Johan love us too?"

Charity tried to think of a way to sound convincing. "I think it will be a long time before he forgives you – forgives any of us," she said. She had her doubts – Johan had made it clear he had no intention of returning to the family – but she kept them to herself. "I'm sure it will come, in time."

Dolman cleared his throat, loudly.

"It's time to go," Charity said. "Goodbye."

The Administrator was waiting for them outside, standing next to a long line of children of between twelve and fifteen years of age. Charity would have recognised them as mundane-born even if she hadn't been told; they wore regular uniforms, with neither the house crests nor the style of someone born to a magical bloodline. They certainly hadn't had the tailoring that any aristocratic student would have used to make their uniforms fit perfectly.

"They'll be escorted out in twenty minutes," Dolman said, after a brief – and silent – consultation with his fellow Inquisitors. "There aren't many horses left in the city, thanks to the army, but there are a couple of farms on the other side of the mountains."

"Good," the Administrator said. He looked at Charity. "Lady Charity, there are a number of magicians waiting to speak with you."

Charity frowned. "Like whom?"

"Lord Arndell appears to be their spokesman," the Administrator said. "But he is accompanied by Lord Ruthven and Lady Hollows."

"I see," Charity said. Arndell was a Great House; Ruthven and Hollows would probably qualify, if they held their place in the Golden City for a few more decades. "Please can you show me to them?"

She followed the Administrator through a set of doors and into a small meeting room. The Arndell was a grey-haired man with a grim expression – she recalled, vaguely, that his son had been murdered shortly after Johan had developed his powers – while Lord Ruthven was a red-headed man carrying a sword and Lady Hollows looked hardly any older than Elaine or Daria. Her father had died young, Charity remembered; she'd had to take up the title of Lady Hollows only a couple of years ago. It was a minor miracle she'd survived Deferens' rule, when older and more powerful women had been targeted for elimination.

"Lady Charity," the Arndell said. If he knew of her experience under Deferens, he showed no sign of it. "I have been ... *requested* ... to demand the return of the hostages."

Charity blinked before remembering. Deferens had taken a number of hostages from the Great Houses, but where *were* they? Elaine hadn't said anything about them living in the palace; she doubted they would have been sent to the Peerless School. They might even be dead ... but that would have alerted the Great Houses that Deferens was not to be trusted. No, they had to be hidden somewhere ...

"When we find them, we will return them," she said. She made a mental note to check with Elaine before she ordered a search for the hostages. They might have been caught up in the Imperial Palace, after all. "There's a great deal you have to know."

She insisted that Lord Arndell cast a truth spell, then ran through the whole story for the second time. The Arndell looked shocked; Lord Ruthven looked determined to fight, while Lady Hollows looked disbelieving. Charity understood; if she hadn't seen the Witch-King, she would have doubted that a figure from half-forgotten legend had returned to walk the earth once again. But the truth spell made it impossible for them to doubt her.

"The Empress needs your help," she said, once she'd finished. "We need you to send your people to assist us ..."

"For a price," Lady Hollows said. Her voice hardened. "We barely survived *one* Emperor. We may not survive an *Empress*."

"This isn't the time," Lord Arndell snapped. He looked at Charity. "We'll discuss the price later."

"I believe the Empress intends to abdicate the throne after the battle is over," Charity said, before Lady Hollows could object further. "But unless we defeat the Witch-King now, everything we've done will be wasted and our hope of freedom will be lost forever."

Chapter Thirty-Six

Johan was feeling rather useless.

It had been a familiar feeling, when he'd been a child. He couldn't use magic, so he couldn't assist his father or go to the Peerless School; he couldn't work in the kitchen, so he couldn't even help the servants. But he'd felt better about himself when his powers had developed and they'd fled the Golden City. He'd been *useful*. Now, with hundreds of civil servants hurrying into the palace to pledge their loyalty to the new Empress, he felt useless again.

He leant against the wall in the Throne Room and watched, sourly, as Elaine issued orders in her quiet voice. She was growing more assertive the longer she sat on the throne, he realised, as if the Golden Throne was slowly shaping her into a stronger ruler. He could feel her presence in his mind, but there was something else there, something that had come between them. It didn't take much imagination to realise that the Golden Throne was now part of her, at least until she put it aside.

If she can, he thought. He understood the desire for power – and, even though Elaine had never shared it, he had a feeling she would come to like it. Hundreds of men and women were bending the knee to her; there would be thousands more, including entire *kingdoms*, if she stayed on the throne. He found it hard to imagine that she *would* surrender power so tamely. *Magicians always want more power*.

"Hey," Daria said. "You want to go help some kids?"

Johan jumped. He'd been so lost in his own thoughts that he hadn't heard her slipping up next to him. The werewolf looked tired, but surprisingly happy. Johan took one last look at Elaine and followed Daria through a side door, into yet another maze of corridors. A man was standing in the middle, frozen in time. It would be weeks or months before anyone got around to freeing him.

"I could smell you from right across the room," Daria said. "She *will* have time for you soon, you know."

"I know it, but I don't believe it," Johan admitted. Daria looked ... *different*, somehow, although he couldn't put his finger on it. "What happened to you?"

Daria grinned, showing sharp teeth. "The pack didn't want to believe me," she said, "even though I could hardly lie to them. I wound up having to challenge the alpha male for leadership of the pack."

Johan stared at her. "You ... you could have *lost*!"

"Yeah," Daria said. "If I'd lost, it would have been pretty bad. Good thing I didn't."

"Yeah," Johan echoed.

He felt sick. He wasn't an expert, but if he recalled correctly the loser of a leadership challenge would be knocked right to the bottom of the hierarchy. Daria had gambled with her freedom, risking everything just to claim the leadership. He felt a bitter stab of shame. He'd been grumbling about feeling useless while Daria had risked a fate worse than death to help them. Elaine was lucky to have her as a friend.

"Don't think about the risks," Daria urged, as she sniffed the air. "Think instead about the future."

Johan nodded. "Are you going to keep the pack?"

"I'll stay away for a few months, afterwards," Daria said, briskly. "A new alpha will arise to take my place. I'll make sure he has enough time to get entrenched before I go back, so he won't feel obliged to challenge me."

She sniffed the air again. "This way," she said. "Come on."

Johan eyed her retreating back. It was hard to be sure, but were there *scars* under her thin robe? A fight for dominance between an alpha and a challenger would be *nasty*. Daria had been lucky to survive without serious injuries, even though the pack mentality would preclude other challenges until she recovered. And the fate of the loser didn't bear thinking about, not for werewolves ...

"You mentioned kids," he said. "What happened?"

"Your sister discovered that Deferens took hostages," Daria

said, as she hurried down the corridor. Johan followed, grimly aware that her legs were scarred badly too. "They were never returned or sacrificed."

"Because there would be a blood-tie," Johan said. "Their families would know the instant they were killed."

"Correct," Daria agreed. She pulled her wand from her belt and tapped it against a door, carefully. "Let's see what's inside."

Johan tensed as the door opened, revealing a small dormitory. There were twenty-seven bunks, stuffed into a room smaller than Jamal's study. Johan had the feeling that most of the kids would have complained, loudly, even though they still had more room than the average mundane worker in the city. A dozen children, ranging in age from eight to sixteen, were frozen in time; some lay in the bunks, others were reading or trapped in poses that suggested they were trying to work magic. His eyes narrowed as he recognised some of the family crests. Deferens had collected a hostage from almost every major magical family or bloodline in the city.

"They're safe, at least," Daria said. She paced between the hostages, looking for signs of trouble. "Elaine can release them, once their parents arrive. It should make matters easier for their families."

"Their families may want to resist Elaine," Johan pointed out. "Do *you* want to run the risk of surrendering our only guarantee of good behaviour?"

"They're *children*," Daria snapped, angrily. "They shouldn't be held *prisoner* because we don't trust their parents."

Johan sighed. He'd known, of course, that hostages were regularly exchanged amongst the Great Houses, but the hostages were generally treated like honoured guests. It would have been a breach in etiquette to abuse them, even to the point of insisting they share a tiny room with a dozen other hostages. Deferens, of course, hadn't given a damn. He'd probably thought that the idea of forcing the children to share was funny, if he'd thought about it at all.

You were brought up to accept it as normal, he thought, grimly. *But Daria sees it as appalling.*

"It should be considered," he mumbled. He didn't want a werewolf angry at him, particularly not a pack leader. "I …"

"The kids can go back home," Daria said, firmly. She did a quick head count and turned back to the door. "Let's go find the Empress."

Somewhat to Johan's surprise, Elaine was alone when they returned to the Throne Room, sitting in front of a small table that had seemingly grown out of the floor, and studying a set of diagrams. Daria reported quickly; Johan hesitated, then decided to keep his thoughts to himself. Elaine eyed him sharply – she'd be able to sense his concern – but evidently decided not to ask.

"See they get back home," she said, to Daria. "Johan … stay here, please."

Daria nodded and left. Elaine rose to her feet, caught Johan and pulled him into a desperate hug. Her body felt warm against his, but he could sense the tiredness burning through her soul. The Golden Throne was clearly exacting a price for its services. He wondered, suddenly, just where the Emperors of yore had slept, then dismissed the thought. Deferens would have been the last person to use the royal bedchambers.

"I feel harassed," she said, when she pulled back from him. "Do you think your father felt the same way too?"

"Probably," Johan said. "He always threw a fit when he was interrupted in the middle of the day."

"I don't blame him," Elaine said. "Do you realise just how many minor matters have to be handled by the Grand Sorcerer, *personally*?"

"No," Johan said. He smirked. "Hire minions for that, Elaine."

"I don't have any who can be trusted with this," Elaine said. She pointed a finger at the floor, which bubbled and produced another chair. "Have a seat, please."

Johan hesitated before sitting down, remembering just what the Golden Throne did to people who didn't have the right bloodline. But Elaine wouldn't have made him sit on something dangerous, not knowingly. The chair felt oddly comfortable underneath him; he rubbed the stone thoughtfully as Elaine sat facing him, her fingers tracing out the equations on the papers. They were completely beyond his comprehension.

"This is the Witch-King," Elaine said. "I've been working my way through the web of spells he used to create his new body. It's a fantastically complex piece of work, really."

Johan eyed her, doubtfully. "You sound like you admire him."

Elaine hesitated. "He's a genius, no doubt about it," she said. "But at the same time he's a complete lunatic."

She cleared her throat. "The interesting thing is that he combines both wild magic and traditional spell-casting," she said. "My guess is that the magic I detected in you, when we first met, will actually grow stronger over the years. You may be capable of traditional spell-casting yourself within the next couple of decades."

"Not quickly enough to help us now, then," Johan said. He frowned as he recalled the day Chime had shown her first signs of magic. "I thought the earlier a child showed magic, the more powerful it was."

"I'm not sure," Elaine admitted. "It's quite possible that exposure to magic helps bring magic into the light sooner, creating that myth. What *is* clear is that you can do fantastic things *without* a vast reserve of magic. However, your magic is driven by your emotion and isn't entirely reliable."

"I can try to practice traditional spells," Johan objected.

"We can try," Elaine agreed. "However, right now we have a much larger problem."

She ran a finger down the long line of equations. "The Witch-King appears to have come closer to solving Entropy's Dilemma than anyone else in recorded history," she said, quirking her eyebrows. "You *have* heard of Entropy's Dilemma?"

"Spells decay," Johan said. He'd overheard his father lecturing Charity on the subject, years ago. "Even the most advanced and powerful spells slowly decay and fade away."

"Precisely," Elaine said. "Wardcrafters are very good at anchoring wards to protect homes and keying them to family members, but even they cannot ultimately defeat Entropy's Dilemma. The Witch-King's spells, however, keep magic channelling and rechanneling through him, recycling – if you will – the raw stuff of magic. However, even *he* suffers from Entropy's Dilemma. His rebirth used so much magic that he was forced to head straight for the camp, rather than making sure I was dead."

"Luckily for us," Johan said.

"Quite," Elaine agreed. She gave him a smile that melted all his doubts away. "I think *he* thinks he can solve Entropy's Dilemma with a sufficiently large infusion of magic," she said. "The children at the Peerless School, as we noted, are a potential source of magic, as are the wards surrounding the Great Houses, the Great Library, the Peerless School and the Golden Throne itself. However, I have a feeling he'd prefer the children. The wards are shaped magic that may not be suitable for his requirements."

"Shit," Johan said. "Can we stop him?"

"I believe so," Elaine said. She looked him in the eye, her thoughts shadowed with worry. "I also believe there's a reason the Witch-King left you alive."

It took Johan a moment to comprehend it. "You think he wants *me*?"

"Your body, at least," Elaine said. "He'd have the knowledge I have, combined with the power you have; I think he decided that you'd make a suitable host for his mentality if his original plan fell through. It's the only reason I can think of why he left you alive."

"I won't let him have me," Johan said, shuddering in revulsion. It would be worse than a compulsion curse, he was sure. His mentality would be overwritten by the Witch-King, obliterating Johan from existence. Worse, perhaps, the Witch-King would try to make up with Johan's family and slowly turn them into his puppets. "I *won't*!"

He looked at her. "Can we stop him? Please?"

"Yes," Elaine said.

She tapped the papers, again. "We have two possible angles of attack," she said. "First, we can attempt to starve him. He needs power, so we'll make sure he doesn't get any. The children from the school are already being evacuated; they'll be well out of his reach by the time he arrives. Trying to chase them down will merely drain his power still further."

"Particularly if the children scatter," Johan said. "He'll

have to go after them one by one."

Elaine nodded, rubbing her eyes tiredly. "Yeah," she said. "That will force him to come *here*, where we'll be waiting. He won't have a choice. There simply isn't a larger concentration of magic anywhere in the world and he knows that as well as I do."

"True," Johan agreed. So far, it made an alarming kind of sense. "And then?"

"If we're lucky, we can prevent him from draining power from the wards," Elaine said. "He may come straight here" – she nodded to the throne – "but I don't know if he will be able to steal power from the Golden Throne."

"If it needs permission," Johan said, "Deferens may have already *given* him the permission."

Elaine muttered an oath under her breath and closed her eyes. The Golden Throne glowed brighter for a long moment as she communed with it. Johan waited, wondering just what – if anything – it would say. Ancient artefacts that had somehow retained magic for centuries were notoriously temperamental. His father had been fond of telling his younger children bedtime stories about idiots who found charmed swords or enchanted daggers and the fates that had befallen them. The Golden Throne had survived long enough to have a warped idea of what was acceptable behaviour ...

"He did," Elaine said. She gave him a warm look, but her thoughts were worried. "I'm not sure I can undo it. It's much more capable than anything I would have expected from Deferens."

"The Witch-King must have worked through him," Johan said. If Elaine hadn't taken the Golden Throne, the Witch-King could have walked into the Imperial Palace and drained it dry before proceeding to the Peerless School. "Can't you convince the throne to ignore whatever he did?"

"It's not intelligent," Elaine said, doubtfully. She looked at the throne, her eyes narrowing in thought. "I don't think it is really capable of understanding that one of the Emperors might have fiddled with it. There's a strong aversion to messing with the spells programmed into the throne's acceptance criteria."

She smiled. "But we may be able to deal with it," she

added, looking back at him. "There's a final possibility, though. We failed to stop him earlier because we didn't understand the threat. This time, however …"

Johan leant forward. "You have a plan?"

"We'd be risking everything," Elaine said. "If we combine your power and my knowledge, we can slow him down. But if I start … *tampering* … with the spells holding him together, I should be able to start undoing them from the inside."

"And Entropy's Dilemma will take its toll?" Johan guessed. "He'll die?"

"Something like that," Elaine said. He could sense trepidation in her thoughts. "But it *will* be risky. The Witch-King will be counter-attacking, Johan, and he wants your body. We might die together …"

Johan smiled. "How many times have we almost died since we first met?"

"Too many," Elaine said. She looked down at the table, guilt twisting through the bond. "I … I can ask Dread to be ready to kill you, if the Witch-King takes control."

"Please do," Johan said. He gave her a long look. "How long do we have?"

"Two days," Elaine said. She rubbed the side of her head. "He's walking towards us at a steady pace. I hoped the Lug would slow him down but it looks as though he just walked over the water. Oh, and there are several armies heading towards the Golden City too."

Johan frowned. "Friendly?"

"No," Elaine said. "They've had too much of one Emperor, Johan. They're coming to put an end to the Empress."

"I won't let them kill you," Johan said.

"They might not have to try," Elaine pointed out. She sighed, lifting her hands to rub her temples. "They won't be here until after the Witch-King meets his destiny."

"Two days," Johan said. He looked her in the eye. "You really need a rest."

"You mean you want to make love," Elaine said.

"No," Johan said. It wasn't entirely true – he *did* want her – but he had a feeling that sleep was a better idea right now.

There would be time for lovemaking tomorrow. "I mean I want you to have a proper rest. You've been up for … for over twenty hours, I think."

"Longer," Elaine said. She yawned, resting her elbows on the table. "I think I would have collapsed by now if the throne hadn't been sustaining me."

Johan stood. "You need rest," he said. "Let me take you to the bedchambers, where you can have a bath and then actually *sleep*. I'll sleep next to you – I'll even put a sword between us, if you wish. The Empire will not collapse because you take a few hours to get some rest before the next crisis."

Elaine looked up at him. "It's already collapsed," she said. "The Golden City is even running out of *food*. We're not getting any from Knawel Haldane. People will start starving in a week if either the Witch-King or the armies don't get them. I think we may even have to start evacuating everyone, not just the magical children …"

"Then it doesn't matter if you sleep or not," Johan insisted, holding out a hand. "Come on, Elaine. Please."

Elaine rose, slowly. "Don't bother with the sword," she ordered, as she took his hand and led him towards a hidden passageway. "I think the bed is big enough for both of us."

Chapter Thirty-Seven

"The Witch-King is walking through Knawel Haldane," Dread said, two days later.

Elaine nodded, feeling the Golden Throne's warnings echoing in her mind. The Emperors, it seemed, had wanted the throne to be an early-warning system for wild magicians – or gods. It was hard to draw memories out of the throne – she'd grown too used to having the knowledge of the Great Library in her head – but the flickering impressions she saw only suggested the Witch-King had been telling the truth. The gods had been nothing more than immensely powerful magicians.

And that's something that can never be shared, she thought, as she looked at the scrying pool in front of her. A single glimmer of light danced just above the water, mocking her. The Witch-King wasn't even *trying* to hide; he was the single most powerful source of magical energy on the continent. *The world can never know the truth. They'll all start trying to breed super-magicians.*

"The dragons tried to stop him," Dolman said. "He just ignored the flames."

"Close the northern tunnels," Elaine ordered. "Let him expend energy on the mountains."

She felt a dull tremor shuddering through the ground as the tunnels were collapsed, one by one. The remaining Levellers had been stockpiling Firepowder for one last battle; Hawke had agreed, reluctantly, to use it on the tunnels. Now, the Golden City – with most of the population evacuated – was cut off from the north. There was nothing stopping the Witch-King from walking around to the southern tunnels, but he'd be running short on magic all the time. The direct route was still over or *through* the mountains. Which one would the Witch-King choose?

The pool bubbled, faintly, as the light started to advance

forward and up. She sucked in her breath as she realised he was doing the impossible, climbing over the Seven Peaks. Raw magic flickered and flared around him – she could sense it through the throne – but it wasn't enough to stop his steady advance. Kane and Light Spinner had, between them, destroyed one of the city's strongest protections. There had been no time to rebuild it before the Witch-King arrived.

"Start throwing rocks," Dread ordered. "See if we can get him to slow down …"

Elaine blinked in surprise as the Witch-King reached the top of the peaks and *jumped*. For a moment, she thought he'd committed suicide, before remembering that he was effectively invulnerable to physical harm. Rolling down the mountainside was hugely undignified, but effective. And it took him past one of the improvised defence lines.

"Order the catapult crews to abandon their positions," Dread said, softly. "There's no point in giving him more targets."

"We can fight," Hawke insisted.

"You'll just be another set of targets," Elaine said. She shook her head. The Witch-King's presence was growing stronger all the time. "Tell your people to pull back and head for the southern tunnels. One way or the other, they're out of it now."

"Very well," Hawke said. He bowed. "It was a honour, Your Supremacy."

Elaine nodded curtly, already considering the next step. The Witch-King was standing up and restarting his walk, heading right for the Imperial Palace. It was good to know she'd worked it out correctly, even though it put her and Johan in terrible danger. One way or another, she was determined the Witch-King wouldn't survive, even if it cost her everything.

"Keep harassing him," she ordered Dread. "But don't get too close."

***

Charity had to fight to keep her astonishment under control as the Witch-King stood and started to advance towards the waiting students. Gasps of disbelief echoed through the band as they realised, for the first time, just how powerful the Witch-King actually was. She didn't dare look to see, but she was fairly sure that some of the students were quietly slipping out of the defence line and making their escape. It was hard to blame them.

The Witch-King looked no less intimidating in broad daylight. His aura was far more powerful than any normal magician, even more powerful than the Administrator who'd ruled the Peerless School with a rod of iron when she'd been a student. Part of her wanted to bend the knee to him, even though she hated the *thought* of submitting to someone – anyone – else after Deferens had made her a slave. From the mutterings, it was clear that some of the students were more deeply affected than others. Power was the one thing magicians worshipped and the Witch-King was power given shape and form.

He strode forward, wrapped in blue fire. Charity braced herself and hurled a killing hex towards the advancing lich. He didn't stop, even when the hex struck his chest and vanished in a flash of light. The other students joined in, some cursing him directly – to no apparent effect – while the others concentrated on casting spells on the surrounding neighbourhood, turning the road to mud, ice or even quicksand. But the Witch-King just kept coming, advancing forward with a cold, chilling patience. Charity gritted her teeth as a dragon bore down from overhead, breathing out a long stream of fire that washed over the Witch-King's blue form. But when the dragon swooped away, the Witch-King was still there. He didn't even seem angry.

"Keep throwing hexes at him," a voice ordered. One of the Inquisitors had taken command, throwing several spells Charity didn't recognise at their target. The air turned to ice, then fire; the Witch-King didn't slow, even once. "Don't let him have a moment to do anything."

Charity shuddered. It didn't look as though the Witch-King *needed* to do anything.

A house exploded into a mass of bricks, mortar and dust. An Inquisitor waved his wand, throwing the remains of the house straight into the Witch-King, following up with pieces of pavement, huge iron crates and everything else within range. For the first time, the Witch-King slowed, holding up a hand to raise a protective ward. The debris slammed into the ward and ricocheted off, heading in all directions. Charity ducked, casting a protective ward herself as bricks flew everywhere. Behind her, several students got in on the game and started hurling pieces of debris themselves. The Witch-King stopped altogether, one arm still raised. They had his attention …

… And Charity was sure, all of a sudden, that that was no longer a good thing.

The Witch-King raised his other arm. Charity threw herself to one side as her hair stood on end, moments before blue-white lightning flashed through the air. Her protective ward was actually *attracting* the lightning! She banished it hastily, watching in horror as four students – too slow to realise the danger – were killed by the spell. The Inquisitor seemed to survive, but then a red-green flash of light struck him and his face *changed.* Charity saw something utterly inhuman in it as he turned towards her, his wand slowly raising to strike …

She fired a killing hex at him, desperately. He dropped like a rock.

I've killed an Inquisitor, she thought, as she scrambled to her feet. They'd kill her for it, if she survived. *I've killed an ...*

She pushed the thought aside. The defence line had been shattered. A dozen dead bodies lay on the road; several others looked to have been ripped apart so badly that she honestly wasn't sure just how many people had died. She'd never realised just how much blood and gore there *was* in a human body. The Witch-King had stopped and was now standing in the exact centre of the road, utterly unmoving. It was hard to be sure, but he looked pleased. Slowly, he let his hand fall back to his side.

Charity glanced from side to side, then turned and started to run. There was a second defence line, then a third, but she had the feeling they wouldn't be enough to stop the lich. Elaine had been tight-lipped about her plans … even Johan had said nothing, apart from reassuring Charity – when she'd asked – that Elaine knew what she was doing. Charity hoped to all seven hells that he was right, because she couldn't think of anything else that could stop the monster.

She glanced back, once. The Witch-King was slowly starting to move again.

He was still heading for the Imperial Palace.

***

"One of the armies has stopped," Dolman reported. "The others look skittish."

Elaine bit back a laugh. The Witch-King had torn through the first defence line and was advancing on the second, seemingly utterly unstoppable. It didn't matter – it didn't *remotely* matter – what the armies did, not now. If the defenders won, they could negotiate with the armies; if the Witch-King won, the armies would be nothing more than targets for his power.

He's trying to distract you in the hopes of making you feel better, Johan sent.

It's not working, Elaine sent back.

The Witch-King's presence was growing far, far, stronger. She reached out through the wards, preparing defences that had lain dormant for over a thousand years. Magic crackled through the Golden Throne, charging the spells; she hoped – prayed – they would be sufficient to turn the tide. And even if they failed, they'd expend a great deal of power in trying. The Witch-King wouldn't be able to draw on it for himself.

"Get everyone out of the palace," she ordered. The plan would have to be revised. "You too, Dread."

Dread looked irked. "Your Supremacy ..."

"You have to leave," Elaine said. "The final defence line is not going to hold him for long."

She settled back on the Golden Throne, holding Johan's hand, as the palace's remaining inhabitants were hurried out of the building. She'd taken the time to evacuate the prisoners over the last two days – most of the slaves had been freed – and the hostages had gone back to their families. The building felt oddly uneasy as soon as it was empty, save for Elaine and Johan. It might not be intelligent, in any recognisable sense, but it knew the Witch-King was approaching.

369

Johan squeezed her hand tightly. "I love you," he said. "And thank you."

Elaine smiled at him, feeling an unaccustomed warmth around her heart. "You're welcome," she said. "I'm glad I had the chance to meet you."

She closed her eyes as the Witch-King pushed the final defence line aside. He must be desperate, part of her mind noted; the spells he'd unleashed, unseen for centuries, effectively *ate* magic. Given his limited power, it was a considerable risk to unleash such spells, although it looked as though he was having no trouble in controlling it. The books Elaine had absorbed had made it clear that only a handful of magicians had *ever* been powerful enough to risk using it.

Even an Inquisitor wouldn't take the risk, she thought. Ironically, given some modification, the spell might be very useful indeed. *She* could have used it at the Peerless School ... but back then, she couldn't have hoped to learn it, let alone rewrite it to suit herself. *It might be usable against the Witch-King*.

She tensed, resting one arm against the throne, as the Witch-King stepped up to the edge of the wards and stopped. Elaine didn't hesitate; she triggered the defences, throwing a wave of raw killing power right into his face. The Witch-King showed no reaction; she triggered a whole series of spells, attacking him on a dozen different levels at once. She sensed, at some level, the ground below the Witch-King shuddering, then rising up to crush him under a wave of molten stone. But his presence was still there ... she gasped in pain as he launched a wave of magic upwards, reducing the stone to ash.

"Elaine," Johan said. She sensed his arm, despite the overwhelming presence of the Golden Throne. "You're bleeding!"

Elaine touched her nose. Blood was dripping from her nostrils and staining her shirt. She grimaced, then pushed it aside, refusing to allow it to distract her. The Witch-King's presence was growing stronger, pushing against the wards; she felt a sudden surge of inhuman rage before a wave of pain slammed through her, almost throwing her off the Golden Throne. Johan caught her and steadied her, his thoughts flaring with alarm. The Witch-King had burnt through the wards …

Just like Johan did, she thought, as she took control of what was left of the defences and directed them right at the advancing Witch-King. *Whatever he did undermined the spells completely, wiping them out.*

She felt more blood dripping from her nose, but she did her best to ignore it. The once-proud network of defensive wards was in tatters, unless … other spells were activating now, a handful of heavy defences merged with a set of soothing spells. She puzzled over the latter, then realised that they were designed to make the target calm down. If the Witch-King had rendered Johan powerless by the simple expedient of drugging him to neutralise his emotions, there was no reason the defences couldn't do the same. But had the Emperors anticipated a lich …?

He must have programmed himself to feel emotion, she thought, as the Witch-King continued his steady advance. *But they're not real. They can't be soothed.*

"He's almost here," she said, slowly. "If I tell you to run, I expect you to run."

"I'm not going to leave you," Johan said, firmly.

"I'll catch up with you," Elaine said. "If I tell you to run, then run."

The door was already shaking; she opened it, quickly, to prevent the Witch-King turning it into a weapon. She fought down the urge to rise from the throne and kneel as the monster stepped into the Throne Room, its presence beating on the air like the wings of mighty dragons. Up close, the Witch-King looked no different … and yet, was there a faint decline in the blue fire? It was unlikely to matter.

"Run," she ordered Johan. "Now!"

She grabbed for the remaining wards and took control, ripping the floor open and throwing it right at the Witch-King. Physical impacts seemed more useful than magic, she reasoned; the Witch-King had actually been slowed by the earlier chunks of debris. The Witch-King stumbled, seemingly shocked that she would burn so much power in a direct attempt to kill him, then staggered as her will grew stronger, slamming the upper floors into him. He raised a shield of his own, then thrust upwards. Elaine recoiled in pain as the Imperial Palace shuddered and started to disintegrate. But it wasn't important. The only important thing within the palace was the Golden Throne.

And I don't care about keeping myself in power, Elaine thought. *All that I want to do is stop him.*

She stood as the Witch-King stepped towards her, sending one final command to the Golden Throne. The Witch-King looked at her, his face twisted into what might have been a cold smile, then crooked a finger. An invisible force picked her up and threw her right across the room, her wards threatening to break as she slammed right into the wall. Johan – she thought she'd told him to run – caught hold of her as the Witch-King touched the throne …

… And stumbled backwards as golden light flared around him.

Work, Elaine thought, as she felt the wards dying, piece by piece. *Please work.*

Johan helped her to walk towards the remains of the wall as the magic grew stronger. It had been simple enough; she'd rekeyed the Golden Throne to project *all* of its remaining power into the Witch-King, tuned enough to be completely unusable. It would be like drinking poisoned water; he needed the water to survive, but if he drank it the poison would kill him. And he *wasn't* of the Emperor's bloodline. There was no way he could undo the commands she'd given the throne.

The entire palace shook, pieces of debris crashing down in the distance. A painting of some ugly woman fell from the wall, hitting the ground with an almighty crash. Elaine wanted to raise a ward, but she couldn't focus her mind. It felt very much as if part of her were dying too. The surges of power behind her were getting stronger …

"Run," Johan shouted. The roof caved in, just ahead of them. "Hurry!"

Elaine tried, but she couldn't muster the energy. Johan grabbed her, threw her over his shoulder and carried her rapidly towards the nearest hole in the walls. Elaine's mind was spinning in all directions; the last traces of the Golden Throne were fading from her mind, leaving her just …

Elaine. It was a relief, yet … part of her had almost enjoyed the two days of absolute power.

A thousand years of history just died, she thought. And yet, it didn't feel like *her* thoughts, or Johan's. *And …*

The Imperial Palace disintegrated. Johan's power flared, shielding them both as he stumbled through the debris and out into the garden. It was tiny, compared to the great estates outside the Golden City, but a symbol of wealth and power. Johan put her down and helped her to stand upright, her head spinning from the sudden loss of the wards. The Golden Throne had practically overwhelmed her while she'd sat on it, steering her into being more of an Empress.

Maybe that's why Deferens chose to leave the Golden City so quickly, she thought. *He knew the dangers of remaining on the throne …*

"No," Johan said, dully. Raw shock suffused his thoughts. "Elaine …"

Elaine looked up. The dust was clearing, revealing a figure standing in the exact centre of where the palace had been. She stared, unwilling to believe that the Witch-King had survived. It seemed impossible that *anything* could survive. And yet, there could be no mistaking the glowing figure. She'd burnt away the Golden Throne – her birthright – and vast reserves of magic, for nothing.

But it wasn't over yet.

"We need to get to the library," she said, as the Witch-King turned to look at them. "We'll make our stand there."

Chapter Thirty-Eight

Johan helped Elaine to stumble through the remains of the rear wall as blue light flared behind them. The ground shook violently a moment later, the Witch-King's anger manifesting as small earthquakes. Johan remembered everything *he'd* done and shuddered in horror. If the Witch-King chose to be angry, he could devastate the remains of the entire city.

Not that it matters, he thought, numbly. He'd never really cared about the Golden Throne, or the Imperial Palace, but he knew what their loss meant. The Empire was well and truly dead. *There's no way the Golden City can survive without it.*

"We need to get to the library," Elaine said. Blood was still dripping from her nose, even though she'd separated herself from the Golden Throne before its death. "We're going to need the wards."

The Witch-King's presence grew stronger. Johan risked a look behind and saw the monstrous figure striding through the wreckage of the palace, kicking pieces of stone and glass out of the way. He looked unstoppable and yet ... his fires seemed to be lighter somehow. It could have been a trick of the light, Johan thought, but it was *just* possible the Witch-King was reaching the end of the line.

"There's no other potential target now, but us," Elaine croaked. He held her upright as they staggered towards the library. She felt absurdly light, as if something had gone out of her when the Golden Throne had died. "He *has* to come after us."

"There's the Peerless School's wards," Johan said. The ground quivered as the Witch-King stepped into the garden. Johan looked back just in time to see flames licking around his feet, incinerating a garden renowned for its beauty. And just for existing in the heart of the Golden City. "And the Great Houses ..."

"Not enough power to keep him going for long," Elaine

muttered. She leant on him for a long moment, then forced herself to stand up. "He needs *you* now, Johan. It's his only hope of survival."

Johan gritted his teeth, fighting down a wave of anger that threatened to burst loose. "Am I always to be *something*, not a person in my own right?"

Elaine laughed, harshly. "Now you know how I felt after … well, you know."

Johan gripped her arm as they hurried towards the Great Library, understanding precisely what she meant. Her knowledge made her a target; everyone, from the Grand Sorcerer to the merest of Hedge Wizards, would have wanted her, if only to learn how to cast low-power spells. He was surprised that Light Spinner hadn't killed Elaine on the spot – or Dread, even before Elaine's brush with wild magic. Her mere existence was a threat to the status quo.

But there's nothing left of the status quo, he thought. *Whatever happens today, the world will never be the same again.*

He pushed the thought aside as Elaine pulled him forward. The Witch-King was closing in, his magic reaching out to touch them. He should be capable of just snapping them up, Johan thought; it took him several minutes to realise that the Witch-King was using wild magic to hold himself in place. The sheer tenacity surprised him, although it shouldn't have done. A person who had managed to live for over a thousand years would know *precisely* how to prolong their life as long as possible.

And he may believe that death is truly the end, Johan thought. His father had told them that they would go to the Household Gods when they died – Jamal had sneered that the gods would turn their backs on powerless Johan – but the Witch-King might think differently. If he'd *been* a god, or an immensely powerful being, he might genuinely believe there was no life after death. *He thinks there are no real gods to take his soul.*

"Nearly there," Elaine said. The Great Library rose up in front of them. Despite himself, Johan felt a pang at the thought of destroying it. The Great Library was the first place he'd ever felt welcome. "The wards are already reaching for me."

"Good," Johan said. Elaine straightened up as she drew on the wards, allowing them to heal her. It wasn't a serious expenditure of magic – and besides, it was power the Witch-King wouldn't be able to use. "What now?"

Elaine squeezed his hand. "We make our last stand."

Johan looked at her, feeling a surge of love and tenderness that surprised him. Elaine wasn't as pretty as Charity or Jayne, the girl he'd thought he could court before his father had ruined everything – again. And yet, she had character and a grim determination to do what she had to do that outshone him. She'd taken him into her home and into her heart, risking everything she had to protect him and study his magic ... he wanted to take her in his arms and kiss her, but there was no time. Instead, he merely squeezed her hand tighter.

"I'm ready," he said, as he turned to face the Witch-King. The Great Library's wards flared between them, but he knew they wouldn't stop the lich for longer than a few seconds. "And I love you."

Elaine smiled at him, tiredly. "I love you too."

***

The Witch-King paused on the far side of the wards. Elaine suspected it didn't bode well, but she was almost grateful for the brief hesitation. Doing two things at once was hard enough when she wasn't under a staggering amount of pressure; now, with the Witch-King's sheer presence bearing down on her, it was nearly impossible to balance the wards with Johan's power. If they hadn't been bonded so closely, if he hadn't trusted her completely, it would have been almost impossible.

She studied the Witch-King carefully through the wards, considering the spells that he'd woven into his wild magic. It was a fascinating piece of work, all the more so because he'd lacked the comprehensive knowledge he'd granted her. Even now, after stealing her knowledge from her mother, he hadn't had the time to sit down and improve his work. But it barely mattered. His spellwork had lasted for over a thousand years without falling apart.

But it has glitches, she thought, as she readied herself. *It can be broken.*

"Fallen Empress," the Witch-King said. Or thought; she wasn't sure if he was speaking normally or through a form of telepathy. "You will die today."

Elaine ignored him. There was no time to do anything but muster the spells she needed, the spells she had to put together at terrifying speed. It would have been completely impossible without the library ... it struck her, suddenly, that the Witch-King had outsmarted *himself*. If he'd been a little less of a planner, if he'd been a little less willing to adapt circumstances to suit himself, he would have won by now. Or merely taken her, then launched his bid to place his tool on the Golden Throne. Trying to do it too quickly, in the end, had crippled him.

"You know this," the Witch-King said. "I have an offer for you."

"No," Elaine said. It was hard to slip her attention from the wards, but she had no choice. "I don't want your offers."

"If Johan comes to me, you will live," the Witch-King said. There was an awful sincerity in his words that tore at her mind. "I will swear an oath, if you wish; you will survive."

Elaine didn't need the bond to sense Johan's horror. She didn't blame him, either. There would be nothing left of him after the Witch-King subsumed his mentality. And it was quite possible that snapping his neck, afterwards, would be futile. The Witch-King might well manage to turn Johan's body into another lich, then keep himself going long enough to find a third wild magician. And even if he didn't, it was quite possible that the bond would kill her as well as Johan ...

... And she couldn't betray him.

"No," she said, coldly. Beside her, she felt Johan's horror becoming anger. Had the Witch-King thought he'd surrender himself to save Elaine? Her survival would come at an immense cost, paid by the remainder of the Empire. "Give up. Your long life is over."

"The Empire will die without me," the Witch-King said. She wasn't sure if he was talking to her or Johan. "Countless kings will snatch power for themselves, killing thousands as they build their armies and ravish the neighbouring kingdoms. Millions of lives will be destroyed. Centuries of tradition will be obliterated. If you truly wish to preserve the Empire, you will surrender yourself to me."

"It's already happening," Johan said. His anger was pulsing beside his words. "The Empire is dying!"

"Then let me save it," the Witch-King hissed.

"You won't," Elaine said. "You'll round up every magic-user you can find and butcher them to power yourself. Then you'll start everyone worshipping you as a reborn god. And then you'll start sacrificing thousands of people every year to summon monsters as your madness grows worse. You'll become an evil ruler who can never be removed."

The Witch-King sneered. "Do you really believe the Emperors were that much better?"

"I think they were right to turn on you," Elaine countered. "You're not even remotely human any longer. The worst blood-crazed vampire is more human than you."

The Witch-King's face didn't change, but she felt his rage. She gritted her teeth as the wards melted, fragments of spellwork scattering everywhere. Thankfully, some of her earlier work – after Johan had damaged the wards a couple of months ago – held firm, starting the task of regenerating the wards. Beside her, Johan held her arm tighter as the Witch-King stepped forward. The wards fell back ...

... And there was nothing standing between them and the monster.

***

Johan felt his anger burning through his mind, demanding release. It wasn't just that the Witch-King wanted his body in the worst possible way, it wasn't just that he'd thought that Elaine would roll over and throw Johan to the monster, it was the sheer certitude in the Witch-King's emotions that they'd surrender for the sake of the Empire. Johan hadn't taken as much interest in political affairs as his father, not since it had become clear that *he* wouldn't be claiming any power of his own, but the Witch-King's arrogance shocked him to the core. It was the Witch-King who had been responsible for the string of atrocities Deferens had committed: the sacking of a dozen cities and towns, the slaughter of countless men, the rape of thousands of women …

… And he expected *them* to believe he would preserve the Empire?

Now, Elaine sent.

Johan drew on his rage, on his hatred, and threw it at the Witch-King. Last time, it hadn't worked; this time, he had help. The Witch-King seemed to wilt for a long moment, his form flickering slightly as Johan's magic dug into his very being, before he stood up. Magic boiled on the air between them, reflecting or absorbing Johan's power. Johan clutched his hatred to his breast, forcing himself to remember all the horrors the Witch-King had committed …

"How many children were killed because they were believed to be powerless?" he shouted, as his power grew stronger. "How many young magicians died because they didn't know how to handle their powers? How many people died because of you?"

The Witch-King stood there, impassive. Johan felt a calming spell shimmer into existence, moments before it was pushed away by the wards. It was a tactic that had worked once, Johan recalled; it couldn't be allowed to work again. He dragged up all the memories, all the humiliations that Jamal had subjected him to, and threw them at his target. The Witch-King eyed him with cold hatred, but seemed otherwise untroubled.

He wants me intact, Johan thought. The idea of being controlled was bad enough, but having his whole personality scrubbed and replaced by something ancient was quite another. *He's trying to find a way to neutralise me without actually doing any harm.*

A piece of rock was pulled from the ground and hurled towards him. Johan was too angry to care, or to take much note when the rock slammed into the regenerating wards and dropped to the ground. The Witch-King took a step forward, pressing against the wards; Johan refocused his anger, but it no longer seemed so effective. Cold fear darted down the back of his mind, mocking him. If he couldn't stop the Witch-King …

The ground shuddered, violently. Johan fell, dragging

Elaine with him. The stone turned to liquid; he tried to pull himself out before it solidified over his hands and knees, trapping him. But it was too late. They were both trapped and helpless.

"You don't know how to use what you have, boy," the Witch-King said. "For all your power, you are nothing to me."

Johan cursed. He had a knife at his belt, but his hands and feet were stuck. Killing himself was no longer an option. The Witch-King peered down at him, his face expressionless …

… And then his burning hands reached for Johan's face.

***

Elaine had known – she had *always* known – that they wouldn't be able to match the Witch-King in a direct fight. Her magic was weak, Johan's magic was undeveloped; the Witch-King had over a thousand years of experience in using both wild and high magic. The complex web of spells that surrounded him only proved it. Valiant had been a genius in his day, she recognised; indeed, she couldn't help wondering if he'd used a modified version of the Bookworm spell himself.

But he doesn't have the knowledge I have, she thought, as she launched the first set of spells into his spellwork. *Nor does he understand how it all fits together.*

She felt Johan's panic as the Witch-King reached for him, but refused to allow herself to be distracted as her spells went to work. Beating the Witch-King directly was impossible, yet if he kept his attention focused on them he wouldn't have time to notice what *she* was doing …

It was hard, so hard, to focus, but the library's wards held her steady. Elaine clung to Johan, feeling his panic lashing out at the Witch-King, and watched her spells go to work. The Witch-King's web was so complex that only a handful of tiny changes would be enough to twist it out of shape. And he'd start to lose control … she drew on the wards, turning the stone to dust, and yanked Johan free a second before the Witch-King could touch him. She had no idea if he could be saved, once the Witch-King wormed his way into his mind, but she rather doubted it. The Inquisitors probably wouldn't even let her *try*.

"There is no escape," the Witch-King said. "I …"

He broke off. *Too late*, Elaine thought, vindictively. *Far too late.*

The Witch-King's fires flickered, growing brighter for a long second. Elaine pulled Johan back as the Witch-King stared at his hands, confused. And then he looked back at her, his gaze trapping her where she stood.

"What have you done?"

"You crafted hundreds of spells together to make your new form," Elaine said. She couldn't *not* answer, not when the sheer force of his presence was pushing against her mind. "But you didn't really understand what you were doing, any more than the idiots who cast *your* spells understood what *they* were doing. You gave me the idea, really."

She knew she was babbling, but she couldn't stop herself. "I inserted my spells into your web while you were focused on Johan, using them to tear your existence apart," she added. "You will need more power than exists in the entire world to keep yourself going now – and if you start shifting into Johan, you'll just come apart faster. You're dying."

The Witch-King raised a hand. Johan shoved Elaine to one side as a flash of deadly red light blasted through where she'd been, moments ago. Elaine rolled over, scrambling back to her feet, just in time to see the Witch-King's body start to flicker. The blue fires were searching for magic …

He can drain every magician in the world, she thought. She ran through the calculations again, just in case. No problems surfaced to worry her. *It won't be enough to keep him alive.*

"Everyone I touched will die," the Witch-King said. Blue sparks were flickering off his body now, expending themselves uselessly. She could sense the spellwork slowly coming apart as her magic gnawed through it. He couldn't divert his attention without making it worse. "You'll throw the Empire into chaos."

"It's already in chaos," Johan said.

Elaine nodded in agreement. She had no idea *what* would happen to the Witch-King's tools, although death was as likely an answer as any. But, with or without them, the Empire was already dead. The Golden Throne was gone, the Watchtower was gone; the only surviving institution was the Peerless School. She had no interest in trying to hold the Empire together, not when it had turned into a nightmare. Besides, without the Golden Throne, she might no longer be considered Empress.

"Goodbye," she said, tightly.

The Witch-King lifted a finger, his power holding her in place as he shaped a curse. Elaine waited, resigned to her fate; blue light flickered over his hand, heralding a deadly curse, then vanished as his power finally died. The fires vanished; his presence snapped out of existence, as if someone had cast a darkening spell. And the remains of his skeleton clattered to the ground.

"It's over," Elaine said. Her head was pounding, but she was alive. *They* were alive. "We won."

Johan grabbed her in a hug. "Now what?"

"Good question," Elaine said. She smiled wearily and then kissed him. "Do you know? I haven't the slightest idea."

Chapter Thirty-Nine

"The armies are still unsure over who should claim the city first," Dolman said. "Do you really intend to leave?"

Elaine nodded. Two days after the Witch-King had fallen, the first of the armies had arrived at the Seven Peaks. It had been in disarray, however, after several of its officers had dropped dead, allowing four other armies to arrive and set up camp. The confused reports the surviving officers had received had convinced them to wait and see what happened, rather than trying to force the remaining tunnels.

"There's nothing left for me here," she said. Daria had promised she would eventually meet them in Ida, once she'd sorted out her position in the pack. "They'd probably be happier if I wasn't here, anyway."

"Probably, Your Supremacy," Dolman said. She *still* hadn't been able to talk him out of calling her the Empress. "Do you really intend to just let it go?"

Elaine looked at him. "If I decided to remain Empress," she said, "could the Empire be saved?"

"I doubt it," Dolman said. "But you could patch together an agreement ..."

"One that would, at best, leave me a powerless monarch," Elaine said. "Eight Inquisitors are not enough to force the world to obey me. So many other magicians are dead ..."

She sighed, inwardly. Hawke and Sarah had left the day after the Witch-King fell, taking with them their knowledge of ways to do things without magic. She had a feeling that several kings were in for a nasty shock. They couldn't call on the Inquisition any longer, or the Court Wizards. The balance of power had changed in so many ways.

"You don't have to stay yourselves," she said, carefully.

"We will remain to defend the Peerless School," Dolman said. His voice was very firm. "I suspect the various kingdoms will agree, eventually, to leave the school in place, but politically neutral. It is, after all, the only place to learn magic in the world."

Elaine had her doubts. Sarah and the others knew some of her spells now ... and it wouldn't be long before they started developing new ones of their own. Perhaps there *would* be a balance between the old traditions and the newer insights into how magic actually worked ... or perhaps there would be war, eventually. But it was no longer her problem.

"I've adjusted the wards on the Great Library," she said, instead. "You'll have access to everything, save for the Black Vault. Better to let that remain sealed."

And hope that keeps them out of enemy hands, she thought. The kings would probably start developing war spells of their own, but at least they'd be starting from scratch. *They can't get into the vault without me.*

"You could stay," Dolman said. "A handful of charms and no one would recognise you as anything other than a librarian."

"I *wanted* to be a librarian," Elaine said. She'd resigned herself to leaving the Great Library when she'd planned to take Johan out of the Golden City, but she hadn't been happy about it. "Now ... better to just go."

"As you wish," Dolman said. "You will, of course, be welcome."

"Not to the kings," Elaine said.

Dolman nodded. "The dragons returned," he said. "Deferens' homeland has been invaded by three other kingdoms. They didn't put up much of a fight; the leadership fought like mad bastards, but everyone else practically surrendered as soon as they saw the enemy approaching. I don't think they really wanted to fight."

"Good," Elaine said.

"And many of their priest-kings dropped dead," Dolman added. "They were the ones who steered the society, after all."

Elaine nodded. The worst of kingdoms would still be an improvement, once the last diehards were hunted down and killed. She had a feeling that most of the population would be grateful for a steadier form of government, particularly the women. It was unlikely that anyone – anyone else – related to Deferens would be allowed to live, but the remainder of the population should be fine.

And the Golden Throne no longer exists, she added, silently. *They don't pose a real threat.*

"You can take control of the city now, if you wish," she said. "I'll be leaving in an hour or so, with Johan and Dread."

"Keep the remaining dragons in Ida," Dolman advised. "They're too dangerous to be left around."

He paused. "Is there nothing your partner can do for Dread?"

"Dread didn't want Johan to try to restore his powers," Elaine said. She'd been surprised, but Dread *was* in his forties. He'd been an Inquisitor longer than Elaine had been alive. She couldn't really blame him for wanting a rest. "I think he wants to retire."

"He'll be welcome back, whenever he wishes," Dolman grunted. "As will you."

But not Johan, Elaine guessed. Figuring out what to do with future wild magicians would be tricky as hell. Let them live – and risk them turning into monsters – or kill them out of hand? And yet that too was no longer her problem. *The prospect of super-magicians scares everyone.*

"I thank you," she said, formally. "You'll spread the cover story?"

"You'll be going to the Summer Isles, if anyone bothers to ask," Dolman said. "I hear it's quite warm down there."

Elaine smiled, then surprised herself by giving the older man a hug. "Take care of yourself," she said, as she took one final look around the office. "And try not to get the school taken apart and scattered over a hundred kingdoms."

Dolman escorted her as she walked through the silent school. It had been the place she'd learnt magic, and yet … it had also been the place where she'd been a laughing stock. She understood why Sarah had left, all right; if things had been different, it wouldn't have been *hard* for her to have taken Sarah's place. The classrooms looked oddly empty; it would be weeks, if not months, before the Peerless School reopened. If, of course, it ever did.

"You *will* be welcome," Dolman said, again. "There's no

way to know what will happen in the future."

Elaine nodded. The Empire might be gone, but the spy network was still in place. There were a dozen minor wars already underway, along with two revolutions and a series of political assassinations that could easily lead to civil war. Any agreement Dolman and the Administrator reached with the kings could be changed, within days, as the kings were replaced by other figures. And, without the force needed to compel everyone to behave themselves, it would only get worse. Ida, at least, would be relatively immune to chaos; the mountains would provide some protection, as would the dragons.

And us, Elaine thought, as she stepped out of the doors. The Great Library could be seen in the distance, calling to her. She resisted it firmly; there was no time, whatever else happened, to give in to the urge to return to the library and stay there. *We'll be living there too.*

"Thank you," she said, gravely. "And good luck."

***

"So," Chime said. "When are you getting married?"

Charity smiled as Johan flushed at the question. It wasn't a stupid question – their younger siblings knew that Johan and Elaine were bonded together – but it was definitely an *embarrassing* one. And it raised the question of just who would be walking with Elaine down to the altar …

"When we feel like it," Johan said, finally. He tossed a pleading look at Charity. "But it probably won't be here."

"You should stay," Chime said, seriously. It wasn't hard to see she wasn't being entirely sincere. "You're *family*."

Johan shook his head. "I can't stay," he said. "And I don't want to stay."

Charity nodded as she chased their younger siblings out. She'd been surprised when Johan had agreed to come and meet them; indeed, she'd made the offer partly to soothe her guilty conscience. And it had taken hours of gentle but firm insistence to convince their siblings to be in the same room as Johan for more than a few minutes. But it hadn't been a complete disaster, thankfully. Their family deserved something after everything they'd endured.

"We'll be staying here," she said, once the door was closed. "I did think about heading to the estate, but … they still need to go to school."

"Just don't rebuild too much of the Great Houses," Johan said. "And don't try to overthrow the government."

Charity nodded. Between Deferens and the Witch-King, thousands of magicians were dead and the Empire was gone. She, for one, would be happy merely keeping the family secure; Jay, if he wished, could try competing for supreme power. But with the Grand Sorcerers no longer in existence, the ultimate prize was impossible to capture. Who knew *what* would happen in the future?

"I'll do my best," she promised. She *was* young, but at least she had a war record now. It would wipe away the stain of being a slave, she hoped. "And Johan … if you do have children, let them know about us."

Johan visibly hesitated. "It would depend, I suppose," he said. "If they don't have powers at first …"

Charity winced. "I understand," she said. "But it would be better for them to know their relatives."

"Maybe," Johan said. "Because I am *not* going to allow my children to be tormented as they grow up."

"I won't let it happen," Charity assured him. "I *swear*."

"Then stick to it," Johan said.

Charity nodded, once. She didn't really understand why Johan wanted to go to Ida – he could easily have talked Elaine out of going to Ida, if he'd wished – but in some ways she was grateful. Johan was just *too* disturbing. It would be better for the world if he was hidden in a mountain kingdom, rather than all too visible in the Golden City. Besides … he'd been calm over the last two days, but who knew when he'd next lose control of his emotions?

She looked up as the wards tingled. "Your partner is here," she said. She rose to her feet. "I do think they're planning the wedding now …"

"We're not marrying for power, if we marry," Johan said, firmly. "It shouldn't be a great event …"

"You're marrying the *Empress*," Charity said. "Just think what that would do for the family name."

Johan surprised her. He smiled. "Just think of who *else*

she's related to," he said. "It won't make us very popular."

***

Johan hadn't been sure what to expect when Charity had invited him to House Conidian. A whole series of apologies? Threats? Or pleas for him to stay in the city and work for the family? But instead, they'd had a small dinner and chatted about nothing. He'd almost felt like he belonged.

It wouldn't last, he knew, as he rose to greet Elaine. They were scared of him – he could see it in their faces – in a way they'd never been scared of Jamal. But then, Jamal had been powerful and yet understandable. Johan ... was something altogether different. The killing of Powerless children had now been forbidden, but Johan wondered just how much notice would be paid to the law. The prospect of another wild magician would scare the Great Houses quite badly.

He gave Elaine a peck on the lips and smiled at her. "Are you ready to go?"

"The dragons are waiting for us," Elaine said. "Do you have anything you want to bring?"

Johan shook his head. He'd had few possessions over the years; his parents hadn't exactly deprived him, but Jamal had found it amusing to damage, hex or simply destroy anything Johan had owned. He still had nightmares about his teddy bear coming to life in the middle of the night and trying to strangle him. No matter what he'd been told, he was still sure that Jamal had intended to murder him that night. A Powerless wasn't entirely *human*, after all ...

Elaine squeezed his hand, gently. "It's over," she said. "You don't have to worry any longer."

"I hope that's true," Johan said. He looked at Charity, who was pretending not to listen to them. "I think you'll be fine, really. Just let them think I died."

"They may not believe it," Elaine said. "Too many people know we're bonded. If I'm not dead, they'll assume you're not dead too."

"But you're going off to the Summer Isles, officially," Johan reminded her. "Let them file a report you're dead in a month or two."

"We can try," Elaine said. She turned to look at Charity.

"I thank you for your service."

"I thank you for helping my brother," Charity said. "And for not surrendering to the Emperor when he held you in his clutches."

"I don't blame you," Elaine said. "He would have killed you if you hadn't submitted."

Charity lowered her gaze. "I would have sooner died than become ... than become his slave," she said. "But I didn't realise what he'd do, once I was in his power."

Johan nodded in sympathy. The Emperor hadn't *touched* Charity, but he'd played with her mind and damaged her self-confidence. Chime had told him, when they'd been alone for a moment, that Charity had been having nightmares – and that she was drinking a glass of potion to help her sleep every night. They had to be bad nightmares if the potions weren't helping. But she'd been completely at Deferens' mercy. He could have killed her – or worse – at any moment.

"You had no way of knowing," Elaine said. "Don't blame yourself."

"I do," Charity said. She curtseyed, lifting her dress slightly. "I thank you for everything, Your Supremacy. And I wish you both the very best of luck in the future."

Johan gave his sister a hug, then followed Elaine as she walked out of House Conidian and into the streets. Half of the once-great mansions were in ruins; a number were being slowly dissected by fortune-hunters, hoping that the defunct Great Houses had left behind books or artefacts of value. He felt a pang of guilt as he looked towards the pile of rubble that had once been House Lakeside, where he'd dumped his younger siblings before fleeing the Golden City. Lady Lakeside had taken them in and tried to do right by them.

But the Emperor burnt through her wards and destroyed her family, he thought. If there were any surviving members of House Lakeside, they were keeping their heads down as they sought to either hide or rebuild their family. *She deserved better.*

He looked at Elaine as they made their way down to the gardens, where the dragons were waiting. "Are you sure you want to go?"

"I can't stay," Elaine said. "They'll *all* want me."

Johan winced. Elaine was the last *Empress*. The person who married her – if he happened to be a king – would have a claim to the title. He rather doubted that any of the kingdoms could set out to take the entire world, but it probably wouldn't stop them trying. Elaine ... would be safer in Ida, where the ruling monarch was female, than anywhere else. If, of course, they realised she *wasn't* in the Summer Isles. They were large enough to force anyone intent on finding her to search for years.

"We can come back later, in disguise," he suggested. "No one will know who you are."

"We will see," Elaine said. She gave him a tired smile. "I have a book to write, you know."

"The true history of the Witch-King," Johan agreed. "And perhaps a book of spells?"

"I'll have to rewrite the basics, at least," Elaine said. She frowned as they entered the gardens, the dragons turning their heads to peer at them. "The Witch-King might not be the only person capable of crafting spells that slowly corrupt a user's mind."

"At least they'll be more aware of the dangers," Johan pointed out. He waved to Dread, who was already sitting on a dragon and waiting for them. "They'll be more careful, won't they?"

"It won't be easy for them to separate the potentially-dangerous spells from the others," Elaine said. She shook her head slowly. "I could use the spells myself, with a little effort; it won't be long before someone else tries, if there are still vulnerable magicians around. And there will be."

Dread slipped down to join them. "Are you ready to go?"

"Yeah," Johan said. "I wasn't planning to bring anything from the house."

"I just have a handful of books," Elaine said. "The last of the Witch-King's personal spellbooks, as far as I know. I don't want to leave it lying around."

"As long as you can't resurrect him," Johan said. "You can't bring him back to life, can you?"

"He's dead and gone," Elaine said. "What he did ... I don't think there was a difference between his mentality and his soul any longer. It was torn apart so completely that there shouldn't be any real hope of rebuilding it."

"Let us hope so," Dread said. "And as long as most people are unsure about what really happened, there shouldn't be anyone trying to bring him back."

Johan nodded. There were stories about magicians trying to resurrect the dead, but they always ended badly. What came back was rarely human, let alone sane. Who knew what would happen if someone tried to resurrect the Witch-King?

He scrambled onto the dragon and smiled as Elaine clambered up behind him and wrapped her hands around his chest. Moments later, the dragon flapped its wings and rose up into the sky above the Golden City. It looked different now, with so many buildings gone; the Watchtower, in particular, no longer dominated the skyline. And yet … it cost him a pang to leave.

And Elaine felt worse. He could feel her growing dismay as the dragon rose higher.

"We could stay," he said, quietly. "No one would need to know."

"We don't dare take the chance," Elaine said. She hugged him for a long moment. "Let's go."

Epilogue

Dread and Queen Sacharissa were married, two weeks after Dread's return to Ida, in the Great Hall of the Royal Castle.

It was, Elaine had to admit, a lovely wedding. Dread made a dignified nobleman – all Inquisitors were considered nobles, although few lived long enough to retire and enjoy the perks – while Queen Sacharissa was beautiful as well as wealthy and royal. The long white dress she wore showed off her curves, as well as asserting her virginity. Some of her nobles didn't look too pleased at this turn of events, but most of them seemed accepting of their ruler's choice. If nothing else, Elaine thought cynically, only one of them could have married the Queen.

"They're a little surprised we're here," Johan noted afterwards, as they joined the dancers swirling around the dance floor. "They don't really *know* us."

Elaine shrugged. Officially, she was a magical researcher and teacher while Johan was her husband and an engineer, working with the Levellers to find more ways of doing things without magic. Apart from Dread, Queen Sacharissa and a handful of her noblemen, everyone believed the cover story; Elaine had a sneaking suspicion that no one would bother to look for Johan among the Levellers. Why would the most powerful magician in the world choose to associate with powerless mundanes?

She smiled at the thought. Johan was fascinated by the possibilities of creating and building without magic – and she had to admit she shared his fascination, even though her own research kept her busy. And he had a knack for designing steam engines, spinning wheels and other interesting pieces of work. If his father had just let him go, she was sure, he would have made a decent life for himself. The powers that had both saved and blighted his life might never have materialised.

And then the Witch-King would have won, she thought. *The entire world would be enslaved.*

The thought made her frown. Dolman had been quietly keeping her – and Dread – up to date with events outside Ida. The Golden City had managed to preserve a precarious neutrality – aided by the fact that it was *still* the host of the Peerless School – but other parts of the Empire were steadily collapsing into war. There were pirates on the high seas, invading armies looting, raping and burning their way through helpless cities and a number of kings who'd declared themselves supreme rulers of the entire world. It would be years, Dolman had said, before everything settled down, leaving a handful of countries where the Empire had once been. And then ... who knew *what* would happen?

Johan squeezed her hand, gently. "You don't need to worry about anything," he said. He could sense her feelings from across the room. "Just ... relax and enjoy yourself."

"I'll try," Elaine said.

It wouldn't be easy. There was always the feeling, lurking at the back of her mind, that it had all been *her* fault. If she'd tried to remain Empress, she might have been able to stop the decline into war ... or, more likely, she would have found herself a prize for whoever captured the Golden City. Maybe Johan and the remaining Inquisitors could have protected her, but they were already badly weakened. She might have wound up unwillingly married to a whole succession of would-be rulers.

She closed her eyes, mentally touching the knowledge at the back of her mind. It was still there, waiting. She'd *always* be the Bookworm, unless she wiped her mind completely. And if anyone else knew where she was, or what she had ... she'd be lucky to wind up merely kidnapped and slowly drained of knowledge. Just like her mother ...

"You're thinking of her again," Johan said. "I can tell."

"Yeah," Elaine said. Her mother had remained in a coma, even weeks after the Witch-King had died. Dread had worried that she might be part of a *very* long-term plan – everyone else touched by the Witch-King had died with him – but Elaine hadn't been able to bear the thought of simply cutting her mother's throat. There was so much she wanted to ask. "Is it wrong of me to wonder what sort of person she is?"

"My mother never cared for me," Johan said. She could sense the hurt through the bond, tempered by the knowledge that he'd outlasted both of his parents. "If your mother woke up ..."

He shook his head, firmly. "Dance with me," he added. "Tomorrow, if you wish, you can go back to your books."

Elaine smiled at him. She'd lived with the mystery of her parents – and the shadow of the Witch-King – for years. Now, at least, she could relax and think about the future. She wasn't the person she'd been when she'd become the Bookworm ...

... And who knew what would happen in the future?

"I do have to finish the first textbook before the students go back to school," she said. The Peerless School needed it, particularly for magicians who didn't know – who couldn't be allowed to know – about the dangers. "But, just for the moment, I can put my books aside and be myself."

"Good," Johan said. He kissed her gently on the cheek. "And so too can I."

The End

Afterword

It may not surprise some people to know that I was a librarian.

Frankly, it's a job that always interested me. I love books. There's a certain pleasure in both being a guardian of a large collection of books and helping people find the book or piece of information they want from the shelves. I had a library card almost as soon as I could walk and was borrowing books above my age range – as if there really is such a thing – almost as soon as I started school.

When I finally *became* a librarian, we joked that most students didn't actually *read* the books. I worked in an academic library and the patterns we saw were large borrows on the first month, relatively few borrows over the next few months and then a steady ramp-up of borrows towards the exams. Students were taking the books they needed, but not always reading them. We joked that sleeping with a book under one's pillow didn't automatically impart the knowledge to the reader.

I think the concept of *Bookworm* was born then, although it wasn't until many years later that I actually started to write.

Being an intensive reader actually allows you to cross-reference pieces of data from several different fields. A great deal of human history, for example, can only be truly understood if looked at from several different points of view at once. Not to put too fine a point on it, some writers slant works one way; other writers, slightly more honest, try to put forward a neutral point of view. From a technological point of view, being a chemist as well as a biologist may lead to newer insights that would otherwise be missed.

For a librarian (or an archivist) who lived and worked before computers, it was incredibly hard to cross-reference data from numerous different pieces of work. Historians struggling to put together an account of what actually happened in Ancient Rome, for example, will find it a difficult task. There are several primary sources – writers who wrote during the time and shortly afterwards – but their works are incomplete, refer to other works that are now lost and sometimes biased in the extreme. (Primary works concerning Mark Antony tended to be written by people who wanted Augustus' favour and as such were slanted against Antony.) I wondered what would happen if someone dug through textbooks of magical lore – and if they somehow gained the ability to assimilate *everything* in the library at one fell swoop. And so the concept of Elaine the Bookworm was born.

Elaine is not, in a conventional sense, a powerful magician. (Her low status in society comes from her very limited power.) However, most spells in the Bookworm universe are actually very poorly written. (I tend to think of it as the difference between websites produced by a WYSIWYG editor and websites produced by writing HTML from scratch; the former looks nicer, but the latter gives you *much* more control.) Elaine, granted the insights needed to actually break spells down to the bare basics, actually becomes a double-edged threat. On one hand, she knows spells that were buried for a reason; on the other, she knows ways to reshape spells so more magicians can cast them.

And both make her immensely desirable.

The rest of the universe slowly fell into place. Emotions were strongly linked to magic – logically, I figured, a very emotional magician should be supremely powerful. Johan was designed, then the Witch-King and his long-term plan; the story kept expanding until it finally covered four volumes.

I do not intend to return to Elaine as a character. She has grown and developed, but neither she nor Johan really want to leave where they are now. However, there is plenty of room for future stories in this universe. I do have one idea involving the Peerless School …

… Well, we'll see. Until then, if you liked this story, please leave a review and let me know.

Thank you very much to the readers who read the first volume and requested sequels <grin>.

And, again, a very big thank you to my beta readers. I couldn't have done it without you.

Christopher G. Nuttall
Kuala Lumpur, 2015

Elsewhen Press

delivering outstanding new talents in speculative fiction

Visit the Elsewhen Press website at elsewhen.press for the latest information on all of our titles, authors and events; to read our blog; find out where to buy our books and ebooks; or to place an order.

Sign up for the Elsewhen Press InFlight Newsletter at elsewhen.press/newsletter

More titles by Christopher G. Nuttall
from
Elsewhen Press
an independent publisher specialising in Speculative Fiction

Bookworm

Elaine, an inexperienced witch in Golden City, has her life turned upside down when she triggers a magical trap to end up with all the knowledge in the Great Library stuffed inside her head. Avoiding the Inquisition she tries to understand what has happened to her. But she is a pawn in the dark plans of one who wants the Grand Sorcerer's power.

Bookworm won the Gold Award in the Adult Fiction category of the 2013 Wishing Shelf Independent Book Awards.

ISBN: 9781908168320 (epub, kindle) / 9781908168221 (368pp, paperback)

Visit bit.ly/Bookworm-Nuttall

Bookworm II – The Very Ugly Duckling

Not every ugly duckling becomes a swan ...

In the wake of the disastrous attack on the Golden City, Lady Light Spinner has become Grand Sorceress and Elaine, the Bookworm, has been settling into her positions as Head Librarian and Privy Councillor.   But any hope of vanishing into her books is negated when a new magician of staggering power appears in the city, one whose abilities seem to defy the known laws of magic.

ISBN: 9781908168382 (epub, kindle) / 9781908168283 (432pp, paperback)

Visit bit.ly/Bookworm2-Nuttall

Bookworm III – The Best Laid Plans

Elaine and Johan prepare to leave Golden City, with Daria and Cass, to search for the Witch-King. But Elaine is arrested on the orders of a new Emperor, puppet of the Witch-King. She must escape and destroy him. Privy Councillors and Heads of the Great Houses have bowed to the Emperor. Only Elaine and her friends can prevent an all-out war.

ISBN: 9781908168764 (epub, kindle) / 9781908168665 (400pp, paperback)

Visit bit.ly/Bookworm3

You might also like

A series of novels attempting to document the trials and tribulations
of the **Transdimensional Authority**
Ira Nayman

If there were Alternate Realities, and in each there was a version of Earth (very similar, but perhaps significantly different in one particular regard, or divergent since one particular point in history) then imagine the problems that could be caused if someone, somewhere, managed to work out how to travel between them. Those problems would be ideal fodder for a News Service that could also span all the realities. Now you understand the reasoning behind the Alternate Reality News Service (ARNS). But you aren't the first. In fact, Canadian satirist and author Ira Nayman got there before you and has been the conduit for ARNS into our Reality for some years now, thanks to his website *Les Pages aux Folles*.

But also consider that if there were problems being caused by unregulated travel between realities, it's not just news but a perfect ~~excuse~~ reason to establish an Authority to oversee such travel and make sure that it is regulated. You probably thought jurisdictional issues are bad enough between competing national agencies of dubious acronym and even more dubious motivation, let alone between agencies from different nations. So imagine how each of them would cope with an Authority that has jurisdiction across the realities in different dimensions. Now, you understand the challenges for the investigators who work for the Transdimensional Authority (TA). But, perhaps more importantly, you can see the potential for humour. Again, Ira beat you to it.

Ira Nayman is the creator of *Les Pages aux Folles*, a Web site of political and social satire that is over 10 years old (that's positively Paleolithic in Internet years!). Five collections of Alternate Reality News Service (ARNS) stories which originally appeared on the Web site have been self-published in print. Ira's Web Goddess tells him he should make more of the fact that he won the 2010 Jonathan Swift Satire Writing Contest. So, Ira won the 2010 Jonathan Swift Satire Writing Contest.

Welcome to the Multiverse[*]
[*] Sorry for the inconvenience
Being the first
ISBN: 9781908168191 (epub, kindle)
ISBN: 9781908168092 (336pp paperback)

You Can't Kill the Multiverse[*]
[*] But You Can Mess With its Head
Being the second
ISBN: 9781908168399 (epub, kindle)
ISBN: 9781908168290 (320pp paperback)

Random Dingoes
Being the third
ISBN: 9781908168795 (epub, kindle)
ISBN: 9781908168696 (288pp paperback)

Visit bit.ly/TransdimensionalAuthority

THE BLUEPRINT TRILOGY
KATRINA MOUNTFORT

The *Blueprint* trilogy takes us to a future in which men and women are almost identical, and personal relationships are forbidden. Following a bio-terrorist attack, the population now lives within comfortable Citidomes. MindValues advocate acceptance and non-attachment. The BodyPerfect cult encourages a tall thin androgynous appearance, and looks are everything.

A dark undercurrent runs through this story; the enforcement of conformity through fear, the fostering of distorted and damaging attitudes towards forbidden love, manipulation of appearance and even the definition of beauty, will appeal to both an adult and young adult audience.

BOOK 1
FUTURE PERFECT

In spite of severe governmental and societal strictures Caia, an intelligent and highly educated young woman, finds herself becoming attracted to her co-worker, Mac, a rebel whose questioning of their so-called utopian society both adds to his allure and encourages her own questioning of the status quo. As Mac introduces her to illegal and subversive information she is drawn into a forbidden, dangerous world, becoming alienated from her other co-workers and her resmates. In a society where every thought and action is controlled, informers are everywhere; whom can she trust? When she and Mac are sent on an outdoor research mission, Caia's life changes irreversibly.

BOOK 2
FORBIDDEN ALLIANCE

More than sixteen years have passed since Cathy and Michael fled their oppressive lives in the Citidomes. They have three children, but for Cathy village life is no longer idyllic. While Michael is famed as the leader of the Alliance of Outside Communities, she is left holding the baby. When a chance arises for her to fulfil her potential, will she make the right choices? Michael, however, is too preoccupied to notice Cathy's personal struggles. This is also the story of Cathy and Michael's sixteen year-old daughter Joy. Fiercely intelligent but with limited career options, she fights against the future her father has planned for her. Forbidden from seeing Harry, the nomadic boy she has loved since childhood, she finds friendship from an unexpected source: BodyPerfect ex-citizen Ryan. And her illusions about life in the Citidomes are about to be shattered.

Visit bit.ly/Blueprint-FuturePerfect

LiGa series
Sanem Ozdural

A thought-provoking series of books in an essentially contemporary setting, with elements of both science fiction and fantasy.

LiGa™
Book I

Literary science fiction, LiGa™ tells of a game in which the players are, literally, gambling with their lives. In the near-future a secretive organisation has developed technology to transfer the regenerative power of a body's cells from one person to another, conferring extended or even indefinite life expectancy. As a means of controlling who benefits from the technology, access is obtained by winning a tournament of chess or bridge to which only a select few are invited. At its core, the game is a test of a person's integrity, ability and resilience. Sanem's novel provides a fascinating insight into the motivation both of those characters who win and thus have the possibility of virtual immortality and of those who will effectively lose some of their life expectancy.

ISBN: 9781908168160 (epub, kindle)
ISBN: 9781908168061 (400pp paperback)

Visit bit.ly/BookLiGa

THE DARK SHALL DO WHAT LIGHT CANNOT
Book II

We find out more about the organisation behind LiGa as we travel with some of them to Pera, a place which lies beyond the Light Veil on the other side of reality. There are light trees there that eat sunlight and bear fruit that, in turn, lights up and energises (literally) the community of Pera. There are light birds that glitter in the night because they have eaten the seed of the lightberry. The House of Light and Dark, which is the domain of the Sun and her brother, Twilight, welcomes all creatures living in Pera. But in the midst of all the glitter, laughter and the songs, it must be remembered that the lightberry is poisonous to the non-Pera born, and the Land is afraid when the Sun retreats, for it is then that Twilight walks the streets…

ISBN: 9781908168740 (epub, kindle)
ISBN: 9781908168641 (400pp paperback)

Visit bit.ly/Darkshalldo

Jacey's Kingdom
Dave Weaver

Jacey's Kingdom is an enthralling tale that revolves around a startlingly desperate reality: Jacey Jackson, a talented student destined for Cambridge, collapses with a brain tumour while sitting her final history exam at school. In her mind she struggles through a quasi-historical sixth century dreamscape whilst the surgeons fight to save her life.

Jacey is helped by a stranger called George, who finds himself trapped in her nightmare after a terrible car accident. There are quests, battles, and a love story ahead of them, before we find out if Jacey will awake from her coma or perish on the operating table. And who, or what, is George? In this book, Dave Weaver questions our perception of reality and the redemptive power of dreams; are our experiences of fear, conflict, friendship and love any less real or meaningful when they take place in the mind rather than the 'real' physical world?

ISBN: 9781908168313 (epub, kindle)
ISBN: 9781908168214 (272pp paperback)

Visit bit.ly/JaceysKingdom

The Janus Cycle
Tej Turner

The Janus Cycle can best be described as gritty, surreal, urban fantasy. The over-arching story revolves around a nightclub called Janus, which is not merely a location but virtually a character in its own right. On the surface it appears to be a subcultural hub where the strange and disillusioned who feel alienated and oppressed by society escape to be free from convention; but underneath that façade is a surreal space in time where the very foundations of reality are twisted and distorted. But the special unique vibe of Janus is hijacked by a bandwagon of people who choose to conform to alternative lifestyles simply because it has become fashionable to be "different", and this causes many of its original occupants to feel lost and disenchanted. We see the story of Janus unfold through the eyes of seven narrators, each with their own perspective and their own personal journey. A story in which the nightclub itself goes on a journey. But throughout, one character, a strange girl, briefly appears and reappears warning the narrators that their individual journeys are going to collide in a cataclysmic event. Is she just another one of the nightclub's denizens, a cynical mischief-maker out to create havoc or a time-traveller trying to prevent an impending disaster?

ISBN: 9781908168566 (epub, kindle)
ISBN: 9781908168467 (224pp paperback)

Visit bit.ly/JanusCycle

About the Author

Christopher G. Nuttall has been planning sci-fi books since he learnt to read. Born and raised in Edinburgh, Chris created an alternate history website and eventually graduated to writing full-sized novels. Studying history independently allowed him to develop worlds that hung together and provided a base for storytelling. After graduating from university, Chris started writing full-time. As an indie author he has self-published a number of novels, but this is his seventh fantasy to be published by Elsewhen Press. The fourth and final instalment in the bestselling *Bookworm* series, *Bookworm IV: Full Circle* concludes Elaine's story. Chris is currently living in Edinburgh with his wife, muse, and critic Aisha and their son.